FLIGHT PLAN

FLIGHT PLAN

TB MARKINSON
MIRANDA MACLEOD

Flight Plan

CHAPTER ONE

T his is it. This is how I die.

Reggie clenched her fingers around the armrests of her seat as the Swiss Air 777 plunged anywhere from ten to ten thousand feet toward the earth. She was seated in the middle section of the plane, and the lack of a window made it impossible to know exactly how much altitude they'd lost. At least she'd be spared the sight of the rapidly approaching ground in those final seconds before she died a fiery death.

A small blessing.

"Regina?" Her father barked across the partition that separated his seat from hers. "Are you even listening?"

The plane bobbed up and then down, like a drunk fishing lure, and Reggie's stomach followed suit. God, how she regretted indulging in that second Bloody Mary at the first-class lounge before the flight. She didn't want to spend her last precious minutes of life feeling like she was going to puke.

"I heard you," Reggie managed to say. "I'm simply left speechless."

"Stop letting your emotions control you." Her father's expression, though annoyed, betrayed no hint of fear. Somehow, not a single piece of his thick silver hair was out of place. Either the man was an even better liar than Reggie already knew him to be, or he didn't share her pessimistic assessment of their survival odds.

If she were brutally honest with herself, Reggie would have to admit there was a greater than zero chance she was overreacting just a smidge to what was possibly nothing more than a bad patch of turbulence.

Reggie relaxed her vice-like grip of the armrest, doing her best to control her voice and project the confidence her father demanded of her by virtue of their shared DNA. "This isn't emotions talking. I've spent seven years as chief executive at Spotlight Entertainment. How could you consider selling it to Phoenix Media after everything I've done?"

Spotlight had become the jewel in Hawks Corp's crown thanks to her. The least he could have done was negotiate an executive position for her with Phoenix. Instead, he expected her to scurry back to the company's New York headquarters at the snap of his fingers. She hated herself for playing right into it the way she had.

"Phoenix is offering seventy-four billion, which is an absurdly high price, and you know it."

"That's because they thought they were getting the news division," Reggie pointed out.

"I will never give up the news. But with Spotlight sold, that works out to nearly two billion for each member of the family trust." He fixed her with a sharp look that took all her control not to shrink from. "Would you like to explain to everyone at the next family dinner why they can't have their money? It's just business, Regina. That always comes first. Feelings never."

"No, Dad. It's more than business as usual this time." Reggie took a deep breath, staring straight ahead as the plane gave a violent shake. Her father's request—no, make that demand—helped take her mind off her impending doom, at least momentarily. "This goes beyond anything you've asked of me before, and we both know it. I'm leaving a position of authority to clear hurdles for Trevor all the way to the CEO's office while I get stuck doing the real work from the shadows."

"He's my eldest son." Her father's jaw clenched, and it was his turn to stare straight ahead to keep his emotions in check. "There was never a doubt he was the heir apparent before…"

Before the accident.

Those were the words her father couldn't bring himself to say. Before that summer evening seven years ago when the bronzed, muscular body of Reggie's twin brother had been scooped, nearly lifeless, from the salty waters off Montauk Point. All because of her. This was her punishment for the role she'd played.

"It isn't fair to Trevor," Reggie argued, switching tactics as she pushed her guilt over her brother's accident into the same abyss she used to banish all weakness and fear. It was a very deep abyss. Escape was impossible, or so she liked to tell herself.

"Do you have a better idea?" He turned his head ever so slowly. "Hawks News is our golden goose, and I need to make certain it's in the hands of someone I trust completely."

"You're the only person you trust completely," Reggie

3

said with a snort. "Why this sudden concern over shoring up the succession plan?"

"Because I'm not getting any younger." Reginald closed his eyes, the lines across his brow lending truth to his words. "It's possible I'm thinking about retiring."

"You? Retiring?" Despite his apparent sincerity, Reggie couldn't believe he was serious. A man who had worked eighteen hours a day for more than half a century didn't simply trade in his jacket and tie for a Hawaiian shirt and piña colada.

Not without a reason.

"Has the cancer come back?" Reggie gasped as the possibility struck her.

"Don't be ridiculous," her father snapped. "Cancer wouldn't dare try to get the best of me for a second time."

Maybe, maybe not. Whatever his reason, Reggie was determined to get to the bottom of it, all while doing everything in her power to make sure her dad made the obvious succession choice: her.

But before she could press him further about his plans, a particularly violent shaking caused the cabin lights to dim. She wished she believed in a deity so she could send out a prayer to make the plane stay in the air. Talking to her father about this shit was hard enough. If they ended up dying in the middle of it, she'd be good and pissed.

"I hate flying commercial," Reggie muttered through clenched teeth. "Why didn't we take the private jet?"

"We all have to make sacrifices if your cousin Dwight is going to win his senate bid. The voting public isn't exactly fond of billionaires these days." He managed to say this without a trace of irony, as if he honestly believed people could be tricked into thinking the Hawkins family—media royalty for over a century—were a bunch of ordinary folks just because they kept their fleet of private jets grounded for a few months.

"We're literally flying home from attending the World Economic Forum in Davos. Do you really think we've got the unwashed masses fooled?" She sounded exactly as spoiled as she'd intended, a subterfuge to throw her dad off the scent of blood in the water.

The truth was, with every bump and shudder, Reggie's fear of flying intensified. In the privacy of their corporate plane, she could down a couple of tranquilizers large enough to knock out a herd of elephants before takeoff and wake up refreshed on the other side. Even in the world's best first class—which this arguably was—the service wasn't so accommodating that the flight attendants would be willing to carry her comatose body off the plane. Inconvenient, considering she was about one more loss of altitude away from losing consciousness.

"Stop being a sissy," her father snapped, not fooled in the least and incensed over her bullshit attempt to cover up her terror. "I've never treated you like a girl, so stop acting like one."

"Ha! Since when?" Reggie's voice was louder than she'd intended but at least yelling at her dad took some of the edge off her fright. When it came to distracting oneself from impending mortality, there was nothing like a good old-fashioned argument. "The obvious succession plan is staring you right in the eyes, and you're too distracted by my lack of a Y chromosome to notice."

"You?" Her father's shoulders shook with angry laughter. "Impossible."

"Why?" Reggie sucked in a breath, bracing herself even

though she already knew the answer. There'd been a time when he'd been less narrow-minded and more willing to overlook her gender in favor of her brilliance for business, which was so much like his own. A time when she'd been the heir apparent instead of her brother. Until she'd dealt him what he'd considered a personal betrayal. It had been more than fifteen years, but the man could hold a grudge longer than a dog with a locked jaw and a favorite squeaky toy.

"Your monumental lack of judgment already cost me a ton of political capital once—not to mention cold, hard cash. I had to jump through fiery hoops just to keep your name out of the papers—"

"We *own* most of the papers—"

"The board will never take you seriously as a candidate," he insisted, steamrolling over her in his typical way. "I mean, an escort service, Regina? And with a *woman*, no less."

There it was. The real reason he would fight tooth and nail to keep her from occupying the corner office. Her father had no moral qualms about prostitutes that Regina knew of, even if he did enjoy exposing a good sex scandal in some of Hawks Corp's seedier tabloids whenever he could. No, it was the gay thing that had gotten his boxers so twisted they were still in a bunch all these years later. Good old-fashioned homophobia for the win.

"I was barely out of college." Reggie smoothed the anger from her tone, keeping her voice from trembling despite her rage.

There was no point arguing with her father over the rest of it. They'd covered the same ground enough times to wear a hole through the carpet. Two ex-husbands later, her father still didn't trust her heterosexuality one hundred percent. That just meant he was smart. A couple decades had made Reggie a hell of a lot better at hiding, but no less queer.

"Are you truly saying you'd rather put my brother in charge of the company, even though we both know mentally and physically he can't do it?"

"You'd be at his side the whole time," her father insisted with an impatience he couldn't hide. "You'll have control of everything."

"But I won't have the title. I won't be CEO."

"You don't need a title. You can do the job just fine— maybe better, even—from the background."

Reggie clenched her fists. "I'm not fucking wallpaper."

How could he not see why that particular detail was so important to her? She hadn't worked this hard for the family business her whole life only to be denied her place at the top. It would be different if Trevor wanted it, or at least Reggie told herself so. But he didn't. He would hate this plan as much as she did.

"You have three strikes against you." He held up three gnarled fingers.

"I'm a lezzie who sleeps with hookers. That's only two." Reggie refused to blink, her eyes boring into him, willing him to flinch at her crudeness. He didn't. "What's my third sin?"

"You betrayed my name."

Reggie's gut clenched as if she'd been punched. Her father had never come out and said it so bluntly before. Forty-two years ago, Reginald Hawkins had faced a choice; bestow his name on his firstborn, a daughter, or on his son, who'd had the gall to trail his sister's entrance into the world by a full thirty minutes. In that moment, her father bucked convention and chose her. He'd taken a monumental gamble, and she'd let him down.

Before she could fully react to the pain of this realization, a bell dinged throughout the cabin, the prelude to an announcement from the pilot.

"Attention passengers," a man's voice sounded over the speaker. "We apologize for the bumpy ride. We're going to be changing our cruising altitude to try to outrun this storm. Please remain seated with your belts securely fastened. All cabin meal and drink service will be suspended for the time being."

"Even in first class?" Reggie's eyes slid to the wine glass she'd drained right after takeoff. She cursed herself for not ordering something stronger. Her father's hands tightened around his whiskey glass, and Reggie nearly cried when she realized he still had a good couple of swallows left beneath the ice. "I'll arm wrestle you for it."

"You see? This is why I can't trust you with the company."

"Because I want a drink?" Reggie's stomach tightened as the plane's engines revved, but even her heightened nerves couldn't keep her from rolling her eyes. "You have one, and God knows Trevor drinks enough for both of us."

"It's different for men." Sadly, as her father had aged, he'd actually come to think this was true, along with believing that businesses, like kingdoms, should be handed down from father to son. His mind seemed to narrow with each passing year. "I'll make you a deal. You can have the Hawkins Foundation."

"The family charity?" Reggie could no longer hold back the vitriol that was overtaking her. "Come on, Dad. Fuck that shit."

Reginald pounded the fist that wasn't holding his glass against the partition, making Reggie jump. "I've worked too hard concentrating the power at Hawks Corp in the hands of our branch of the family to see it slip away because you're stubborn."

"Then give it to me," Reggie pressed, trying not to sound weak or desperate, two qualities her father abhorred. "You know I'm the best choice. I already run everything anyway."

"Your uncle Carl would push so hard for Dwight to be CEO it would squeeze the air out of your lungs. Why do you think I'm working endlessly to get that useless nephew of mine elected to the Senate? Do you think I *like* flying commercial? I've always done what has to be done, and I expect you to do the same."

"And I will," Reggie promised. "If I agree it's what needs to be done. But having me shadow Trevor as an invisible puppet master for the next forty years is in no one's best interest. So give it to me straight, Dad. What do I have to do to prove I'm worthy to be CEO?"

"Straight?" Her father erupted into bitter laughter. "An excellent choice of words. You want to know what you can do to prove to me you have what it takes? Run the Hawkins Foundation and be grateful. My mind is made up."

"You're unbelievable." Reggie crossed her arms, the hugging sensation providing more comfort than she'd expected. It was everything she could do not to start rocking herself like a baby right there in her seat. "If you don't want me in charge, fine. But you have to realize Trevor isn't an option. The board won't be fooled much longer. Aunt Val, for one, is starting to suspect he's worse off than she's been told. She won't—"

"Valerie?" Her father laughed, which turned into a

hacking cough, the kind that made Reggie's insides nearly revolt. She was queasy, and the plane jouncing all over the sky like a cat toy on a string didn't help matters.

"Yes, Valerie. Your sister. You remember her, right? Even if she is a girl?" Reggie shook her head, wondering how her dad could be so dense. He accused her of being stubborn, but he was a mule when it came to seeing anything from a perspective other than his own. "Aunt Val may have a soft spot for Trevor as her favorite nephew, but she won't back him if it means hurting the company."

"You think *you* would be her choice?"

"In case you missed it—which I don't know how that's possible since every newspaper we print has the date written right across the top—it's the twenty-first century. I know you're all from a different generation, but I'm sure by now even Aunt Valerie has figured out that women are just as capable of leadership as men."

"I don't know any." Reginald delivered his rebuttal like a petulant child, a sign that Reggie was more correct in her assessment than he wanted to let on.

"If that's true, why is your sister even on the board?"

"That was my father's idea. Besides, Val's loyal. I need her vote." He shook his head. "It's like you haven't been paying attention at all. I'm surrounded by idiots."

"Funny. Me, too." Reggie shot her dad a pointed look.

"Watch it. I can end you."

"I don't buy that threat anymore. Who will prop Trevor up when you're gone if you have me bumped off?"

"You're impossible. You know that?"

"Ditto, Daddy dearest." Reggie took several short breaths as the jet engines began to whine, her body tensing.

The next moment, the plane fell.

Her stomach dropped, the contents within—mostly alcohol, if she was honest—threatened in earnest to move in the wrong direction. As sweat broke out across her brow, Reggie flung apart her seat belt with trembling hands.

"Where are you going?" her dad demanded.

"I need to stretch my legs."

This was a lie. Her pressing need was to hurl, and she prayed she could make it to the bathroom in time. Barfing into a paper baggie in front of her father was a display of weakness she couldn't bear.

The plane jerked to the left, and she latched onto the bathroom door with one hand. She wasn't sure which would be worse, vomiting all over the aisle or landing in it face-first while her father looked on.

Because the flight hadn't already been horrible enough, the door to the toilet was locked. Reggie fought back tears. She didn't even feel sick anymore, just terrified. They were going to crash, and nobody could convince her otherwise.

Perhaps her father was right. Maybe she didn't have what it took. It might be better if the plane went down after all, putting her out of her misery before she could fail for the whole world to see.

The bathroom lock clicked as the person inside slid the bolt open. Relief flooded Reggie's chest, but before she could do anything else, a solid crack like a bomb exploding went off in Reggie's ears. The cabin lights went dark. All-around her, people screamed as the plane dropped and kept on dropping. Losing her balance, Reggie's arms flailed in front of her as she fell, searching for something, anything, to break her fall.

Her prayer was answered as her hands and head landed on something impossibly soft, like a cloud.

This could only mean one thing.

The plane had gone down. She was dead, and this cloud she had landed on was heaven. It certainly felt like heaven and smelled like it, too. Apparently, heaven had a vanilla and lavender aroma.

"Excuse me?" It was a woman's voice speaking.

Reggie smiled. She'd always suspected if God did exist, she'd be a woman.

"Excuse me!" This time, God sounded a little peeved.

Slowly, Reggie opened her eyes and found herself chin deep in the most luscious pair of boobs she'd ever laid eyes on.

CHAPTER TWO

There's a woman lodged in my cleavage.

Gwen's life had been far from ordinary of late, but it was safe to say she'd never found herself in this particular situation before. A complete stranger had latched onto Gwen's breasts, buried her face between them, and showed no intention of letting go. Velcro had less sticking power.

"Would you mind takin' your paws off me?" Gwen's stomach churned, and not from the turbulence. After years in the UK, she'd been certain her Texan drawl was long since gone. But there it was, slipping into her speech when she could least afford it. She was supposed to be from Chicago. That was the backstory Solène had given her, along with the counterfeit passport in her purse.

Being from Texas instead of Chicago was one of a million slipups that could get Gwen into a heap of trouble.

"Don't you know we're dead?" the strange woman mumbled from the depths of Gwen's bosom. Instead of letting go, the woman had tightened her grasp, a feat that defied every known law of physics. She'd shoved her face so deep into Gwen's chest that nothing showed beyond a mop of dark brown hair.

"We're not dead." Not yet, anyway. For months now, Gwen had been doing everything in her power to stay alive, including altering her appearance with the help of more hair bleach than should be legal, and she wasn't about to stop now.

"Ladies!" A frazzled flight attendant waved at them, his head peering out from an alcove where he was seated in the jump seat close to the cockpit. "This is not the time for trying to join the mile high club. You can't be out of your seats."

Mile high club? Heat rushed through Gwen as she took in how compromising their position must appear. Her temperature spiked higher when it registered that instead of pushing the stranger away, she'd leaned into the intimate contact like a starving person with a steak dinner.

Under different circumstances, she might enjoy this. Gwen had a thing for women in expensive suits. But it was hardly the time or place.

Perhaps coming to the same realization, the stranger released herself from Gwen's tits, revealing a perfectly oval face, smoothly bobbed hair, and brown eyes as stormy as the weather outside. She was older than Gwen by at least a few years. Shorter, too, with full lips that Gwen instantly regretted were no longer pressed to her chest.

What a missed opportunity.

"We'… no, I'm…" the stranger stuttered, her flustered behavior at odds with the type of put-together elegance that signaled she was normally a *take no prisoners* kind of woman. Gwen's favorite type. "The plane—"

"Was struck by lightning," the flight attendant finished in an oddly calm way, considering the shocking news he was delivering. Even Gwen, usually a fearless flyer, became lightheaded at the revelation. "Which is why you must be seated at once."

"Did you say lightning?" The stranger's already pale skin drained of what little color it had held, giving her a corpse-like pallor that was startling, though not unattractive. She sank into an empty seat, and for a moment, Gwen feared the woman had fainted, but the man in the seat next to her didn't seem concerned. Surely, he would have been if she was unconscious, right?

"Your turn." The flight attendant had unbuckled himself from his seat and was walking toward her with an expression that made Gwen feel like a naughty child.

"I'm sorry," Gwen rushed to say. "I had to use the toilet."

Americans say bathroom, not toilet, Gwen chastised herself as her heart beat wildly. Yet another blunder. It was like she didn't know who she was or where she came from anymore. She would never survive being on the run if she couldn't remember simple details. Then again, the plane had been struck by lightning, so maybe survival wasn't an issue anymore. Maybe they'd all be dead in a minute, like Ms. Boob Grabber had predicted.

"I don't care what you think you had to do." The flight attendant scolded with a ferocity that would've given a nun with a ruler a run for her money. "You're a grown woman. You can hold it."

Rendered too meek to argue or even reply, Gwen turned to make her way back to her seat, but the flight attendant clicked his fingers loudly. "Where do you think you're going now?"

"Back to my seat." Gwen gulped. "22D."

"Coach?" The flight attendant's nose wrinkled like he'd caught a whiff of microwaved fish. "This area is restricted to first class passengers."

"I'm sorry. Like I said, I needed the bathroom, and the first one I tried was—" *Like the pea soup scene from The Exorcist.* It had been one hell of a bad flight.

For a moment, the attendant looked ready to drag Gwen by her ear all the way to the rear of the plane, but another violent shudder reminded them both of the very real danger they were still in.

"Sit," he barked, pointing forcefully to the seat on the opposite side of the aisle from the boob grabber. "I'll deal with you later."

Gwen's hands shook almost as violently as the plane as she attempted to clasp the seat belt around her waist. She was rattled, but not so much that she failed to appreciate the luxuriousness of her surroundings. The seat was huge, and—were those slippers on the shelf in front of her? A small box of chocolates, too. Maybe the stranger was right, and they were already dead because this sure looked like heaven.

"Attention passengers," the pilot's voice crackled through the cabin, "I'm sorry to announce that we have been ordered to return to Zürich immediately. There's no cause for alarm."

Yeah, right.

Gwen snorted, suppressing a giggle as an almost identical noise emanated from the seat across the aisle.

Apparently neither she nor the woman in the cream cashmere turtleneck and soft beige mohair jacket had been convinced by the pilot's pep talk.

"Back to Zürich?" came the gruff voice of a man, presumably the one who'd been seated beside the boob lady, although the way the first-class seats were arranged to maximize privacy, it was impossible to see.

So this is first class, huh? Gwen had been upgraded to business class a few times, but never first. Simon, her boss, had been a big talker, but he was a cheap bastard at heart. She'd been a fool to believe a word he said. If this all worked out and she remained alive, Gwen relished the opportunity to testify in front of whichever world governing bodies would welcome her presence.

Her eyes shifted toward the box of fine Swiss chocolates she'd spied earlier. If she ate one, would the stern flight attendant try to charge her for it when they landed?

"I don't have time for this!" The man continued to rant loudly about how inconvenienced he was as he attempted to get a message to someone he referred to as Charlene, whom Gwen assumed was a beleaguered assistant in an office building somewhere in Manhattan. Given that it was a little before three o'clock in the morning in New York, Gwen doubted Charlene would be pleased if her boss succeeded in making contact.

As he continued to carry on, Gwen's eyes narrowed, her hackles raised by the businessman's display. Did he honestly think he was the only one on the plane with someplace to be? Gwen recognized the type. He was no different than the dozens of Kensington Datalytics clients who'd patted her on the butt and demanded a cup of coffee, not realizing she was the Director of Business Development they'd traveled all that way to meet. All they saw was a leggy young woman with a nice rack, as more than one of them had said directly to her face like it was a compliment.

"Put the phone down," the woman beside the man said stiffly. "I don't know if you noticed, but the plane is barely staying in the air. You can call Charlene when we land."

Completely unbidden, Gwen's brain conjured an image of lush, naturally pink lips settling into a pout. But, no. That wasn't right. The woman hadn't seemed the pouting type. Not that Gwen knew much about the woman—like her name, for instance—but you could tell a lot about a person by having their face on your boobs. From Gwen's vantage point, the stranger had come across as every inch a take-charge woman. The kind who grabbed hold of what they wanted and didn't let go.

Gwen closed her eyes, giving into the full body shiver that engulfed her at the memory of the woman's hands doing precisely that, grasping Gwen's breasts like her life depended on it. Considering Gwen was on the run from people who wanted her dead and might very well be snuffed out on impact if their plane fell from the sky, there were certainly worse things she could be ruminating about.

Gwen couldn't quite put her finger on why the experience of a woman she didn't know grabbing her breasts was so very different from a would-be client's butt pat. But it most definitely was.

Leaning forward in her seat so she could see around the privacy partition, Gwen cast a furtive glance toward her hidden neighbor. She was met with a pair of dark eyes doing exactly the same thing. With a gasp, Gwen pulled back. For more than two months, she hadn't dared to make even fleeting eye contact with anyone, not even the other journalists on Solène's team as she'd let them record her story. Now, she was seeking it out and getting caught in the act.

Why was the stranger trying to look at her?

And who was the pompous guy seated next to her, anyway? Her husband?

No. Not likely. Granted, Gwen's gaydar might not have been firing on all cylinders while being groped in the aisle earlier, what with the impending doom of a fiery crash and all that. But even if the stranger hadn't been as into fondling Gwen's nipples as it had seemed at the time, she couldn't see a woman like that being married to a man like him.

Bottom line, arrogant assholes who tried to call their assistants from 35,000 feet—or whatever altitude they'd dropped to by this point—were usually more into acquiring trophy wives. Boob lady was nobody's trophy. Of that, Gwen was certain.

What was infinitely more confusing was why Gwen was giving so much thought to the matter. The plane she was on, if it didn't crash on the way there, was about to take her back to the last place on the planet she should be. Hadn't Solène told her so in no uncertain terms? Get out of Europe, now. Go back to America. Lay low until the story breaks. She had information that could seriously compromise the heads of at least a few governments. Yet here she was, obsessing over an attractive stranger like a schoolgirl with a crush.

Throughout the cabin, a series of dinging bells offered an unmistakable sign that they were about to make the final approach into Zürich. The lights brightened. Gwen's hands tightened around the armrests as she squeezed her eyes shut, keeping them that way even as the plane thudded down and bumped along the airport tarmac. A burst of applause sounded from the cheap seats in the back. Gwen remained frozen in fear, a million times worse now than when they'd been in the air.

The plane may have landed safely, but Gwen's troubles were only beginning. If anyone from Kensington Datalytics had tracked her to Switzerland, they could be waiting at the airport to snatch her. She needed someplace safe to hide until she could get on another flight.

The second the plane came to a stop at the gate, even before the seat belt sign could turn off, the loud businessman—whom Gwen had taken to calling Mr. Boob—leaped to his feet, a black leather briefcase clutched in one hand.

"I'm catching a ride with Elon," he declared. "They're holding his jet for me."

"What about me?" asked the woman who had become Boob Lady.

"No room." Mr. Boob was already halfway down the aisle to the door. "You'll have to make your own arrangements."

"Gee, thanks, Dad. Love you, too," Boob Lady muttered just loud enough for Gwen to hear.

Gwen's lips twitched in a half smile. At least that was one mystery solved. Not an important one, like what she was going to do with herself now that she was back on European soil with less than twenty Swiss francs in her pocket and without a functioning credit card. But a mystery nonetheless.

Solène's less than savory underworld contacts had arranged to have a stack of cash waiting for her in a storage locker at a bus station near JFK Airport, but a hell of a lot of good that did right now.

Drawing a deep breath, Gwen closed her eyes again. Maybe if she tried really hard to meditate, an answer to her problems would materialize when she opened them again. Instead, as seat belts all around her began to click open and passengers prepared to deplane, Gwen opened her eyes to find the scary flight attendant glowering down at her.

"I told you I would deal with you later." He brandished a portable credit card machine. In her current financial situation, it was the most frightening item on the planet. "No one flies in first class without buying a ticket."

"I didn't choose to fly in first class. You made me!" Gwen spluttered, her throat constricting as dark splotches floated in front of her eyes. How much did a ticket for first class cost? "Look, I didn't even eat the chocolates. I just needed the bathroom."

At least she'd remembered it was called a bathroom this time. No one would question she was an American as they dragged her ass off to a Swiss debtor's prison.

"I assume this will take care of it?" Still shrouded in the depths of her seat, Boob Lady held up her hand, a shiny piece of black plastic stamped with a stoic silver centurion pinched between her index and middle fingers.

The flight attendant stared at the card and blinked several times but didn't make a move until the woman wiggled her fingers. As if snapping out of a trance, the man took the card and inserted it into the machine as Gwen looked on. She was too stunned to say a word. Was the woman who had groped her boobs now honest-to-god paying for her first-class upgrade with an Amex Black, the most prestigious credit card in the world?

That settled it. The plane had definitely broken into pieces during the storm, and this was some crazy final attempt of Gwen's dying brain to make sense of the senseless as her body plummeted to earth. It was the only rational explanation.

Boob Lady took the card back, giving no outward indication as she did so that she was a mere figment of Gwen's imagination. "And tell the lounge I'll need the same accommodations as this morning."

"Yes... yes, ma'am."

Without a backward glance, the formerly menacing flight attendant returned to his alcove like a dog who'd been kicked. Gwen supposed she should feel sorry for him. If her plane crash theory was correct, he was dead now, too, same as her.

"You may as well eat them."

Gwen jumped as Boob Lady's face appeared from around the seat partition, her cheeks rosier than the last time Gwen had seen them. "What?"

"The chocolates. They're very good." The woman extended a hand, and for a moment, Gwen thought she was reaching for the candy, until the woman added, "I'm Reggie, by the way."

"Wen—Gwen. Gwendolyn Murphy. But, uh, Gwen's fine." Gwen swallowed hard, praying she'd covered her monumental blunder in time. Thank goodness the fake identity Solène had concocted for her was similar enough to her real name that she could attempt a recovery. Maybe Boob Lady—or Reggie, since it suddenly seemed rude to keep calling her that now that introductions had been made —hadn't noticed the slipup.

"Nice to meet you." Reggie stood, passing her hand over

her herringbone trousers to smooth wrinkles that were imperceptible to nonexistent.

Gwen scrambled to her feet, searching all around for her own carry-on bag. "I can't believe you paid for my ticket like that. I'll pay you back. I mean, I can't—" Gwen's heart clenched as she realized her carry-on was still in the overhead bin above seat 22D. "My bag!"

"Excuse me." Reggie snapped her fingers in a way that was reminiscent enough of how the flight attendant had done it before that Gwen wondered if it was intentional. "My friend will need her suitcase retrieved from her old seat and brought here. Thank you."

The man nodded.

"I... that was..." Gwen didn't know what it was, really, that display of total dominant authority that had sent the flight attendant bully scurrying back toward the bowels of coach without a word of protest, saving the day before Gwen even had a chance to truly start freaking out.

The only word to describe it was hot.

Yeah, that was it.

Fucking hot.

But she wasn't about to say that out loud so Reggie could hear her.

"Gwen?" Reggie tilted her head slightly, and for a terrifying moment, Gwen feared she had said all that out loud. Every single word.

"Uh, I..."

"If you're trying to offer to pay for the upgrade again, please stop."

"But, why?" Gwen managed to ask. Indeed, why would a total stranger, no matter how rich, go out on a limb like that without a reason?

23

Ever since she'd handed over the credit card, Reggie had acted every bit the take-charge woman Gwen had imagined her to be. However, as she paused to take a breath, a slight flush of pink colored her cheeks, hinting at a vulnerability hidden beneath the surface.

"The incident earlier, with the, uh"—Reggie's gaze faltered almost imperceptibly, slipping to Gwen's chest before bobbing back up. "I don't want there to be any misunderstandings. Or trouble."

"Of course not," Gwen said, even as she realized she'd understood exactly what was going on between them all along.

There'd been nothing wrong with Gwen's gaydar, no matter how Reggie was trying to cover it now. Those circles that had blossomed from pink to crimson on the woman's cheeks after taking in the swell of Gwen's breasts were proof enough.

Gwen followed Reggie to the aircraft door, where the once surly flight attendant waited to hand over her carry-on bag with an ingratiating expression befitting a page handing over the crown jewels.

"This lounge you mentioned…" Gwen lifted her chin as she took it, hoping to channel even a fraction of Reggie's confident attitude. She was going to need every ounce of it. "Can I buy you a drink there?"

"It's the first class lounge. Drinks are free."

"Good, because that's about what I can afford." Gwen pressed her lips together, suppressing a triumphant smile. That hadn't been a no, which was as good as a yes. "What do you say?"

A hundred emotions flitted across the woman's face as they stood motionless on the jetway. Gwen's stomach tightened, but just as she anticipated being shot down, Reggie's shoulders raised in a slight shrug.

"Why not? You've got a first-class ticket, same as me." With that, the woman sashayed toward the terminal like she owned the place. For all Gwen knew, maybe she did.

CHAPTER THREE

The uniformed attendant behind the reception desk looked up as Reggie and Gwen approached. Recognizing Reggie from earlier that morning, she offered a smile that was at once warm and sympathetic. "Welcome back, Ms. Hawkins. While I'm pleased to see you again so soon, I imagine you may not feel the same."

"It's not how I thought my day would go," Reggie admitted with a sigh. Now that her feet were safely back on solid ground, her busy schedule swirled in her head, a hundred things that needed doing while she was stuck, unable to address a single one. Damn her father for leaving her to navigate her way home alone.

"I've booked you on the next available flight to New York, but I'm afraid with the delays, it's not likely to depart until six o'clock tonight. Everything's grounded at the moment because of the storm. You should get into New York around nine o'clock tonight." A flash of worry marred the attendant's welcoming expression.

Reggie had seen similar looks plenty of times before.

While she was adept at keeping her own temper under control, the last time this woman had seen her, she'd been in the company of her father. Delivering unpleasant news to Reginald Hawkins carried significant risk of having one's head bitten off. The difference between Reggie and her father was she preferred to save her wrath for people who deserved it.

"It's the best you can do. I know you can't control the weather, Lauren." While Reggie hadn't remembered the woman's name from that morning, it was right there on her name tag. The importance of using people's names was another point on which she and her father differed. She could be as hard-assed as the old man, but she was smart enough to know a little decency went a long way. "Could you tell me which flight my friend here is on? Gwendolyn Murphy."

That name Reggie *had* remembered. And not just because of the cute way her new acquaintance had stumbled over it when introducing herself. Something about the woman had gotten a hold of her and wasn't letting go. The wise choice would be to cut her loose this instant. Emotional entanglements of any kind were a total nonstarter for her, considering her father's views on all things gay.

But Reggie couldn't bring herself to walk away. At least, not yet. After the ugliness with her father on the plane, anything that made her feel good was a blessing to be savored while she could. Knowing how pissed it would make him if he knew was a bonus.

As Lauren's gaze shifted from Reggie to Gwen, her chin tilted noticeably upward, emphasizing their height difference. Now that they were side by side, it appeared that

Gwen was nearly a half a foot taller than Reggie. They made an odd pairing, especially considering the contrast between Reggie's luxurious cashmere and Gwen's yoga pants and hoodie.

Although, despite her companion's casual attire, Reggie couldn't help noticing that Gwen didn't seem intimidated by her surroundings. She stood with her head held high and steady. Her confidence was striking, especially considering the long string of unusual circumstances that had led her here. Gwen had every reason to feel insecure, yet she was holding her own.

Reggie admired a confident woman.

"I see Ms. Murphy had a last-minute upgrade, but there are no seats left on the flight you're on, not even in coach." Lauren's fingers clacked along the keyboard, a scowl settling over her features. "I'm sorry. All the tricks I usually use don't seem to be working. There are too many people looking to rebook. The best I can do is a nine-thirty tonight on one of our partner airlines. Sadly, it's business class, and there's a long layover in Paris. But you don't change planes, so you can stay onboard and sleep if you'd like. You'll arrive early tomorrow morning."

"That will be fine," Gwen assured Lauren, whose answering smile spoke volumes. She'd probably had a hellish time of it with pushy customers trying to get their way.

Not that Reggie would have thought twice about throwing her weight around if it was necessary, but it wasn't like she was looking forward to New York anyway. She'd much rather spend some time getting to know the pretty stranger with the nice tits whose charming laugh hit her in all the right places.

"I've reserved the St. Moritz day room for you," Lauren said. "Housekeeping is seeing to it at the moment, but it should be ready soon."

"Is the other room available, too?" Reggie asked, seeing no reason Gwen shouldn't have a place to rest but not comfortable with the idea of sharing. It was impossible to predict what Gwen would think of an offer like that, coming so soon after the breast fondling incident on the plane.

"The Montreux is occupied at the moment, but I'll see what I can do. Perhaps you'd care for some food while you wait? I can put your bags in the luggage room to unburden you, and I'll keep you updated on the status of both flights." After taking their bags, Lauren waved them down a long hallway, at the end of which was a set of wide glass doors.

"That's quite a wine collection," Gwen said, taking in the massive humidor on the other side of the door where over a thousand bottles of wine were stored.

"It is." Reggie shot Gwen a curious glance.

Once again, the woman seemed less overawed with the obvious display of excess than might have been expected. Granted, flying commercial was a letdown compared to your own private jet, but Reggie wasn't so out of touch as not to recognize that this lounge, with its rich wood tones, white linen draped tables, and fully stocked bar was pretty goddamn impressive by most people's standards.

"Do we grab a bottle and bring it to our table?" Gwen laughed at her own joke.

"I suppose no one would stop us, but then how would we open it?" Reggie countered, eager to continue this line of conversation, if only to make the woman laugh some more. It was an infectious laugh, full of sincerity. That quality was rare in Reggie's world, and she found herself drawn to it, eager for more.

"Here I thought you were so put together," Gwen teased. "Do you not carry a corkscrew for emergencies?"

Reggie made a show of patting her pockets. "I must have left my Swiss Army knife in my suitcase."

"Pity." Gwen batted her lashes flirtatiously, or at least Reggie liked to imagine that was the intent. "You never know when you'll need a good screw. I could sure use one."

Now, hold on there…

Eyebrow arching, Reggie examined the woman's face for a sign, however subtle, that she'd heard her right. Or more importantly, that the flirtatiousness she'd been wishing for was real. "Are you always this spicy?"

"Only after near-death experiences," Gwen said with a grin. "Now, I seem to recall I promised to buy you a free drink."

"I think I'll take you up on that." Reggie stepped over to the bar, a long, sleek slab of curving wood mixed with steel and under counter lighting. More important than being stylish, it was well-stocked, with every kind of alcohol imaginable and a bartender who could make anything.

"Another Bloody Mary?" The bartender asked as he dried a glass with a towel before setting it back on its proper shelf. One would think she was a regular from how quick all the staff were to remember her. But it came along with the territory of obscene wealth. Sometimes it was a blessing, other times a curse. Reggie could never be certain of her privacy and, therefore, trusted no one.

At the mention of the acidic drink that had been churning in her gut all morning, Reggie nearly convulsed. "Maybe you could suggest something else?"

"How about a Holdrio?" the bartender suggested. "It's plum schnapps with rosehip tea and sugar."

"The tea would be perfect to settle my nerves," Reggie agreed. "And I won't say no to schnapps, either."

She turned to Gwen, who was eying a glass bowl on the bar filled with Lindt chocolate. "Would you like one?"

"A chocolate?" Gwen reached in, snatching a foil wrapped ball from the bowl. "I never pass up free chocolate."

"You did on the plane," Reggie pointed out, feeling playful. "I don't know how you managed it. I ate every last piece; keto diet be damned. Of course, I was convinced we were going to die."

"Whereas I figured if we didn't die, I would soon find out the chocolate wasn't free." Eyes downcast with embarrassment, Gwen giggled. "And I was right."

"Yes, you were," Reggie said, laughing as well. "Although when I asked if you wanted one, I meant one of those tea drinks."

"I think I'd like a coffee." Gwen grabbed a handful of Lindt balls, each with a different colored wrapper.

"She'll have a Flämmli." Reggie swiped a chocolate for herself. After a near-death experience, a little self-indulgence was in order. "I think we'll grab a table."

"Of course." The bartender nodded his head. "I'll bring the drinks out to you when they're ready."

On the way to one of the more private tables around the other side of the bar, Gwen asked, "Flämmli? Is that a Swiss coffee?"

"No. It's more of a Swiss surprise."

"I don't know you very well yet, but you seem to be full of surprises."

Reggie's pulse stuttered at the word yet. So full of possibility. "Is that good or bad?"

"Time will tell." Gwen's eyes skittered to the side, intent on the view of a plane landing, but Reggie didn't think that was the real reason for pulling those stunning blue eyes away.

"That sounds a little dramatic." Reggie took her seat, crossing her long legs with deliberate slowness, curious to see if she could regain her companion's attention. The ploy worked, and a slight smile tugged at Reggie's lips. "I've never seen anyone look so wary over the promise of a surprise. Are you expecting ninja assassins to drop from the ceiling and carry you off?"

There was no mistaking a moment of raw panic on Gwen's face as she struggled to control her features. "Now who's being dramatic?" she asked with an airy laugh, but it wasn't genuine enough to erase the memory of what Reggie had seen. Was the woman in trouble? Probably not from ninja assassins, but maybe she had a possessive ex she was trying to put behind her.

"You needn't worry while you're with me," Reggie assured her, joking but also not. As the daughter of a wealthy and controversial man like Reginald Hawkins, Reggie had made self-defense training a priority. "I have a specific set of protocols I can engage to counter any would-be ninjas."

"That's a relief." Gwen laughed as she said it, but Reggie couldn't shake the feeling the woman did, indeed, appear more relaxed.

The bartender arrived with the drinks, and a glum look settled on Gwen's features. After the promise of surprises, she seemed disappointed by the plain cup of coffee set in front of her. But the next moment, her eyes sparkled with delight as the man lifted some of the liquid out of the cup and set it on fire, tipping it back in as the flame continued to burn. He placed sugar on the spoon, letting it caramelize over the flame.

"Is this your assassin protocol?" Gwen asked when they were alone again. "Set them on fire?"

"Not many would expect death by coffee." Reggie placed her hand over the flame, the fire going out. "Now it's ready."

"Do you buy flaming coffees for all the women?"

"Who said there were other women?" she found herself asking, though she'd intended to tease Gwen about having to pay the imaginary bill. As silence settled around them, Reggie stared deeply into Gwen's eyes, surprised by the depth of the connection. Her heart pounded, and she sought for any way to lighten the mood. "Of course, everyone knows setting a drink on fire is the surest way to get into a woman's pants."

"Here I thought I was special." Gwen's pouting smile stirred Reggie's insides in an unexpected way.

"Time will tell." Reggie lifted her cup to sip her tea, hoping to hide cheeks that were surely scarlet based on how much they were tingling. "I'm famished. You?"

"A little." Gwen opened the menu, squinting, making Reggie wonder if the woman usually wore glasses. However, the real issue soon became clear. "There aren't any prices. That happened to me once at a business dinner, and let me tell you, that wasn't a fun conversation when I turned in my expense report."

"I imagine not, but you don't have to be concerned with prices."

"I appreciate your generosity," now Gwen's cheeks were burning a hot red, "but I can't let you pay for anything else."

"I'm not," Reggie insisted then thought better of what she'd said. "Well, it comes with the ticket. All of this is included."

"The food, too?" Gwen turned her attention back to the menu, a smile on her face. It seemed her enthusiasm was no longer hampered by the looming specter of a sky-high credit card bill. "What's good here?"

"I'm fond of the smoked salmon tartar." She'd chosen the item out of some misguided need to impress the woman, but Reggie's still-delicate stomach flipped at the mere thought of eating raw fish. Unfortunately, her own pride would force her to follow through on ordering it. Pigheaded stubbornness was a quality she hated about herself sometimes but couldn't figure out how to eradicate.

"Maybe something more down to earth for me," Gwen said. "They have a Swiss hot dog. It comes with coleslaw and fried onions."

"You may be a few years younger than I am, but you're not five." Reggie paused, mentally trying to calculate the woman's age but coming up with uncertainty. Her youthful glow was unmistakable, but the woman had a troubled air that suggested worldly experience. "I'm vetoing the hot dog."

"Who says you have that power?" Gwen playfully crossed her arms.

"Everyone," Reggie deadpanned. "I'm used to being in charge."

"I've noticed. But if you get to veto my meal choice, I'm going to veto yours. Anything *tartar* is out of the question."

"Fine." Reggie feigned being annoyed, but relief

whooshed through her. She was off the hook, no thanks to her own idiocy.

Gwen gave her a quizzical look. "I was expecting more of a battle."

"Sorry to disappoint, but that flight—it did a number on me." Instantly, Reggie regretted sharing this detail. It made her seem weak, which was the one thing above all else she was not allowed to be. "I know. Pathetic."

"It's not pathetic," Gwen insisted with a gentleness that Reggie found oddly touching. "I was terrified. The plane was struck by *lightning*."

Reggie felt almost lightheaded as an immense weight seemed to lift itself from her chest. Was she really being given permission to feel afraid, like any normal person would be? Despite the gravity of the subject matter, Reggie laughed. "My father would say it was pathetic."

"No offense, as I obviously don't know him, but if you're referring to the guy who was sitting next to you on the plane, I'm not sure he has his priorities straight."

"Interesting observation." Reggie turned her attention back to her menu, unable to argue. "How about the fondue? We could share. I mean, if you'd like."

"That sounds perfect. Did you hear that?" Gwen smothered her belly with both hands. "I can't remember the last time I ate a good sit-down meal."

"Lots of eating on the run?"

"Something like that." Gwen shrugged. "What's the story between you and your father?"

"I don't know if we have time for *that* conversation." Reggie held up a finger, a server immediately appearing for her to place the fondue order. Were things always this easy for the woman?

Gwen looked out the window, where large flakes of snow swirled with the rain. "I think we might. We're not going anywhere in this."

"Let's just say my father isn't my biggest fan," Reggie said quietly. She hadn't meant to say anything at all, but now that she had, she found herself adding, "He's a good old-fashioned misogynist. I'm the only one who can properly take over for him after he retires, but instead of crowning me his heir, he wants me to babysit my brother in the corner office and thinks putting me in charge of the family's charity foundation is a suitable consolation prize."

"Naturally." Gwen gave a laugh laced with bitterness. "Women always get the unappreciated work."

"Sounds like you know what I'm talking about."

"First-hand experience. I worked for a non-profit agency," Gwen said, answering the implied question.

Reggie noted the use of the past tense, but before she could dig for details, the server arrived with their fondue spread. It was probably for the best. Reggie had already said more about her personal life to this perfect stranger than she had to her own therapist, let alone someone who wasn't bound by a confidentiality agreement.

Spearing a piece of bread with ease, Gwen dipped the morsel into the cheesy sauce. Bringing it to her mouth and closing her eyes, she let out a delicious moan. "You have to try this."

"Tempting." Taking in the sight of this beautiful woman in a moment of complete ecstasy, there were at least a dozen things Reggie could think of that she'd like to try, but none of them were appropriate for a public dining room. She shifted in her seat to squelch the insistent throbbing that was building between her legs. If the chocolate fondue course was as good as the cheese, Reggie might not live to make it back to New York.

"Still feeling sick?" Gwen's genuine concern was touching. If Reggie's father had been there, he would have mocked her for her weakness.

"No, I was..." Reggie's voice trailed off, her throat going dry. Gwen had shifted forward in such a way that the deep V of her hoodie gaped open, exposing quite an eyeful of lavender bra underneath.

Instead of pulling the top back up, Gwen leaned closer still, giving Reggie an even better view. "Does your father know you're such a boob girl?"

Heat engulfed Reggie's face, but she found herself unable to deny it. "Somehow we haven't had that conversation."

"The conversation where you tell him you like to fuck women?" Gwen's teasing tone and raunchy words delivered another jolt of lust to Reggie's core, but there was also a conspiratorial quality that filled her with a sense of trust she couldn't remember ever experiencing so intensely before.

Instead of shutting the conversation down as she knew she should, Reggie proceeded, albeit with caution. "What makes you think that?"

"I'm sorry," Gwen was quick to say. "It's none of my business."

"I have two ex-husbands, you know," Reggie pressed, though she wasn't certain what that was supposed to prove. It might make a stronger argument for her heterosexuality if she was still married to one of them.

"I didn't mean to imply anything." Gwen's eyes slid to the tabletop, and her cheeks seemingly flushed with mortification. "For what it's worth, I know what it's like.

Having that conversation with my conservative grandfather was one of the hardest things I've ever done in my life."

"How did it turn out?"

"Not great. We haven't spoken in a while. My mom, either."

"I'm sorry." Deep inside Reggie's chest, the walls that had held everything in for so long gave way. It was as if this small kindness of sharing a personal trauma from the past was the final straw. Now that the process had started, Reggie couldn't stop until it all came out.

"Do you remember about fifteen years ago when that big sex scandal broke involving several New York state legislators and a high-end escort service?" Reggie's heart thumped so fast she struggled to breathe. Was she really about to go there? Even now that she'd committed, she could hardly believe she was doing it.

"Fifteen years ago?" Gwen's eyes crinkled as she strained to recall.

"What were you, five? Six?" Reggie quipped, apprehension building as she awaited Gwen's answer.

"I was sixteen." Gwen plucked a chunk of bread from the plate and tossed it at Reggie with a playful grin. "I don't recall this particular scandal, though. There have been so many."

"There really have been, right?" Way more relieved than she should have been to confirm the woman wasn't as young as her worst fears, Reggie speared an apple slice and dipped it into the fondue. "My god, this *is* good."

"It is, isn't it?" After the silence dragged on and Reggie didn't resume her story, Gwen prompted, "You were saying something about a sex scandal?"

"Was I?" Reggie chuckled as Gwen prepared to lob

another piece of bread her way. "This is too good a meal for it to end up on the floor. Stop wasting the bread, and I'll tell you."

"Wait. Let me guess," Gwen said. "Did your father get caught with an escort? He seems the type."

Bracing herself, Reggie confessed, "Actually, it was me."

CHAPTER FOUR

"Get the fuck out of here." Gwen nearly swallowed her lips, sucking them in deep to prevent any other stupid exclamations from falling out. But had she heard that right? The daughter of conservative media mogul Reginald Hawkins had hired an escort? No way could she believe this immaculately dressed woman who oozed power and charisma from every pore had ever needed to resort to paying for sex. She had to be pulling Gwen's leg.

Reggie's shoulders folded inward, as if tensing for a barrage of insults to be hurled her way. As the truth sank in that this woman was one hundred percent serious, guilt engulfed Gwen, and she regretted how harsh her outburst must have sounded on the receiving end.

"Sorry! I meant that in more of a *you go, girl* kind of way." Gwen waved her hands like a cheerleader holding pompoms. She couldn't get any dorkier if she tried, but at least it was working. Reggie's lips twitched at the corners, a smile threatening to escape. "You know what? Fuck it. So what if you hired an escort? I'm sure you had your reasons, and men get away with that kind of shit daily."

"Maybe, but my father was livid when he found out." Reggie paused. "This feels strange to ask since we just met, but you do know who my father is, right?"

"I think so." Gwen frowned, revulsion creeping in as she thought of the man on the plane and all he represented. She had so many reasons to hate this woman's father, her whole family, really. Yet for some reason Gwen's attitude toward Reggie was more complex. She was drawn to the woman, even though she shouldn't be. "If I'm correct, I should say right now I don't agree with the Hawks News brand of fear-based politics in the slightest. In fact, I find it abhorrent."

"That's something we most definitely agree on."

"How is that possible?" Gwen demanded, uncertain whether to believe her, though she really wanted to. It would make it easier to justify liking the woman if she wasn't working for the enemy. "Hawks Corp has become synonymous with the most extreme fringes of right-wing propaganda."

And this woman was much too sexy to be one of Satan's minions.

"I'm more familiar with the entertainment side of things. I haven't been involved with the news division for quite some time. I've been in London for the past seven years."

Me, too, Gwen wanted to say but didn't. It was true, and a fun coincidence they would no doubt enjoy exploring, but it didn't fit her cover story. She had to stick to that above all else.

"It's hard to escape the Hawks Corp influence in the States," Gwen said instead. "Especially if you have family living in the middle, away from the coastal cities. Hawks Corp runs just about every newspaper in North America."

"Don't I know it." Reggie came across as anything but pleased. "It was one of our own papers that broke the escort story, ironically. Even being the man at the top, my father had to pull every string imaginable to keep my name out of the scandal. Reporters were tripping over themselves to get ahold of the client lists."

Gwen leaned forward, well aware of how her new position enhanced her cleavage. Reggie's eyes confirmed the effectiveness of the motion by falling to Gwen's chest and sticking like a saber tooth tiger in a tar pit.

"This escort..." Gwen paused, searching for the right wording. "Was *he*—" Her hunch was confirmed when Reggie burst out laughing. "Aha. Not a he?"

"Hell no." Reggie laughed some more. "The funny thing was, I actually convinced my father I wasn't having sex with the woman. I told him I needed a friend to talk to and that I had paid her to be discreet."

"Did he believe you?"

"Probably not," Reggie admitted. "But a few months later, I started dating the son of a potential investor. When we got married, it doubled Hawks Corp's Asia Pacific market share. Dad believed what he wanted to believe. At least for a while."

"That was the last time you hired an escort?" Gwen asked as the waiter cleared the mostly eaten cheese course and replaced it with a bubbling pot of dark chocolate and delectable morsels of fruit and cake.

"Champagne?" Reggie asked as if not wanting to discuss the matter further.

"Yes to the champagne. No to letting you change the

subject that easily." Gwen studied the woman across from her, intent on preventing her from retreating back into that perfect shell she'd crafted for herself. Other people might believe that was who Reggie was, a totally put-together businesswoman with spreadsheets and quarterly reports where her heart should be. But now that Gwen had gotten a glimpse behind the mask, she wanted to see more. "There's way more to this, and I'm dying to know the details."

"I'm not one to kiss and tell," Reggie countered, spearing a cube of cake and dipping it in the chocolate. "Although in this case, I'm also legally prohibited from doing so, as is the other party in question." She twirled the last of the chocolate droplets from the sweet morsel and popped it into her mouth. The tip of her tongue darted out to catch a dribble that clung to her lips. Gwen had never been so jealous of a drop of chocolate in her life.

"I suppose it makes sense your father would get his legal team involved." Gwen selected a strawberry and swirled it in the pot, wondering if Reggie was half as turned on right now as she was. Until today, Gwen had never imagined grabbing a bite to eat in an airport could be so sensual. If only her life wasn't a dumpster fire at the moment, she would love to get to know Reggie a lot better, preferably in a clothing-optional kind of way.

"Getting busted by my dad in a sex scandal in my twenties has taught me to be extra careful. While I admire your whole *fuck that* attitude"—the accompanying grin sent a delicious shiver down Gwen's spine and straight to her clit, reinforcing how disappointing it was that nothing could be done about it—"when it comes to my father and our company, I don't have the luxury. I must be in control at all times."

"Are we talking whips and handcuffs?" Gwen knew they weren't, but now that she'd said it, she couldn't shake the alluring image from her mind. Small but intense, Reggie would make one hell of a dom. Why did the timing of their meeting have to be so cruel?

"We're talking nondisclosure agreements."

"Do go on." Gwen contemplated her companion with a thoughtful expression, hands folded as she waited, hoping for Reggie to continue. The woman managed to make dry legal documents sound sexy.

After a moment of silence, Reggie said, "There's a countess in London. She—"

"Shut the front door! You're courting a countess?" Gwen's estimation of Reggie skyrocketed at this revelation. "I thought that only happened in romance novels. You're my new hero."

Reggie's laugh transformed her face, chipping away its etched-on wariness. "Not to burst your bubble, but I'm not *courting* anyone."

"Dating, then," Gwen corrected, filled with awe. She was having lunch with a woman who rubbed elbows, and probably other body parts, with royalty. "I was trying to be poetic."

"I don't date. Ever." Reggie's face clouded.

"What about those two ex-husbands?"

"I especially don't date *them*." Reggie gave an exaggerated shudder, making Gwen laugh.

"Not now, I suppose," Gwen conceded. "But I have a hard time believing you live like a nun."

"Funny. My brother calls me Sister Reggie." This might have been true, but the look on Reggie's face said her brother was mistaken.

"Why did you mention the countess if you aren't dating her?" Gwen asked when Reggie turned her full attention to the fondue pot, remaining frustratingly mute.

"The countess is a shrewd businesswoman with a list of high-end clients for whom she arranges discreet liaisons."

"Your countess is a pimp?" Gwen's mouth hung open. "But if you don't date, what do you do?"

Heat swept through Gwen's body as Reggie gave her a look that asked *what do you think I do?* She was tempted to pry for greater detail but wasn't convinced she could withstand it without letting out an orgasmic moan worthy of Meg Ryan right there at the table.

"Once contracts are signed and money is exchanged, what a client does is no one's business," Reggie said. "That's the whole point. The secrecy is ironclad. Money is exchanged in a way there's no tracing it back. I have it on good authority certain high-ranking politicians have acquired their spouses this way, though, of course, I have no idea who."

"Is that what you're looking for?" Gwen asked. "A spouse?"

"I'm done with husbands, and my father would disown me if I brought home a wife. Anyway, I see no reason to limit myself. I choose to be with someone different each time. It's easier that way." Reggie shrugged with the same nonchalant attitude that might accompany an explanation of a preferred way to chop tomatoes.

"Does that mean it's all transactional with you?" Gwen asked, her cheeks tingling at her own nerve.

"Of course," Reggie confirmed. "Everything in life is transactional."

"Even human relationships?"

"Especially those." Scowling, Reggie lifted her champagne flute to her lips.

Gwen dipped a strawberry into the chocolate. "In that case, I guess I know a way to pay you back for upgrading my ticket."

Reggie choked, face reddening, until Gwen was convinced champagne would start dripping from the woman's nose.

"I'm kidding! You must think I'm terrible to make fun of your circumstances like that." Gwen whisked her napkin from her lap and handed it to Reggie, whose eyes were two streaming faucets in a beet-red orb. If it weren't for the possibility of third-degree burns, Gwen would've buried her head in the fondue pot. "My grandfather is a Hawks News fanatic, but I can't imagine what it must be like to be the daughter of the man who sits on the Hawks throne."

"No, it's not that," Reggie finally managed to gasp. "It's just—it feels good to make a joke about it. I haven't talked, let alone laughed, about this incident with anyone other than my father, which was the opposite of funny."

"Joking aside, how did you get to be so cynical about relationships?" Gwen could tell Reggie believed what she'd said, though it was possible she had herself fooled. In the short time since they'd met, Gwen had caught glimpses of something softer than the tough exterior Reggie tried so hard to maintain.

"Me, cynical?" Reggie's laugh had a bite to it. "Let's see. My first husband married me to increase the price of his company's stock, and my second was gay and needed a beard. Which was fine because, yeah, me too. My father's second wife started off as my nanny and almost certainly got herself knocked up in the pursuit of a big payday. His third wife was a scheming wench who nearly lost us the company. And his fourth wife was most likely a corporate spy."

"A spy?" Gwen was a little taken back by Reggie's thorough list.

"We're not sure. But probably." Reggie shrugged. "On the other hand, she didn't have any kids with him, so she's also my favorite. With two brothers and a sister, the last thing I needed is another brat wanting to split the family fortune. What about you?"

"No kids, no siblings, no family fortune," Gwen replied, not sure what information Reggie was looking for but trying to cover all the bases. "What about wife number one? That's your mom, I assume. You didn't say why she married your dad."

"For the worst possible reason. She thought she loved him." A deep sadness settled in Reggie's eyes, turning them as stormy as the sky outside. "It ruined her. To the day she died, she never fully recovered from what he did."

"I'm so sorry." Gwen swallowed the last of her champagne, uncertain what else to say.

"What about your parents, Miss Pollyanna? Are they still together?"

"High school sweethearts, married thirty-five years." This was a lie, part of the cover story she'd committed to memory. Though it pained Gwen to be deceitful after Reggie had opened herself the way she had, there was nothing to be done about it. Solène hadn't gone to the trouble of crafting a foolproof false identity so that Gwen could toss it aside on a whim. "They live just outside Chicago."

"Windy City girl, huh? Whatever are you doing in Zürich in the middle of winter?"

"Returning from a trip to Thailand. It's beautiful this

time of year." This time Gwen spoke the truth, although she hadn't been on vacation as her casual tone implied. Bangkok had been her first hiding spot when she'd fled from London almost three months ago. It was exhausting to think of all she'd gone through since then. At least New York represented the end of her journey and a fresh start, even if it was nothing like the life she'd pictured herself having.

"Ladies?" Lauren arrived at their table as they were finishing the last sips of champagne. "The St. Moritz room is ready now. I apologize, but with the storm, we don't have the other available. Would you like me to have it set up for two?"

"I couldn't possibly impose," Gwen rushed to say. She doubted Reggie would want her there anyway, but if the woman did intend to extend the offer, the best thing to do was nip it in the bud. It had been hard enough getting through a meal without fantasizing about what might happen if they were alone somewhere together. Allowing that to happen for real would be a big mistake.

"Are you sure?" Reggie pressed. It was hard to tell if she was doing it for show or actually wanted Gwen to join her. Either way, Gwen's answer remained no.

"We have a nice shower room if you'd like to freshen up," Lauren said to Gwen. "And there are several armchairs in the lounge that are almost as comfortable to nap in as a bed, if not quite as private."

"That's much better than I could have hoped for on my own." Gwen jerked her chin to the window overlooking the terminal where dozens of people could be seen contorting themselves around armrests and suitcases, trying to get comfortable during the long delay. "Look at how miserable everyone looks down there, waiting out this storm.

Meanwhile, I've just had the most amazing fondue and even champagne. This has been the best *stranded at the airport* experience in my life."

The attendant beamed. "I'm so glad to hear it. Now, if you've finished your meal, I can show each of you to your respective destinations."

Reggie drained the rest of her champagne. "Ready?"

"Yes." Gwen applauded herself for keeping the disappointment out of her reply. Since they were on different flights, she wouldn't see Reggie again after this. Already, the next several hours in the lounge seemed longer and less exciting, no matter how much free champagne she had at her disposal.

Lauren led them out of the main lounge and through narrow hallways, using a keycard on a lanyard around her neck to unlock some of the doors as they went.

"Ms. Hawkins, here's your room. Is there anything else I can help you with?"

"Yes. Could I get my outfit freshened and pressed before my flight? I'm out of clean clothing and can't stand the thought of another twenty-four hours in what I have on."

"Of course," Lauren replied. "I'll let the laundry service know."

"I guess this is goodbye, then," Reggie put a hand out for Gwen to shake. "Safe travels, Gwen."

"You too, Reg." Gwen's face went up in flames as the unintended nickname ricocheted in her skull.

Way to play it cool.

And what had she been thinking, making a crack about paying the woman back for the plane ticket by sleeping with her? Talk about a hundred shades of inappropriate. Though it was the businesslike handshake at the end that cut deeper than Gwen wanted to admit. Not that it should have. Theirs was one more meaningless encounter that would be soon forgotten, at least as far as Reggie was concerned. Gwen would try her best to feel the same.

As Reggie disappeared into her room, Gwen followed Lauren through another maze of hallways. The attendant was still speaking, but Gwen was too mortified by her gaffe with Reggie to process any of it.

"—this white bag here, you see?" Lauren looked at her expectantly. They'd come to a stop in the middle of a small room with beige stone walls. A glass-enclosed shower stood at the far end, and there was a toilet and sink with two towels and an assortment of travel-size toiletries arranged on the counter.

"Yes, I think I've got it." Gwen replied after a longer than normal delay. She hadn't in fact caught any of what Lauren had said but given that the item in question was a cotton sack hanging from a hook, in a separate changing nook, Gwen figured she could wing it. She needed to snap out of this brain fog if she was going to make it to New York without doing anything stupid that would get herself caught —or worse.

When Lauren left, Gwen stepped out of her clothing and placed the items in the hanging bag to keep them off the floor. She unfolded the beige terry cloth robe from the vanity and placed it on a hook beside the shower, and then she turned the faucet handle so that a stream of water cascaded from the showerhead like rain. After a few moments, hot steam began to fill the room. Gwen stepped under the steady flow and sighed as the knots in her muscles began to unwind.

Unscrewing the cap from the shower gel, Gwen lifted the

small tube to her nose. She inhaled a blend of sweet orange and cedar wood, tendrils of relaxation spreading through her for the first time in weeks. In seconds, she'd worked the gel into a thick foam, which she spread across her bare shoulders and down her chest.

Suds slipped across her skin as she lathered her breasts, stomach, and legs. She closed her eyes, and her imagination filled with the only thing missing from this heavenly scenario: Reggie.

How much pressure would Gwen have had to apply to coax that petite, dark-haired beauty into the water with her? She could feel the woman's hands on her now, caressing her. Full lips nuzzling her neck, tongue flicking her earlobe.

Gwen sank her front teeth into her lower lip as she imagined what it would feel like to run her fingertips up the length of Reggie's thigh, to slide her hands into the hot wetness between her legs. What sounds would she make as Gwen stroked her thumb along Reggie's slit, teasing her clit with soft circles that promised more to come?

A longing whimper echoed against the stone walls. Gwen opened her eyes in the steamy shower, alone. Streams of water ran clear down her body, the suds long since gone. Gwen shut off the water and grabbed her robe, slipping her arms into thick terry cloth sleeves. After wrapping a towel around her dripping golden locks, she rested her forehead against the slippery wall and fought back tears.

"It's a damn good thing you didn't go to her room," Gwen muttered to herself. It was true, but that didn't mean she had to like it.

Making connections and sharing secrets was how people on the run got caught. Gwen refused to be brought down by such a rookie mistake. The last thing she needed was to get herself mixed up with someone like Regina Hawkins, even if she was the most intriguing woman Gwen had met in years. The woman was high-profile and well-connected, but while that might make Gwen feel safe in the moment, it could lead to disaster. The secret Gwen was keeping was the sort of thing any one of the reporters on Reggie's payroll would give their right arm for.

Nothing was safe.

The best thing she could do was get dressed, drink lots of coffee, and stay alert.

"What the?" Gwen's head swiveled, taking in the entire changing nook and finding nothing but an empty hook. The white bag with all her clothes in it was gone. She poked her head into the hallway and found the space deserted. She couldn't find Lauren without traipsing across the entirety of the first-class lounge wearing nothing but a robe.

That left exactly one avenue to go down, the one place Gwen knew she shouldn't go.

CHAPTER FIVE

Once the door had clicked shut, silence rang in Reggie's ears with an intensity that surprised her, making her nerves buzz unpleasantly. She'd been in this exact room early that same morning, at which time the continual roar of jet engines provided a low and constant hum in the background that was oddly comforting. Now, not a single flight took off or landed as snow continued to fall, large flakes whipping against the floor-to-ceiling wall of windows that overlooked the tarmac.

At least the thunder and lightning had passed.

Reggie's eyes swept the room with its pleasantly muted color palette and elegant, understated furnishings. An unsettled feeling spread in her chest. The room was expensive but impersonal, the type of space that offended no one, nor did it spark much joy. It was a place to exist between two points, to stretch out on a bed that cost more than the average car and watch the seconds tick by on the face of an oversized Swiss clock that glowed with the intensity of an alien sun.

Perhaps it was being surrounded by quiet after hours of conversation, or the aftereffects of lightning striking the plane. Either way, unease weighed on her, pressing in until her lungs hurt when she drew a breath. She massaged her fingers along her sternum, convinced the walls were closing in around her.

"Don't be ridiculous," she scolded herself, but the sensation only intensified, making her breathing become frantic, her eyesight blurring as panic set in.

This was different than on the plane—or rather similar, but not for the same reason. In fact, the very thing that had soothed her at 35,000 feet was responsible for her sorry state now.

What had she done?

That was the wrong question. She knew exactly what she'd done. She just didn't know why. Opening herself up to a total stranger like she was talking to a priest in a confessional was so out of character as to be completely unrecognizable. She'd spilled enough secrets to ruin herself and the company, and she'd neglected her go-to move of getting a signed NDA.

Fuck.

How could she have been so stupid?

Only her father and a handful of lawyers knew about the escort scandal. And Reggie had never told a soul about the Countess, not even those in her inner circle. Not that she had much of an inner circle.

Other than Trevor, and possibly her younger sister, Stephanie, the only other person in her life she even halfway trusted was her Aunt Val. Her baby brother, Logan, was just a kid. Uncle Carl was a greedy bastard. As for cousin Dwight, he was a politician. Enough said.

The one thing the entire Hawkins clan agreed on was that anything as messy as feelings was best shut down with the swift, clean precision of a guillotine blade. Beyond family, Reggie stuck to the topics of business and the weather.

Except, she hadn't done that with Gwen.

Reggie closed her eyes, sucking in a deep breath, trying to stop the panic swirling inside. An image of Gwen appeared behind her eyelids. Reggie squeezed them tighter, not sure if she was trying to shut it out or hold onto every detail of the memory. Those full round breasts, soft and sweet, as if a cloud and a marshmallow had a baby. Piercing blue eyes. Playful smile. Sexy voice. Reggie yearned to claim the woman with her hands, her mouth, her tongue. Tears pricked her eyes, her desires denied.

Reggie needed to do something, anything, to stop dwelling on Gwen. Physical desire was every bit as much a fool's errand as love. There was no point in pining for the woman, no matter how pretty she might have been. Not only was it weak, it wasn't like Reggie would ever see her again. And that was a good thing. Another few hours together and who knew what Reggie might do or say to compromise herself?

It was best to stay the course. Avoid emotional closeness with anyone, and physical, too, for as long as she could stand it until her weak will couldn't take it anymore. And when that happened? That's what the Countess's highly skilled operation was for. She'd find an excuse to get back to London soon enough or have someone sent to New York if her need became unbearable.

Reggie headed into the en suite bathroom, stripping off her jacket as she went. A scalding hot shower would wash her troubles away. If nothing else, the sound of the rushing water was a welcome distraction from the silence.

She washed quickly, avoiding her hair and face. As soothing as the water felt beating on her back, Reggie shut the shower off the moment the last of the soap had been rinsed away. It was too tempting to linger, to let her mind wander under the influence of the pleasurable sensations her body was signaling.

Stepping out onto the bathmat, Reggie buffed her arms and torso with one of the towels, which was soft but not *too* luxurious. Reggie appreciated that, a little reminder of the need to toughen up. She was heading back to New York to face the fight of her life, not to enjoy a spa day.

She slipped on the terry cloth robe that had been provided for her, leaving it untied. After patting her legs and feet dry, Reggie hesitated. Much of her torso was still exposed to the rapidly cooling air, and it was impossible to ignore the way her nipples had hardened or how her body tensed in anticipation of applying the towel to the wetness between her legs. Which was mostly from the shower water. Mostly but not entirely.

It's just a fucking towel.

She stood in front of the mirror to chastise herself, not bothering to wipe the condensation from the glass. It was better that way. When she looked in the mirror, she didn't always like what she saw. Too often there was fear, indecision, or shock in her eyes.

"Stop being a pussy," she muttered, instantly regretting her word choice as a shock of pure lust slammed her core at the same time the towel brushed against her labia. She sucked in air through her teeth, ridiculously close to the brink for having done nothing at all.

Shit. This was getting out of control, and Reggie had rules about that. Luckily, she also had a foolproof cure for what was ailing her.

Digging through the small purse that was the only personal item she hadn't left with the attendant, Reggie quickly located a cylindrical object at the bottom. It was made of metal and shaped like a tube of lipstick, but it wasn't makeup. It would, however, bring some color to her sallow cheeks.

As Reggie wrapped her fingers around the miniature vibrator and removed it from the depths of her purse, she forced herself to breathe in and out slowly, deliberately. This was nothing to get all worked up about. A little self-care, that's all. She pressed the button on the bottom, holding it until the cylinder jiggled to life against her fingers.

Now *that* would obliterate any and all thoughts from Reggie's mind.

Reggie strode to the bed, single-minded in her purpose. She pulled back the covers and lowered herself onto the incredibly comfortable mattress, her robe untied but still clinging to her back and shoulders. With an almost inaudible sigh, she allowed her head to sink into the pillow behind her. Switching off the vibrator and setting it on top of the duvet, she spread her legs and closed her eyes.

You will not think about Gwen, she instructed herself, which was the worst thing she could have thought. Instantly, the only image her brain seemed capable of forming was that of the woman she'd just told it to pretend didn't exist. The fact she also looked like she could be a professional swimsuit model didn't help matters.

No thinking of anyone, she corrected. That was usually how it went, anyway. This was a means to an end, like scratching the itchy spot on the top of her head. She didn't need to produce mental porn to get the job done.

Resolute, Reggie reached down with her right hand, running her finger up and down along her slit. She was already wet, a good sign. This shouldn't take much time at all. If only her own button worked like the ignition on a car, it'd be perfect. Less time spent indulging her weakness. Less time to dwell on how her sex life, if it could even be classified as a life, definitely lacked something.

Reggie continued touching herself, her hips now moving, her center arching for that first brush of her fingertip across the tight bundle of nerves. Just as her hand made contact, an image of Gwen's face tickled Reggie's eyelids. She let out an exasperated sigh.

This need for sex would be her downfall. It already had caused her more trouble than it was worth. Why couldn't she simply go without? She should embrace becoming Sister Reggie once and for all. Maybe even join a convent. Her father, lapsed Catholic that he was, would probably be proud to have a nun for a daughter.

But even now, her every muscle was tense, her nerves pulsing with the need for release. Removing her hand from between her legs, Reggie found the vibrator. She was just about to push the power button when a knock rattled the door.

She cursed under her breath. She'd forgotten to leave her clothing out for the laundry service. "Just a minute," she called out, launching off the bed and retying her robe. Satisfied she'd managed to cover everything that needed covering, Reggie swung the door open.

Gwen stood in the hallway, towering above Reggie even while barefoot, swaddled in an identical terry robe that looked a lot skimpier than it did on Reggie's smaller frame. "Please tell me they're here."

"They're...what's here?" Reggie's tongue stumbled in confusion.

"My clothes. I took them off to shower, and now they're gone. I was hoping someone thought I belonged with you, and...?" Gwen stared wide-eyed.

Reggie couldn't help but wonder if she'd become trapped in a cheesy lesbian porno.

Cue the opening strains of a sexy Barry White song now.

Dear god, Gwen was entirely naked underneath that little bit of terry cloth. What Reggie wouldn't have given to be able to reach out and untie the belt of that robe so she could watch it fall open to expose the treasure beneath. Would the woman's breasts look as good as they had in Reggie's imagination as she touched herself?

Stop thinking about that.

Reggie's head spun at the thought, and it took everything she had to string together a coherent reply. "Where did you put them?"

"In the white bag on the hook."

Finally, Reggie's brain clicked into gear. "Oh no. Lauren probably thought you wanted your clothes laundered along with mine. Hold on. I'll make a quick call to track them down." *And put certain parts of my body on ice while I'm at it.*

After speaking to the front desk, it was as Reggie had suspected. The clothes Gwen had been traveling in were in the process of being cleaned. Reggie put her own laundry bag in the hallway before delivering the rest of the news. "They should be ready in a couple of hours. Do you want Lauren to send in your carry-on bag?"

"It wouldn't do any good. All my clothing was in my

checked bag. Thanks for looking into it, though." Gwen turned to leave.

"Where are you going?"

"To wait in the lounge," Gwen answered.

"You're practically naked!" Reggie exclaimed. "You can't sit in the lounge like that."

"Where should I sit, then?" Gwen demanded. "I can't very well stay in here. You're practically naked too, in case you hadn't noticed."

"Don't be silly." Reggie argued, even though the smart thing to do was let her leave. "Who knows what kind of trouble you might find yourself in if you went into public the way you are right now."

"What kind of trouble do you think I could get into if I stayed here?" The arch of Gwen's brow suggested she had a few ideas in mind. Was that a warning or a challenge in her tone?

Calculating the possibilities, Reggie's clit practically did a salsa dance spin. Not that Reggie could allow anything to happen between them. It wasn't like she carried nondisclosure agreements around in her purse in case she met a random stranger for a sexual encounter in an airport lounge. Although, she just might start.

Let her go, Reggie urged her better nature.

"I'm afraid I simply can't let you leave," Reggie stated in her most authoritative tone, her better nature apparently not listening to a word she said. "It's a legal consideration, pure and simple. If you get harassed while walking around in your robe, you might try to sue me. We can't have that."

"No, I guess we can't." Gwen's lips curled into a devious half smile. It should have frightened Reggie to the core with all that it implied, but hormones had made her too stupid to be scared.

"Then we're agreed. You'll stay here until your laundry is done." Alarm bells were sounding in Reggie's head with all the urgency of a doomed ship sailing straight for an iceberg. What was she doing? No lawsuit was half as dangerous as allowing Gwen to stay in this room right now. And yet, she couldn't stand the thought of watching her walk away again.

A frown creased Gwen's brow as she surveyed the room. "Where should I sit?" Other than the bed, the only piece of furniture was a narrow wooden bench with no cushions.

"The bed is plenty big enough to share." Reggie tried to sound nonchalant but blew it by choking on the final word like it was a spoonful of peanut butter. "You stick to one side. I'll take the other."

"Deal." Before Reggie could react, Gwen bounded toward the bed and took a flying leap onto it. "This mattress is amazing!"

"It should be." Reggie held back a smile and tried to sound grumpy even though she found the woman's moment of childlike glee utterly charming. "It's the best mattress money can buy."

"Uh-oh." Gwen's lips pursed as she moved to sit up and scoot to one side to make room for Reggie. "I think you dropped a tube of lipstick."

"I don't own lipstick." No sooner had the words left Reggie's lips did she remember she *did* own something that was almost exactly the same size and shape. "Wait. Give that here."

Gwen held the metal cylinder with one hand while she tried to remove the non-existent lid with the other. In the process, she pressed the button on the bottom with her thumb, initiating a sudden vibration that made her gasp. "You're correct. This is not lipstick."

"Told you."

Reggie swallowed, unable to pry her eyes off the woman holding her vibrator while sitting nearly naked in the middle of her bed. Gwen pressed the button again. Instead of turning off, the vibrator emitted a stuttering pattern, which Reggie's heart attempted to imitate as it lodged itself in her throat.

Tell her to leave this instant!

Instead, Reggie took a step closer to the bed.

"I interrupted you." Gwen laughed, then the sound ebbed as she seemed to detect a shift in Reggie's demeanor even before Reggie herself became aware of it. "I didn't hear it when I knocked."

Reggie locked eyes with the Gwen, throbbing with a need that grew greater by the second. "I hadn't gotten to that part yet."

This time, Gwen was successful in stilling the humming device clutched in her hand. Instead of handing it back, she slipped it into the pocket of her robe. "Do you want me to go?"

The part of Reggie's brain that was rational and in control screamed yes, but her head shook from side to side, paying no attention.

"Then, what do you want?" Gwen whispered, each syllable weighted with suggestion.

Reggie took another step closer and then another. She didn't speak, nor did she break eye contact. Her legs moved of their own accord. She didn't think she could stop them if she tried.

"I kind of laid my cards on the table back in the lounge

when I offered to pay you back." Gwen spoke slowly, giving Reggie time to make up her mind. "I said I was joking, but it was only partly. If you tell me what you want—"

"Touch yourself." Reggie didn't know where that had come from, and she held her breath, certain Gwen would flee. Why had Reggie barked that order? Other than it being an honest answer to Gwen's question.

Gwen's eyebrow arched, but instead of jumping from the bed and racing out the door, she tugged at the belt on her robe. "As you wish."

"No!" Coming to her senses, Reggie sat on the bed, reaching to still Gwen's hand. "I'm sorry. I shouldn't have said that. I don't want you to think for a minute I would demand something like that—"

"Are you saying you don't want to watch me touch myself?" There was a playful glint in Gwen's eyes. Did she know what that question had done to Reggie's insides?

"You're trying to punish me." Reggie turned her head to the side, desperate to look away.

"Do you want to be punished?" It was almost a statement, and when Reggie didn't answer, Gwen followed up with, "I see. I think maybe you do."

The strange thing was, Reggie was convinced the woman did see, that she saw exactly what it was Reggie craved and was willing to give it to her, too. No lover had ever understood this about her, not unless she was paying them to play a role. No one who knew her would guess that after having to maintain control in every aspect of her life, Reggie longed to let go, to let someone else take charge. To be completely at their mercy.

It was humiliating.

"Maybe I should go." Reggie's knees wobbled as she

stood from the bed. "I can sit in the lounge in my robe. No one will dare to bother *me*."

"You think you're more intimidating than I am?" Gwen leaped to her feet, grabbing the knot at Reggie's waist and holding tight. "I could press you up against this window right now, do anything I wanted, and I bet you couldn't stop me. What do you think of that?"

Desire permeated the air between them, a musky scent that made Reggie's head swim. Whatever caution she'd exercised before was long gone. Reggie held back a smile as she tilted her head to meet Gwen's challenging gaze.

"I think I'd like to see you try." Reggie shivered. She was playing with fire, but she couldn't stop.

"All I have to do is tell you to, and you'll do it." Still holding the knotted robe, Gwen took a step forward, inching Reggie back. "Isn't that right?"

Yes. It's true. Reggie gulped. She'd been right. Gwen knew exactly what Reggie needed.

Step by step, Gwen walked them back toward the window, pressing Reggie's back against the glass. A bolt of lightning lit up the sky, reflecting in Gwen's eyes.

Reggie gasped, her body shaking with the recollection of the terrible turbulence on the plane. With an almost imperceptible shake of her head, Gwen placed a steadying hand on each of Reggie's shoulders. She said nothing, but with each second that passed, Reggie's panic lessened.

"Robe off," Gwen growled, the mood shifting from comfort to something more primal.

"The curtains—"

"No. I want them open." Gwen caught hold of Reggie's belt again, untying it with one strong tug.

Adrenaline surged through Reggie's blood, bringing

every nerve ending to attention. "What if someone sees?" She should shut this down, now, but she lacked the will. She'd never wanted anything so badly as to give herself over to whatever Gwen had in store. At this moment, she didn't care who saw.

"No one is out there in this storm." Gwen slipped one arm of Reggie's robe off, followed by the other, the garment dropping to the floor.

A clap of thunder rattled the glass, but this time Reggie barely noticed.

"Now what?" Reggie whispered, heat enveloping her like a shroud even as her bare skin made contact with the cold glass. Whatever Gwen demanded, her body ached to do.

Long, slender fingers wrapped around Reggie's hand, guiding it lower until it pressed into the cleft between her legs.

"Touch yourself."

CHAPTER SIX

Gwen held her breath as the naked woman obeyed her command, her eyes glued to the movement of Reggie's forefinger as it trailed along her labia and disappeared into her slit. Was this really happening?

Reggie let out a whimper, her fingers moving faster. The woman's eyes were closed, her head resting against the window, her breathing growing heavier by the second as her arousal increased.

This was definitely happening, even if Gwen wasn't certain how it had come to be. Powerful, confident, and rich as fuck, Reggie Hawkins wasn't the type of woman who took orders from anyone. So what had possessed Gwen to take this risk? She had no idea, except her instinct had told her to go for it.

It sure as hell seemed to be paying off.

Keeping her eyes on Reggie's industrious fingers, Gwen used her own hand to cup Reggie's left breast. It sat heavy and rounded against her palm, soft and pliable. Gwen teased

Reggie's nipple with the pad of her thumb, circling it until it came to life.

"Don't stop touching yourself," Gwen said in a breathy whisper against Reggie's ear before fluttering her lips along the woman's jawline and down her neck, stopping to flick her tongue at a small indentation along the collarbone before pulling away.

She squeezed Reggie's breast, kneading rhythmically. "Are you getting wet?"

Eyes still shut, Reggie nodded. Strands of dark hair crisscrossed her forehead, clinging to the skin. Gwen stopped herself from brushing them aside, not wanting to detract from the intensity of the moment.

"Say it," Gwen directed, tensing slightly. Was Reggie still into this game?

"I'm... I'm getting wet," Reggie stuttered, coaxing a smile from Gwen's lips in response.

"Good." Still holding the breast in one hand, she slipped the other between Reggie's legs, her palm against the top of Reggie's hand. "Now stop."

All at once, Reggie's hand went completely still. The woman swallowed hard, a pained expression on her face as Gwen eased both their hands away, but no other signs of protest were forthcoming.

"Good girl." That the woman Gwen addressed was several years older than her was of no consequence. Gwen was in charge, and she would make sure Reggie remembered. The only question was, what should she do now?

There was no end to the list of things Gwen wanted to do. Her body bared in the soft afternoon light, it was clear Reggie Hawkins took care of herself with taut skin and toned muscles she'd worked hard to achieve. No one looked this good, no matter what age, without significant effort.

But for all that Gwen was in control of their encounter, this wasn't about what she wanted. It was about reading Reggie's subtle clues and giving her what she needed without her having to ask. It was a sacred responsibility, and one Gwen wouldn't take lightly.

Touching her tongue to her lips, Gwen retrieved the small vibrator from her pocket. With a press of the button, it jumped into action, buzzing for all it was worth until Gwen could barely feel her fingertips. "Open your eyes."

Reggie's eyes flew open at the command. A hint of surprise rounded her lips into the shape of an O as her focus fixated on the vibrator.

Extending her arm, Gwen touched the vibrator to the space between Reggie's breasts, teasing it down her front before circling one pink aureole and then the other.

"You want this." The huskiness of Gwen's voice came as a surprise to her, as did the jolt of current that shook her deep inside as the intensity of Reggie's desire played out across her features. "How much?"

"So much." Reggie bit down on her lip, trembling but not allowing herself to make a move until she was told to. The restraint was humbling in a way Gwen hadn't expected. It would be so easy for Reggie to take what she needed instead of waiting, allowing Gwen to dish out pleasure with painstaking slowness.

Gwen reached between Reggie's legs, her fingers gliding across slick lips. It felt amazing to know how badly Reggie wanted her, a million times more intense than what she'd imagined in the shower.

Gwen traced the vibrator down Reggie's torso and then

along the crease of one thigh. All the while she explored Reggie's folds with the tip of her finger. Reggie had been wet before, but now she was drenched.

"Put your foot on the bed." Speaking close to Reggie's ear, Gwen ended her sentence by nipping at the woman's delicate earlobe.

Reggie held onto the wall to support herself, placing one leg on the mattress, opening herself wide.

"That's a nice move." Gwen winked, her tongue poking out between her lips.

Gwen locked eyes with Reggie's as the vibrator slowly entered, causing Reggie's hands to leave the wall and dig into Gwen's back for support.

The tip was barely inside, but it lit Reggie up like a pinball machine. There was no doubt she wanted more. Much more.

So did Gwen.

"Get on the bed," she growled, pulling the vibrator away and whipping Reggie around. She pushed the woman's petite body onto the mattress. Reggie made a yipping noise as she landed sideways across the bed with a springy bounce, her legs spread wide as they dangled off the edge.

Gwen lowered herself to her knees and pulled Reggie's legs until they rested on her shoulders. The scent of Reggie's arousal filled Gwen's nostrils, desire overwhelming her.

Kicking the vibrator up a notch, Gwen traced a circle around Reggie's pussy with her finger. The woman's heels dug into her shoulders, drawing her head closer in invitation. Gwen ran her tongue down one labia and back up the other. This was done a few more times before Gwen moved closer and closer to Reggie's clit. It glistened, swollen and crimson, so in need of sweet relief.

With the first flick of Gwen's tongue, Reggie let out a yelp.

The second elicited a groan.

Positioning the tiny yet mighty vibrator at Reggie's opening, Gwen settled in. She was in no hurry. Using her tongue, she circled Reggie's clit with an easy steadiness, tasting her thoroughly. Reggie threaded her fingers into the hair on the back of Gwen's head.

Reggie's hips writhed, pressing her deeper into Gwen's mouth. She drew Reggie's clit in between her lips, sucking hard. Reggie's hips bucked, her ass bouncing off the mattress. Gwen continued, increasing in intensity even as she worked the vibrator deeper inside until it was buried as far as it would go without losing her grasp.

Gwen felt the crest of Reggie's orgasm building, thighs clenching against her ears. As Reggie came, there was a massive clap of thunder. For a moment, Gwen thought they might have been the cause, so great was the energy between them.

But even as Reggie shook with waves of ecstasy in front of her, Gwen was already wondering how she could do it again. She was nowhere near ready to quit.

"All the way up. Head on the pillows." Gwen rose to her feet, watching Reggie adjust herself exactly as she'd been told.

It gave her a thrill, having this control. She'd never expected Reggie to go along with being bossed around for so long. Gwen turned off the vibrator and cast it aside as she climbed onto the bed, sinking into the luxurious softness.

"How much did you say this bed costs?" Gwen asked.

She knew it was breaking character a little to say something so mundane, but she couldn't help it. This mattress was heaven.

"About $40,000." Reggie arched one chiseled eyebrow at Gwen, daring her to react.

"I'll be sure to order one when I get home." She was joking, of course, but Gwen's tone was dead serious. "I'm not sure I've ever fucked in a bed worth that much before."

"There's no time like the present." The hint of a smile creased Reggie's lips. Beneath her facade of obedience, the woman was clearly amused.

"I couldn't agree more." Climbing on top of her, Gwen took Reggie's hands, pinning them above her head. "You have an amazing body."

"You're the one with the boobs." Reggie tried to free a hand, but Gwen didn't allow her.

"I'm not the only one." Gwen licked Reggie's nipple once. Twice. On the third stroke, she sucked the hardening nub into her mouth.

Reggie let out a delighted squeal, so different from her previous low moans that Gwen reared up. Her legs straddled Reggie's hips, which made contact with her pussy in a way that sent a shockwave to her core. She needed more of that, now.

"I want your mouth on me," Gwen demanded.

Reggie swallowed, a seductive gleam blossoming in the dark depths of her eyes. "Where?"

"Everywhere."

The next moment, Gwen was scooting toward the headboard. Reggie's hands cupped the back of her thighs, fingers grasping her ass, until she straddled Reggie's head.

Gwen cried out when Reggie's hot, wet mouth made contact.

Reggie's tongue raked against her clit again and again, merciless in its quest to devour her whole. Gwen clawed at the headboard, desperate to keep hold of her sanity as the world around her spun away. All pretense of being in control was gone.

Reggie slid two fingers into her, curling and stretching from inside even as her lips and tongue worked from outside. Gwen's thighs burned as the strokes intensified, her back arching as she got closer and closer to the edge.

"Make me come," Gwen yelled out, belatedly remembering she was supposed to be in charge here. As if Reggie wasn't doing a thorough job of it already.

Ever obedient, Reggie did as she was told, until Gwen could no longer remain upright and collapsed in a heap on the pillows beside Reggie's head.

THE SHRILL RINGING OF A PHONE PULLED GWEN out of a deep slumber. Prying her eyes open, she didn't immediately recognize the room. The bed was cozy. Too cozy. She had no idea where she was. Though she was alone now, the smell of another woman on the sheets suggested that hadn't been the case all along.

Reggie.

Gwen shot up in bed as memories of earlier that day flooded back to her. She was still in Zürich, in the dayroom in the first-class lounge. The snow had stopped, or at least she assumed it had. It was too dark outside to see clearly, but lights shone, and the tarmac hummed with activity as planes rumbled to and from the runways. Gwen's clothes, freshly washed, sat neatly folded on the bench. There wasn't a trace of her former companion to be found.

The phone rang again. Through her grogginess, Gwen realized the sound was coming not from her cell phone but from one sitting in a cradle beside the bed. This place really thought of everything, even iPhones for their guests to use.

"Hello," Gwen croaked, hoping she was holding the phone to her head the correct way. It had been since she was a teen living in Texas that she'd used one of this style.

"Ms. Hawkins wanted me to ensure you'd make your flight. Priority boarding begins in thirty minutes." It was a man's voice speaking, and it occurred to Gwen that Lauren's shift had probably ended some time ago.

"Uh, thank you."

Gwen sat for a minute after hanging up the phone, waiting for the fog in her head to clear. She'd barely had any alcohol, so that wasn't the cause of it. Only one explanation remained. Mind-blowing sex was an actual thing.

Sure, she'd tossed around the phrase more times than she could count. She'd never imagined it was anything other than another way to say good, satisfying, or enjoyable. She hadn't realized it was possible for an afternoon of sex to physically melt the receptors in her brain like a cell phone left in a hot car.

Apparently, it was, which explained her current state. The mystery of what the hell she'd been thinking, hopping into bed with a total stranger—one of the most powerful women in media, no less while on the run with information that could topple heads of major corporations, and even governments, remained.

It had been reckless. Stupid. But oh, how she'd needed

it. After so many weeks of looking over her shoulder, never fully relaxing, the brief time she'd spent with Reggie in this room had been a refuge. She'd felt safe, normal, even. Now that it was time to leave, she had no idea when she might feel that way again.

With precious time ticking away, Gwen hopped out of bed, rinsed off in the shower, and tossed on her clothes.

"What am I forgetting?" Gwen's eyes swept the room. "My phone!"

Not that she would be keeping it for long. The rules were clear. If anyone was left alone with the phone for even a second, Gwen had to dispose of it. No matter how safe she'd felt with the woman, falling asleep with Reggie was a risk that needed to be mitigated.

Picking up the phone, Gwen frowned. "What the?"

There was a text on the screen and not from a number she knew. All the safety she'd felt evaporated, exposed for the lie it had always been. This was what happened when Gwen let her guard down.

Her pulse racing, she pondered whether to read the message or simply look for the nearest place to dispose the cursed thing. Curiosity got the better of her, and she tapped the screen. It was a text from Reggie, who must've grabbed the number from the burner phone while Gwen slept.

"I owe you for this afternoon, and I always pay my debts. RH."

Why Reggie would think she owed Gwen anything was beyond her, as if paying for her upgraded ticket and then giving her one of the most memorable afternoons of her life didn't put Gwen in her debt instead. Regardless, Gwen was now in possession of a direct line to one of the most powerful, not to mention sexiest, women on the planet.

"Fuck my life." Gwen let out a bitter laugh. It was a number she would never be able to use or even keep.

Gathering her things, Gwen made it to the reception desk with a minute to spare.

"Ms. Murphy?" a man in an airline uniform greeted her, holding out the small carry-on bag she'd left with Lauren that morning, along with a freshly printed boarding pass. "The elevator is right through those doors. You're at Gate 21."

Emerging from the serenity of the past several hours into the hustle and bustle of the crowded airport terminal was a shock to the system. After a few deep breaths to calm her nerves, Gwen made her way toward the gate. She slowed her steps only long enough to take her phone out of her back pocket and casually toss it into a trash bin as she passed.

The flight attendant in the business class section smiled as Gwen boarded the plane. "Good evening. Would you like something to drink?"

Gwen had an intense desire to order whatever that flaming coffee drink had been, just for one last memory of Reggie, but she couldn't remember the name. It was stupidly sentimental and unlikely they allowed open flames on a plane anyhow.

"Red wine, please," she answered instead.

By the time Gwen finished the glass, she was ready for more shuteye. Who would've guessed an afternoon of fucking the hottest woman she'd ever met could be so exhausting?

The next thing Gwen knew, the plane landed with a thud, a tiny hop, and then the brakes were employed. She'd slept right through Paris and was on the ground in New

York City. Not quite home, but the closest she was going to get anytime soon. Or possibly ever.

She collected her checked luggage with ease, one last perk of Reggie's upgrade, and made her way to the ground transportation area. She had no need to consult any schedules. She'd committed the route to the bus station to memory.

When she'd arrived, it didn't take long to track down the locker Solène's contact had arranged. The combination for the lock had been committed to memory, too.

Inside the battered locker was a new phone, enough cash to get by for a while, and a credit card in her assumed name. There were also two keys to the furnished apartment she'd be subletting in Flushing, Queens, along with handwritten directions to the address since looking them up online was too big a risk. She'd have a few glorious weeks to stay in one place and figure out what to do next.

Gwen's new home was in a dingy brick building overlooking a busy street in a neighborhood where most of the signs on the storefronts were written in Chinese. An ornate stainless-steel gate covered the main door, which Gwen unlocked with one of the keys. From there, it was three flights up to her unit, through a stairwell that smelled of bleach alongside fried food from the restaurant next door.

Even without laying eyes on it, Gwen already knew the studio apartment wouldn't be much to look at, but that was okay. She'd been able to afford to prepay the rent out of her savings, which was all that really mattered. That, and the fact no one who'd been to her flat in Notting Hill would ever think to look for her on this side of the proverbial tracks.

Setting down her luggage with a thud, Gwen turned the

key in the lock of apartment number three and stepped inside. She started to take a deep breath but thought better of it as the musty air clogged her lungs. No matter. Her nerves might be frayed, but she'd made it in one piece.

"Hello, Wendy."

"Who the fuck are you?" Gwen whipped around, heart racing wildly. Had she imagined it or had a stranger just called her by her real name? Even she hardly ever mentioned or thought of that name, knowing it wouldn't do her any good to hold onto the past she could never return to not even for a short visit.

A light clicked on over her head, and she came face-to-face with a young woman who was dressed in nondescript athletic wear and leaning against the all-in-one stovetop and sink unit that passed for a kitchen. She looked for all the world like she owned the place, and Gwen prayed that was what was going on here, that it was the landlord showing up to welcome a new tenant. Because the alternative was terrifying.

"I don't have a lot of time, Wendy, so calm down and listen."

Shit. She'd definitely said Wendy this time, which meant this was not the landlord paying a friendly welcome visit. As for calming down, Gwen wanted to run as fast and far as she could, but her feet were made of lead.

"How'd you find me?"

The woman sighed. "Phones are dangerous. I would have thought you'd learn that by now, but fortunately for us, you haven't."

"Us?" Gwen glanced around the space, seeing nothing but a bare mattress on a steel frame and a plastic card table with two folding chairs. There was no place for anyone else to hide, though that brought her little relief. "Are you with Kensington? Did Simon send you?"

"No," the woman claimed, not that Gwen had any reason to believe her. "I'm as interested in stopping the people you're running from as you are."

"Forgive me if I call bullshit."

The woman shrugged. "Regardless, consider yourself lucky it was us who found you, not them."

"I'm not seeing it that way. For all I know, you're with the Polyphemus project and—"

The woman put an urgent finger to her lips, cutting Gwen short. "Do not speak that name. Did you dispose of your phone in Zürich?"

"It's none of your business." Gwen wished she'd never learned the name of her former employer's top-secret project. She rued the day she'd accepted the job. "I don't even know who you are, or what you're doing here."

"Who I am is not something you need to know. As for what I want, that's simple. I need you to get close to Regina Hawkins, or should I say *closer*." There was a mocking quality as she said this that put Gwen on high alert.

"Regina Hawkins, the media vulture?" Gwen forced a laugh through her rapidly closing throat. How the hell did this woman know anything about Reggie? "You expect me to do that? I don't even know her."

The woman rubbed her forehead. "I hate it when people don't understand how much trouble they're in, and I doubly hate liars."

"Whatever, crazy lady who broke into my apartment. I was on the same flight as her yesterday. But I don't know her." Even as her pounding heart tried to knock an escape hole through her chest, Gwen had to bite down on her bottom lip to prevent herself from smiling at all the memories she wasn't owning up to.

Instead of arguing, the woman responded by playing a recording from her phone. Gwen strained to hear it, but it only took a second to recognize the sound of Reggie's scream as she orgasmed.

She grabbed the phone from the stranger and gaped at the image of Reggie sprawled out on the dayroom bed, naked and exposed. Gwen's own head was bobbing energetically between the woman's legs, leaving little mystery as to what she was doing.

"How the fuck did you get this video?"

"How do you think?" the woman asked with a smirk that made Gwen want to smack her across the face. "Maybe you'll get it this time when I say phones are dangerous. The people you're running from have created a monster. They can track anyone. Record whatever they want without anyone's knowledge or permission."

"You think I don't know that?" Gwen shook with rage. She'd already risked so much. What more could anyone want? "I've done everything I can, turned over everything I had. I'll testify when I'm asked. I don't know who sent you here, but you can tell them to go to hell. I'm done."

"I'm afraid it's not that simple."

"Why should I even believe that you're one of the good guys? Because from where I'm standing, you're just as bad." A horrible thought struck her. "Which phone did you get that recording from? Mine or...?"

"You're not in a position to ask questions. We know where you are. We know where your mother and grandfather are. We could use that information to our advantage, or you can do what I ask and nobody has to know anything. It's your choice."

"At least you're not pretending to be one of the good guys anymore." Gwen closed her eyes, rubbing her temples to ward off a sudden intense pounding. "I can't do what you're asking. I don't even know how to contact her."

"As it happens, I can give you her private number. Wonder where I got that? Hmm." The woman smirked at her own joke.

"I won't seduce her on false pretenses," Gwen declared, sickened by the thought of betraying someone she'd been intimate with in that way.

"I have no interest in making you sully your virtue." Sarcasm dripped from the stranger's lips. "Besides, I know enough about Regina Hawkins to know it wouldn't work. She doesn't date. Or have basic human emotions."

"Then how—"

"Must I spell it out? She promised you a favor." The woman held up a hand, stopping a stream of expletives from spewing from Gwen's mouth. "We saw the text. One thing I know is Regina always fulfills a promise. That, and as of a few days ago, the Hawkins Foundation is in need of an associate director. You're going to ask her to give you the job."

"You want me—" Gasping, Gwen clapped a hand to her mouth. "Did you do something to them?"

"Do something to...? Oh, you mean the former associate director?" The woman laughed, a sound that might have been pleasant if the circumstances didn't make it so sinister. "Trust me; Bitsie Donaldson, the foundation's director, can run off her staff all by herself. This is the fourth one in two years. Reggie will be desperate to fill the vacancy once she finds out Bitsie's done it again. And you're more than qualified for the job, especially considering the fake background your reporter ex-girlfriend cooked up for you."

Gwen tensed. Was there anything about her private life this woman didn't know? "If I get the job, what then? What is it you expect me to do?"

"That's a detail you don't need to know right now." The woman brushed past Gwen as she made her way to the door.

"You're a fucking bitch. You know that?" Gwen called after her.

The woman paused in the stairwell. "That's the way of the world, Wendy. You're either a bitch, or you're dead. Which do you want to be?"

CHAPTER SEVEN

A wall of hot air blasted Reggie's face as she ducked through the door of the temporary vestibule that shielded Philippe Chow's front entrance from the pelting rain. The weather since her return had been obnoxious: dark, damp, and freezing cold without the charm of falling snow. London in winter wasn't much better, but at least there she didn't have the obligation of attending monthly family dinners. And there was always a trip to the Countess's den of iniquity to keep her warm.

As if Reggie needed more reminders of everything she'd given up to obey her father's orders to come home. The one bright spot in all of it had been the hours she'd spent with a total stranger in an airport lounge. If that wasn't an indictment of her entire fucking existence, she wasn't sure what was.

And yet, even three days later, Reggie sneaked an occasional glance at her phone in the vain hope that Gwen had answered her text. It was pathetic. Even worse was how many times each day her mind wandered back to that room, reliving every moment, every inch of that gorgeous body, in excruciatingly vivid detail.

She would likely never feel so good again. And especially not tonight, as she was forced to endure an entire evening with her relatives.

The restaurant's interior was boxcar narrow. Reggie had to press her puffy winter coat to her body and turn sideways to squeeze past the packed bar until she reached the even narrower set of stairs that led to the prep kitchen. On the other side of all the frantic sizzling and steaming was the wine cellar where the Hawkins family gathered once a month at the whim of their patriarch, whether they wanted to or not.

After handing over her coat to a server, Reggie stood outside the entrance to the private dining room. As she smoothed the wrinkles from her suit, she strained to determine if she had timed her entrance right. If she heard her father's booming voice, she'd know at once that she'd failed miserably. After ten seconds without any yelling, she knew he wasn't present yet, but every other family member seemed to be accounted for.

Perfect. Just perfect.

A single, long table was set up in the center of the dimly lit room, tea lights flickering in glass holders on the white cloth. A fire in the fireplace burned brightly in the semi-darkness, sparkling off the bottles that filled the floor-to-ceiling wine racks flanking both sides. Red velvet draperies softened the walls and matching upholstery covered the chairs. There were eight place settings instead of the expected seven, causing Reggie to frown.

Trevor and Julie. Stephanie and Brandon. Aunt Val. Dad. Me. Reggie counted them out on her fingertips as she went, locating her siblings, their spouses, and her aunt as she did so. Seven, and all accounted for. So why…

"Look who decided to show up," Trevor, her twin, groused as he spun around from the table. He held a whiskey snifter with two hands, the glass only slightly trembling. It was either one of his better days, or he had yet to take a sip of the alcohol his neurologist frowned upon.

"I'm five minutes early," Reggie pointed out, which was the truth, though it still made her late by Hawkins' standards. Arriving anywhere after the old man did was the kiss of death. "I'm not the only one who got here with time to spare." She stared pointedly at the drink in his hands. "You haven't eaten yet."

"Because we can't fucking touch the food until his holiness arrives!" Even in the shadow-laden brick cellar Reggie detected the unmistakable redness of Trevor's face. Was it the whiskey or his brain injury that had him so riled up? It was impossible to tell sometimes. Trevor pounded the table, making the silverware rattle. "I'm starving."

"He'll be here soon," Julie, his wife, rested a hand on Trevor's arm in a practiced move meant to calm him.

He wiggled free like a petulant child and slammed his drink down his gullet in two hearty gulps. Reggie stared daggers into her twin's eyes, trying to convey one thought: *Pull yourself together, Trev.*

This only made him bristle even more. He'd picked up on her meaning, as usual. It was a twin thing. Even after seven years away, it was impossible to deny the connection. The others in the family hated how they could read each other's thoughts sometimes. But they were jealous, and honestly, it was far more often a curse than a blessing to know what her brother was thinking these past few years.

Deliberately forcing her thoughts from the darkness of her brother's accident, Reggie strode toward the fireplace, holding out her frozen fingers. The warmth from the roaring flames helped combat her nerves as she awaited her father's arrival.

Her last chat with her father, if one could call it that, had left a bitter taste in her mouth. Some might think there was safety in numbers and that having all her closest family members in the room would protect her from her father's sharp tongue or brash ways, but Reginald Hawkins never cowered or held back.

Why had Reggie agreed to come back to New York? She was forty-two and no longer needed her father's approval. Yeah, right. Everyone in this room did.

"It's good to see you." Coming up beside her, Aunt Val, her father's older sister, gave Reggie's shoulder a quick squeeze. "How was Switzerland?"

For a moment, all Reggie could remember from Switzerland was getting laid. Heat flushed her face, but fortunately she was left with enough functioning brain cells to recognize that nothing about her encounter with Gwen was appropriate dinnertime conversation.

"A blur, really," she answered evasively. "Everything seems to be that way these days."

"Wait until you reach my age," her aunt said with a laugh. "Any news on the Phoenix deal? I heard you met with their head of European operations in Davos."

"It's still on track for seventy-four bil, although they're pissed the news isn't part of the deal, but Dad refused to push for an executive position for me at Phoenix." Reggie balled her fists as the familiar anger swelled. If she had her way, the whole deal would go up in flames.

"Yes, I heard your father's giving you the Hawkins Foundation," Val remarked. There were no congratulations forthcoming, and Reggie knew it was because her aunt, like her, recognized the move as the insult it was.

"I guess now that Uncle Carl has decided to become a full-time Texan, Aunt Madge doesn't feel she has the time to devote to being the foundation chair." Reggie shrugged. "Or, you know, Dad took it from her so he could saddle me with it and anchor me to this side of the Atlantic."

"I'm sure you'll manage to make some good come of it." Aunt Val's legendary diplomacy was on full display. "Did you hear Bitsie Donaldson scared off another associate director? Considering the woman only got the job because she was sorority sisters with Madge and has never done a day of work in her life, you'll have a challenge starting on day one."

"Shit." Unwilling to think too hard about this unwelcome development, Reggie cast a surreptitious glance at the extra chair. "Is Uncle Carl coming tonight? Or Dwight?"

"Not that I'm aware. Carl's at the ranch, and your cousin's on the campaign trail nonstop, what with the special election looming. But his poll numbers are up, so it's paying off." There was a hint of pride in Val's tone as she spoke of her nephew.

"That's good news." For a moment, Reggie wondered why her aunt had never had children of her own. She was of the generation where it was almost a requirement, and yet, despite a marriage of over thirty years before her husband had died, she'd remained child-free. Reggie looked again at the table with its extra chair. "What's up with the eighth seat?"

"Your father has invited a lady friend." Aunt Val said this through clenched teeth, not bothering to hide her distaste.

"Dad's bringing a girlfriend?" Stephanie, Reggie's younger sister, said in a voice that was several notches too loud.

"A new one?" Julie shook her head, which was the only possible response to a man in his late seventies who dated more than a teenage boy.

"Not new," Trevor said. "I'm trying to think of her name. It starts with an R. We met her after Thanksgiving, I think."

Trevor and Reggie briefly locked eyes, and instantly, she knew this was another example of her brother's injury.

"Rovena," Reggie supplied because, of course, she did. It helped the woman's name was so similar to Regina. But aside from remembering every little detail, covering up for Trevor's shortfalls was what she did best. That was why she was here in New York instead of doing a job she actually cared about in a city she enjoyed. "He's still dating her?"

Trevor smothered his face with a palm. "We're going to have a new mommy."

"You know what they say, why stop at four failed marriages when you can bomb on the fifth." Brandon, Stephanie's husband, chuckled over his joke, receiving the stink eye from his wife.

"I'll have you know, wives play a very important role in any man's life, including yours." Stephanie meant this as a warning, and Brandon was smart enough to lean in for a quick peck on the lips.

"They do," he agreed in his typical kiss-ass way, cementing Reggie's impression that Brandon arrived in this world with his lips puckered.

"What exactly are your wifely duties, Sister dear?" Trevor

craned his neck to see Stephanie standing behind him. "Last I heard, you were interviewing yet another nanny. How do you go through them so quickly?"

"I don't go through them. I'm hiring an additional one." Stephanie rested a hand on her growing baby bump.

"A nanny for a kid that hasn't even taken a breath?" Trevor jabbed a finger toward Stephanie's swollen midsection, prompting her to scoot backward, out of reach.

"You try managing four children with only two nannies," Stephanie huffed, returning to her seat.

"The fourth isn't out yet," Reggie balked.

"No, baby will make five. You're forgetting my man-child husband. Do you think this one does a thing around the house?" The accusation wasn't so much lobbed in Brandon's direction but hurled with enough might Brandon, if he had any sense, would have fallen to the ground like a dog playing dead.

Instead, he tried another appeasing kiss, but it didn't have the same placating effect. Reggie smothered a laugh. As far as she was concerned, Brandon was a brown-nosing interloper who needed to be put in his place a little more often.

"How old is Rovena? Fifties?" Trevor closed his eyes as if that helped him divine the answer.

"Mid-forties," Val said. "I'm pretty sure."

"Oh, thank god." The relief was evident in Trevor's face. "Way past her prime."

"Excuse me?" Reggie directed her irritation squarely at her twin. "We're approaching our mid-forties, you dolt."

"I meant, she can't get, you know, pregnant," Trevor said sheepishly.

"I'm with you there, Bro," Reggie agreed.

"Why is it no one is mentioning that Dad is past his prime?" Stephanie demanded in a huff. "He's nearly twice Rovena's age. Sure, forties are the new thirties. But he's almost eighty, and that's still ancient as ever."

"Guys can have kids well into their eighties," Trevor pointed out with a level of boasting that was truly obnoxious. "Robert De Niro just had a kid, and he's seventy-nine. It's why we're superior."

"I'm so sick of the attitude in this family." Stephanie's voice trembled. "If you ask me, none of the men in this room would be half as successful if it wasn't for their wives."

"Maybe I should get a wife, then?" Reggie joked.

Instead of the expected laughter, the room fell dead silent. The only thing missing was the sound of a needle scratching across a vinyl record. One glance to the doorway made the reason evident. Her father stood in the opening with a murderous expression on his face.

"How dare you?" He strode directly over to Reggie and slapped her once across the face.

"What was that for?" Reggie rubbed her stinging cheek, blinking back tears.

Shit. Had he heard what they were saying about Rovena and him?

"That was for your dirty mouth," he bellowed. "You want people to think you're an-honest-to god lesbian?"

"I'm not a child," Reggie whimpered, too shocked by his irrational anger to process anything. "You can't slap me like that."

"Who's going to stop me?" Her father made eye contact with everyone in the room, each and every one of them dropping their gaze. "That's what I thought. Now, shall we eat?"

Rovena smiled at Reggie, not out of sympathy, but with a shark-like quality, sniffing blood in the water. She wore a skirt that was simultaneously too tight and too short, with unnaturally bleached hair and too much makeup. Her father's girlfriend looked like a prostitute.

If anyone should know about that, it's me.

Reggie nearly fell over at her own joke, using every ounce of strength not to laugh. She was shaking from the whole ordeal, half out of her mind with shock and anger. As the others dug into the food, Reggie poured a glass of wine to the brim, her appetite gone.

When the chatter around the table put the slap out of everyone's minds, Reggie got up for the bathroom. Staring in the mirror, her cheek still reddening, Reggie willed the tears not to fall, but they didn't listen.

The bathroom door cracked open, and Reggie let out a groan. Why couldn't everyone leave her alone?

"Are you okay?" Aunt Val's tone matched the sympathy in her eyes.

"I don't know what I am." *Other than a lesbian.* According to her father, nothing else mattered.

Reggie splashed water on her face in an attempt to cover the evidence of what had transpired moments ago.

Val leaned against the bathroom counter. "I thought you should know there's a lot of rumbling going on with the Hawks Corp board."

"About?" Reggie reapplied lip gloss, trying not to read too much into her aunt's gossipy tone. It was just as likely she was fishing for information as bearing important news.

"Trevor, for one thing. People are starting to notice he's not like he used to be. His temper is getting worse."

"All the Hawkins men have tempers," Reggie said with caution, not wanting to reveal more than her aunt already knew. "The apple doesn't fall far from the tree."

Her aunt met her gaze in the bathroom mirror, wearing a look that made it clear she would not be dismissed. "It's more than that. You know it. And so do I. Ever since that incident on the boat you all think I don't know about. Isn't that right?"

Swallowing hard, Reggie nodded.

"Withholding that from the shareholders is unethical, you know. There's also talk about Reginald." Val met Reggie's eyes. "Robert De Niro may be having kids in his seventies, but he isn't running a multi-billion-dollar company. More than a few of the board members think a man within a stone's throw of eighty has no business in the corner office. He's out of touch. Tonight's performance proves that."

"Which one, the homophobia or the corporal punishment?" Reggie's voice cracked despite every effort she made to stop it from doing just that. "It was quite the double feature."

"Take your pick. Violence is never appealing, and neither is thinking society should be stuck in the past." Val's disgust was plain on her face.

"Why are you telling me this?" While Reggie was grateful for the pep talk, Aunt Val hadn't always been her biggest champion. She was kind to a certain degree, befitting her role as a loving auntie, but she was still her brother's sister. That made her a dangerous ally.

"Because I know you, my darling niece. Right now, you

want nothing more than to torpedo your father. You'll burn it all to the ground if you have to."

Reggie stood silent. Her aunt wasn't wrong.

"Don't light the match just yet. Not when I can get you what you really want." Aunt Val proceeded in a conspiratorial whisper. "I've been hinting around to key members of the board that someone else might be better suited for CEO."

"You?" Reggie guessed.

"Heavens." Val laughed. "I'm even older than your father. No, I'm thinking the company needs to pass to the next generation. But you'd have to make some changes."

"Me? You think I have a shot at it?" Now Val had Reggie's full attention. "Tell me what kind of changes you have in mind."

"As you know, there are six members of the Hawkins family on the board and seven outsiders. The family has generally been in thrall to Reginald's whims, but the rest of the board craves stability more than loyalty. Let's assume we vote together against your father." Val held up two fingers. We need five of the seven on our side to override my brother's wishes. Right now, I know for certain how to get you three. When we flip them, at least two others might wobble."

"It's a longshot, but…" Reggie bit her lip, weighing the risks. What did she have to lose? "Tell me what I need to do to win over the three."

A victorious expression slid over Val's lined face. "They'd like you to settle down, here in New York, where they can keep an eye on you. And frankly, while Stephanie is usually an idiot, sometimes she's not wrong. Getting married would do wonders to rehab your reputation with some of the naysayers."

Reggie rolled her eyes at this straight out of the 1950s advice. "I've got two ex-husbands already. I'm not like my father. I can't do it again."

"Reggie, you can't fool me." There was a hint of sadness in her aunt's tone, and an unreadable expression on her face. "I know, okay? I know."

"Know what?" Reggie rubbed her cheek as her body tensed. If her aunt called her queer in so many words, Reggie would have to deny it. Again. She was running out of strength to keep lying.

"That what you really need is not a husband but a wife." Instead of rage or disgust like Reggie's father would have shown, Aunt Val's demeanor was gentle and understanding. All at once, it struck Reggie. Was this the answer to the true cause of her aunt's childless state? Were the two of them more alike than Reggie had realized? It would explain a few things, to say the least.

Reggie couldn't trust it. It might be a trap.

"Yeah, the board would love that," Reggie said with a snort.

"A few of them would," Val countered. "And more than a few of the others wouldn't care."

"And the average Hawks News viewer?"

"Hawks Corp is much more than that crackpot, tinfoil hat wearing bunch of conspiracy theorists, even if that is all people think we are any more. The truth is, putting an openly queer woman in the top spot could do wonders for the company's less-than-stellar reputation where diversity is concerned. It's not just the liberal-minded members of the board, you know. According to our polling, more than half of the country wants positive change on that front."

"I'm not *openly* anything." Reggie folded her arms across her chest. That wasn't exactly a denial, as her aunt almost certainly knew, too. "Can you imagine if I married a woman? Forget being disowned. Dad would have me shot, and he wouldn't hire someone to do it. He'd pull the trigger himself."

"Even he wouldn't go that far, but he might do something very stupid, and I think that could work to your advantage."

Aunt Val might actually be serious.

Reggie let out a shaky breath. "How?"

"A rage like he showed tonight would alienate him even further from several key voting members." It was clear she'd thought this through, a realization that left Reggie terrified. If she went through with what her aunt was suggesting, it would turn her carefully crafted life on its head.

It could possibly set her free.

Was Reggie ready to open herself up to such scrutiny?

How much was her freedom worth? Would it just be her father who turned his back on her? What about Trevor? Stephanie? Could Reggie stand on her own two feet without the might of the Hawkins name?

"It's not like I can conjure a woman out of thin air and make her my wife." As if rising to the challenge, an image of Gwen flitted through Reggie's mind. Instantly, she banished it to the shadows where it belonged. "Even if I could, Dad might die from the shock."

"That'd be the icing on the cake." Aunt Val's eyes twinkled at the thought. "I love my brother, and I'm not saying I wish him ill..."

"But?" Reggie arched a brow, wondering how far her aunt would take this line of thought.

"He's not good for the company; that's all." Aunt Val rummaged in her handbag, emerging with a tube of concealer. "Now put some cover up on that before the bruise starts to show, and get back in there."

If Reggie didn't know better, she'd think she'd stumbled into the middle of a coup. Much as she relished the prospect of beating her father at his own game and securing the top job despite him, she'd have to watch her back lest she end up with a knife in it.

"Ready to return to the lion's den?" she asked her reflection in the mirror.

Instead of waiting for an answer, which might not be the one she needed to hear, Reggie plucked her phone from her bag, her finger tapped the screen, her eyes scanning for the same thing they'd been searching for since landing in New York.

One new message from an unknown number.

Reggie let out a deflated sigh. When would she give up and accept the text she hoped for would never come?

She nearly tossed the phone back into her bag without another thought, but her curiosity got the better of her. Unknown callers on her private number were rare. She opened the message, and her heart sprang to her throat.

Reggie, this is Gwen.

I need you.

Funny. Reggie was thinking exactly the same thing.

CHAPTER EIGHT

"I'll let Ms. Hawkins know you've arrived. Have a seat." The stern-looking receptionist jerked her head toward two neutral gray armchairs grouped around a short, round table with a vase full of fresh flowers on its gleaming glass surface. Her nose wrinkled as she gave Gwen the once-over, as if the bright yellow clearance tag from the discount store was still hanging from the armpit of Gwen's no-name suit jacket.

"Thank you," Gwen effused, trying to keep her nerves from fraying under the office worker's scrutiny. She was dressed appropriately for an interview at a nonprofit organization, regardless of how much (or little) she'd spent on her attire. She had every right to occupy this space.

Besides, Reggie had seen her wearing a hell of a lot less. If that weren't true, Gwen wouldn't be here right now. Reggie had promised her a favor, and Gwen needed to collect on it. Her safety, and her family's, depended on it.

Hawks Corp's corporate headquarters were a stone's throw from Times Square, in the part of Manhattan where high-rise buildings lined the streets like the walls of a deep, narrow canyon. Even forty-six floors up, there was no expansive view to be had, just the shiny windows of other equally tall buildings so close Gwen was convinced she could reach out and touch them.

Her breathing was shallow, her shoulders hunched under the claustrophobic sensation caused by those buildings pressing in. Or maybe it was the vague threat of exposure from the strange woman who had violated the privacy of her apartment and forced her on this fool's errand that had Gwen feeling a little on edge.

Go figure.

Despite the lack of exterior vistas, the executive floor where Reggie's office sat emitted a spacious and sophisticated aura. It whispered of a level of money and influence most mere mortals couldn't dream of, let alone achieve. If the Hawkins family was an 18-wheeler on the highway of life, Gwen was a gnat that could get squashed on its windshield, and no one would notice.

Maybe texting Reggie had been a colossal miscalculation.

"Ms. Hawkins will see you now." The receptionist's tone did not invite argument, and Gwen hurriedly made her way to the office door. It was quite a reversal from the dominant role she'd enacted in Zürich, but this was Reggie's domain, and it was Gwen's turn to do as she was told. Besides, whoever it was who'd videoed them together had left Gwen with no alternative. She would beg, plead, or whatever it took to get a job that would give her access to Hawks Corp.

The corner office was at least five times the size of Gwen's studio apartment, with walls that were nothing but glass. The views that had been lacking from other parts of the floor were present here, and then some, stretching all the way to the Hudson River in the distance. Gwen took it all in with the practiced indifference she'd learned through interacting with the super-rich while working at Kensington, masking her awe. Besides, what was outside the window paled in comparison to what was in front of it.

Reggie sat with her back to the panorama at a desk that was sleek and functional. She was dressed in a light gray suit that blended so well with the neutral tones surrounding her that Gwen wondered if it was intentional. Her head bent over her work, dark hair falling forward and catching a ray of sunlight from the window, making Gwen long to brush it back.

The woman appeared to be unaware of Gwen's presence, but she suspected this was a power play. The seconds ticked by, Gwen seeming to shrink in stature with each one, until she was very small, indeed, despite the advantage of her height.

"Hello again." Gwen's voice was no more than a mouse's squeak.

After what seemed an eternity, Reggie lifted her head. The moment their eyes met, a switch was thrown, and Gwen's body hummed like a live wire. It'd only been a week since Zürich, but even so, Gwen had forgotten the intense effect this woman's presence had. It was unnerving, and inconvenient, considering what Gwen had been sent here to do.

"Thank you for waiting, Ms. Murphy." Reggie's demeanor was pleasant but detached. Nothing about her gave the slightest hint they'd met before, let alone become acquainted in the most intimate of ways. Either Reggie was even more of a master at hiding her natural reactions than

Gwen, or the time they'd spent together in Zürich had left absolutely zero impression on her.

And what the hell did Reggie mean by referring to her as Ms. Murphy?

"I… uh…" Damn it. Five seconds in and Gwen was shaken to the core and not in a good way.

"I assume you had a reason for asking to meet today?" Reggie arched an eyebrow, a simple facial tick that wobbled Gwen's knees. "Would you like to take a seat? You look unsteady."

The woman would have to notice something embarrassing. Not that Gwen could argue. High heels had been a poor choice. Without waiting to be asked twice, Gwen took a seat in a cream and steel chair that sat directly across from Reggie. It was more comfortable than it looked, but nerves kept her from sinking in.

"As I explained in my text, I'm looking for a job. I understand there might be an opening at the Hawkins Foundation." Gwen focused her eyes on the view as a way to calm her nerves. After how quickly the sparks had flown before, she hadn't expected Reggie to be so hard to read.

"Yes. I got that much." Reggie studied Gwen in silence, showing no inclination to help move this dialogue along. Had she not been serious about owing Gwen a favor? She almost seemed angry, in a totally neutral way.

"I brought my resume." Gwen's fingers were all thumbs, and she fumbled with the zipper on her bag.

"No need. I had my people run a background check on you last week."

"Last week? But I only texted you yes—"

Oh.

Gwen stopped short as the truth of the situation sank in.

99

The background check had nothing to do with a job. Reggie had been doing her due diligence after the fact to make sure Gwen was who she'd said she was. Which, she was not. Gwen resisted the urge to cough, her throat suddenly parched. Her discomfort must have shown clearly on her face.

A ghost of a smile appeared on Reggie's lips, as if watching Gwen squirm brought her pleasure. Was it just a perverse enjoyment of having the upper hand, or was Reggie about to spring a trap? If so, Gwen had walked right into it.

"I have to admit"—Reggie flipped through the contents of a folder on her desk—"I was surprised by the quality of your experience."

"Not used to people asking for jobs they're qualified for?"

"I assure you nothing about this is typical." Reggie closed the file. "In situations like ours, I usually pay in advance."

Gwen stiffened. Was that Reggie's ultra-smooth, Ivy League way of calling Gwen a whore? *I think she's actually angry with me.* For some reason, the possibility lifted Gwen's spirits. At least the woman wasn't as icy as she tried to make it seem.

"I wouldn't have contacted you at all, except my need for employment became urgent."

"Oh?" Reggie leaned back in her chair, threading her fingers behind her head. It was a casual pose, but a sudden hardening of her jaw said Gwen's comment about not contacting her had landed hard. Was that what the hostility was about?

"Yes. Circumstances can change surprisingly quickly. Life, eh?" Gwen shrugged, but inside she was dancing a jig.

She'd gotten under the woman's skin for sure. Clearly, when Reggie gave a girl her phone number, she assumed it would be impossible to resist using it.

"They can, indeed." When Reggie said nothing else, Gwen became spooked.

"Is that your way of saying you don't want to help me anymore?" Gwen curled her fingers tightly around the arms of her chair, urging herself not to panic. She needed this job, but she wasn't out of cards yet. It wasn't like she wanted to drop the fact that some crazy bitch had Reggie and Gwen's tryst on video, but she'd use it if she had to. This was what her past had forced her to become. Primal.

"I don't like owing," Reggie said, not really clarifying anything.

Did anyone like owing? Gwen doubted it. But the real question was whether this woman was the type to pay her debts or wriggle out of them. Considering she was a Hawkins, it could go either way. But suddenly, Gwen couldn't stomach the game another second. So much for being the one to do anything to survive.

"You don't owe me anything." Hoisting herself out of the chair, Gwen squared her shoulders. Consequences be damned, this was wrong. She'd figure out some other way, even if it meant going on the run again. "I'm sorry to have—"

"Sit," Reggie barked. She had the decency to look shocked over her own tone, her cheeks blushing pink. "Please. I haven't finished with what I was going to say."

The fire in Reggie's tone proved she was angry, but her folded shoulders told a different story. She was completely mortified by her outburst. And maybe something more. She'd almost seemed frantic to make Gwen stay. But why?

"I shouldn't have asked," Gwen couldn't keep herself from saying, even as she retook her seat, more confused than ever. If Reggie hated owing, Gwen wasn't too keen on being owed, at least not for this. Despite what Reggie seemed to think, having sex had not been transactional. At least, not to Gwen.

Did Reggie's steely silence agree with Gwen's statement?

"Me being here has nothing to do with what happened last week, okay? I need you to understand that. You really don't owe me anything. But I do think I can help where the foundation is concerned." The first truth, or so it seemed, since stepping into this office.

"Oddly, I agree." Reggie's face pinched, and with as miserable as she looked, her need for Gwen's assistance was almost palpably real. "I suddenly find myself in charge of an organization that can't keep an associate director for longer than six months."

"Forgive me for asking, but is there a reason for that?"

"I hope it's a run of bad luck and nothing more." There was sincerity in Reggie's tone that was hard to fake. "To be honest, I don't know very much about it yet. Up until recently, my uncle's wife had been in charge of it. Between you and me, she was as useless as the ditzy friend of hers she appointed to handle the day-to-day operations. I need someone I can count on to tell me what changes need to be made."

"Really?" Despite this being a setup, genuine excitement surged through Gwen. Something that offered value to society, instead of destroying it. "Do you mean you're going to offer me the job?"

"I'm not even sure I can count this as your favor," Reggie admitted. "With your background, you're actually perfect."

"I am?" Gwen couldn't be bothered to play it cool. Thank goodness Solène had insisted on a cover story similar to who Gwen really was. The specifics had been changed, but the experience was her own. This was a job she could make a difference doing, and maybe wash away some of the stain of working for Simon in the process. "I can't believe you're going to give me the position of associate director."

"I'm surprised by it myself," Reggie admitted. "But yes, I think you're exactly what I need."

"I thought you would laugh, and I'd be lucky to get a job answering phones." All at once, Gwen found herself blinking back tears. After everything she'd gone through, her luck was finally changing.

"That would be a waste of your considerable talents. Before we finalize things—" Reggie straightened, scooting some papers across the desk. "I need you to sign this NDA."

"For...?" Gwen didn't finish the sentence because she wasn't sure of a polite way to ask how extensive this agreement might be. Not that it mattered. The last thing Gwen intended to do was tell a soul that she'd basically blackmailed a billionaire into handing over her dream job after fucking her in an airport. "Never mind. Whatever it is, I'll sign it."

Reggie offered her a nod. "I appreciate that. It's standard verbiage, but take your time reading it."

Gwen fanned through the stack of densely worded legalese. "There's a lot here."

"I like to cover my bases." For the first time, there was more than a hint of humor in Reggie's tone, like the woman Gwen remembered from Zürich.

"You know what? I'm sure it's fine. I trust you." Gwen

took the pen and signed Gwen Murphy, wondering how much that would hold up in court.

Reggie studied the papers, clearing her throat. "Now that we got that out of the way, I feel like I should tell you the truth."

Gwen went stone-cold. Maybe she'd been too hasty with her trustfulness. "The truth about what? Are you not giving me this job?"

"It's not that," Reggie assured her, seeming almost sorry for making her worry. "I was serious about the job. I need some eyes and ears over there, and yours are perfect for it. I've got the paperwork here. Salary and benefit package, the works."

Gwen took the folder that Reggie offered, her eyes widening at the dollar amounts listed. It was a good offer in the low six-figures, more money than she'd ever made at a nonprofit, even if it paled in comparison to what Kensington had promised. Not that they'd delivered half of what they'd said they would.

"Seems in order." Gwen closed the folder, bobbing her head.

"Then there's this." Reggie handed her a different folder. This time, when Gwen scanned what was inside, her jaw dropped.

"What the fuck is this?" Gwen's vision blurred, and she had to count all the zeroes again to make sure she had it right. "Fourteen million dollars? No associate director makes that much, or even a director, unless they're crooked. Do you want me to cook the books or something?"

"Is that something you'd do?"

"Absolutely not!"

There was the smile Gwen continued to picture in her head.

"That's good to hear. No. This has nothing to do with the foundation." Reggie touched the tip of her tongue to her lips.

Instantly, Gwen crossed her legs in response. "What then?"

"Something more personal."

"What personal services do you think you'll be paying me for?" She played it as prim and proper as she could, with a hint of outrage befitting a chaperone in a Jane Austen novel thrown in for good measure. The last thing she wanted Reggie to know was how that simple flick of the tongue and all that it implied had set off a tidal wave that threatened to soak through her panties.

"Not what you're thinking, so calm your tits." Reggie had the audacity to ogle the aforementioned body parts quite openly at that moment. The hunger in her eyes suggested she was every bit as impressed as when she'd landed face-first between them, even if she was trying to claim otherwise.

"You can't blame me for assuming." Embarrassment on top of arousal set Gwen's body alight like a can of lighter fluid over hot coals at a Fourth of July cookout.

All the while, that number flashed in her head, more zeroes than she could imagine. Even before she'd had to drain her bank account to go into hiding, she could never have dreamed of a number this big. It was insanity.

Yet, what might she be willing to do for that much money? It would change her life for certain. And her mother's, who was trapped with Gwen's spiteful grandfather for lack of any other options. But anything worth that much had to be illegal, immoral, or both.

"I'm sorry, but I can't possibly imagine what could be worth fourteen million dollars."

"I can think of a few things," Reggie mumbled, her eyes landing on Gwen's breasts again. "Like a prenuptial agreement, for instance."

"A what?" Gwen knew what a prenuptial agreement was, but not what it had to do with the situation at hand.

"You see, my brother has a wife. Julie, lovely girl. She's stuck with him through… well, through a lot."

"If your brother already has a wife, I'm assuming you aren't intending for me to…" Honestly, Gwen couldn't even finish the sentence. It was too absurd. She'd never met Reggie's brother, and she had no interest in a polygamous, sister-wives type of arrangement. Were the Hawkins part of a cult? It would explain a lot about their so-called news organization.

"It's been suggested to me from someone in the know that being single is my primary disadvantage in the quest for the corner office."

"Is this not a corner office?" Gwen's gaze swept the space. It sure seemed corner-shaped to her.

"It's not the one I want." Reggie swept a hand vaguely to her right. "The CEO's office is on that side of the floor. And it should be mine."

"Uh-huh." Gwen would've liked to respond with more eloquence, but she was too confused. "So, you need my help finding you a husband?"

"Good God, no." Reggie shuddered, her nose twitching like Gwen had placed a bag of dirty socks beneath her nose. "I won't make that mistake again. This time, I need a wife."

"And you want me to help you find one?" Gwen was fairly sure she'd lost the thread of the conversation some time ago, along with her ability to think coherent thoughts.

"Are you okay?" Reggie's stare radiated incredulity. "Do you need some coffee or something?"

"Do you have that kind you can set on fire?" Gwen whimpered. She was so far in over her head it wasn't funny. "Better yet, can you just spell it out for me? This guessing game is making me dizzy."

"Gwen Murphy,"—Reggie clasped her hands together in a pleading gesture that was ridiculously melodramatic, even under these bizarre circumstances—"do you agree to be my wife for a period of eighteen to twenty-four months, as needed for me to secure the position as my father's successor, after which we will divorce, and you will be given fourteen million dollars?"

"Uh…" Gwen pressed a hand to her chest, almost the way she might have if Reggie had made some grand romantic gesture. That was definitely not what had happened. Reggie's proposal was insane. Insulting, even. But if Gwen wanted access to the inner circle, and to keep herself and her family safe for as long as possible, there was no better way. "I do?"

CHAPTER NINE

"You do?" Reggie half expected confetti to rain down on her head while a bridal march began to play. "I mean, you accept?"

"Yes. I think so." Gwen, too, seemed stunned. "That is what you wanted me to say, right?"

Reggie couldn't believe she'd heard correctly. Gwen Murphy—looking every bit as amazing today, despite her ill-fitting, off-the-rack black suit, as she had while lying naked and flushed in the bed in Zürich—had agreed to be her wife. The impact of it was unexpected, and Reggie shifted in her desk chair, unable to rein in her nervous energy.

She'd been dead serious about her proposal, but never in a million years had she expected it to be this easy to get a yes. Or to experience the surge of adrenaline from it that she had. What was she supposed to do now?

"This is excellent news." Gathering her wits, Reggie picked up a pen and shifted a legal pad into an empty space on her desk. She had a hard time strategizing unless drawing circles with arrows. "I guess now we need to plan our attack."

Gwen's color shifted from rosy to ghostly. "This sounds less like a wedding and more like a war."

Reggie couldn't hold back a smirk. "You've never been to a Hawkins wedding."

"Ominous, considering what I've just agreed to." Deep lines creased Gwen's forehead, giving her an almost studious look. "What have I agreed to, exactly? Because I came here hoping for a job, and I thought I had one, but now I'm confused."

"Let me see if I can explain." Reggie frantically sketched a circle, putting an F in the middle. "You'll start working at the foundation, here." She made another circle, but Gwen held up a hand to stop her before Reggie could add a label.

"You're going to need to elaborate. Like, a lot. To be honest, I don't even know exactly where the Hawkins Foundation is located—you know, on a map—let alone how me working there leads to us getting married."

Reggie tapped her pen on the pad, but despite leaving a few dozen black dots on the yellow sheet, she couldn't come up with a way to express her plan in a neat diagram. Probably because it was batshit crazy.

"The foundation headquarters are on Fifth Avenue, near Bryant Park." Reggie set the writing implement down and folded her hands, fixing a steady gaze on Gwen. Having imparted that single piece of information, she was fresh out of easy answers and had no idea how to proceed.

"Welp, that clears up everything. Thanks." Gwen's eyes were as unfaltering as Reggie's own, the sarcasm as thick as the cheese fondue they'd once shared. "Is this an inheritance scam?"

"Excuse me?"

"You know, where your grandfather left you a trust fund but you have to be married before you turn forty to collect it?"

Reggie chuckled, partly spurred by the serious way Gwen had delivered her absurd question, but mostly because she was tickled at being mistaken for younger than reality. Far be it from Reggie to disabuse Gwen of that right away.

"I think what you described only happens in the movies." Reggie sucked in her cheeks to keep from laughing more. "But no, this has nothing to do with a trust fund."

Gwen scowled. "Yeah, well, I wouldn't know. We're not really the trust fund type in my family."

"No, but you've been around people with money." Reggie surprised herself by putting this observation into words. "I noticed it in the airport, and again here in this office, surrounded by all the trappings of wealth. You catch on quickly and blend in."

"Instead of gawking at everything like a middle-class tourist on holiday?" Gwen's shoulders had tensed, and Reggie feared she'd stepped in it.

"I didn't mean to imply any sort of criticism. It's just unusual. And, frankly, helpful, considering what I'm asking of you." Reggie offered a reassuring smile. "Being able to fake it under pressure will be a huge asset as my spouse."

"Don't be too hard on yourself. You did just fine in Zürich." Humor glinted in Gwen's eyes, and it was her turn to laugh.

Reggie caught on to what was being implied, her cheeks burning. It was the elephant in the room, and it needed to be addressed at once. "I want to be clear. This deal has nothing to do with sex. That is to say, I don't want sex. Or, I mean—"

Jesus, Reggie. Stop before you combust.

Gwen crossed her arms and pursed her lips. "You might think you're making the situation better right now, but just so you know, you're digging that hole deeper by the second."

Yeah, Reggie was aware.

Of course, some part of Reggie—a very physical part— wanted to have sex with Gwen again. Preferably soon and often. But simple logic told her a fake marriage would be difficult enough without complicating it with sex. On top of that, her pride was stubbornly opposed. After all, Gwen would never have texted her if she hadn't needed a favor. Their time together had left zero impression on the woman, and Reggie wasn't about to humiliate herself by pretending otherwise.

"You said you wanted details. I'm trying to provide them." There was no hiding her testiness, but Reggie didn't care. She had every right to feel hurt. Gwen's indifference had wounded Reggie more than she cared to admit.

"I'm sorry. Please, continue. I want to know everything about your plan." At least Gwen's contrition for interrupting seemed sincere.

Yes. The plan. Reggie glanced at the legal pad, but her incomprehensible doodles offered no assistance whatsoever.

"I can't emphasize this enough. My family isn't the type that can be easily fooled."

"No pressure, then. Sorry." Gwen grimaced at her sarcasm. "Can I ask, am I what they expect?"

"No." At last, a question that didn't leave Reggie stumped.

"I didn't think so. I haven't forgotten about that countess of yours, you know. The one who arranges things like this, who could probably find exactly the person your family would want." Gwen tilted her head thoughtfully. "Why me?"

A damn good question. One Reggie couldn't answer because she wasn't sure she could put it into words. Gwen was right. Contracting with an expert like the countess would have made way more sense. But Gwen's text had arrived at exactly the right moment, like a sign. Marrying anyone else had never crossed Reggie's mind. But it wasn't like she could say that.

Instead, she shrugged. "You said you needed a job. As careful as we need to be to convince them, part of me likes the challenge of doing it my way." With Gwen.

"That is consistent with your reputation," Gwen agreed. "But tell me, are they even expecting you to marry a woman?"

"No, and that's the best part." A smile spread across Reggie's lips as she imagined what her father had in store over the next few months. He'd crossed a line, slapping her the way he had. Finally, he would get what he deserved. "I fully expect certain members of my family to lose their collective shit over it. But with the votes in place to override my father's choice of successor, there's nothing they can do. And I'm fucking sick of hiding who I am."

"You seem committed." Gwen leaned forward, elbows on Reggie's desk. "Give me the battle plan."

"Later today, I'm going to have my brother's office send your paperwork to the foundation. That way, I have nothing to do with it. No fingerprints. You'll have to go through the proper channels, sit down for an interview and all of that, but with it coming from our executive offices, you're a shoo-in." Reggie paused so Gwen could absorb the information. When there were no questions, she continued. "There's going to be an event in a few weeks for the top donors. It'll be my first one as the new chairperson. That's where we'll officially meet."

"And you'll sweep me off my feet?" Gwen arched a brow. "Or should I be the one to sweep you?"

"Not even close. For my family to find this remotely believable, I'm going to have to deny it for weeks. That's what I would do if this were real." She tapped her pen against her front tooth. "At the party, you stick close to the director, and I'll introduce myself to you both when I have a chance. We'll be seen together, talking, maybe laughing."

"Will you be saying something funny, or should I come prepared with some jokes?"

"Good question. I think we can just—" Belatedly, Reggie absorbed Gwen's smirk and realized she was teasing. "I see you're already the comedian."

"I couldn't help it. You're very thorough." Gwen smothered her laughter with a hand across her mouth. It was way more charming than it should have been, and Reggie found herself mesmerized until Gwen prompted her. "You were saying?"

"Uh, right. The point is, we want people to see us together. A few nights later, I'll take you to dinner. Strictly business, or at least that will be the official line. But I'll arrange for some photographers to be in the area. Not anyone associated with Hawks Corp. It'll have to be one of our rival newspapers, the trashier the better. We'll need to juice the media circus."

"I'm sorry, but are you suggesting having paparazzi

follow us around?" Gwen's alarm seemed genuine, catching Reggie by surprise.

"Do you know a better way to get tongues wagging?"

"No, but I'm not sure how I feel about having my face in all the papers."

"Just the tabloids." As someone who had grown up in this business, Reggie failed to see the problem, but it was obvious Gwen felt otherwise. "What if I promised to arrange it so none of the photos showed your face? Would that be better?"

"I guess, but—"

"You're going to have to trust me, okay? At least on this part. One benefit of being a Hawkins is I know how this all works. I could probably orchestrate a media storm while in a coma. For the most part, not many know who I am. New York is filled with rich assholes. I'm hoping to catch the eyes and ears of just those few who do pay attention to my family and company." Picking up her discarded pen, Reggie drew another circle on the paper, not for any purpose, but to feel more grounded. This was the part of the conversation where things got surreal. "We'll keep meeting up, getting people whispering, and denying it all. Sometime in May, we'll get caught kissing on camera. Bam. Plausible deniability up in smoke." Reggie blew on her fingertips.

"I thought you said no sex," Gwen objected.

"Since when is kissing sex?" Reggie countered, hating that the very word *sex* was enough to turn her brain to mush when Gwen was the one saying it. "A reasonable amount of PDA is expected to sell the story, but if you would be more comfortable, you can add a clause to the contract spelling out what is and is not acceptable to you in detail."

Gwen held up her hands, shaking her head. "I'll be fine."

"In that case, we'll announce our engagement on the Fourth of July."

"So soon?" Gwen swallowed.

"It has to be. My father hosts a party in the Hamptons every year for Independence Day. Everyone will be there. The entire board. My family." Reggie met Gwen's eyes. "Everyone."

To her surprise, Gwen didn't flinch. "Just so I've got this straight, I'll have a corporate job, and I'm attending a donor event and a party in the Hamptons? I'm going to need to do some shopping. Any chance of getting a small advance on my first paycheck so I can hit the mall?"

"Don't be ridiculous. I'll have my usual stylist courier some appropriate options to your apartment. Where is it you live?" Reggie tapped her pen on the paper, ready to jot down an address.

"Queens."

Reggie looked up from her legal pad. "Please tell me you're joking."

Gwen shook her head, this admission leaving her too timid to speak. Rightfully so, as far as Reggie was concerned.

"The only time anyone goes to Queens is to sit in box seats at the US Open."

"Box seats at a golf tournament? How does that work?"

"The US Open is a tennis tournament." Reggie blinked, suddenly terrified this was a huge mistake. Maybe Gwen wasn't as sophisticated as Reggie had believed and wouldn't be able to fit in with the Hamptons crowd after all.

"I was joking." Gwen winked, provoking a visceral response in Reggie's body that was very inconvenient in light of the no sex clause in their contract. "Do I need to brush up on my tennis? I used to be decent, but it was years ago."

Reggie shook her head. "Only if you want to. But you'll definitely need to move to Manhattan."

"You expect me to move to Manhattan just like that?" Gwen's eyes widened as she snapped her fingers. "I spent every penny on the apartment I have, so—"

"Leave it with me. You won't have to worry about money. At least, not for the next eighteen to twenty-four months." Reggie shivered. It sounded like they were discussing a prison sentence. She wondered if Gwen thought of it that way. Damn her father and his stubborn refusal to see reason without her resorting to desperate measures.

Gwen sat back in her seat. "This is a lot to take in."

"I know it is." The compassion in Reggie's tone was genuine, and she stayed silent for a moment out of deference to the turmoil that must be raging in Gwen's mind. But only a moment. There was too much work to be done. "My assistant, Janet, will get your address and have the final contract sent over later today. In the meantime, I'll contact my realtor and stylist. Do not call or text me. Remember. We haven't met. You got that?"

"We've never met," Gwen repeated.

Reggie wondered how badly the woman wished that were true.

MOST OF THE OFFICE DOORS ALONG EXECUTIVE row were firmly shut as Reggie passed. Either their occupants were away at lunch or too engrossed in their work for distractions. It was just as well. Reggie didn't want to be seen. The fewer people who could connect her to the new-hire paperwork for one Gwen Murphy, currently clutched in her hand on its way to Trevor's office, the better.

"I'm not a baby." Trevor's voice reached her ears while she was still several yards from his office. "You don't have to tie my fucking shoelaces."

There was a thud. A moment later, Charlene, administrative assistant for both Trevor and Reginald, darted out of the office and shut the door behind her.

"Careful Reggie," the woman warned. "It's one of your brother's bad days. Clark Maxwell's contract is up for negotiation, and that rabid little weasel is out for blood."

"I assume you're referring to Clark and not my brother?" Reggie asked wryly.

The assistant laughed. "I'd give that man a swift knee to the family jewels if his show wasn't basically bankrolling my salary."

"You and me both," Reggie admitted. She gave a nod toward her brother's office. "Is that the only thing that set him off?"

"He's having some hand coordination issues." Charlene's hushed tone was typical of whenever Trevor's condition was being discussed. Outside the immediate family and his medical team, the assistant was the only one who knew the full extent of his difficulties. "His shoelace came undone, and he was struggling, so I..."

Reggie nodded. She didn't need the details. The scene had played out similarly before.

"Thanks for the warning." Reggie sucked in a deep breath before opening his office door, nearly tripping on the stapler that apparently Trevor had chucked across the room.

"Hey, Trev, I have a problem I'm hoping you can help me with." Reggie stepped over the stapler. *Mental note, remove all possible projectiles from Trevor's desk.*

"Does it involve shoes?" he growled. He was standing behind his desk, his chair pushed back, too riled up to sit.

"Uh, no. When have I ever given a flying fuck about shoes? It's Dad. Oh, and these papers need your John Hancock, if you don't mind." With a twinge of guilt, Reggie slid Gwen's paperwork onto her brother's desk. He signed without so much as a glance, as she'd known he would. His hand trembled badly. It was the most telling sign of the hypoxic brain injury he'd suffered from his accidental drowning.

"What about Dad?" Trevor shoved the papers toward her, the excessive force sending them flying onto the floor. All at once, her brother looked like a scared kid. "I'm sorry, Reg. I didn't mean to—"

"I know you didn't," she soothed as she retrieved the papers and slid them into the envelope, which she sealed and placed in the outgoing mail tray on Trevor's desk. "So, yeah. Dad. There's this donor thing they're throwing in a couple weeks to mark my taking over the foundation, but you know how people get when he attends things."

"He's about as much fun as a rotting corpse at a kid's birthday party."

"Not sure I would have phrased it like that"—Reggie stifled a laugh—"but you're not wrong. I want people to have a good time. He's the opposite of that."

"Do you remember our high school graduation? He made you dance with the mayor."

"I can still feel that creep's paws all over my rear end." Reggie shook off the memory.

"I punched him in the men's room for you."

Reggie arched an eyebrow. "For real? I always wondered how he got that shiner."

"What was his name?" Trevor closed his eyes, concentrating so hard Reggie felt bad for him but knew not to rush to his aid. He'd take it about as well as he had Charlene trying to tie his shoe.

Even before the accident, Trevor had been proud. He was even more sensitive now to people thinking he wasn't up to the task. Reggie could understand that. Her father's shadow was long and cold, and both of them had spent their lives living in it. Unfortunately, her brother truly wasn't up to it now. If he had been, Reggie would never have tried to take it away, no matter how badly she wanted to be top dog.

Trevor pounded his fist on his desk. "I fucking hate that I can't remember a simple thing like the former mayor's name."

"I think that says more about the politician than you."

Her brother offered a rare smile. Coming out from behind his desk, he made his way to the leather couch by the window. He lifted his foot onto the cushion and proceeded to tie his shoe. It was a painstaking task that took many uncomfortable seconds, but in the end, he got it done.

"Oh, I know." Trevor grinned, regarding his shoe with pride. "I'll plan a dinner with Clark. Dad will feel compelled to go in my place. We have to wine and dine that lug nut, so he doesn't jump ship, and you know Dad won't want me doing it on my own. I might make a mess of it."

"Yeah, I heard Clark's contract is nearly up." Reggie scowled. "God, I hate that blowhard."

"Dad loves him."

"Naturally. He's a misogynist, through and through."

Trevor stopped mid-nod. "Wait. Which one?"

"Ding! Ding!" Reggie tapped her finger on the tip of her nose. "Winning answer. Both of them are, equally. Dad's gotten so much worse with age, but Clark is too young to use senility as an excuse. He's just a piece of shit in a suit."

"People love the guy, though. Clark, that is. Well, Dad, too, of course." Trevor's expression clouded with doubt. "I mean, we love Dad, right?"

"Yes, and he's contractually obligated to love us in return," Reggie deadpanned. "Mom wrote it into the divorce settlement, along with the deeds to our cottages in the Hamptons. As for Clark, I've been digging into the numbers, and it's not as much of an audience lovefest as you seem to think."

"What do you mean? His show draws in the biggest audience of the evening lineup."

Reggie suppressed a sigh. Just once, she would love for her brother to surprise her by being on top of things without her help. "Clark's bringing in people but not the right people."

"You mean the Nazi element?" Trevor asked in earnest.

Reggie snorted. "I wasn't even counting them into the equation—how terrible is that?—but good point. No, I meant he's weak in some of the key demographics."

"He's number one with men fifty-five and over," Trevor argued. "I know because he's told me so at least a dozen times this week."

"And trailing heavily in the twenty-five to fifty-four demo, not to mention women of every age," Reggie countered. "Not sure you've heard, but half the population has a vagina. They do not love him. We should can him now before he causes a lawsuit."

"I don't make the rules, Reggie. I just play within the lines." Trevor paused several seconds before grinning and adding, "At least sixty-five percent of the time."

Reggie glared at Trevor before she started laughing, too. "You'd better be joking, little brother. For a minute there, I was afraid you'd been taken in by all that *good people on both sides* bullshit. How is it I'm back working in a place where we actually try to peddle that insanity? It's fucking toxic, like a disease."

She'd been away from it all in London, surrounded by a mostly progressive-leaning crowd on the entertainment side of things. Now that she was back in New York, it was a shock to the system to see how hard the news division was leaning into the lunatic fringe.

"You don't have to worry," Trevor assured her. "This place won't turn me. I don't even like the news anymore. I wish I could go off to London like you did and work on the entertainment side of things. Probably why Dad's selling it off, to reduce the temptation."

Reggie refrained from reacting but filed this information away for safekeeping. Was that the real reason their father had been so adamant about selling Spotlight? Reggie wouldn't be surprised. She and Trevor were a lot alike. If she'd loved the entertainment division, it stood to reason her brother would, too. There was no doubt her father knew that. It was a shame, really. Trevor would have flourished someplace like Spotlight, where the idiosyncrasies of his behavior would be less noticeable in the general swirl of artistic temperaments.

"Nevertheless, I'd love it if we could give Clark the heave-ho. Three major advertisers are threatening to walk after that segment he did about immigration last week. If nothing else, he needs to be reined in." Reggie gave her brother a thoughtful look. "Did you really punch the mayor for me?"

"No one takes advantage of my sister. I don't care if he was running for president at the time."

"That's right. He was." Reggie's face registered disgust as she recalled the man and his wandering hands. "He flamed out soon after if my memory serves."

"Yeah, well. Dad wasn't pleased with him either, the perv."

"Dad?" Reggie was taken aback. "He never said anything about it. He was one of the mayor's supporters, as I recall."

"That's what makes Dad so great. He doesn't have to say a word in public. Step out of line, and one phone call will clip anyone's wings." There was real hero worship in Trevor's eyes, which filled Reggie with unease. She appreciated that her dad had been on her side when it came to the mayor, but should anyone have that kind of power in a democracy? Her father could ruin a person with a single well-placed call. Could he also slot in a despot?

"Hey, if you're bowing out of the Clark dinner, what are you going to wear to my fancy charity party? I hear it's going to be on a boat."

Trevor's eyes lit up. "I love boats!"

"I know you do." Reggie hated boats, but she'd never admit that to Trevor. It would crush his spirit to know how much she blamed herself for what had happened to him. They'd never discussed it, and Reggie wasn't even certain how much of the day he remembered. "What do you think of this outfit?"

"For you?" Trevor took a look at the picture on the phone that Reggie was holding out to him and frowned.

"That's a guy. I know Dad thinks you're secretly a lesbian and all, but if you dress in men's clothing, I think he'll murder you."

Reggie gave her brother's head a playful smack. "I was thinking for you, numbskull. I love the shoes."

"I thought you didn't care about shoes." Trevor squinted, taking a closer look.

"I think they'd look sharp on you." Reggie held her breath as her brother continued to study the picture. Had he noticed the shoes didn't have laces? "Prince William was wearing a pair just like that at a charity thing we were both at before Christmas."

"Prince William, huh?"

"Yeah. I guess they're Italian. I don't know. They seem to be a big thing in Europe." Reggie held back a smile. Her brother was a sucker for royalty and all things European.

"Send me the link." He got off the couch. "Time for the afternoon meeting. You coming?"

"I'll be there in a second."

When Trevor was gone, Reggie swallowed hard, closing her eyes to keep back the tears. Managing her brother and his moods was a full-time job on its own, let alone running the business. She couldn't do it much longer. As she left the office, she glanced back at the envelope in Trevor's mail, the one with Gwen's paperwork inside.

This plan has got to work.

CHAPTER TEN

Gwen rounded the street corner, double checking the directions that had been scrawled on a scrap of paper and delivered by a bike courier to her apartment in Queens. There was no address, only the name of a park: Tudor City Greens. She'd been instructed to arrive at 2:00 p.m. on Saturday and take a seat on the second bench past the sign, next to the lamppost. What would happen then was anyone's guess.

The location was easy to find. As Gwen sat on the park bench, a woman passed by with a baby in a carriage and an older child by her side. Though it was only the beginning of February, a brightly-colored banner announced an Easter egg hunt to be held in the spring. As Gwen stretched her legs in front of her, she pictured how the space would look when warmer weather coaxed flowers from the ground and bright green leaves covered the still-bare trees. A sudden longing to stroll through a park on a beautiful day without looking over her shoulder in fear squeezed her heart. Would she ever have a normal life?

"You made it."

Gwen froze at the unexpected voice but managed not to jump. Appearing out of nowhere, Reggie stood in front of the bench. A wide brimmed hat was pulled low on her head, and oversized sunglasses covered her eyes. A long trench coat completed the ensemble. The tension flowed from Gwen's body at this comical sight, and she laughed before she could think better of it.

"What's so funny?" Reggie demanded, her lips—the only feature Gwen could see clearly—forming a thin, angry line.

"You look like a spy in a comic book." Gwen sucked in her cheeks but couldn't keep the grin off her face. "Is this your idea of going undercover? Your trench coat is buttoned all the way to your chin."

Reggie folded her arms across her chest. "I don't see anything wrong with it."

"Seriously? Unless this is a 1940s detective mystery, you might as well hang a sign around your neck that says I'm trying to hide my identity." Despite the ridiculousness of her companion's outfit, a shiver traveled Gwen's spine as she recalled the reality of being on the run. Lost in thoughts of spring flowers, she'd nearly forgotten the danger that hung over her daily. "With this whole cloak and dagger routine, please tell me you at least left your phone at home."

"My phone?" Reggie sounded horrified as she pulled the device in question from her pocket. "I'm in charge of a multi-billion-dollar media company. I can't drop off the map for several hours at a time."

"Maps are exactly the issue," Gwen explained, experiencing a sense of déjà vu. Not too long ago, Solène had been the one in her position, patiently explaining the modern digital landscape, while she had been Reggie, clutching her phone like it was an extension of her body that she would die without. "Are you aware how many ways there are to track a person just by using their phone's mapping apps, even with security protections in place?"

Not to mention sophisticated spyware like the Polyphemus program that worked outside the boundaries of the law. But that wasn't a conversation she wanted to have right now.

"What do I do with it?" Reggie's voice trembled slightly as she looked warily at the device in her hand, a welcome sign Gwen's point had hit home.

"For now, turn it off. You can't be tracked if the phone isn't on." Gwen rose from the bench as Reggie complied, her screen going dark. "Where are we heading, anyway?"

"Your new apartment. The realtor sent over the keys this morning." Reggie's imperiously nonchalant tone raised Gwen's hackles.

"Just like that?" Gwen found herself taking unusually large strides to keep up with the shorter woman's pace. "Don't I need to take a look at it first and sign a lease if I like it?"

"It's a one-bedroom, short-term sublet in the appropriate price range for your current salary. What's to like or not like?" Reggie continued walking another several yards before she turned, finally noticing Gwen had stopped dead, her hands on her hips. "Why are you looking at me like you want to rip my throat out?"

"You may think all the peasant hovels are alike," Gwen said when Reggie had returned to her side, "but I have to live there."

"You're being unreasonable," Reggie chided. "I'm told

this neighborhood is very desirable and is just the place for an associate director of a charitable foundation."

"You're told? You mean you haven't seen the apartment either?" Gwen's anger mounted. Since leaving London, she'd lost control of her life. Was she a real person anymore or merely a pawn for others to move around?

"I saw the photos," Reggie frowned, clearly baffled by Gwen's outburst. "It's fully furnished and has all the necessities, like a 24-hour doorman and a gym."

"I'm glad *you* find it acceptable, since it's only my life we're talking about." Gwen balled her fists at her sides. "I don't even like gyms. I prefer to get my exercise outside."

"Gym or not, it's a step up from a third-floor walkup in Queens, I assure you." Reggie's icy tone and masterfully layered sarcasm were insufficient to mask her frustration and possibly something bordering on hurt feelings. "Do you know how hard it is to get a decent apartment in this city on a budget?"

"Welcome to the real world." Gwen let out a bitter laugh. "Enjoy your visit. Some of us live here."

"Sure, laugh if you want at how out of touch I am, poor rich girl, but I was honestly shocked. It took most of this past week to accomplish what I thought would take a few hours. The majority of the places were terrible, and I had three other good ones that got snatched away before I could even make it to a showing. When this one came up, I knew I had to grab it for you, sight unseen."

"I'm sorry." All at once, Gwen was filled with guilt as she realized how much Reggie had actually done. The woman could've delegated these details to someone else. The fact she saw to it herself, even if it was just to keep their secret more secure, deserved a little gratitude. "I'm sure it's nice, and I appreciate you taking the time to handle everything personally."

Not to mention providing the money to pay for all of it. There was no question Gwen had stumbled into amazing good fortune. Now to learn how not to be such a bitch about everything just because her life was in shambles. Meeting Reggie was one of the brighter spots lately. It wouldn't hurt to let the woman know that, even if their relationship was nothing more than contractual.

"Come on. Let's go take a look." It was clear from Reggie's tone that she wasn't quite over their tiff, but Gwen's apology seemed to have taken the edge off. As they started to walk, Reggie removed the floppy hat and unfastened the top three buttons of her coat, exposing her chin and neck. "Better?"

"Much." Gwen's lips twitched, but she dared not smile. She'd taken the teasing as far as was wise, at least for now. Hurting Reggie's feelings, now that she knew it was possible to do so, wasn't something Gwen relished doing again.

As they approached a prewar building with an ornate facade—standing maybe twenty stories tall but nowhere near the skyscrapers that were common in other nearby neighborhoods—Reggie reached into her pocket and pulled out a set of keys.

"Home sweet home." The keys jangled as Reggie placed them in Gwen's palm. "The doorman already has your details, including a photo, and he thinks I'm your realtor. He should wave us through to the elevator."

They passed beneath a long green awning and through an arched front entry. The Gothic style reminded Gwen of the architecture in London, sparking an unexpected sense of coming home. The lobby lived up to its Tudor name, with oak paneling, stone floors, and leaded glass panes in the windows. As Reggie had predicted, a friendly looking doorman raised a hand in greeting but let them pass without further ado.

"You're on the tenth floor, number 1005," Reggie announced as she stepped into the elevator. She hesitated, her finger hovering above the button as Gwen joined her. Her expression was almost timid. "I hope that's okay. I've realized I don't know how you feel about heights. I should have asked."

"As long as it's not 35,000 feet in an electrical storm, I'll be fine." Gwen was gratified to see Reggie smile at the little inside joke. If they were going to pretend to be a couple soon, it wouldn't hurt to get along.

"Would you like to do the honors?" Reggie stood to the side as Gwen located the appropriate door and put the key into the lock.

Letting the door swing wide, Gwen passed through the small foyer and into the living room, pausing to take in the details of her new home. As she took stock of the traditional furnishings—two armchairs with striped upholstery, a slate blue sofa with curved wooden legs, a cozy print rug on the floor, and a large gilt-framed mirror on one wall—a sense of peace overtook her. The apartment lacked the pretense she'd expected Reggie to gravitate toward. It was surprisingly livable. Best of all, it was a fresh start. No one would know she was here, which made her feel safe for the first time since she'd found a stranger waiting for her in Queens.

The look on Reggie's face made it clear she didn't agree. "I'll have a decorator come by next week and—"

"No." Gwen surprised herself with the forcefulness of her refusal. "I like it the way it is."

"Are you sure? It looks like a grandmother lives here."

Was that what Gwen was reacting to? The furnishings were nicer than her working-class grandmother could have afforded, but she would have loved the style.

"I'm sure." Gwen swallowed the homesickness that rose like a lump in her throat. "What else is there to see?"

"Looks like the kitchen's through there." Reggie pointed to a space about the size of a walk-in closet that nonetheless managed to offer the cooking essentials, including a full-size refrigerator and a small dishwasher. "Bedroom and bath must be that way."

Gwen sized up the next room quickly, nodding with approval at the queen bed and the desk by the window. "Do you think I can get an extra computer from the foundation so I can do some work in the evenings?"

Reggie's brow furrowed. "Why would you want to do that?"

Gwen tilted her head. "Do you not do work after you get home?"

"Yes, but it's my job."

"This is my job, too." Gwen tamped down the anger that threatened to spill over like a boiling pot at Reggie's easy dismissal of Gwen's work. Instead, she switched on the bathroom light, her mood instantly improving.

"A clawfoot tub! It's a deep one, too. And what's in here?" Gwen opened a door to find a closet filled with clothing. "Oh no. Did the previous tenant forget to take their things?"

"Oh, good!" Reggie's delight at the clothing made Gwen rethink her theory that it had been left behind. This was confirmed when Reggie explained, "I had Hector, my personal stylist, drop by Bergdorf's and send over a few items."

"A few?" Gwen stared at the packed hanging bar, counting at least fifty items before her brain shut down.

"There should be more in the other closets." Reggie opened a door on the other side of the bedroom. "Yes, here we go. It looks like work clothes are over there and evening wear is in this one. I assume the third has shoes and accessories."

"There's so much." Gwen struggled to take it all in. It was like standing in a store, but one where she hadn't been allowed to pick out anything herself. "What if it doesn't fit?"

"I gave Hector a rough guess of your size based on— well, that doesn't really matter." Reggie's cheeks flamed red, and her lips were pressed tightly shut, as if to keep any other indiscretions from slipping out.

"Based on what?" Considering her own awkward discomfort at the entire situation, Gwen saw no reason not to let Reggie in on some of it, too. "Based on the detailed measurements you gleaned while we were in bed together? That's quite a party trick."

"Look," Reggie said stiffly. "Try on the pieces you like tonight. The tailor will be by tomorrow so you're ready for the office on Monday."

"I thought you said they were my size. Why do I need a tailor?" At this point, Gwen was peevish and didn't care if Reggie knew. She'd never felt more like a Barbie doll, being dressed according to someone else's whims.

"Spoken like a woman who's tall enough not to need her pants hemmed." Based on Reggie's exasperated tone, Gwen did not have a corner on the market when it came to being peeved. "You know how I can tell a person who comes from money and someone who's just pretending? It's the way their clothing fits. A pinch here, a tuck there, until everything's perfect. Nothing is ever worn straight off the rack. If we're going to get married and make people believe it, you have to fit the part of someone they think I would choose."

Gwen knew this, of course. She'd observed enough rich people during the years she'd spent working at Kensington Datalytics. She'd learned to pass and blend in so she could get her job done. Just because she knew what was expected of her didn't mean she had to like it.

"Apparently, I'm doing a lot of fitting. Like I'm a puzzle piece." The statement made Gwen queasy. For the past few months, she'd felt less like she was living and more like she was watching a movie about someone she faintly remembered. How long until the real her—Wendy Mancini from Plainview, Texas—disappeared completely?

"I like puzzles." It was impossible to tell what Reggie intended by this comment, uttered so far under her breath as to barely be heard, so Gwen decided to ignore it.

Opening the third closet, Gwen stopped short, too stunned by what she saw to process what she was feeling. The whole space was filled with lingerie, most of it more suited for a strip club than a charity. Gwen grabbed a red lace bustier and held it up to her torso. "Did Hector understand the assignment? Or did he think he was shopping for one of your floozies?"

Reggie's lips thinned, meaning the punch landed. Immediately, Gwen regretted it. Reggie had told her about that part of her life in strict confidence, and now she'd hurled it back at the woman like it was an insult.

"I didn't mean it like that. I'm a little overwhelmed. It's all so—" Gwen blinked back tears, not wanting to look any more ridiculous to Reggie than she already must. "The apartment, the clothing, you, all of it. It's a lot to get used to."

"Of course. Moving is difficult. I should have thought of that." Reggie thought for a moment, chewing on her lower lip in an uncharacteristically self-conscious way. "I'm sure once you bring your things over from your old apartment, this will feel a lot more natural to you. I know I'm still out of sorts waiting on my own boxes from London. Those will take weeks to ship. Luckily, it's a lot easier for you."

If only Reggie knew the truth.

"Actually, I don't really have a lot to move over at the moment." The two suitcases she'd checked on the plane were about all Gwen currently had left to her name, though she didn't want Reggie to know that much about her situation. "I'm pretty minimalist."

"What if we go shopping?" Reggie blurted out, surprise registering on her face as if she hadn't realized what she was going to say. "Not now, of course. But in a few weeks, once the cat's out of the bag about us. Would that make you feel more like yourself?"

"It's really not necessary," Gwen protested. "I'm sure your stylist did a great job. I'm acting like a brat. I think I'm hungry."

"Hungry?" Reggie's face lit up. "I'm starving. Do you like Chincsc?"

Gwen raised her eyebrows. "Does anyone not like Chinese?"

"Thank goodness. If you'd said no, I would've had to call off the wedding. My family would never accept you." Reggie pulled out her phone, frowning at the blank screen. "Shit. I forgot I'd turned it off, and no one in my circles can know I'm here with you."

"Who are you calling?" Gwen pulled out her phone and unlocked the screen.

"Philippe's on the Upper East Side." Reggie held out her hand. "Can I use yours?"

"Sure, it's okay to call the restaurant with mine. But that won't get you in trouble?"

"I doubt my company has that reach." Reggie laughed over the ridiculous thought.

"Here. I dialed the number. It's ringing." Reggie's laugh didn't put Gwen at ease, and she silently acknowledged that this was technically against Solène's protocols, but then again, so was getting sham married to a famous billionaire. Probably. Gwen hadn't shared this particular bit of news with her coconspirator—who also happened to be her sometimes jealous ex-girlfriend—quite yet. It wasn't exactly a conversation she looked forward to.

"It's Regina Hawkins." Reggie spoke loudly into Gwen's phone, using a falsetto tone that seemed specially calibrated to make the person on the other end feel like a close friend even though they weren't. "Is this John? Hi. I'm going to need a delivery. Could I get—wait. Let me check something."

Reggie turned toward Gwen covering the phone. "Is there anything you don't eat?"

When Gwen shook her head, Reggie continued. "Let's do chicken satay, hot and sour soup, spring rolls, kung pao —actually, why not just go with the tasting menu, right?

Way easier. No, the one with the Peking duck. There's two of us. Oh, minimum four? That's fine. Make it for four, and add the usual tip. I'm not at the office, so let me get you the address."

Gwen put her hand out to retrieve her phone when Reggie ended the call. "How much food did you order?"

"No idea," Reggie answered with a shrug. "But you'll eat leftovers, right? Now, back to the shopping. You'll need summer clothes soon. We can go together, and you can pick out what you like. Will that make you feel better?"

"Sorry, what? Oh, clothes. Yeah, that sounds good." It had taken a beat or two of silence for Gwen to realize Reggie had asked her a question. She'd been too engrossed studying the restaurant's online menu. Apparently to a billionaire, existential angst was easily addressed by a shopping spree and about a thousand dollars worth of gourmet Chinese takeout.

"What else do you need?" Reggie didn't elaborate, and Gwen got the impression that there was little within reason that wasn't on the table if she asked. The problem was, what Gwen needed now wasn't something money could buy.

"I need to feel normal. I get that this marriage farce is some type of war between you and your family. Considering who your family is, I understand if you've been conditioned to view everyone else on the planet as chess pieces. But I'm not a chess piece."

"I understand." Reggie's voice was quiet, and a hint of compassion warmed her eyes. "What can I do?"

"Tell me what I need to know. About your family. About my new job." *About you*, Gwen nearly said, but held back, fearing Reggie would take it the wrong way. "I want to do my best."

"I respect that. How about we see if this apartment has plates in the kitchen, and we can talk all about it over dinner?"

The sincerity in Reggie's tone filled Gwen with an indescribably sweet feeling of pride, and a buoyant sensation seemed to carry her along behind Reggie as they made their way to the tiny kitchen. Halfway there, Gwen had to give herself a mental shake.

As much as she might feel like there was a connection between her and Reggie, it was an illusion. Reggie needed her services to get what she wanted, but that was all. In Reggie's mind, Gwen knew there was little difference between her and John at the Chinese restaurant. It would be best for her to remember that.

CHAPTER ELEVEN

A sharp wind whipped at Reggie's body, cutting through her thickest wool coat as she boarded the Mark Twain-style riverboat the Hawkins Foundation had chartered for tonight's top donor event. She was deeper into Lower Manhattan than anyone ever ought to be. Another inch and they might as well call it Brooklyn.

But tonight's event was too important to miss, and not only because it was being held in her honor to welcome her as the foundation's new chair. Gwen would be here, and engineering a memorable meet-cute was all part of the plan to get their fake relationship rolling. How she would do it, Reggie hadn't yet decided, but she wanted to make a splash.

Poor choice of words.

Reggie drew her coat tightly around her as she stepped from the gangplank onto the vessel. She hated boats, ever since Trevor's accident. She wouldn't go near a yacht, which was why this event was being held on an old-fashioned steamboat better suited to a cruise down the Mississippi than the East River. Even so, it left her uneasy. This had all better be worth it.

"May I take your coat?" It was one of the ship's crew in a stark white uniform, his shoes shined to mirror-like perfection for the occasion.

She wanted to keep it wrapped around herself like a security blanket, but now that she was inside on one of the ship's three enclosed decks, Reggie was sweltering. Either the heat was working overtime to make up for the foul weather or her body had picked a hell of a time to start having hot flashes.

"Thank you." Reggie handed over the coat, revealing an ankle-length jumpsuit of gray chiffon. It was technically pants but flowing enough that it could pass for an evening dress if no one looked too closely. Though the foundation was supposed to be her own domain, Reggie walked a fine line between what she wanted and what would have her name crossed off her father's will so fast her head would spin.

If tonight went as planned, it would be the first step toward never having to be cautious about her personal life again. She'd either be triumphant, free to do as she pleased, or she would blow up her future into so many pieces she'd never find them all. After forty-two years under her father's thumb, it was worth the risk.

A server with a tray of champagne whizzed by, and Reggie grabbed a flute, her eyes panning the interior. There was a piano and jazz singer because every event like this was required to have those, apparently. It promised to be another cookie-cutter soiree filled with dull people more concerned with looking good than doing good.

The ship's horn blared, and the engines kicked on.

Reggie reached out to steady herself with a hand against the wall. She drew a deep breath, tamping down the first sparks of anxiety as she got her sea legs under her.

Stop being weak. It's just a fucking boat.

It was her father's voice in her head, but he wasn't wrong. The last thing she needed was a stupid phobia sparking a repeat of her embarrassing behavior on the plane. Although falling face-first into Gwen's boobs in front of two hundred and fifty donors would make for a memorable story.

Speaking of Gwen, Reggie locked eyes on her intended target.

Holy moly.

Gwen, already five foot ten when barefoot, was positively giant in tonight's pair of ultra-high heels. Reggie smiled at the flash of red sole that subtly identified their brand. Paired with a sheath dress of peacock blue silk, the whole outfit was stunning. It should be, considering what it had probably cost Reggie, but a single glimpse of it on the wearer made it the best money she'd ever spent.

Suddenly, it didn't matter where Reggie was. Boat, plane, or a rocket ship to the moon. Who cared? There wasn't enough room in her consciousness to be aware of such mundane details. As Reggie's heart pounded and her throat went dry, there was no question where her attention was, and where she wanted to be, too.

"Reg!" Trevor bounded up to her, not looking the slightest bit wobbly despite the choppy water that had Reggie wishing she was back on shore. "Got a sec?"

"Hey, Trev. What's up?" Reggie checked her brother's face for signs of trouble. His temper seemed in check, fortunately.

"I got cornered by Bitsie a minute ago, and she congratulated me on the new hire I sent her way. The thing is, I have no idea what she's talking about."

"Gwen Murphy." Reggie supplied. "She's the new associate director."

"Yeah, I got that, but I... I think I'm getting worse, Reg. My hypox... uh..." He shut his eyes, trying to focus. "You know, the brain thing."

Tension stiffened Reggie's frame. "Okay, but why?"

"Because I have zero recollection of nominating Ms. Murphy for the position. Do you think—should I tell Dad?"

"No!" Immediately, Reggie regretted her panic. What she'd unwittingly done to Trevor was bad enough without making it feel a hundred times worse. "I mean, you know Bitsie. Details are quaint little things she never pays attention to. Frankly, this is why the foundation is a mess."

"But she said the paperwork came from my office."

"Charlene probably stamped it with your office info when she meant to put Dad's." Reggie hated herself for lying to her brother. Not to mention putting him in this situation. She would never have used him for cover if she'd thought Bitsie would rat her out. "Spiffy shoes, by the way."

He glanced down at his new loafers, the same ones she'd shown him a couple of weeks ago. "My awesome big sister led me to them."

Guilt flooded her, not that he noticed. He was too busy being sweet.

"I knew they'd look great on you."

"Did you hear about Clark?" he asked, lowering his voice.

"No. What?"

"He's given up with the pretense of a dog whistle. He

went on an antisemitic rant last night during his show, and now a sponsor pulled out."

"Figures," Reggie said in disgust. "Clark's the kind of guy who would relish the opportunity to polish Hitler's shoes with his tongue."

"Even Dad's getting concerned. He thinks it's only a matter of time before Clark gets us sued. I know you're worried about it as well, but now that Dad is..." He seemed to lose track of his words. "He's worried it will weaken our position in arguing for an increase in cable carriage fees."

Reggie offered a grim smile. Of course, that was why their father was concerned. Clark might cost them money. Dog whistling could be explained. Outright hate speech complicated things. Her father didn't care one way or the other about racism, fascism, or any of the other -isms, but he hated complications.

"Dad's going to talk to Clark tonight. Tell him to come back to the line and continue to bump up against it but not bolt over."

"Interesting." The thing with rabid dogs was they didn't listen to reason.

"The captain said he'd let me observe things. I'll see you later." Trevor kissed her cheek.

Reggie immediately sought out Gwen, sighing when she spotted her target speaking to Bitsie. If it wasn't for Gwen, Reggie would go in the opposite direction, but she steadied her patience, pasted on a fake smile, and headed toward the lion's den.

"Sister Regina, I wasn't expecting to see you tonight."

For the second time that evening, Reggie's path to Gwen was blocked. This time it was her cousin Dwight who stood between her and her goal. Instead of the perfunctory air kiss, he raised a champagne flute.

Reggie raised her glass in reply, forcing herself to smile. "Haven't you heard, Tiny D? I've just been named the foundation's new chair."

She held back a smile at the way her cousin flinched. Now that he was a grown man and over six feet tall, he was inordinately concerned others might assume the "tiny D" in question referred to something other than his lack of height as a child. That was what made it so amusing. What was good for the gander was doubly good for this goose.

"Guess this means the old man's made up his mind about the succession plan." Her cousin's gloating expression made Reggie wish she could punch him in his capped teeth.

"I'm not sure why you would think that." Reggie's eyes followed Gwen as the woman slowly made a move in her direction. It was nearly time to put project meet cute into action.

"Ah, come on. Chair of the Hawkins Foundation? Ouch." He might be an idiot in many ways, but even Dwight could see how her father had slighted her.

"I thought you were perpetually campaigning right now," Reggie said, changing the subject.

"Taking a quick break from it. I couldn't miss a chance to show my support for the family's important charitable work."

"And rub elbows with several hundred top donors who might write you a check for your campaign," Reggie added with a snort.

"Hold on now—" Part way through whatever he was going to say, Dwight's head swiveled, distracted by Gwen's imminent arrival. "Woah, hottie alert."

"Cool it with the sexual harassment vibes, or I'll have you removed from the party."

"We've already left the dock," Dwight pointed out. "Then again, throwing family overboard is your specialty, or so I hear."

Reggie stiffened, her hands clenching. Was he really going to bring that up now? He wasn't even supposed to be in the know about Trevor's condition or the circumstances surrounding it. That meant there was a leak. The only thing she could do was not react. Pretend she hadn't heard.

"How goes the campaign? Aunt Val said your poll numbers were up."

"Yeah, thank goodness. I'd rather win outright in May. A runoff would suck, and if I lose, Uncle Reginald will have my nuts in a vice."

It was all Reggie could do to refrain from rolling her eyes at her cousin's dramatics. "He'll be disappointed, but a vice might be taking it too far, even for my dad. Besides, you can always run again next November."

"No way. If I'm not seated before the FTC confirmation vote, then it's bye-bye Dwighty." Dwight dragged a finger across his throat, presumably in illustration of what good ol' Uncle Reginald would do to him.

"Mm. Uh-huh." Reggie was much more interested in the tasty morsel her cousin had let slip. Was that what this whole senate run was all about? What interest could her father have in who was confirmed to the Federal Trade Commission? Unless he had reason to believe the Phoenix Media Spotlight acquisition wouldn't go through without an ace in the hole.

Reggie's pulse ticked faster. If everything hinged on one

FTC commissioner, that meant the deal was way more fragile than she'd thought. Was killing it worth a try?

If CEO was out of the question, scuttling the sale of Spotlight would at least safeguard a job Reggie wanted. None of this charity bullshit. As long as her father never found out who torpedoed the deal. If he ever knew she'd worked against him, he'd find something much worse than her tits to put in a vice.

Reggie's eyes caught Gwen's. Instantly, she regretted calling the foundation bullshit, even in her mind. The more they'd talked about it at Gwen's place over Chinese, the more she'd come to realize how much passion the woman had for her new job. Reggie liked that about her, and it was far from Gwen's only good quality. Considering she planned to spend the next few years with this woman as her wife, it was probably a good thing they got along so well. But honestly, it left Reggie a little shaky. Human connection wasn't her strength.

"If you'll excuse me, Dwight, I think this woman is coming to talk to me."

"In your dreams."

He said it with the type of knowing snicker that made Reggie even more certain someone deep within Hawks Corp was talking out of turn. But there was no way her father would have told Dwight about Reggie's youthful indiscretions. As far as he was concerned, his cousin was as straight as the day is long. So, who was telling tales about her? She made a mental note to find out.

"Hello. Are you Regina Hawkins?" Finally making it to where they stood, Gwen stuck out her hand to Reggie in greeting. "I'm Gwen Murphy, the new associate director at the foundation."

"Yes, of course." Reggie shot her cousin an *I told you so look*, as if he would actually stand a chance with this woman. The man was in his mid-fifties, and a politician, for God's sake. "Please, call me Reggie. I hope you're enjoying it here."

"I'm Dwight Hawkins, Reggie's cousin and the future senator from the great state of Texas."

Gwen smiled. "I thought I noticed a family resemblance."

"Really?" Dwight jutted out his square jaw. "Most compare me to JFK, Jr."

"I thought he was dead," Gwen said with a frown.

"Well, actually—"

Reggie butted in. "Let's save your bizarre conspiracy theories for your voter base, shall we?"

At that moment, the ship lurched. Reggie took the opportunity to stumble into Gwen, spilling champagne down the front of her dress. All part of the plan.

"Oh my goodness. I'm so sorry." Reggie apologized loudly, attracting the attention of several party goers, as she'd intended. She wanted everyone on the boat tonight to have heard this story before they got back to the pier. "Does anyone see a waiter to bring us a towel?"

"Here, allow me to help." Dwight pulled his pocket square out with a flourish, making a move as if to sop up the bubbly liquid from Gwen's dress himself. Not letting him have the opportunity, Reggie snatched the silly fabric from his grasp and dabbed Gwen's bust line.

"Don't just stand there," Reggie chastised, trying hard not to laugh at the jealous look that camped out on her cousin's face. "Bring us some napkins from the bar."

Dwight started to complain, but Gwen piped up with, "Thank you so much for the help, Dwight."

He blushed like a virgin on prom night and scurried off. How anyone could take him seriously as senate material was a mystery to Reggie.

Once he was out of sight, Gwen laughed, lowering her voice to say. "I know you have a thing for boobs, but I didn't know you planned to drown them in champagne."

"I was improvising," Reggie glanced around to make certain no one was close enough to overhear. "It seems to have worked. If you haven't noticed, all eyes are on us. And cameras."

"No wonder. If I saw the chair of a foundation I was donating money to fondling a woman in public, I would probably stare, too," Gwen quipped.

"The important thing is for a few of the photos to make it to social media, start building a buzz," Reggie explained.

"In that case, mission accomplished, I think."

"I'm so very sorry," Reggie said, even louder than before. "Oh, your dress is destroyed. What can I do to help you repair the damage?" She swiped the sodden pocket square across Gwen's chest once more for good measure.

Gwen's cheeks twitched as she held in her laughter. "You're incorrigible."

"One of my better qualities," Reggie agreed. She turned to one of the long-time donors she recognized standing nearby, an older woman in a pashmina. "Excuse me. Would it be possible for me to borrow your lovely shawl for the evening? I'm afraid I've made a disastrous mess of our associate director's dress."

"Oh, you poor dear." The woman quickly removed the

long rectangle of wool and handed it to Reggie, who placed it carefully over Gwen's bare shoulders.

"There. You look absolutely lovely. The blue green brings out your eyes." Reggie's fingers lingered on the soft shawl, lost for a moment in the slight flush of Gwen's cheeks. With much greater effort than it should have taken, she brought her hands to her sides and forced herself to stop thinking about how wonderful it felt to touch Gwen's skin again. She was supposed to be selling an infatuation to the people in the crowd, not herself.

Dwight returned like a St. Bernard, with the requested napkins in hand. "I was assured these are very absorbent."

"I think we're all set, but just to be sure." Reggie took the napkins from Dwight before he got any ideas. No one else was going to be mopping up Gwen's boobs tonight but her.

"I'm so sorry about your dress," Reggie announced, her voice booming so the curious folks on the other side of the boat wouldn't miss it. "Please, you must let me pay for the dry cleaning. And maybe take you out for dinner to make up for my clumsiness."

"That's really not necessary." Gwen fluttered her lashes like a southern belle.

"I insist." Reggie smiled inwardly as more heads swiveled and additional sets of eyes became riveted on them.

"Well, if you really insist"—Gwen's lids closed halfway, her gaze dropping modestly to the floor—"how can I say no?"

It was a meet cute worthy of Hollywood, and Reggie had no doubt the public would soon be dying to read all about it in every tabloid in town.

CHAPTER TWELVE

Gwen's eyes swept the interior of the French restaurant, taking in the white Roman-style pillars reaching to a ceiling hung with glittering crystal chandeliers. It was the type of place where most people couldn't afford to order water. Even so, a surprising number of the impossibly chic diners had given in to the once-a-year temptation to buy bouquets of red roses and heart-shaped boxes of chocolates.

"I can't believe you booked our so-called business dinner for Valentine's Day," Gwen said under her breath as a server in a black jacket and tie led them to a table in the very center of the main room.

"Isn't it perfect?" Reggie whispered, leaning in close so her breath tickled Gwen's ear.

Paired with the swishing of Reggie's black taffeta palazzo pants—another outfit that walked a fine line between feminine and masculine, Reggie's signature look—it was so seductive Gwen nearly swooned. She was saved only by the server pulling out her chair mere seconds before she hit the ground.

"You've definitely outdone yourself," Gwen said, working hard to catch her breath without being obvious about it. Who knew black pants could have such a strong effect on the senses? "If tongues aren't wagging about this, the society pages can be declared dead."

"The chef would like to know if you'll be having your usual, Ms. Hawkins," the server said, still holding two menus in his hand.

"Are you feeling adventurous?" Reggie asked. "I usually do the seven-course menu and leave it to Daniel to choose the dishes and pair the wines."

"I'm game if you are." It took everything Gwen had not to let her eyes bug out at the prospect of seven full courses. Who ate like that? But one of the traits Reggie valued in her was her ability not to gawk like a yokel, so she refrained. That didn't mean she wasn't gobsmacked on the inside.

"Do you get this treatment everywhere you go?" Gwen fought to keep her tone neutral, not giving in to judgement on the one hand—because who the hell deserved to be treated like royalty just for existing—and awe on the other, because let's face it, the kind of raw power that demanded such treatment was intoxicating to be around.

"Not everywhere, no." Reggie bit down on her bottom lip, her thoughts clearly focused on something specific.

Gwen was intrigued.

"Name one place where people don't bend over backward to please you."

"1009 Fifth Avenue," Reggie replied without hesitation. "My father's house."

"Screw that asshole." It came out more confrontational than she intended, and her timing couldn't have been worse. No sooner had the obscenities flown out of her than the server had returned with their first course.

"The rabbit chaud froid with a basil-sorrel reduction." The main server set a plate in front of each of them while a second person brought a basket of bread. A third, looking very official, filled their glasses with a white wine that had a French name on the bottle. Gwen assumed it probably cost more than her dress, a relatively simple black and embroidered floral number with a price tag dangling from its off-the-shoulder sleeve that had nearly stopped Gwen's heart when she'd removed it earlier in the day.

"While I love your spirit, please don't ever tell my dad to go fuck himself."

"I won't," Gwen promised, fighting a nervous giggle, "but don't you ever want to?"

"Sometimes." Reggie lifted her wine glass and took a slow, steady sip. "My father took me to this restaurant on my twenty-first birthday."

"Oh?" Gwen wasn't sure what had prompted the change in topic, but she was curious to see where the conversation went.

"It was still at its old location back then." Reggie's features softened as she reminisced. "He ordered a bottle of the best champagne. The whole family was there. Trevor, Aunt Val, whichever wife he was on at the time. Was it Karla? No, it must have been Irene."

"Was that the spy?" Gwen took a bite of her first course, the flavors melting together delightfully in her mouth.

"No, the nanny. But good job trying to remember my complicated family tree." Reggie lifted the fork to her mouth, sighing with satisfaction.

"All in a day's work." Gwen's lips curled into a half smile. "Sounds like you have good memories of this place."

"I brought Lydia here a few times. We used to get a private table in the back room." Reggie gestured vaguely to a corner of the restaurant.

"Lydia?"

"Yes, my hooker."

Gwen's jaw dropped. "Don't call her that!"

"Why not?" Reggie arched her brow in that sardonic way that made Gwen's toes tingle. "I'm pretty sure you've said it at least once."

"That was before I knew her name," Gwen reasoned, guilt pricking her conscience. "Now that I do, it feels insulting."

"Impeccable logic. You'll fit right in with my family." Reggie's tone left it unclear whether this was a compliment. Gwen thought probably not.

"Were you in love with Lydia?" Gwen sucked in her lips, but it was too late to keep from letting the question out. "I'm sorry. I shouldn't have asked that. It's not my business."

"It's okay."

Reggie didn't seem mad, but as the silence dragged on, she also didn't seem likely to answer. She'd taken three full bites of her food before she said, "I was never under any illusions when it came to Lydia."

"How do you mean?" Gwen sat still, almost afraid to breathe, lest Reggie think better of sharing. Considering how similar her own situation was to the former escort, Gwen wanted to know everything she could.

"She was paid to listen when I talked, to laugh at my jokes. She kept her problems to herself."

"You could have paid her to argue with you," Gwen teased. "It would have felt more realistic that way."

"No matter how you slice it, playing the role of a girlfriend is not the real thing," Reggie responded. "I was okay with how it was. It was good while it lasted."

"After your father found out, did you still see her?"

Reggie shook her head. "No. Never."

Gwen mulled over how easily Reggie was able to let Lydia go, even though she was almost certain the woman's feelings had run deeper than she let on. What kind of woman had Gwen agreed to marry? How cold did you have to be to drop a person you cared about—maybe even loved, in a way—and never look back?

"If that was your way of convincing me your dad's really a good guy after all, your argument could use some work." Gwen reached for her wine glass, draining the remaining contents.

"I would never try to convince anyone my dad is a good guy." The bitterness in Reggie's voice was impossible to hide. "A great leader, perhaps. He never fails to make the right move for the company, no matter the cost to people. Making him rarely good on the human front."

"I don't get it." Gwen shook her head.

Reggie slanted her head. "What?"

"You're obviously angry with him, yet you still do his bidding like a puppet." *Geez, Gwen. Don't hold back.*

Fortunately, Reggie didn't appear to take offense, simply sipping at her wine again as she pondered what Gwen had said. "He has a way of getting his children to step in line."

The server returned with a new course and fresh wine.

"What's the one memory of your father from childhood that stands out the most?" Gwen sat back slightly as the server came to remove her plate, replacing it with another. *One down, six to go.*

The sommelier filled new glasses with a different wine, which Reggie tasted before answering. "A childhood memory? Let me see. There was the time I jumped out of a swing when it was at the highest point."

"Was your father proud?"

"No, furious." Reggie let out a little laugh. "He might have been proud if I'd stuck the landing, but I didn't. Not by a long shot. Landed right on my tailbone. At the time, I was convinced I'd broken my scrawny ass."

"What'd he do?" Gwen clenched, her voice little more than a whisper as she anticipated the response. Odds were it hadn't been good.

"He charged across the backyard. I can still feel the ground vibrating under me." A light shudder moved Reggie's shoulders, a reaction she covered by reaching for her fork and knife, pausing to take a bite of the second course. "He was screaming, 'Stop this weakness right now!' I was crying, you see. Bawling, really."

"Of course, you were." Gwen's heart broke for the young Reggie, with a father who couldn't show her love. At least her grandfather had been kind when Gwen was growing up, even if his temperament had curdled like milk as he'd aged.

"After that, he gave me a spanking I'll never forget." Reggie laughed, an incongruous reaction to what had to be a traumatic memory. "It hurt like hell. But it taught me a lesson that carries me through to this day. When you're at your weakest, that's when it's most important to look strong."

Gwen stared at her untouched plate, no longer hungry. "How old were you?"

"Five? Thereabouts, anyway."

"That's your childhood memory?" Gwen wiped her mouth with a hand, not sure how to proceed. "I don't know if you know this or not, but your father comes across as an even bigger asshole than I thought."

"I'm sure he meant well… deep down." Reggie stared at the flickering flame of the candle in the middle of the table, her expression unreadable. "He wanted to toughen us up."

"He wanted to demoralize you. That seems to be his mission for the entire world." An image of Gwen's grandfather flashed through her mind, the broken and bitter man he'd become, aided in no small part by the vitriol he'd absorbed watching the programs he was spoon-fed by Hawks News.

"That sounds personal. What do you mean?" Reggie sat back in her chair, crossing her arms.

"Nothing," Gwen lied. "Maybe I just have a hard time seeing you as the future head of a company like Hawks Corp. You don't seem like you've been red-pilled like the rest of them."

A man at a table across from them not so discreetly snapped their photo.

Reggie winked, and Gwen's stomach tightened. She'd known this was the plan, to be seen together by paparazzi and get their photos out into the world, but having it come to fruition while in the middle of an intensely personal conversation made her feel queasy. Even the assurance that her face would be obscured in the papers did little to ease Gwen's nerves. She understood Reggie couldn't control everyone with a phone, and Gwen's face would be out there. She banked on people focusing more on Reggie and the Hawks News connection, not on Gwen's fabricated past.

Not wanting to think about her fishbowl moment, Gwen pressed on. "Do you believe Hawks News is good for the country? Democracy? The planet? Human rights?"

"Sure, Hawks is a conservative-leaning news organization. But so what?" Reggie's shoulders tensed as if preparing for battle. "Throughout US history, there've always been partisan news outlets. Look at the election of 1800. John Adams and Thomas Jefferson tore each other to shreds in the press."

"No offense, but that sounds like something your father's press secretary made you memorize." Gwen took another drink before saying, "I've been digging into the Hawkins Foundation, and I'll admit to being surprised by the list of charities on the books."

"What did you expect?" Reggie remained cautious, but her body started to relax.

"Honestly? Giving money to lawyers and judges who want to strip away whatever remaining human rights there are to make soulless corporations more powerful. But from what I gather, it's nothing like that."

"Let me see if I understand." Reggie leaned forward, and there was a spark of humor in her eyes. "Are you saying we're not greedy enough in our capitalism?"

"Not at all, but it's confusing as hell."

"I know what Hawks Corp is," Reggie said, her tone hushed, most likely so the paparazzi masquerading as dinner guests couldn't overhear. "Do you think I don't? But I'm not my father, and I'm not on board with what he's done with certain parts of the company. I'm not the only person in my family who feels that way, who disagrees with some of the things that are done in our name. The family foundation has always been a way to offset the harm that might be done—"

"Might be done?" Gwen couldn't believe her ears. "Hawks News is halfway to installing that fuckwit Clark Maxwell as the next president."

"Fuckwit!" Reggie burst into laughter. "I love it. Do you know he walks around the studio referring to himself as The Talent? I'm pretty sure he wants people to call him that, but from now on, I know how I'll be thinking of him."

"You see!" Gwen tossed a hand in the air. "I knew you weren't a true believer. So why are you fighting to take over a company that's so tainted with hate?"

"Because I want to change it. Move it more to the center." Reggie walked her fingers from the side of the table to the middle as if it would be that easy.

"Do you honestly think you can steer the Titanic of white nationalism like it's a dinghy after three decades of stripping your viewers of their common decency?"

"You're taking this way too personally." Reggie's disapproving expression bordered on irritated schoolmarm. "It's business, Gwen. Plain and simple."

"No, it's not." Gwen's hands clenched at her sides, and she had to actively work to relax them, to take a calming breath so her pulse didn't skyrocket out of control. "You want to know what my childhood memory is? It's my grandfather helping me learn a few words in Spanish so I could ask the little girl across the street if she wanted to play. Her family was from Mexico, and I found out later her dad was a doctor, but his certification didn't count in the US, so he was a janitor at the same meat processing plant where my grandfather managed one of the lines."

"He sounds like a nice man." Reggie's eyes drifted away, like she wasn't sure what Gwen expected her to say next.

"He really was. When I was a kid, my grandfather was kind, loving, and compassionate. After his company shut down his plant, he lost hope in life. The only thing he did was watch Clark Maxwell and whatever else was on Hawks News." Gwen pinched her eyes to cut off the memory, but it only made it worse.

Reggie quietly waited for Gwen to continue.

"The transformation was slow. Questioning things he never had before. It went from 'Isn't it a shame Dr. Gonzalez across the street isn't allowed to do what he was trained for?' to 'Those immigrants are stealing our jobs.' And don't get him started on LGBTQ rights. He froths at the mouth at the mere mention of gays, or people of color, or God forbid women. He's terrified a horde of immigrants are going to swarm the border and take over his home."

Reggie frowned. "This is in Chicago?"

A cold lump formed in the pit of Gwen's stomach as she realized she'd been talking freely about her real Texan grandfather, not the cover story she was supposed to stick to at all times.

She rushed to cover the blunder. "Crazy, right? He's practically in Canada, but it doesn't matter. Hawks News has all their viewers terrified over things that won't happen. And for what? To win the ratings war?"

"Don't forget the money." It was said as a joke, but it was also the truth. Reggie had the decency to blush with embarrassment.

"That brings up a good point. You can't donate money to progressive charities as if that balances the scales, because it doesn't come close." Gwen let out a breath in a huff, hoping her anger and frustration would go with it. She'd been working herself up over this topic all week, and she doubted Reggie wanted to hear her thoughts.

"It's not like I believe money can wash away all the Hawkins family sins," Reggie said quietly, surprising Gwen by speaking at all. There was no reason for the woman to engage in the conversation. Much like Lydia, Gwen was there for Reggie's comfort and convenience, not a lecture on society's ills.

Yet here she was, encouraging Gwen to let her have it. It was an opportunity Gwen couldn't resist.

"There are more important things than money," Gwen said, attempting to strike a balance between being honest and hitting Reggie with the full force of a fire hose. "Like not living in fear. Not having fascists take over local governments and school boards. No amount of money can justify that. In some ways, the fact none of you even believe in it makes it worse."

"I wouldn't say none." Reggie grimaced, and Gwen wondered if it was her father she was thinking of or someone else. "But I do get what you're saying."

"Do you? Because even the way the foundation is going about trying to mop up your family's mess is half-assed. Do you even know how much that donor event cost compared to the donations that were brought in?"

"I'm assuming the ratio is less than ideal." Instead of anger, something like amusement flashed in Reggie's eyes, though Gwen had no idea why. Did the woman enjoy being flagellated?

It was probably best not to ask. That could definitely be taken the wrong way.

"Let me just say that for optics, it's probably not the best to put a bunch of rich white people on a steamboat like they're taking a day off from overseeing their plantations to cruise the Mighty Mississippi."

"That was my fault," Reggie admitted. "But not for the reason you gave. I hate boats. Yachts, especially. The steamboat was the only other choice. But I have to say I'm not used to people talking to me like this."

"Let me guess. I'm fired for speaking my mind?"

"Absolutely not. I'm serious about making changes with Hawks Corp. I don't want to be surrounded by yes-men. Or yes-women, in your case."

"Pretty sure it's not in my DNA." Now that the heat of her passion had cooled a little, Gwen was mortified. Had she really said all of that to Regina Hawkins?

Reggie laughed. "No, I'm seeing that. I want you to know you can always speak whatever's on your mind to me."

"Really?" Gwen had her doubts. Wasn't this the same person who had admitted earlier in the evening to paying her last fake girlfriend specifically not to talk about anything important?

"I'm serious, Gwen. You may not believe me right now, but I want to do what's right." Reggie reached across the table, placing a hand on Gwen's. The connection was instant, making Gwen stifle a gasp. "Maybe having someone outside of my bubble will help."

Gwen forced her attention from the tingles that traveled up her arm from where Reggie's fingers were and looked her in the eyes. "You'll need more than me. You need to see the damage that has been done. Families and relationships have been ruined. Giving a hundred thousand dollars to your favorite cat charity so they can wear fancy bow ties doesn't absolve you from that."

"Do we do that?" Pulling her hand away, Reggie clasped it to her mouth to stifle a laugh.

Gwen grinned. "That may have been an exaggeration. If it turns out that is a real charity, though, I'm here for it. The world needs more cuteness."

"Oh, I agree. One hundred percent." Reggie's shoulders continued to shake with silent laughter for several more seconds. Finally, she settled down and asked in a serious tone, "Would it be too much for me to ask you to do a report on the foundation? I'd like to figure out what can be changed to make a bigger impact."

"Why would that be too much to ask? It's literally my job."

"We both know it's not really your job." Reggie's eyebrow arched, and Gwen twisted in her seat as a spasm of desire shot through her.

Damn it. Why did her soon to be fake wife have to be so attractive? Especially since everything about her should have made Gwen want to run screaming.

"Whatever happened to Lydia?" Gwen asked. Maybe a cold splash of reality would knock some sense into her. Hadn't Reggie herself said human relationships were nothing but transactions? A woman who believed that would have no idea.

"Lydia?" Instead of a dismissive shrug, Reggie's shoulders slumped ever so slightly as her expression grew wistful. "She used the severance package I gave her to finish college. She's married now, living in Connecticut, and has a little boy who's learning to play the cello."

What kind of person had Gwen agreed to marry? One

who gave a severance package to a call girl. One who, even after fifteen years, still kept tabs on the woman's life, making sure she was okay. In other words, one who cared way more than she let on. That told Gwen everything she needed to know.

CHAPTER THIRTEEN

"Well, look who we have here." Reggie walked up alongside Gwen, who had been strolling several yards ahead of her along a path in Central Park. "What a coincidence."

"Isn't it?" Gwen giggled at the obvious lie. "What is this, the eleventh such coincidence since Valentine's Day?"

"Twelfth," Reggie corrected. "I believe it's been one completely accidental, very public meetup per week, every week, like clockwork."

"Weird."

Gwen tittered again, making Reggie's head go a little fuzzy. It wasn't like laughter had been a staple in Reggie's life up until recently. Hearing it was a bit like drinking alcohol with a low tolerance. More than a taste and the world started to spin.

"Do you think anyone's still buying the coincidence cover story?" Gwen asked.

As a runner jogged past, they moved in tandem to the side, their bare arms brushing. Reggie's skin went bumpy all over like a plucked goose. The month of May was off to a warm start, meaning lots of temptingly exposed body parts that hadn't been taken into account in the dead of winter when she'd proposed this fake relationship scheme. A major oversight, and one that was wreaking havoc on her frustrated libido. If only her brother's stupid nickname for her had been even remotely based in fact.

"They'd have to be idiots to believe us," Reggie said, forcing herself to focus on the conversation instead of the surge of hormones roaring through her veins like the first hit of an illicit drug. "But just in case, today's performance should remove all doubt."

"The big day has arrived. The undeniably public kiss." This time Gwen's laughter had a decidedly nervous quality to it. "Are you sure you're ready for us to out ourselves?"

Reggie's stomach twisted at Gwen's phrasing, but she kept her head high. "Of course."

When in doubt, pretend you're not. Someone should translate that into Latin and slap it on the Hawkins' family crest.

"Are you, though? For real?" Gwen slowed her pace. Reggie, who had gotten better over the past several weeks at recognizing this move before she'd walked a full block alone, followed suit. "You don't have to pretend with me. It's a big deal. This isn't just a picture in the paper. Your father is going to see it, which makes it a declaration of war."

"I'm not saying it will be pleasant, especially if he's seen the photos before we go to his house tonight for the election results, but it had to happen eventually." Reggie stopped walking, drawing a shaky breath. The whole family would be there, minus Dwight and Uncle Carl, who were watching the results at campaign headquarters in Houston.

"He'll threaten to disown me, I'm sure. But I'm counting on him needing me too much to actually go through with it."

Gwen's raised eyebrows seemed to ask *And if you're wrong?* Reggie looked away to avoid answering the unspoken question.

"Anyway, the timing couldn't be better," Reggie continued. "Aunt Val has alerted me to three board members who are most likely to be swayed to my side by our little romantic revelation, and they'll all be there tonight."

"Who are they?" Gwen asked. "I want to make sure I do my part to charm them."

A smile stole across Reggie's lips, silly and sentimental, as she registered the eager determination in Gwen's face. In so many ways, the woman was proving to be a perfect partner, quick to learn and determined to please. Not a bad listener, either. A lot like Lydia had been, but Gwen had an opinionated streak a mile long. Of course, her former confidante might have been like that, too, and simply held her tongue because she was paid to. However, Reggie doubted there was enough money in the world to make Gwen do the same when she truly had something to say. Another plus for Gwen. Spicy turned out to be a huge turn-on.

"Their names are Thomas Riess, Richard Clay, and Harold Bryson," Reggie said.

Gwen shot Reggie a suspicious look. "Are they really called that?"

"Yes. Why?" They'd begun walking again and were approaching Loeb Boathouse at the edge of Central Park Lake. Reggie scanned the water's edge, wondering what Gwen would think of the surprise she had in store.

"They're Tom, Dick, and Harry. Could it get any more

absurdly generic?" Gwen shook her head with an air of disbelief. "More and more, I'm realizing the people who are supposed to be the smartest guys in the room are a bunch of clowns who were in the right place at the right time."

"Are you lumping me in with the other circus folk?" Reggie asked jokingly. Her smile widened as she finally spotted the special boat she'd arranged for the afternoon.

Paying no attention to the water, Gwen tilted her head to one side and then the other, studying Reggie's face intently. "No, I can't quite picture you with a red nose and white paint."

"Way too much makeup for my taste," Reggie agreed with an exaggerated shudder.

"And you'd need to acquire a sense of humor," Gwen teased.

"Very funny." When Gwen continued to stand with her back to the lake, Reggie's patience gave out. "Aren't you going to turn around?"

"What? Why?" Even as she questioned it, Gwen automatically turned, her eyes lighting up when she saw the result of Reggie's planning. "Is that for us?"

"A rowboat on the lake, complete with picnic basket and champagne." Without thinking, Reggie reached for Gwen's hand, grasping it in hers and dragging the stunned woman the rest of the way to the ramp where an attendant waited to help them into the vessel.

"You've got to be kidding." Gwen stood on the dock, her fingers clasped tightly around Reggie's.

Reggie's smile drooped. "Do you not like it? I was trying for something romantic, but that's not really my strength."

"Reggie, no. It's amazing. It's just—you hate boats."

"Not rowboats!" Reggie let out a burst of relieved

laughter. "It's yachts I don't like. Not since… a bad experience."

"Are you sure? I really don't mind if we do something else." As she continued to gaze at the boat with its checkered blanket and bouquet of bright yellow sunflowers, Gwen's longing was clear.

"You're a terrible liar. Now get in the boat." It was only at the point when Gwen tried to move that Reggie realized she'd been holding the woman's hand this whole time. Her fingers sprang open, letting it drop like it was on fire. "Hurry, they charge by the hour."

"Good thing I don't." Gwen stepped into the rowboat and settled onto one of the seats.

"Smart-ass." Reggie was grinning from ear to ear as she climbed in after, taking the seat directly across from Gwen. She grasped an oar in each hand as the attendant gave the boat a shove, setting it afloat in the green-tinged lake.

"You love that about me. Admit it." Gwen spied a paper parasol on the bottom of the boat. She picked it up and opened it, holding it over one shoulder. "Do I look like a Victorian damsel?"

"Are you not going to grab the other set of oars and help me row?"

"I didn't want to hurt your pride by out rowing you. You're very competitive. Is it because you're a twin?" Gwen twirled the handle of the parasol, making it rotate behind her head like a miniature Ferris wheel. "Look. There are two swans, and their necks are making a heart. I love it when they do that."

"Swans are mean." Reggie grumped, not appreciating Gwen's observation about her competitive nature. It was a trait that had caused damage in the past, especially with her brother. The last thing she needed while surrounded by all this water was to start thinking of Trevor jumping from the deck of their boat because of her teasing.

"How can you not like swans?" Gwen honestly seemed baffled, and like she might be about to launch into a full presentation on the benefits of swans.

"I like them plenty. In fact, I love that swans are mean. No one ever messes with a swan." Reggie dipped the oars into the water and pulled hard to put some space between them and the swans. Being with Gwen was like spending the day with Snow White and her forest animals. Reggie feared the woman would lean out to pet one and tip the boat over.

As they neared one of the bridges that spanned the water, Reggie caught a glint off in the distance.

Gwen noticed as well, asking, "Telephoto lens?"

Reggie's brow furrowed as she squinted for a better look. "If we're lucky."

"Photographers or not, I don't care. It's magical out here, and it's lovely to feel the sunshine on my skin." Gwen leaned her head back, face toward the sky. It was a pose that sent her ample bust jutting out even more than usual, leaving Reggie disoriented until she turned away.

"I was thinking we should count to three." Reggie kept her eyes along the shoreline and away from Gwen's heaving bosom. Which may not have actually been heaving since she was just sitting there and not even exerting herself by rowing, but it sure was heaving in Reggie's imagination, like the woman on the cover of a Harlequin.

"Count to three for what?" Gwen inquired sleepily.

"For the kiss."

"A three second kiss?" There was definite disapproval in Gwen's tone.

"Too long?"

"Are you serious?" Gwen scoffed. "People kiss their grandmothers for longer than three seconds."

"So, five?"

In the silence that followed, Reggie spotted mallard ducks floating on the water. All she saw was green from the leafy trees and their reflection on the water's surface. It wasn't until she looked skyward that she saw skyscrapers off in the distance. Without that reminder, they could've been out in the countryside instead of the heart of one of the world's biggest cities.

Gwen was right. It was magical.

Also, the guy on the bridge definitely had a camera pointing their way.

"Right," Reggie announced with the enthusiasm of someone heading to the dentist for a filling. "Time to kiss."

"Just like that? No warm-up?" Gwen pouted, ironically positioning her lips in a perfectly kissable shape at the same time. She moved closer, touching her tongue to her lips and leaving behind a slick sheen that glistened in the sun. "I know. It's in the contract. So, I guess we should kiss."

Reggie froze. Now she wanted to kiss Gwen. A lot. And that wasn't part of the deal at all.

Reggie wasn't sure what to do. She needed to kiss Gwen, but she wasn't supposed to want to. How could she do it without giving herself away? Because the only thing on Reggie's mind was the memory of Gwen's mouth on hers as the snow swirled outside. And now she wanted to do so much more than kiss...

On second thought, maybe this was a bad—

Gwen's lips landed on Reggie's, soft and full. Vanilla and lavender flooded her senses, so overpowering and sensual that Reggie held her breath to keep her wits.

One. Two... had they agreed on three? Or five?

It didn't matter. Reggie had forgotten how to count.

It was difficult to determine which of them forgot first that this was supposed to be staged. Was it Reggie who moved from sweet to blow your socks off? Or was it Gwen? The only thing Reggie knew—or would have known, had she been thinking, which she most certainly wasn't—was that one of them had.

Once they did, there was no going back.

Reggie's mouth opened, allowing Gwen's tongue to sweep inside, tangling with hers. Gwen's hands were clutching her shoulders, clasping her back, fisting her hair. Reggie grasped the oars like they were the only things rooting her to this world, keeping her from catapulting into the sun. Neither seemed willing to break away.

At least not until the boat tilted, nearly pitching them into the water.

Fighting to regain her senses, Reggie steadied them with the oars. "That... uh, that should work for tonight."

"It worked for me." Gwen stared deeply into Reggie's eyes, lust shifting to humor that ended in a saucy wink. "By the way, that was definitely more than five."

"HOLY SHIT. THIS IS YOUR DAD'S HOUSE?" GWEN tilted her head back to stare at the intricate five-story limestone and red brick facade of Reginald Hawkins's stately Fifth Avenue home, steps from the Metropolitan

Museum of Art. Her jaw slackened with awe, and Reggie couldn't blame her. It wasn't every day you went to visit someone who lived in their very own Gilded Age mansion. "You grew up in this place?"

"No," Reggie was quick to assure her. "This is a more recent acquisition. It went on the market a few years ago, and my father couldn't resist. It's one of the last authentic mansions in Manhattan that hasn't been subdivided into condos or turned into a museum. Deep down, he's always wanted to be a robber baron."

"That does fit the impression I have of him." Gwen's voice cracked with uncharacteristic nervousness. The woman had managed to hold her own in every situation Regina had thrown at her, but in Reginald Hawkins's 20,000 square foot shrine to capitalism, she appeared to have met her match.

Reggie gave Gwen a searching look. "Are you sure you're ready for this?"

"Now you're asking? We're literally at your father's doorstep." Gwen laughed and gave Reggie's hand a squeeze. "Whether or not I'm ready isn't the point. It's happening. Besides, didn't you say your dad has cameras everywhere? He's probably watching us right now. Oh shit!" Gwen dropped Reggie's hand. "Sorry."

"It's okay." Reggie took her hand again, holding it tightly. She wasn't sure whether the gesture was more for Gwen's comfort or her own. "That's the whole point of coming here tonight. Phase two, remember?"

"The point of no return." There was no trace of Gwen's usual joking.

"You're right. It is. The tabloids may have the photo, but I have one last chance to spin it."

"How?" Gwen tilted her head in disbelief. It was a valid response.

This wasn't fifteen years ago when there was still time to negotiate, or threaten, so that damning evidence never left the newsroom. It had been less than six hours and already the pictures of their kiss had reached every corner of the internet. And thanks to how carried away they'd gotten, there was really no way to pass the images off as anything other than what they were. That didn't mean Reggie couldn't do it if she had to.

"You leave that to me. Look, Gwen. I know we have a contract, but if you're having second thoughts, you need to tell me right now. Once we go through that door, there's no turning back."

"Like you'd let me back out of a signed contract," Gwen scoffed. "I'd be out of a job and on the streets by morning."

Reggie's heart clenched. After all these weeks they'd spent getting to know each other, did Gwen truly think she was as ruthless as her father?

"I'm serious." Reggie grabbed Gwen's other hand, holding them both as she tried to telegraph with her eyes that this wasn't a trick. "We can turn around right now. You can keep your job at the foundation, the apartment, everything. Hell, from what Bitsie tells me, you're the best associate director they've ever had. I couldn't get her to fire you if I tried."

"She really said that?" Gwen flushed with pride, their precarious mission momentarily forgotten. But after a moment, her brows drew together, and she gave Reggie a searching look. "Are you not ready? Is that what this is all about? Because I understand if you aren't. I would be terrified in your position."

"I hate this. I really do. I'm a grown woman. If I want to bring a date to a family function, I should be able to. Right?"

"You're kinda adorable right now." Gwen sucked in a breath. "Whatever you want to do, I'm here for you."

Emotions Reggie barely recognized and would've been hard-pressed to name welled in her chest. Had anyone ever offered their support so unconditionally to her before? Their dating relationship might not be real. There was the issue of a fourteen-million-dollar payment upon completion of the task. Deep down, though, Reggie sensed this sentiment was genuine. Her throat constricted to the point she couldn't respond. Not that she had any idea what to say.

Reggie was spared the need to speak as the door swung open, and Trevor greeted her with a grin. "Hey, Sis! I guess I can't call you Sister Reggie anymore, huh?"

For a moment, Reggie feared her brother was going to pull her into a bear hug or possibly get her in a headlock and give her a noogie like he did when they were kids, but instead he stepped aside and motioned them in with a deep bow, as if he'd been transformed into a butler for the evening.

"I have no idea what you're insinuating." Reggie did her best to play it cool, but she wasn't remotely calm inside. She knew all too well the madness that was to come. "This is Ms. Gwen Murphy from the Hawkins Foundation. We were conducting some business nearby and—"

"Oh, is that what we're calling it these days?" Trevor offered her an exaggerated wink. "I may not be all there sometimes"—he tapped the side of his head—"but don't insult my intelligence. I saw the photos. May I say, Ms.

Gwen, you're even lovelier in person. Sometimes in the pictures, I can't quite see your face."

Because I worked my ass off to make sure of it, Reggie thought, proud that she'd been able to keep her word. Mostly. There were rogue cameras out there, which made Reggie hopping mad. As she had once before, Reggie wondered if Gwen had a jealous ex in her past she was hiding from. Certain things made her skittish, Reggie had noticed, and she didn't want anything to happen to Gwen.

"Thank you for the compliment. You must be Reggie's twin brother, Trevor." Gwen offered her hand to shake. To her credit, she'd handled this slightly unorthodox introduction with perfect grace and decorum. It was a pity Reggie's father was sure to be too blinded by his own prejudice to recognize what an asset the woman could be for them.

"Uncanny resemblance, right?" Trevor pulled himself up to his full six-foot stature, towering over Reggie. He nudged her in the side. "Just so you know, I'm happy for you, but Dad's been looking ready to commit murder ever since the first photos hit the socials."

"Great." Reggie cast a sideways glance at Gwen, but it was too late to pull the ripcord. "Where is he?"

"War Room, of course," Trevor answered, adding for Gwen's benefit, "That's the meeting area in his home office where he has several television screens, all tuned to different news channels. The polls just closed in El Paso."

"I guess there's no sense putting it off." Reggie let out a sigh. She'd timed it perfectly, if such a thing were possible in this case. "Trev, can you get Gwen settled while I go to meet my doom?"

As her brother led Gwen toward the living room with its

fully stocked bar—a stop she definitely regretted not making first—Reggie made her way up the sweeping, curved staircase with its iron and gold railing. She turned right when she reached the landing, pushing her shoulders back and lifting her chin as she approached the room where her father was gathered with a handful of his top advisors. The room was dimly lit, glowing with the light of six different flat screens, all showing election coverage.

"Get in here." Reginald glared at her from where he sat, dead center, at the long table that faced the wall of screens. Three men sat on each side of him, and it did not escape Reggie's attention that the only other woman in the room was Rovena. Apparently, that relationship was still going strong.

"Let me get a drink."

Reggie took a step toward the liquor cart in the corner but froze as her father barked at her again.

"Now, dammit!" This was not a request but a command.

Reggie blinked once. Twice. On the third time, she made her way across the hardwood floor. She counted each step to calm her nerves.

"What game are you playing, girl?" her father bellowed. His companions shifted their eyes to the televisions or to the tabletop. Basically, anywhere but Reggie's face. It was somewhat gratifying to know they were as uncomfortable as she was.

"Game?" Reggie willed her lips to curl upward, just a little bit. She refused to look as terrified as she felt. "I was thinking of working on my tennis game this summer. Would you like to join me?"

"Shut your dirty mouth."

Reggie cocked her head to one side. "Tennis offends you?"

"You offend me!" He stabbed a chubby finger at Reggie's chest, and despite being several feet away, Reggie could almost feel its impact. "You and that woman."

"You mean Ms. Murphy? She's the associate director of the Hawkins Foundation." *Keep smiling, Reggie.* "We had a meeting that went late. I would've told you she was coming, but—"

"Don't bullshit a bullshitter. The photos of you two kissing in the park are everywhere. Even on our news sites. Do you know what this is going to do to our brand? Hawks News doesn't stand for perverts."

"Neither do I." As Reggie stood there, face-to-face with her father, her heart thumped so hard in her chest she thought it might leap out. Outwardly, she showed no fear.

"Your actions prove otherwise," he growled. "And now the whole world knows. You're a fucking disgrace! As for Ms. Murphy, she's fired."

"I'm afraid you can't do that." Reggie's head swiveled toward one of the men at the table, whom she recognized as her father's personal lawyer. "Isn't that right, Ron? As chairperson—a role you put me in, Daddy Dearest—only I can decide what happens at the foundation. Tell my father I'm right, won't you, Ron?"

"Er... uh..." Ron turned the color of an eggplant.

"Never mind. Get out! I can't stand to look at you." Her father dismissed her with a grunt, turning back to the others at the table as if his daughter no longer existed. "Ready for Hawks Corp history? Our boy Dwight is going to single-handedly close this merger for us."

Moving to the edge of the room but not quite leaving,

Reggie scanned the programs being broadcast on the wall. Her attention was caught by the words scrolling along the Hawks News chyron at the bottom of the screen. "I'm no genius like you, Dad, but those numbers aren't adding up."

He whipped his head to the appropriate screen, turning up the volume as the Hawks News anchor was saying, "It's official, folks. The Texas senate special election is heading to a run-off."

"Don't call the race, you morons." Now her father was the one who looked like an eggplant as he jumped from his seat and nearly lunged across the table. "Only eighty-six percent of the vote has been counted."

"Pretty sure the numbers don't lie," Reggie remarked, even though inside she was stunned. Her father had been so certain of Dwight's victory. This was better than she could have hoped.

"Rovena!" Reggie's father screamed at his girlfriend, who responded with a classic deer in the headlights imitation. "Get me my phone! Heads are going to roll."

CHAPTER FOURTEEN

Despite the sensation of walking through a museum filled with priceless art and antiques on display, the library-style room Gwen entered was a scene of domesticity. As she followed a few steps behind Trevor, she let out her breath in a slow, steady stream, finally allowing her muscles to release some of the tension they'd held since she'd set foot in the house. Though the room was extraordinary, the people occupying it seemed friendly and approachable.

In one area, a man and woman sat on a sofa, the woman holding a bundle of blankets that hinted at a baby within. Meanwhile, a silver-haired, grandmotherly type in vintage Chanel was filling a small plate as high as she could with hors d'oeuvres from the tiered servers that were arranged on a console table in front of one of the room's many floor-to-ceiling bookcases. Three men, all middle-aged or beyond and distinguished in appearance, wearing suits and ties, occupied a trio of leather club chairs. A fire crackled cheerfully in a marble fireplace to ward off the spring evening chill.

Trevor brought her first to the couple on the couch. The woman looked expectantly at Gwen, not bothering to hide her curiosity. Something about the woman's expression told Gwen she'd seen the photos and knew exactly who she was about to meet.

"Gwen, this is my sister, Stephanie," Trevor said. "And Little Baby D."

Stephanie's cheeks puffed in protest. "I wish you and Reggie would stop calling him that. His name is Dominic."

"Which starts with a D." Trevor said this as if he had no idea why his sister was upset with him, though Gwen had a feeling he was playing dumb. "We already have a Tiny D in the family, so we couldn't use that."

"My siblings think they're so clever," Stephanie fumed. "Just because my other children are named Archer, Bentley and Caden, they started calling this one Little Baby D as soon as we announced I was pregnant."

"Well, darling, you did insist on naming him Dominic," the man beside her remarked in perhaps the blandest tone Gwen had ever heard. She assumed this man was Stephanie's husband, though no introductions were offered.

"Whose side are you on, anyway?" Stephanie demanded. Just then, a resplendent farting noise rose out of the blankets, along with a terrible smell that instantly assaulted Gwen's nostrils. Stephanie promptly handed the baby over to her companion. "Brandon, love, would you mind?"

Gwen watched, mildly impressed, as Brandon disappeared into the next room without a protest.

Stephanie watched, too, a smug smile on her face. "He doesn't think I do much as a stay-at-home mother, so I've been teaching him exactly how much needs doing all the time."

"Serves the men in this family right." The grandmotherly woman came up to join them, her plate in one hand and a scotch in the other. "Hello, my dear. I'm Reggie's aunt Val. You must be Gwen Murphy. Bitsie has told me what a marvelous job you're doing at the foundation. I'd offer you my hand, but they're both full at the moment."

"Reggie might get mad, Aunt Val," Trevor teased. "Based on what I've seen, I think my sister has plans of her own for Gwen's hand."

"You impudent pup," Val scolded, a fond expression belying her words. "Why don't you make yourself useful and find a place for these." She handed her nephew both the plate and the glass while keeping her attention glued to Gwen. "Now, why don't I take you over to meet our other guests."

"Who is this?" The oldest looking of the three men squinted at Gwen as she approached.

"Tom, this is who I was telling you about earlier," Val explained, leaving Gwen to wonder exactly what had been said. "Tom's on the board of Hawks Corp, along with Richard and Harold."

The infamous Tom, Dick, and Harry, Gwen thought as the other two men offered friendly nods.

"Did you know Tom's son is gay?" Val asked in a pointed way that made Gwen believe this was being brought up for a reason, and not because the woman, like so many people Gwen had encountered, believed all people on the rainbow spectrum must know one another and be great friends.

"Is that right?" Gwen remarked, playing along.

"My daughter's nonbinary," Richard chimed in, clearly not wanting to be outdone. As soon as he'd said it, a look of confusion came over him. "Wait. I've got that wrong. My child? My offspring? Neither of those is sounding right."

"I'm sure they'd be pleased you're trying," Gwen offered, finding it sweet how determined the father was to get it correct.

"The world is changing. That's for sure," added Harold. To Gwen's relief, he sounded pleased by this fact, instead of threatened. "And your brother is becoming a fossil, Val. He can't see what's right before him."

"I think he can," Val said. "And it scares him."

"You might be right about that." Harold shifted, pulling his phone from the inside pocket of his jacket. He held the phone at arm's length to read the screen. "Speak of the devil. It's Reginald. The results must be in. Shall we head upstairs?"

"You go ahead," Val said. "I'll be right behind you, but I need my booze and nibbles to power me through." She turned to Gwen as the others rose and made their way out of the room. "Care to join me when I go up?"

"Are you sure that's wise?" Gwen had thought she'd heard yelling coming from upstairs a few times and could only imagine what was waiting for them.

"I won't lie," Val said. "It's not going to be pretty. But you're lovely. I don't know how my niece did it, but you're perfect."

As Gwen followed Val to the staircase, she wondered exactly how much the woman knew about the arrangement between Reggie and her. There was something about how she'd said it, along with how pointed she'd been in her small talk with the board members, that made Gwen think Reggie's aunt knew a lot more than she was letting on.

However, she didn't have much time to ponder this because as soon as they arrived on the second floor, it was clear pandemonium had broken out.

"Will someone get me on the air? I have to fix this mistake!" A man bellowed, a vein in the middle of his forehead, sticking out to the point Gwen was sure she could see the blood rushing through. Though they had yet to be introduced, there was no mistaking Reginald Hawkins.

"You can't go on air and say there's something wrong with the election." Reggie looked frantically around the room, making eye contact with her brother. It was a subtle exchange, but Trevor reacted as if his sister had jumped around waving a red flag.

"Let's not be rash, Dad," Trevor soothed. He put his hands on his father's shoulders but the old man instantly shrugged them off.

"Rash? My idiot son and traitorous daughter think I'm being rash?"

"Come on, now," Trevor said. "It's a run-off. Dwight's still in it to win it."

"I didn't pour millions of dollars and the full force of Hawks News into that boy's campaign for a goddamn participation ribbon," Reginald roared. He snapped his fingers at no one in particular. "Get me Clark on the phone. They need to retract the results. I demand it!"

"That's not how democracy works, Dad." Somehow, Reggie managed to speak firmly but still maintain a respectful tone. How, Gwen had no idea. The man was acting like his after-dinner coffee had been replaced with rocket fuel. One more outburst and he'd blast right through the beautifully crafted plaster ceiling above his head.

"You're supposed to be the smart one." Reginald did nothing to hide his disgust. "Fucking fix this now!"

"Despite what you may think," Val said, "we're not actually king makers. We have to work within the parameters of the laws."

"Of course, we're king makers!" Reginald slammed his fist into the table.

"You need your medicine." A dark-haired woman with a trace of a foreign accent approached Reginald with pills in hand.

"I don't want my medicine, Rovena," Reginald railed. "I don't need a goddamn nursemaid. You're always hovering over me with my fucking pills!"

Rovena persisted, and Gwen was impressed. Was this woman a nurse? Never had anyone looked so close to a deadly heart attack as Reginald Hawkins did right then. Part of Gwen wished the woman wasn't trying so hard. Considering the harm this man had done, the world would probably be a better place without him.

"Now, now, my love," Rovena cooed. "Just take them."

Gwen arched an eyebrow. Had this woman, who was half Reginald's age if she was a day, just referred to that crotchety old bear as *my love*?

Gross.

Reginald slapped Rovena's hand away, not accepting the pills. "Reggie. Talk to Chuck. What are our pollsters seeing? Trevor, get Dwight on the line. Tell him not to concede. We'll do whatever it takes to get him across the finish line."

Reggie and Trevor went into action.

Gwen drifted to the side of the so-called War Room, the televisions blaring with pundits reacting to the election upset. She pressed her fingers to her temples, hoping to ward off a migraine.

"How are you holding up, dear?" Joining her, Val's expression brimmed with sympathy.

"Is it always like this? Is he?"

"This is quintessential Reginald right now."

Stephanie, approached, the baby squawking. "Brandon can stay if Dad needs him, but I'm going to take Dominic home. He's getting fussy."

"Yes, get the baby away from here. Your father's not fit company right now." Val kissed Stephanie's cheek, wishing her a safe journey home.

In Gwen's opinion, Little Baby D wasn't the only cranky infant in the room. Gwen's eyes laser locked on Reginald, who only now was finally swallowing the pills Rovena had insisted he take. He had one phone pressed to his ear, and Brandon held another phone ready for Reginald to bark orders into as soon as he was ready.

"How bad was he on the 2020 election night?" Gwen asked Val.

"Unhappy but not like this. Dwight's election is much more important to him."

Gwen was curious to hear more, but before she could ask, Reginald demanded Val's assistance with something. Mostly forgotten, Gwen sank into a corner chair and watched the spectacle unfold as Reginald berated, coaxed, and threatened everyone in his orbit.

Everyone except Gwen. He only glared at her whenever he had a second to spare. Luckily, there weren't many of those. Still, it was unnerving. More than once, Gwen wanted to bolt from the room.

She couldn't leave Reggie, though. Not now in her time of need.

It was around three in the morning when Reggie finally admitted there was nothing more she could do, and it was time to go.

At the door, Val pulled Gwen in for a quick peck on the cheek. "I guess we'll be seeing you in the Hamptons soon, yes?"

"Y-yes," Gwen nearly choked on the word, shocked that this was her life.

It was going to be quite a summer, if Gwen made it that far.

———

It was silent in the SUV as Reggie's driver maneuvered into a spot along the curb in front of Gwen's apartment building. Gwen stared out the window into the predawn stillness, uncertain what to say.

Finally, she settled on, "It was an ugly night."

"Not the first I've experienced, but yes." Reggie's tone was flat, whether from hiding emotion or lacking it, Gwen couldn't say. "Come on. I'll walk you to your door."

Gwen hopped out of the car. "I feel so guilty."

"Why?" Reggie joined her on the pavement, shutting the car door. "It's not that far. I can use the exercise."

"Not that." Gwen gave Reggie's shoulder a playful nudge. "I feel like I caused all this. He hates that you're with me."

Stopping outside the door to Gwen's building, Reggie placed her hands on each of Gwen's shoulders. "You did not cause this. And what's more, there is no this. I'm allowed to be with whomever I want to, and it's time I started remembering that. I'm angry with myself for not standing up to him sooner. None of this was your fault. Please tell me you understand."

"I'm not sure I do." Tears stung Gwen's eyes as some of the biting things Reginald had said to his daughter echoed in her memory. On impulse, she pulled Reggie into a hug.

Instantly, Reggie's body went stiff. "You don't have to do that. There aren't any photographers around at this time of night."

"This has nothing to do with the paparazzi." Gwen continued to hold Reggie tightly, smiling to herself as she felt the woman's body relax, leaning into the embrace. "I've wanted to do this all night."

Instead of fighting to get away, Reggie rested her head against Gwen's shoulder. "Why?"

"To let you know everything's going to be okay."

"Do you really believe that?" Reggie whispered, clearly not believing it herself.

"Of course, I do." Gwen brushed her fingers through Reggie's hair, smoothing the wayward strands. If only every one of life's tangles were so easy to straighten out. "If you don't have hope that things will work out for the best, what's the point to life?"

"I've never thought of it that way."

"I know. I just might be able to teach you a few things." After an extra squeeze, Gwen let Reggie go. "Thank you for walking me to my door. Very gallant of you."

Reggie shrugged, looking embarrassed. "You never know what danger could be lurking within ten feet of your front door."

"Would you like to come upstairs?" Gwen asked softly,

exhausted but not quite ready to let Reggie go. "It's too late to get any sleep. I can make us some coffee."

"That sounds lovely, but I need to head directly to the office." It was hard to say if that was an excuse Reggie was using to get away, but Gwen hoped not.

"You're like one of those ducks we saw on the pond yesterday. Always looking perfectly calm but paddling like hell beneath the surface."

"Don't tell anyone I'm a duck. I want them to think I'm mean, like a swan." Reggie kissed Gwen on the cheek. "I'll call you soon for our next date."

"Looking forward to it." She truly was. In fact, despite the traumatic evening, Gwen practically skipped inside the lobby, feeling light and free.

She crashed to earth as soon as she laid eyes on the woman waiting for her in the lobby. Solène's tall, muscular form was hard to miss.

"What do you think you're doing?" Solène demanded in a harsh whisper, keeping one eye on the doorman who was looking their way with an expression of concern on his face.

"Me? What the fuck are you doing in my lobby?" The adrenaline pumping through Gwen's veins made her words blunter than they might usually have been. "It's the middle of the night. How did you find me?"

"Are you kidding me?" Solène pulled several sheets of paper from her shoulder bag, brandishing the latest photos of Gwen with Reggie in the rowboat, plus some older ones, too. "Look at this."

Gwen did, and what she saw were two women looking very much like a couple, laughing and enjoying each other's company. They looked so sweet and happy that Gwen's heart ached to be them, or rather for what she saw to be real.

"Come on. We should go upstairs where we can have some privacy." Gwen started toward the elevator, and Solène followed. They remained silent until they were inside Gwen's apartment. As soon as the door clicked shut, Solène let loose.

"You're being an idiot." Solène's accent softened the blow of her criticism, and Gwen couldn't help but respond with a goofy smile, because her friend was right. She felt like an idiot, through and through. "Do you care to explain why you're grinning like a fool?"

"Nope. Do you want to explain why you're here?"

"Me? I'm just doing a little thing called my job. I'm an investigative journalist, you might recall." It was clear Solène's mood had not been improved by Gwen's silliness. "You know, trying to expose the people who have you on the run. Make it so they don't try to kill you or something. No big deal. Clearly it isn't to you."

"I'm sorry." Gwen smoothed the smile from her face. "I may not have thought it through when I agreed to be so public with Reggie. I didn't think anyone at Kensington would read the gossip sheets."

Solène raised an eyebrow at the word *agreed* but didn't question it further. "I thought we had *agreed* you would lay low in Queens. Live off savings for a while and disappear off the radar. We vetted that apartment for you, worked out the prepayment. Instead, you take a job at a high profile charity? It's a good thing your background story held together. It wasn't necessarily designed for that kind of scrutiny. Plus, you move without telling me? It took some work to find you."

Gwen shivered, recalling how it had felt to walk into what was supposed to be a safe place to discover a stranger waiting inside. "Yeah, it turned out that place in Queens wasn't to my liking. Anyway, isn't it good you had a difficult time? It means it wouldn't be easy for Simon to find me, either."

"Maybe." Solène didn't sound convinced. "Speaking of Simon, I've been traveling between Brussels, London, and DC to get—"

"I'm sorry, Solène, but I'm too tired for the details right now. Can you just tell me how much longer I have to live this way? When I first told you about Kensington when we met up in Edinburgh, well over a year ago now…" Gwen's voice faltered. "I didn't realize how hard it would be. How long things would take. How absolutely fucking terrifying it would be. Until I go on the record and give my testimony to someone in authority, I'm a target." She choked back a sob. "I don't know how much longer I can be in this holding pattern."

"I know." Solène took hold of Gwen's shoulders, making eye contact. "I'm trying to get through to the proper agencies, get someone high enough up to listen to me. It's why I've been flying everywhere I can think of. But without a smoking gun, it's a challenge."

"I thought I was the smoking gun."

Solène took a deep breath. "You're playing a huge role. You are. But we need more documentation. We need ironclad proof to bring Kensington down."

"I don't know how much more I can do."

"You've already done enough. Not many would be this brave. What you need now is to be smart." Solène took another steadying breath. "And by smart, I mean perhaps not gallivanting on the arm of Reggie Hawkins with your photo in the press every day. She's a celebrity, for fuck's sake."

"Maybe to a news geek like you, but she's hardly a Kardashian. The average person doesn't give a fuck about the Hawkins family, and most might know the name but couldn't tell you why they mattered." Gwen argued, leaving out that Reggie had been planting their photos in the press to get the attention of an audience of one. "Besides it's not every day. It's once a week."

"Yes, I noticed. For twelve weeks." Solène's jaw tightened, and Gwen detected jealousy in her tone. "You know, I've looked into this new girlfriend of yours. She has some interesting things in her past, including rumors that somehow never made it to the papers. Not like this fling of yours did, like wildfire. Curious, no? Maybe I need to dig some more. I can't have her using you for... whatever it is she's using you for. Same thing she always does, yes?"

"Solène, no." There was no doubt in Gwen's mind what her ex thought was going on, and she needed to nip it in the bud. Not only was it incorrect, it was unfair to Reggie to let Solène believe Reggie was behaving inappropriately. "You don't understand what's really going on."

Solène crossed her arms. "Then explain."

With a heavy sigh, Gwen briefly summarized her encounter with the woman who had been waiting for her in Queens. "So, you see? I had to move. And I had to take the job. She told me if I didn't, she knew where my family was. My mom and grandfather. I'm doing all of this to get my life back. To get my mom back. I have to believe she doesn't hate me but is being manipulated by my right-wing troll of a grandfather. If I can just afford to take care of her..."

Gwen pinched her eyes as tightly as she could to stop the tears.

"This stranger, she threatened your family?" Fire burned in Solène's eyes. "What did she look like?" After Gwen gave a brief description, her friend's lips pressed into a grim line. "I think I know who this woman is or at least the political activist group she's with. A few of their members have been sniffing around, so I'll look into possible leaks. What did she want?"

"She didn't tell me. And don't give me that look. It's the truth."

"But you're working for her?"

"No. Not really." Gwen shifted uncomfortably. With everything else going on, she'd nearly forgotten the original reason she'd contacted Reggie for the job. "It's been months. Maybe whatever it was, she doesn't need me anymore."

"Are you really so naive?" Solène took a deep breath, letting it out as a sigh. "Okay. I'll add this to my list of things to investigate while I'm in New York. But I don't like it one bit."

"It's not like I'm living my best life either." Except, as Gwen closed her eyes, she could practically feel the warm sun on her skin and hear the gentle sloshing of the water as the rowboat skidded along the surface. If that wasn't her best life, what was? The only thing that might be better is if it wasn't all for show.

Having said all she'd come to say, Solène made her way to the door. "Please be careful, Wendy."

Gwen nearly gasped at hearing her real name. She'd become so used to being who she was now that her old self almost felt like a dream.

Once she was alone, Gwen went into the bathroom and turned on the water in the clawfoot tub, letting it run as she stripped out of the clothes she'd been wearing for far too many hours.

Just as she was poised with one foot lifted, ready to step under the hot shower, her phone rang. Her heart skipped a beat as she saw Reggie's name appear on the screen.

Gwen cleared her throat. "Hello?"

"What are you doing?"

Gwen's heart beat even faster. Had Reggie somehow known that Solène had been there and was checking up on her? The last thing she wanted was for Reggie to think she'd been betrayed.

"I was about to take a shower," Gwen stuttered, adding somewhat awkwardly, "I'm naked."

"You are?" There was more than a hint of wanting in the hitch of Reggie's voice. Clearly, that had not been the answer she'd been expecting. Was it surprise? Or was there something else there, too? Gwen had to find out. She couldn't care less at this moment about the no sex clause in their contract. Ever since the kiss on the boat, Gwen had been dying to know if it had impacted Reggie as much as it had her.

"Completely naked. Someone got me all sweaty today out in the sun." There was a husky quality to Gwen's tone that was very deliberate. And, she hoped, effective. "I'm about to get all wet."

"Oh?" There was a pause, and Gwen could almost picture Reggie trying to pick her jaw up off the floor. "Maybe I should take you boating more often."

"I wouldn't say no. So, I'll see you soon?"

"Uh… yeah." Reggie cleared her throat. "Definitely."

Gwen grinned as she hung up the call. She'd succeeded in making Reggie Hawkins speechless at the prospect of seeing her. The thrill of victory sent a delicious shiver down Gwen's spine, landing in the cleft between her thighs. For a difficult night, it was a glorious conclusion. She couldn't wait to see what would happen next.

CHAPTER FIFTEEN

"What's the big emergency? I'm still getting caught up from my Australia trip." Reggie entered Trevor's office with a sinking feeling in her gut. It had started with her brother's urgent text of *Mayday*—almost certainly not a reference to the current month of the year—and had grown more pronounced with every step she'd taken through the nearly empty executive floor.

"Oh, hey. How was it Down Under?" Trevor wore a confused expression, and Reggie wasn't sure if this meant he'd forgotten why he summoned her or if he'd just wanted to say hello.

"It was two weeks of cold weather and meetings that could have been emails. Kind of like this could've been, apparently." Reggie tossed her hands in the air, more exasperated at her brother than usual. "It's two o'clock on the Friday of Memorial Day weekend. The office is already a ghost town. Can this honestly not wait until after the holiday?"

The haunted look on Trevor's face told her the answer was no. "I have two words for you. Know what they are?"

"Ice cream?" Reggie guessed hopefully. "There's a double scoop of Kahlua chip from John's Drive-in with my name on it, and I intend to be on my way to collect it as soon as Gwen gets here."

"Braving Memorial Day in the Hamptons with the new lady friend, eh?" Trevor's eyes widened as he shook his head. "She must've been good and pissed at you to get you to agree to that. Can't blame her, really."

"Why would Gwen be mad at me?" Reggie's insides quivered. She'd spent two weeks justifying to herself why leaving had been okay. It had nothing to do with the kiss she and Gwen had shared, or the overwhelming temptation she'd faced during Gwen's teasing late night phone call. She'd had important business to attend to. But the look her brother was giving her said all that self-delusion had been in vain.

"You left for Australia, what, the day after your whole relationship bombshell hit the tabloids? For two weeks?" Trevor tapped his fingers on the desktop, waiting for her to catch up. Each rapping sound drove the words deeper until they finally hit home.

"That probably wasn't the best timing on my part." An understatement if there ever was one. She'd flown halfway around the world and left Gwen alone to deal with the aftermath, both in the press and her own emotions. Even for a fake girlfriend, Reggie's move had been really shitty. She took one last stab at self-redemption. "It was an important trip, though. I couldn't put it off."

"You told me it could've been an email." Trevor tilted his

head, studying her in an uncomfortably penetrating way. "Did you get cold feet? Is that why you ran off?"

"No. Of course not." The idea was preposterous, yet suddenly, Reggie was reminded of that feeling of panic she'd had after hanging up the phone call with Gwen. The one where Gwen had been naked. And wet. And completely inaccessible, no matter how much Reggie might wish otherwise. They had a no-sex clause in their contract, and it was there for a reason. No matter how much it tormented her after that kiss on the pond had gotten so out of hand.

Be honest with yourself, Reggie. That was why she'd developed the irrepressible urge to check in on the Hawks Corp operations in Sydney. And Gwen had every right to be livid about it.

"Shit."

"Yeah," Trevor agreed. "So, where are you going for dinner tonight?"

Reggie frowned. "I told you already. John's Drive-in."

"Oh, you sweet summer child. Charlene!" Trevor's assistant appeared almost instantly. "Charlene, I need you to set my sister up with the standard Julie Hawkins Hamptons Weekend apology protocol."

Reggie boosted an eyebrow. "You have your own apology protocol for your wife?"

"I fuck up a lot."

Reggie couldn't hold back a chuckle. "What's in this protocol of yours?"

"Dinner reservations at Harvest, a 90-minute couples massage, plus a full-day spa treatment," Trevor explained. "Have you seen her at all since Dad's?"

"Not since I dropped her off that night," Reggie admitted. "But I texted from Sydney."

"No Facetime, at least?" Trevor turned to Charlene. "Do the upgrade. You remember, like that time two years ago when I thought Julie was going to serve me with divorce papers."

"Upgrade? What does that entail?" Reggie asked, then sighed. "You know what? It doesn't matter. Do the upgrade."

"Good job, Sis," Trevor said after Charlene left. "Learning how to grovel for forgiveness is the first step toward a happy relationship. But if you're willing to submit those claw feet of yours to a pedicure, this thing with Gwen must be true love."

Reggie's knee-jerk reaction was to tell him he was wrong, but then she remembered the goal was to sell this relationship as the real deal. "I mean, what if it was?"

"Then I'd be happier for you than I've ever been."

"That's it? That's all you have to say?" Reggie lowered herself onto the sofa by the window, refusing to sit in one of the chairs across the desk from her brother like she was his subordinate. "No teasing? No torture?"

"Me?" Trevor placed a hand over his chest in what could have been mistaken by some as a sincere gesture, but only if they'd never actually met her brother before.

"You were merciless to my ex-husbands."

"Good old Chip and Dale."

"See? You can't even get their names right." Reggie folded her arms across her chest in triumph. "Chip was a nickname. And it wasn't Dale. It was John. You make it sound like I was married to cartoon chipmunks."

"Here I was going for exotic male dancers," Trevor said with a smirk. "That you didn't pick up on the reference is making way more sense now that I've seen you sharing goo-goo eyes with Gwen."

"When have I ever?" Reggie protested. It was one thing to sell it. But goo-goo eyes? That was taking things too far. And what did he meaning *sharing*? Was he suggesting Gwen was doing it, too?

"When? How about in every single photo of the two of you together?"

"Whatever." Inside, Reggie sighed with relief. For a minute there, she'd been afraid Trevor had been picking up on something with his twin-tuition spidey senses. Some spark between her and Gwen that Reggie herself wasn't ready to look too closely at, let alone discuss with her brother. But he was talking about the tabloid photos. Those were supposed to be convincing, so she should probably be glad her brother was fooled and leave it at that.

Trevor raised his left hand. "I solemnly swear if you marry Gwen, I won't tease her more than is absolutely necessary to maintain my reputation."

"You're supposed to swear with your right hand, you dolt." As soon as she said it, the shadow that crossed her brother's face alerted Reggie to her mistake.

"Yeah, well, it was a joke anyway." Trevor's cheeks burned brightly.

Reggie could have sunk all the way under the sofa cushions. This had to have been one of those moments when the ravages of brain hypoxia had left her brother unable to tell his right from his left. She wished with all her heart she could turn back the clock, if not seven years so the accident wouldn't have happened at all, at least a few minutes so she wouldn't have added insult to injury by embarrassing him unnecessarily. Sure, she enjoyed giving her brother crap, but she never wanted to be cruel. Not like their father.

"You said earlier you had two words for me," Reggie prompted, feeling it was best to move on. "Care to share? And neither one of them better start with an F."

Trevor responded with two raised middle fingers. But as he lowered his hands, his forehead creased, and he let out a troubled sigh. "Clark Maxwell."

"Fuck me." Reggie groaned, breaking the rule she'd given Trev. "What has the fuckwit done now?"

"He's gone and said something he shouldn't have." Trevor swallowed, looking like he might be sick. "I'm not sure what to do."

"He says something he shouldn't at least once every twenty-four hours," Reggie pointed out, trying to hide her frustration. If her father was so set on Trevor being in charge, it would be nice if her brother could handle the job without running to her at every turn. "Artistic license is the company line. Hawks Corp has never seen the need to do anything about what he's said on his show before. Why start now?"

"This doesn't involve his show. Well, it does, but not something he said on air. There's been a leak. A clip of Clark losing it during commercial breaks." Trevor picked up a remote to turn on a TV screen on his office wall.

Clark Maxwell's heavily made-up face appeared, his features twisted, frozen mid-rant. When Trevor hit the play button, Clark's familiar voice filled the office.

"Who the fuck is talking into my ear piece during my segment?" he roared. "I can't think if someone is talking into my ear."

"The man thinks?" Reggie cracked.

"News to me, too," Trevor said with a laugh. "Keep watching. There's more."

"If someone doesn't stop that goddamn drilling..." There was a five-second pause during which it appeared Clark was listening to someone speaking in his earpiece. Out of the blue, he exploded again. "I'll take that fucking drill and make the person rue the day he messed with me." Clark followed up this threat with an obnoxious drill sound—buzzzzt, buzzzzzzt—as he mimed using a drill, on what, Reggie couldn't tell.

"Is that supposed to be someone's head he's drilling into?" she guessed.

"Maybe their ass?" Trevor suggested with a shrug.

Reggie laughed. "He needs to up his game in the threat department. That's not remotely scary. Nor is it legally actionable. It's clear the guy's a puffed-up buffoon. So why did you go all red-level on this like he's a threat to national security all of a sudden?"

Trevor's face went ashen, his tone grim. "Because it gets worse."

"Oh, I know." Clark exaggerated his words the way he tended to do when he thought he was being super clever. "Is that Reggie Hawkins up there? Did she just get a new set of power tools in her lesbian welcome bag and couldn't wait to try them out? She'd better knock it the fuck off."

"Ha-ha. So smart of him." Reggie rolled her eyes, trying to keep her temper in check as the man did a grotesque gyration that was clearly supposed to be sexual in nature. "It's obvious he thinks drills and sex toys are the same thing, and he has no idea what to do with either."

Trevor put his finger to his lips. "This is the part where it gets bad."

Clark's face was bright red as he ranted into the camera. "It's bad enough that lesbo's ruining our brand. Now I can't think with this racket." There was another pause. "I don't care if she's not in the building. Yeah, I know it's not her drill, you moron. I'm saying perverts like her should be frog-marched out of here in handcuffs. Being in the same building—it's disgusting." He exaggerated a cringe. "She's disgusting. All of 'em. They belong in prison. Send 'em all to a deserted island where they can fuck each other all they want until they die off. Or there's option three."

Clark pointed a finger at the camera in what was undeniably supposed to be the shape of a gun. But in case anyone didn't get his meaning, he added a "pew-pew" sound effect, just to be sure. Reggie's body went cold as she stared at the finger that was pointed straight at her.

"I'm so sorry." Trevor's voice wavered between a whisper and a whimper. "That was terrible. You see why I don't know what to do?"

Reggie felt the shaking coming on, starting in her core and traveling to her extremities. If she didn't stop it, she'd be a quivering heap on the floor. She couldn't let one horrible man reduce her to that, especially when her brother needed her to hold it together.

"Yeah, it was terrible. That's the worst fucking gun imitation I've ever seen." Reggie tossed up her hands, the exaggerated motion helping to release some of the pent-up energy threatening to bring her to her knees. "Is it supposed to be a revolver? A space laser? Pathetic."

"Heads are going to roll!" Their father burst into Trevor's office, practically frothing at the mouth. He stopped short at the sight of Clark on the screen, frozen in the act of firing his gun finger. "Goddamn it! Turn that off. If anyone sees you watching that we can't deny we've seen it. Don't you know anything?"

Seething, Reggie clenched her fists until her knuckles hurt. "I should have known you would be more concerned about liability than the fact one of your rabid dogs threatened to kill your first born."

"What is she doing here?" It was clear her father was speaking to Trevor and ignoring her. "Tell your sister this has nothing to do with her role at the Hawkins Foundation, and therefore, her presence is not required."

"But I, uh…" Trevor's breathing grew heavy. "I invited her, Dad."

"In that case, tell her she's been uninvited. Effective right this fucking minute. Got it?"

Reggie shook her head in disbelief. "Real mature."

She stood her ground, determined that nothing would make her move from her spot until she was good and ready to go.

Trevor looked from Reggie to Reginald, and back again. He continued like he was watching a tennis match, with the sound off, until finally breaking the silence.

"I think we need to put out a statement on behalf of Hawks Corp, saying we don't condone language like that," Trevor suggested. "We can say Clark is leaving for his *regularly* scheduled vacation for a week." He made quote marks to accompany the word *regularly*.

"Absolutely not." Both Reggie and her father said this at the same time, like they'd been programmed to respond in unison. Reggie suspected they'd said it for very different reasons.

"He can't threaten my life, and others, with his incendiary language and get off with a slap on the wrist."

Reggie moved into her father's direct line of sight. "If you don't stand up to him and one of his lunatic followers acts on this, Hawks Corp is complicit."

Her father's lip curled into a snarl. "I'd like to see that stand up in court." He twisted around, unsteadily, turning his back on her so he could talk to Trevor. "I want the leaker found and flogged."

"I think you mean fired, Dad," Reggie taunted. "It's not the seventeenth century, and you aren't the captain of a pirate ship."

"Dad—" Trevor stood a little taller—"respectfully, I think we have to say something. This clip has been picked up by every media company. It's a meme on the socials. There are photos of Reggie's face with crosshairs over it. Clark has finally gone too far. We have to cut him loose. Not renew his contract."

"Over this?" The old man sneered. "Don't be a pussy. This is nothing."

All at once, Reggie couldn't get Gwen's grandfather out of her mind. It was bullshit like this that had led this company so far down the wrong path. It needed to stop.

"What about all the viewers he's brainwashed?" Reggie demanded. "Clark Maxwell serves up fear and hatred like his own flavor of cult Kool-Aid, and his followers drink it down each week. Because we allow it."

Reginald crossed his arms defiantly. "It makes money."

"At what cost?" Reggie swallowed her emotion, struggling to keep her tone even so her stubborn mule of a father might hear a word or two of what she said. "Real people, real Americans, have lost friends, family, and loved ones because they've blindly followed Clark down every crazy rabbit hole."

"Do these people keep watching his show?" Reggie's father held his hands out to either side, as if there was nothing more to say. "They do. They tell their friends to watch, too. Win. Win."

"How much ad revenue have we lost?" Reggie demanded. "Millions and you know it. Advertisers won't touch his show, except for the crazy My Buddy guy with his stupid dog beds. Cable viewers are cutting the cord so they don't subsidize the Clark Maxwell show by paying their monthly bills. The guy is toxic. It's only a matter of time before we get sued for millions, if not billions."

Reginald glared at her. "No one in their right mind will ever try suing us."

"Fine. Forget about being sued. How about firing him because he's destroying the social fabric of society." Reggie was close to tears, but she held it in. If she let a single drop fall from an eye in her father's presence, this argument would be lost. "Words carry weight. We are giving this man his bully pulpit, and someone is going to get hurt."

Reginald's face was the portrait of a volcano ready to explode, but instead of erupting, he turned his back on Reggie once again. His next words were directed to Trevor with terrifying calm. "Tell your sister I don't need her input."

"If you want to speak to her," Trevor yelled, blowing up where his father and sister had not, "she's standing right there. I'm not the fucking messenger boy."

"I have nothing else to say," Reginald announced. "This wasn't on air. Clark Maxwell is free to say whatever he wants in private. Whoever leaked this tape is the problem. People should be able to trust their coworkers. At Hawks Corp, we're a family."

"That does help explain the trust issues around here." Reggie said it under her breath, but the old man still had uncanny hearing for his age.

He whirled around, eyes sharp as daggers. "If you didn't have a vote on the board, I would cut you out of my life. As a daughter, you're dead to me. Do you understand?" The man stormed out of the office, shouting, "Get me the leaker!"

Trevor let out an anguished sigh before putting his head down on his desk. His entire body shook.

"You okay?" Reggie asked softly, approaching his desk and placing a hand on his shoulder.

"No. You?"

"No," Reggie admitted. "But it doesn't matter. I knew when he found out about Gwen, it would be a declaration of war. Dad likes to think he's a maverick, but he's so fucking predictable in his old age, so full of fear and brainwashed by his own propaganda, that he's losing touch with the world."

"What can I do, Reg? Tell me what to do." Never before had Trevor looked so much like a man unsuited for his position. It seemed to Reggie it would swallow him whole. Another few years of this and there would be nothing left of him.

"I need time to think." Just as she said this, Reggie's phone buzzed with a text. She checked it quickly, her spirits lifting slightly seeing Gwen's name on the screen. "Gwen's here. Can we continue this when I get back?"

"Yes, of course. Have a good weekend." Still seated, Trevor wrapped his arms around Reggie's waist, the same way he used to do with their mother when he was little. "I'm glad you have Gwen. I'm truly happy for you."

Reggie forced herself to smile, but inside, she was

hollow. She wished she had Gwen, in the way her brother had meant it. The person who stood by you, who defended you in times of trouble. Instead, she had a woman who'd signed a contract to make it look like that was what Reggie had. Reggie stood alone, and considering how terrible she was at managing even a fake relationship, she probably always would.

Reggie sucked in a deep breath and pulled away from her twin. "I'll see you Tuesday, Bro. Are the kids home this weekend? You tell those little shits of yours to start practicing now because their aunt Reggie's going to destroy them at Marco Polo this summer, okay?"

She left in a hurry, barely making it to the refuge of the women's bathroom before she broke down and sobbed.

CHAPTER SIXTEEN

Gwen sat inside Reggie's office, trying not to grind her teeth to dust as she stared at the array of clocks on the wall that told the time in a dozen different cities around the globe. In every single one of them, Reggie Hawkins was running late.

Reggie Hawkins was never late, or so Gwen had been told more than once by the woman herself. But upon finally resurfacing from her two-week absence, Reggie was once again MIA. Not even her assistant, Janet, had a clue where she could be.

Two weeks in Australia and barely a text.

Gwen kicked her toe at the carpeted floor, pretending it was Reggie's shin. *Fucking Australia?* That was about as far as you could fly from New York before you actually started circling back. And Gwen knew exactly how Reggie felt about planes.

Gwen wasn't a hundred percent certain it was the kiss that had sent Reggie packing, but chances were high. What else could explain it? Well, the smoking hot kiss had been followed by a little harmless flirting as Gwen was getting into the shower. But nothing more. Nothing that should've spooked a grown woman who wanted to run a multinational company.

I was trying to unwind!

Meeting Reggie's family had been hard. Had it even occurred to the woman how difficult that had been? And then with Solène showing up unannounced... Well, she'd needed to let off some steam. Gwen hadn't meant to cross any lines with the flirting. It had just felt natural. And fun.

Regina Hawkins is a fun hater!

Honestly, if one hotter-than-intended kiss and some relatively innocent banter was enough to send the woman running to Australia, maybe she should have stayed there. How were they going to pull off a sham marriage if they couldn't get through a single day as a "real" couple? And then to leave without talking it through? Unacceptable.

If she's not here in five minutes, I'm leaving.

Gwen scowled at the clocks again, picturing the traffic they would face. Friday afternoon on Memorial Day weekend? Only a fool would leave now to drive all the way to Montauk. It was at the very tip of Long Island. They'd be lucky to arrive by morning. Gwen didn't even want to go anymore. Not if Reggie was going to be like this.

"Sorry I'm late." The office door opened, and Reggie strolled in, her chipper voice making Gwen want to scream. "There was a work thing."

"You mean like Australia was a work—" Stopping midscolding, Gwen slanted her head to better assess. The stress lines on Reggie's forehead didn't match her singsong greeting. And her eyes were pink and puffy like she'd been crying. "Are you okay?"

"It's… not a big deal. Someone leaked a video that shouldn't have been made public." Reggie said dismissively, but Gwen wasn't buying it.

"What video?"

Instead of an answer, Reggie closed her eyes and swallowed. Her face had gone green.

"What video?" Gwen repeated, firmer this time. Her stomach knotted as Reggie approached, holding out her phone.

Oh God. Not the sex tape. Don't let them have leaked the sex tape.

But after Gwen watched what was on the screen, one thing was certain. It was most definitely not the sex tape.

"I don't even know what to say." Gwen paused, allowing time for Clark Maxwell's hideous diatribe to sink in.

"Don't worry." Reggie was stiff, shocked. Why wouldn't she be? One of her own employees had gone off the rails, threatened her very existence. That was some serious shit. "We're already on it. Hawks Corp will find the leaker and fire them."

"Who cares about the leaker?" Gwen was aghast. "What about Clark? Those reprehensible things Clark said are the real issue. And that way he pointed at the camera at the end. That was a direct threat. Do you not agree? You should be calling the police."

"A company like ours has to be able to trust the people on our team. If we can't, things break down." Reggie had broken down from what Gwen could tell. She'd become a poorly functioning, robotic version of herself, parroting her father's wishes. If she didn't snap out of it, Gwen wasn't certain what to do.

"What about Clark?" Gwen repeated, anger boiling right

to the top and threatening to spill all over Reggie's tastefully neutral rug. "Will anything happen to him?"

"Clark is Clark." Reggie's jaw clenched, but the spell that had her spouting the Hawks Corp company line went unbroken.

The space around Gwen went from beige to a hazy red. "That's bullshit, and you know it!"

Gwen's fury was unleashed, but instead of responding in kind, Reggie took a forced breath. Gwen recognized the move. It was the same thing the woman did every time she was trying to bury healthy human emotions in the deepest depths of her soul.

"I think I could use a weekend away," Reggie said in an even tone. "Shall we get going?"

"Really? You think we should *get going*? Just like that?" Whatever control Gwen might have been able to muster had evaporated the moment that suggestion had left Reggie's lips. "Just run away from the problem, like the way you high-tailed it out of town the day after we kissed?"

"I didn't mean for that…" Something approaching emotion flashed in Reggie's eyes. Finally, a crack in her icy veneer. "I was… I was…"

"You were what?" This time Gwen did manage to calm herself enough to avoid snapping like an angry turtle. Whatever Reggie was struggling to say, Gwen wanted to hear it. Whether or not she'd want to murder her afterward remained to be seen.

"I thought I knew what to expect." Reggie's voice was a shaky whisper. "This plan was my choice. It was under my control. But it all became so *real*. And that kiss…"

"Yeah, that kiss…" Gwen echoed.

That kiss had been achingly real, and both of them knew it.

"This brilliant plan of mine has set off a firestorm. I knew my father would be angry, but I thought I wouldn't care." Reggie choked back a sob, and Gwen's heart clenched. "I thought I wouldn't care about... a lot of things. But I was wrong."

What else did Reggie care about? Gwen's heart stuttered, but she reined it in. Their relationship was an illusion. A lie. This was the worst possible time to forget it. Yet it was also the most real thing Gwen had in her life. Even her name was a lie. And witnessing the usually stoic woman's unraveling was like gazing into a mirror that reflected the twisting of her own restless soul.

"So, you figured the best way to deal with it head-on would be to get on a plane and fly halfway around the world?" It was said gently, with humor, and to Gwen's relief, a tenuous smile tugged at Reggie's lips.

To be fair, when her own life had gotten to be too much, Gwen had run, too. How could she blame Reggie for doing the same?

"It made so much more sense at the time." Reggie pressed her hands to her temples, as if trying to make sure her head didn't come flying off. At least that was how it seemed to Gwen. "Please believe me. I didn't mean to abandon you. You have every right to be angry."

"Do I?" Gwen wasn't convinced. She'd given it a lot of thought over the past two weeks, and she truly didn't know. "I signed a contract. You have a right to expect me to behave a certain way. To listen to you, to laugh at your jokes, to keep my opinions to myself. Like Lydia did."

"You're not Lydia, and I don't want you to be." There

was an edge to Reggie's voice, almost an angry tone, that made Gwen shrink back. But it was gone in an instant, replaced by a heavy sigh.

"What do you want?" Gwen asked, not sure she wanted to know. The very mention of Lydia had sent Reggie back to the edge. It was clear the depth of her emotions for the woman she'd loved and lost was something Gwen could never compete with. It wasn't until the stabbing pain sliced through her heart that Gwen realized how desperately she'd hoped that wasn't the case.

"Honestly, right now, I'm looking forward to our weekend." Reggie closed her eyes. "Maybe it's running away, and maybe I should stay and fight, but... I made reservations at a nice restaurant."

"You did?" Gwen was touched by the revelation, as well as the way Reggie had called the weekend theirs. She might never take Lydia's place in Reggie's affections, but maybe whatever this was between them, this sweetness, would be enough.

"I had planned to take you to this drive-in with amazing ice cream, but Trevor vetoed that idea. He said I should take you to a fancy dinner, as a way to say I was sorry. About, you know, Australia. I can't believe I'm taking relationship advice from my brother."

"I can't believe you willingly stayed in a plane long enough to fly to Australia." Gwen searched Reggie's face, wondering if she would ever fully understand this woman. "You hate planes."

"Wanna know a secret?" Reggie opened her eyes, and Gwen shifted her gaze so it was less obvious she'd been staring. "I took the private jet. Fuck flying commercial. My doctor gave me enough sleeping pills that I was knocked out the whole way there."

"I don't want a fancy dinner." Gwen had spoken her mind before she'd realized her mouth was open.

Reggie's face fell. "I understand. I completely freaked out after one kiss. And I have a terrible family. Not to mention an employee who apparently wants to kill us. I don't blame you for not wanting to spend more time with me than you have to."

"No. Reggie, look at me." Gwen held Reggie's gaze, trying not to laugh. With all those problems, and this crazy woman seemed more concerned with Gwen's feelings than anything else. How was that possible? "I want to go to the ice cream place. Do they have burgers, too?"

"The best burger you've ever had." For the first time since entering the office, Reggie's face boasted a genuine smile. "You're sure you want to go?"

"I'm not saying no, but traffic is going to be brutal," Gwen replied. "I understand you probably want to make sure the paparazzi see us and get photos together this weekend, but should we wait until the morning? It'll be a much shorter drive."

"Drive?" Reggie laughed heartily, making Gwen wonder where she'd gone wrong. At least the laughter released some of the tension in the process. "I think you should follow me."

Baffled, Gwen followed Reggie as she led the way to the private executive elevator, hitting the button for the parking garage.

"Is this like the elevator in *Charlie and the Chocolate Factory*?" Gwen joked, feeling a bit uneasy by this odd turn of events.

"Not exactly." Reggie's eyes twinkled with mischief.

A car and driver were waiting for them in the garage, and after a short drive, they turned into the East 34th Street heliport. A helicopter waited beside the water, its blades already spinning.

"There's your magical elevator, princess." Reggie chuckled as Gwen's mouth dropped open.

"We're going in that? You hate flying!"

"I hate planes," Reggie corrected. "Don't ask me how, but it's different with helicopters. Maybe because this baby will get us all the way to Montauk in under forty minutes."

"I guess you were right about me having a lot to learn." There was no hiding the awe in Gwen's tone. "You live in a totally different world."

"Not different enough," Reggie said, a hint of sadness beneath her words. "I wish there was a world I could take you to where we wouldn't have to deal with assholes like Clark Maxwell. And my father."

"No amount of money can work magic," Gwen said.

Reggie exited the car and ran around to open Gwen's door. Taking Gwen's hand, she helped her from the car and pulled her along toward the helicopter. "Don't duck down when you climb aboard. Everyone who rides in one, probably for the first fifty times, they always duck. Don't. The blades won't come close to you."

"Don't duck." Gwen swallowed as they got closer to their ride. "Got it."

"You hold your head high," Reggie encouraged, giving Gwen's hand a squeeze. "Remember, this is where you belong."

Gwen held her head high as she climbed into the helicopter, but there was heaviness in her heart. No matter how much she pretended to belong, how good at it she became, as long as they had the terms of their contract and Lydia's ghost between them, it would never be true.

———

GWEN'S BODY FLOATED ON A CLOUD. SHE STIRRED slightly, keeping her eyes firmly shut as the silky sheets caressed her bare legs. The sound of waves crashing pulled Gwen from her sleep and she reached for her phone to shut off the sound machine app. With one eye cracked just enough to see the screen, she pressed the off button, but the sound of waves continued.

Gwen's eyes flew open.

Everything around her was white, from the lighter-than-air comforter that surrounded her, to the slipcovered chaise lounge beside her bed, and the floor-to-ceiling sheers that softened the glow of sunlight beyond the window. For a moment, she thought she might be in heaven. Then she remembered the helicopter trip to Montauk. And the ice cream for dinner. It wasn't heaven, but it might be the next best thing.

Gwen climbed out of bed reluctantly, too relaxed to ever want to leave, and slipped on a kimono-style robe of deep turquoise over a crisp, button-down sleep shirt of white cotton lawn. The shirt had been waiting for her in a lavender-scented drawer when she'd arrived, the robe hanging neatly on a hook near the door to her ensuite bathroom. There were slippers, too, but she didn't bother with them, preferring to remain barefoot as she slid open the glass door that led from her bedroom to the cobblestone terrace outside.

"Morning." Reggie's voice was husky with sleep, the coffee mug at her elbow half gone, her attention focused on the phone in her hand.

She sat at a bistro table with the ocean behind her, the glorious colors of the sunrise lighting up the sky above the water. Suddenly, Gwen understood why so much inside had been white. Who needed color on the walls when this was waiting a hop, skip, and jump away?

"What time is it?" Gwen couldn't contain a yawn, belatedly covering her mouth with a hand.

"A little after five." Reggie tore herself away from the screen in her hands, her eyes lingering on Gwen's legs and breasts before finding their way to her face. "That robe's the perfect color on you."

"This old thing?" Gwen joked. She bit her lower lip, contemplating her ensemble. "Actually, I have no idea where this came from. It was in my room, so I assumed it was for me to use. We were halfway here when I realized we hadn't brought any luggage, but I was so tired by the time we finished our ice cream that I forgot to ask about it."

"I never bother to pack for these weekends," Reggie explained. "It's easier to keep my summer wardrobe here for when I need it. As for the clothes in your room, they're for you. I had a few essentials sent over from my favorite local boutique, but we'll go shopping sometime this weekend for the rest. I haven't forgotten my promise to let you choose for yourself."

"That isn't necessary," Gwen argued. "I already have more clothing back in my apartment than I will ever be able to wear."

"You'll need a summer weekend wardrobe that fits in with the Hamptons crowd. This is the obvious place to buy it." There was a warning in Reggie's tone that this was not an argument Gwen would win. "Did you sleep okay?"

"Better than okay," Gwen answered, accepting the change of subject without comment. It wasn't worth the fight or spoiling such a glorious morning over. "That bed is absolutely amazing."

"I should hope so," Reggie said with a laugh. "I'd hate to think the Hästens mattress I ordered for your room wasn't to your liking."

"Is that the bed from—" Gwen stopped herself from saying the airport in Zürich. Their past was a secret. Even here at Reggie's house where it felt like they were alone, they really weren't. When they'd arrived the evening before, Gwen had been introduced to a house manager and the head of security, just to name a few. They would never be completely alone, and though she had no doubt Reggie's staff was all trustworthy, it was better not to take chances.

"It is. Does that mean you liked it?"

"I slept like a rock." Gwen massaged her neck, sucking in her breath as her fingers hit a tender spot. "Maybe too deeply."

"Are you in pain?" Reggie's eyes flashed with concern.

"No." Gwen sucked in air through her teeth as she tried to shake her head, prickles shooting along her neck. "It's just really tight."

"I have the perfect thing for that later. Are you ready for breakfast?"

Gwen's eyes lingered on the water, not wanting to leave this spot. "Sure. I guess we can head in."

"Are you kidding? And give up this view?" Reggie tapped at the empty chair beside her with her foot. "Come sit down. Sherri will bring it up for us."

Gwen took a seat at the table, letting out another impromptu yawn. "How long have you been awake?"

"I always wake up at half past four, no matter where I am in the world."

"Because of work?" A coffee cup appeared beside Gwen's arm as a woman, whom she assumed was the aforementioned Sherri, rolled a cart laden with coffee and tea service into position beside them.

"It goes back further than that," Reggie said. "When we were kids, every morning our dad would get us up as soon as the early papers arrived. He'd spread them out on our big dining room table and explain why certain stories were placed where."

"Job training?" Gwen reached for the milk until she realized the coffee in her cup already had it in there.

"Milk and one sugar, right? I saw you fix it that way when we were at dinner, so I told Sherri what to do."

"Very observant." To be honest, Gwen was deeply touched. It was little things like that that made it so hard to remember sometimes that none of this was real.

"My father would tolerate nothing less. Everything we did was a lesson," Reggie explained, "prepping us for this life."

"It's kinda sweet that your dad spent that time with you when you were kids." Gwen took a sip of her coffee, letting out a satisfied sigh. "Perfect."

"I'm sure it wouldn't surprise you to know that in typical dad fashion, it was more cutthroat than sweet."

"How so?" Gwen leaned forward, intrigued but also horrified in anticipation of what new torment she would discover. From what she could tell, Reginald Hawkins should never have been allowed to reproduce.

"We had to analyze all the headlines and diagramming—er, that's the layout, and then we had to answer rapid fire questions."

"Like a quiz show?" Gwen asked, relaxing a bit. That didn't sound so bad. "Was there a prize?"

"Yes." Reggie took a sip of her coffee, which Sherri had warmed up from the fresh pot. "Whoever scored the highest got to eat breakfast that morning. The loser had to sit at the table with the winner and watch them eat."

Gwen gasped. "Please tell me you're fucking kidding."

Reggie shook her head. Gwen shut her eyes. Whatever she'd expected, the reality was worse.

"I don't even know what to say to that. I can't believe your father would deprive children of food. He's a billionaire, for Christ's sake."

"It wasn't so bad. Our housekeeper packed granola bars in our backpacks every day for school. So no one was going to starve. The one who got breakfast just got an extra treat." Reggie stared at the waves. The pain etched on her face told Gwen she wasn't buying her own rosy interpretation of the past. "It wasn't until we were in high school that we realized just how messed up it was. Until then, Trevor and I were active participants in the daily battle."

"What about your other sister?"

"Dad didn't play those games with Stephanie, or Logan, either, for that matter."

"Logan?" Gwen frowned, trying to remember if she'd met another brother.

"He's fourteen. You'll meet him this summer when he's home from boarding school."

"Neither of them is involved in the family business?"

Reggie shook her head. "Steph wasn't interested. The business has never intrigued her. Sometimes, I admire that. As for Logan, he's too young for Dad to train the way he'd want. The downside of having a kid when you're an old man."

Gwen's heart ached as she contemplated the seemingly put together woman in front of her, realizing once again how much pain she kept buried beneath her aloof exterior. Anyone who thought she was cold and emotionless simply didn't know shit. "Do you have any fond memories of your dad?"

"I must." Reggie licked her lips, opened her mouth, and then shut it again with a frown. "Hmm. I'll have to think about that some more."

"Do you always work in silence, or were you being polite, not wanting to wake me?"

"I do better with quiet. You?"

"I'm a music gal. Shane Paris is my go-to. Her love ballads speak to my soul." Gwen smothered her heart with both hands.

"That's pretty country for a Chicago girl." Reggie leaned forward in her seat, contemplating Gwen.

Another slip about Gwen's true Texas background. *Shit, shit, shit.* The more comfortable she became in Reggie's presence, the easier it was to forget she was supposed to be hiding.

"I notice you don't have a morning paper now, despite owning half the ones in this country." Gwen waved to indicate the absence of paper on the table. "Is that why?"

"I never thought of that, but..." Reggie settled back into her chair, leaning against the cushion and holding her coffee cup. "I'll deny this to my dying day, but I can't stand newsprint. Who wants to have ink-smudged fingers? Give me a phone or a tablet any day."

"Wow. You must really trust me." Gwen cradled her fingers around the coffee cup, grinning over the rim.

"Why do you say that?" The smile Reggie returned had a hint of nervousness at the edges.

"I could probably kill any hope of you ever being named your father's successor if I let that juicy morsel out."

"Even more than I already have by being outed to all our viewers via an angry rant from one of our most unhinged on-air personalities?" Reggie's smile, wide and warm, spoke volumes. Despite the ugliness, she seemed to have cast aside the deepest of her regrets over their plan. "You're probably right. The board members who are on my side because I'm gay would drop me in a hot minute if they found out I don't like newsprint. Somehow, I feel like you won't tell anyone."

"Because of the NDA I signed?"

"I wasn't even thinking of that." Reggie gave a little laugh, like she was amused at herself for forgetting a silly detail like the woman who was sharing her house had signed a contract first. "You don't seem the type to spill secrets."

Gwen's guts tightened. If only Reggie knew the truth. Considering how adamant she'd been about firing the person who had leaked the Clark Maxwell video, Gwen wondered what Reggie would think if she knew her future wife was a whistleblower on a much higher level.

Sherri returned to the terrace with a tray in her hands. Gwen's eyes landed immediately on a magnificent selection of fruit, displayed like it was being served at a top-rate hotel. The pineapple chunks had been cut into stars, and the kiwis halved to look like flowers. Gwen spotted blood oranges, berries, melon balls, and—"What's that?"

"Dragon fruit," Reggie answered, spearing one with a fork, as if that was a totally normal breakfast option.

"Do you need anything else?" Sherri asked Reggie as she set a basket of baked goods down between them.

Reggie turned to Gwen. "Do you want pancakes, waffles, or—?"

Gwen interrupted Reggie, "I think the croissants, muffins, and scones are plenty."

Reggie dismissed Sherri with a thank you.

"I love fresh fruit," Gwen said, using a pair of silver tongs to make a plate. "But I never have more than one type in my fridge at a time. I can't eat it all before it goes bad, and who has time to cut everything up like this? I mean, are these stars from, like, cookie cutters or something?"

Reggie shrugged. "I've never given it a moment's thought, but now I feel like maybe I should have. I've taken a lot for granted."

As Gwen studied the guilt that lined Reggie's face, she wondered if she'd ever met anyone, let alone someone as rich and seemingly entitled as the daughter of a billionaire, who carried so much personal responsibility for every little thing around her. What would it take for her to let go of some of that burden?

"Considering what you told me about breakfast when you were growing up," Gwen said softly, "I think you deserve to be pampered a little."

Reggie's face lit up. "Speaking of, I hope you're ready for some pampering yourself. We have a full spa day planned. Facials, massages, manicures, pedicures, and the sauna."

Gwen's eyes drifted back to the water. She wished they

could sit here all day and soak it in, but of course Reggie would want to go out and be seen. That was the whole point of the trip, to make their relationship look like the real deal by being photographed together as much as possible.

Gwen gazed at the ocean, the waves breaking on the sand, and a handful of seagulls bobbing in the water. It was no use pining. She had her half of the bargain to keep up. She sat straighter in her seat, steeling herself for the day ahead. "What time do I have to be ready to go?"

"Go where?" Reggie tilted her head, wearing a truly puzzled expression. "We're not going… Oh! No, honey, we're doing that all here."

"Here?" Gwen wasn't sure if she was more dazed by the idea that a full spa day could happen in your own home or by the fact that Reggie had called her honey. Was that in case the staff was listening, or was that for real? No, it couldn't be for real. Reggie was just very good at playing her part.

"I hope you don't mind. It gets so crowded in town. We don't have to leave the compound at all this weekend, other than the shopping I mentioned. Unless you want to go somewhere," Reggie quickly added.

Gwen thought for a moment. "Are we allowed to walk on the beach?"

"Why wouldn't we be? I own it, after all." Reggie chuckled. "Well, the family does, anyway. It's part of the compound."

"I can't believe you have a family compound. I thought only presidents had those. Who lives over there?" Gwen pointed in the direction of a somewhat larger house that was in a similar Hamptons colonial style as Reggie's, with wooden shingles and white trim.

"The big one on the other side of the tennis courts is my dad's. Trevor's house is over that way."

"What about Stephanie?"

"She, Brandon, and the kids stay with dad. Which she hates." Reggie's lips twitched, and Gwen got the impression the woman found her younger sister's disappointment amusing. "Steph has always resented being a half sibling, like she thinks Trevor and I are the chosen ones."

"You sort of are," Gwen pointed out. "You even got your own houses when the others didn't."

"That was my mother's doing. She made sure of it in the divorce, that Dad would have to give the cottages to us when we came of age." Reggie wore a faraway look that Gwen couldn't quite penetrate.

"You don't talk much about your mother," Gwen said softly. "What was she like?"

"A shell of herself, after my father was done with her." Emotion cracked in Reggie's voice, and it made Gwen feel honored that she didn't try to hide it this time.

"Loving Reginald Hawkins ruined her, you once said."

"It did. And I'm my father's daughter," Reggie added darkly.

Gwen wondered what that was supposed to mean.

CHAPTER SEVENTEEN

"I could get used to this lifestyle." Gwen stretched her legs out in the steam-filled sauna as Reggie did her best not to gape.

As it turned out, her best wasn't all that successful, and it was entirely her fault. What had she been thinking, picking out that barely there swimsuit for Gwen?

Actually, Reggie knew exactly what she'd been thinking, and it hadn't had anything to do with the cute polka dot print. Like so many other parts of her plan, Reggie discovered Gwen wearing that suit in real life, in an enclosed space where Reggie could see every glistening droplet of sweat on her bare skin, was very different than how she'd imagined. It was way sexier, to the degree of causing physical pain.

"What's wrong with getting used to it?" Reggie asked, focusing her eyes on a spot above Gwen's head as she tried to get her libido under control.

"Nothing at all," Gwen replied with a laugh. "In fact, as

soon as we're back home, I'm going to make sure to have a sauna built in my pool house, too."

"Don't stop there. My father has a two-lane bowling alley in his basement next door. I'd take you over and show you if I didn't think he'd have me shot for trespassing." Despite the intense heat, a shiver worked down Reggie's spine. She could still see Clark Maxwell's gun-like fingers pointing at her through the TV screen. "I think I need to get some fresh air."

"I'll join you." Outside the sauna, Gwen put on her flip-flops and slipped into a terry cloth robe, obscuring Reggie's view of the swimsuit. Definitely for the best. She pointed to a cedar wood enclosure near the sparkling pool. "Is this an outdoor shower? Maybe I should rinse off."

As Gwen stripped off the robe she'd only recently put on, Reggie tore her eyes away. She'd thought the couple's massage was difficult to endure, knowing Gwen was only a few feet away, totally naked, with some other woman's hands all over her. Now the woman was going to take a shower in the great outdoors with nothing but a screen between them. Reggie wasn't sure she'd survive.

There was a squeak as the faucet was turned on, followed by the gentle splash of water on the ground. A polka dot bikini top and matching bottoms appeared on top of the screen.

Oh dear God. Reggie shut her eyes, trying to block out the memory of a naked Gwen from her brain. She failed miserably.

"This is amazing," Gwen enthused. "Maybe I should have one of these installed back home, along with the sauna and bowling alley. Too bad I don't have a balcony for it. Do you think I could have one inside?"

"I think that would make it, you know, a shower." Reggie laughed, grateful for a way to release some of the tension within. She'd never guessed spending the weekend alone with Gwen would be so difficult to endure.

"That's a good point." The water shut off, and the bathing suit pieces disappeared. A minute later, Gwen—her robe on and tied tightly, thank goodness, and hopefully with the swimsuit on underneath—reappeared. "That was sublime."

"Glad you enjoyed it." Reggie's brow creased as worry descended over her. "You're not bored, are you? Staying here all weekend and doing nothing instead of exploring?"

"Bored!" Gwen laughed. It was a sound that Reggie would never get enough of. "We're spending an entire day together, and there isn't one camera in sight. Unless you have a drone overhead, catching me unaware for tomorrow's tabloids?"

"Drones. Why didn't I think of that?" Reggie, choosing a lounge chair in the waning sunlight near the pool, winked at Gwen before pulling her shades down. "Given the Clark Maxwell leak, I didn't think either one of us would want to feel too exposed. But I'm realizing now that I made all the plans without consulting you. I'm sorry about that."

"Reggie, stop. It's been a lovely day." Sinking into the lounge chair beside Reggie, Gwen put her hands behind her head. "I was thinking I might take a dip in the ocean a little later. You up for it?"

"You're on your own for that one," Reggie said quickly, swallowing the unease that instantly overtook her at the mere thought of going into the waves. "I prefer to stick to the hot tub."

"Are you sure?" Gwen pressed. "I can't believe you live within steps of the ocean and never go for a swim."

"Believe it." Reggie didn't mean for her response to sound so curt, but it was either speak quickly or start hyperventilating. Talk about something that would be difficult to explain. But this was yet another reminder of how her instinctive harshness would lead to her ending up alone. Most didn't enjoy having their head bitten off for a simple question.

Reggie closed her eyes, her body finally relaxing as the accumulated exhaustion of the past several weeks overtook her. She drifted off, and the next thing she knew, it was nearly dark.

"Gwen?"

There was no answer.

Reggie sat up, removing the sunglasses that still covered her eyes. The lounge beside her was empty.

"Gwen? Are you still out here?" Reggie spoke a little louder this time, but still no reply came.

Assuming the other woman had headed inside, she stood and collected the towel she'd been laying on. As she straightened up, she caught sight of a shadowy figure, struggling in the waves that had grown choppy with the shifting tide. The person's arms flailed, and their head bobbed beneath the water.

"Oh my God! Gwen!"

Reggie's heart was in her throat as she raced down the path to the sand. In her mind, she saw a different stretch of beach, not far from here, and her brother's body being dragged beneath relentless waves. She couldn't let it happen again.

"I'm coming! I've got you!" Reaching the water, Reggie

plodded in, not noticing or caring about the way the cold spray stung her legs.

Gwen rose from the water but was dragged under an instant later. Blinded by panic, Reggie dove in headfirst. Salty water sliced her eyes. Her lungs burned as she reached as far as she could with her arms. She would have cried out in relief as her hand grasped the waistband of Gwen's bathing suit if she hadn't still been underwater at the time.

"Gwen! Are you okay?" Reggie demanded as soon as her head was free of the waves. With her arms around Gwen's waist, she pulled with all her might. They toppled onto the sand, safe from the water.

"What the hell was that all about?" It was Gwen, sounding surprisingly feisty for someone who had nearly drowned.

"You were... the waves..." Reggie could barely breathe as she struggled to sit up and untangle her limbs from Gwen's.

"I was going for an evening swim. I wasn't going to drown." Gwen's eyes were wide as Reggie continued to gasp. "Reggie, what's wrong?"

"I..." The edges of Reggie's vision were going black. She couldn't get enough air. "I..."

"You need to get inside. Right now," Gwen commanded. Jumping to her feet, she put an arm around Reggie, trying to lift her. "You're shaking like a leaf. Let me help you into the house."

Mortified, Reggie brushed away Gwen's arm. "I can do it myself." But after two wobbling steps, she was back in the wet sand.

"Stop fighting me." Gwen's arms encircled her, the warmth of her body blocking the cold air. "Please. I know I can never be to you what Lydia was, but I care. I want to help you. Don't push me away."

Reggie went limp, unable to fight anymore. She took one step, and another, leaning on Gwen for support until they were off the cold sand and up the walkway. Reggie's mind whirred, trying to make sense of what was going on.

Gwen slid the glass door to the guest room open and ushered Reggie inside. In an instant, Reggie felt a soft blanket on her shoulders as she collapsed against the bedroom wall. Next came the friction of Gwen's hands as she tried to pat Reggie dry. "We've got to get you warmed up."

Reggie's brain finally seemed to click into gear, dragging itself from a deep fog. "What did you say?"

"About getting you warm? I think you're going to need a hot shower."

Reggie shook her head, her wet hair dripping. "No, earlier. What does this have to do with Lydia?"

"I know how much you loved her," Gwen said softly, even as she struggled to get Reggie to start walking again. "And I know if you'd been able to stand up to your father before, it would be her you'd be marrying. I'm a poor replacement, but—"

"A poor replacement?" In a burst of adrenaline, Reggie found the strength to walk again, making her way across the room while leaning against Gwen for support. "Are you kidding?"

Gwen was on the verge of tears. "I'm sorry. I—"

"When I saw you in the water, saw you struggling in that wave—" Reggie's words came between gulps of air, and she tightened her grip on Gwen's waist. "I thought it was happening again. I thought I was going to lose you. And the only thing I knew for certain was nothing on earth could ever be a replacement for *you*."

"What's so special about me?" Gwen pulled back the shower curtain and turned on the water. "You're the take-charge woman who runs a multi-billion-dollar company. I'm a nobody."

"How can you say that?" Reggie grasped Gwen's shoulders, more for emphasis than support this time. "You're the kindest, sincerest, bravest person I've ever met. I knew you were special from the moment we met on the plane outside Zürich."

The water started to steam, and after a quick adjustment, Gwen urged Reggie, still in her swimsuit, to step into the tub. "There you go. All the way under. Can you stand on your own?"

"I think so. I'll be—" Reggie wobbled, and Gwen hopped into the tub before she could finish her lie.

"I'm right here," Gwen soothed. "Just lean against me, and let the water warm you up."

Reggie let her body relax, her back against Gwen's front, as blistering hot water pelted her skin.

"Is that better?"

"Getting there." Reggie tried not to think about how her bare back was pressed to the exposed skin of Gwen's bare midriff, but it was impossible not to. Now that she was aware of it, she might as well have told herself not to think of a pink elephant.

"I thought Zürich didn't mean anything to you." Gwen's comment was out of the blue, bordering on accusatory.

"What?" Disoriented, Reggie had no idea how to respond.

"You were so cold, so formal, when I went to your office.

You called me *Ms.* Murphy." It was obvious exactly how much Gwen had disliked *that*.

"Because *you* only responded to my text when you needed a job," Reggie shot back, her blood getting good and warm now but only partly from the heat of the shower. "That sucked, you know. I did what I always do when hurt."

To Reggie's surprise, instead of continuing the fight, Gwen laughed softly in her ear as she pulled Reggie tightly against her. "You silly, silly woman."

Closing her eyes, Reggie leaned into the embrace. "Is that all you have to say?"

"I'm sorry I didn't text you sooner." Gwen brushed her lips against Reggie's ear, whispering, "I wanted to."

"You did?" Reggie let out a soft mewl as Gwen traced the curve of her face with the tip of a finger.

"I have a confession." At the feel of Gwen's hot breath, goose bumps erupted along the nape of Reggie's neck. "At the airport, after you went to the room, and I went to take a shower…"

"Yes?" Reggie breathed.

"When I was naked under the water, kind of like right now, only *completely* naked…" Gwen paused mid-sentence to skim her lips along Reggie's neck, sending a searing bolt of pleasure straight to Reggie's core. "All I could think about was you."

Gwen's arms loosened from Reggie's waist, her hands beginning to roam. While one moved downward, caressing Reggie's hip, the other climbed upward, circling Reggie's right breast.

"In that case, I should probably tell you…" Reggie swallowed, near distraction as Gwen's fingers pushed under the crotch of her swimsuit and brushed playfully at the hair beneath. "When I was in my room, on my bed..."

"With the vibrator?" Gwen pinched Reggie's nipple, rolling it between her finger and thumb until it pebbled beneath the tight spandex that encased it.

"Mm-hm." Reggie's breathing grew shallow as Gwen nipped at her earlobe, as if demanding for her to continue. "When I was on the bed... with the vibrator... all I could think of was you."

"If that's the case"—Gwen's lower hand plunged deep into the crevice between Reggie's thighs, causing her back to arch—"what the hell were we thinking with that no-sex clause?"

"I have... no fucking... clue."

Reggie twisted her torso, her hungry mouth not satisfied until it grabbed hold of Gwen's full lips. The steady stream of the shower engulfed them. Reggie undid what was left of Gwen's messy ponytail, threading her fingers through the soaking blond locks. "I really thought you were going to drown out there."

"I might still if we stay under this shower head much longer." After another kiss, Gwen maneuvered toward the wall, turning off the water. "Feeling warmer now?"

"On fire." Reggie lunged for Gwen, wanting every inch of their bodies to be together.

Gwen hooked a finger under one of Reggie's bathing suit straps, slowly lowering it down Reggie's arm. "You need to hook me up with your trainer."

Reggie tightened her bicep, feeling foolish but sexy. A new sensation. Sure, Reggie had slept with many people, but when you pay a woman, it was little more than a simple physical act.

This didn't feel simple at all. More like... what was the word?

Overwhelming? Delightful? Scary?

That was just the tip of the iceberg.

"Are you sure?" Reggie asked, needing to hear Gwen say it.

"I'm assuming you don't mean about calling your trainer," Gwen joked. Reggie loved the way she teased, especially when she was nervous. "Actually, I'm realizing I was wrong about something."

"Oh?" Reggie's face fell as her insides clenched. This was the part where Gwen changed her mind and left Reggie broken.

"Yeah. When I said the mattress was perfect, it wasn't."

"It wasn't?" Reggie's brain swirled, not making sense of anything.

"No, it was missing something." Gwen held Reggie's gaze with hers, not letting go. "You."

Gwen broke into a grin, and Reggie returned it, lighter inside than she'd been in a long time. They remained in the tub, clinging to one another as droplets of water dripped from their bodies and rolled toward the drain.

"I'm not sure what to do," Reggie admitted, wanting to take this amazing woman in her arms to bed but feeling like her feet were welded to the tub. "I mean I know what to do, but—"

"Just so you know, you're really adorable when you're vulnerable."

"Don't tell anyone."

"I would never." Gwen kissed Reggie's shoulder, her mouth making her way along the collarbone and across to the far side as she slid the other strap down Reggie's arm, kissing her arm as the strap lowered. Past her elbow, over the wrist, and off her fingers, Gwen kissing each fingertip.

"I seem to recall," Gwen said between kisses, "that you like it better when I take charge."

"Mmm," was the only response Reggie could manage, so lost was she in her desire to be fully possessed by this woman.

The hint of a smile curved on Gwen's lips, like she'd understood exactly what Reggie's whimper meant. Turning Reggie's arm to expose the underside, Gwen kissed her way up before tugging the suit off Reggie's chest, exposing nipples that were hard as diamonds. Gwen took one in her mouth, sucking and teasing it, causing Reggie to sway on her feet.

"Don't fall over." Gwen laughed. "Let's get out of this tub and get you fully naked on the bed. I don't want anything to happen to you."

With the last of her swimsuit off, Reggie stopped at the edge of the bed but would go no further, despite Gwen's prodding.

"Nope. Not until you remove yours, too." She pointed to Gwen's bikini. "Play fair."

"Who said I was playing?" A seductive gleam flowered in Gwen's eyes as she peeled off her wet suit and let it fall, first the top and then the bottoms, onto the bedroom floor.

Reggie swallowed, Gwen's body on full display before her. This wasn't a game. Not for her. And not for Gwen, or at least that was what Reggie was starting to believe. Should they put a stop to this before it went too far?

A sexual relationship—the real kind, with a full array of emotions tied in—was a major complication to her plan. It wasn't what either of them had agreed to. Once feelings were involved, it was easy to get hurt. And there were feelings, all right. The type that were so intense, one couldn't put words to them. But she could see the depth of the meaning in Gwen's eyes. There was no way Reggie could stop this if she tried.

"You see me, don't you?" Reggie asked. "I don't mean that like is your vision okay, but—"

"I knew what you meant." Gwen cupped Reggie's cheek, regarding her steadily. Though Reggie was completely exposed, inside now as well as out, she lacked the power to look away. "And, yes I do."

Pain and shame formed a knot in Reggie's stomach. "Then you know how damaged I am."

Gwen held a thumb and forefinger an inch apart in the air in the most generous underestimation of psychic trauma Reggie could imagine. Circling her fingers around Gwen's wrists, Reggie moved her arms as wide as they would go. A much more realistic depiction.

"I don't understand how you can still respect me, knowing how I crumbled over the Clark Maxwell thing. Or how I can barely stand on my feet in front of my dad." Despair twisted Reggie's heart at the prospect of the rejection she deserved.

"Reggie. Stop torturing yourself." Even as she admonished, Gwen's eyes devoured Reggie's body.

"But, I—" The argument was cut short as Gwen placed a hand in the soft valley between Reggie's breasts, just above her pounding heart.

"Do not say Clark or mention your father again. This is not the time or the place for them." Gwen's exaggerated look of revulsion made Reggie smile. "This may come as a

TB MARKINSON & MIRANDA MACLEOD

shock to you, but no one is perfect. We're all doing what we can to get through life."

A tear snaked down Reggie's face, and she was powerless to stop it. "I'm a mess, Gwen. A fucking mess and most of the time I don't know how I'm not crumbling into pieces that can never be put back together. You don't want that."

"How do you know? Maybe that's what I like about you." Gwen gave Reggie's chest a gentle push, sending her body backward until she was sinking into the mattress. Replacing it for Gwen had been a spur-of-the-moment indulgence, and it was worth every fucking penny.

"How is that possible?"

"Because perfect is boring. And persevering is a turn-on." Desire lighting up her eyes, Gwen straddled Reggie, the weight of her nearness as comforting as it was provocative. "You're very good at persevering. In case you didn't know, I'm very turned on right now. Are you?"

"Yes," Reggie managed to choke in response, so filled with desire she could taste it. Her heart raced and stuttered at the edge of authority in Gwen's tone, wanting to do anything and everything she could to please her.

"How turned on are you?" Gwen slipped her hand between Reggie's legs, sliding a finger along her wet slit, teasing her clit. Instantly, Reggie's back arched in invitation. "That should do. Now touch me. Here."

Gwen took Reggie's hands and positioned them on her hips, guiding them along her thighs until Reggie took over the motion on her own, reveling in the touch. Gwen had made a good point about perfect being boring, but Reggie was hard pressed to identify a single flaw. Right now, in this moment, perfection had been achieved.

Pinned beneath Gwen's thighs and pelvis, Reggie began

a slow and rhythmic undulation. Gwen rocked in time with Reggie's motion, her pussy hair tickling Reggie's belly like a downy feather. Their eyes locked, digging deep into each other's souls.

Gwen slowly lowered herself, stretching her entire body until she enveloped Reggie fully.

Their mouths locked in a kiss, both sweet and passionate, neither trying to conquer the other. They were equals in every way. Reggie had never felt so complete in her entire life.

"I've missed the taste of you," Gwen murmured. She ran her tongue across her lips, whether to savor what was there or prepare for more, Reggie wasn't sure.

Propping most of her weight on one forearm, Gwen's free hand roamed down Reggie's side as far as it would go before traveling up again. Down and up. Hypnotically so.

Gwen turned her attention to a nipple, biting and teasing it. She moved to the other, biting harder, but not too much. Reggie wanted to feel it. To really give in to everything happening. Not wanting to skip everything to get to the payoff. No, Reggie wanted to take each step as slowly as possible. To give herself completely to Gwen.

Gwen.

Gwen.

Gwen.

How would Reggie ever survive with her Gwen?

Before leaving her breasts, Gwen dropped a kiss between them. Then she struck a path downward along her belly. She went ever so slowly, paying special attention to each patch of skin like it mattered more than anything else in the world. Reggie was nearly brought to tears as she considered the time she'd spent with others who didn't make her feel like every part of her mattered.

That she mattered. All of her. Not just her money. Not her name. Not her power.

Gwen shifted onto her knees, centered between Reggie's legs as she folded herself with the languid grace of a cat stretching its back in the sun. The first touch of Gwen's tongue between Reggie's legs made her gasp.

How could she have ever expected herself to resist this? She spread her legs wider to allow Gwen access to every inch.

Soon, Gwen's mouth was replaced by a finger as she entered Reggie, stretching the tight, wet opening ever so slowly. Reggie could feel every inch as Gwen worked her way deep, until the heel of Gwen's palm pressed against Reggie's clit. A slight crook of Gwen's finger put her in exactly the right spot.

Reggie gasped with a need that overwhelmed her, a desire she'd never experienced before. Not even in Zürich. Then, she'd wanted Gwen to take her. She wanted that now, too. But she also wanted more. So much more.

Everything. Nothing. The world.

She wanted to be filled, to be healed, to never want anything again.

The silky feel of Gwen's damp hair brushing against the insides of her thighs caused a part of her, low and deep, to coil like a tightly wound spring.

"Oh, God," Reggie whispered. "Don't stop."

She lifted her hips, a little at first, then higher and faster. Her thighs clenched as she drove Gwen's finger as deep as it would go.

"More!" she cried.

"Say please," Gwen gently chided.

"Please," Reggie whimpered.

A second finger entered her, filling her to overflowing as hot wetness spilled out and down the insides of her legs. Almost instantly, Gwen's tongue was on her, following the trail, until she flicked the tip across Reggie's clit.

Reggie's toes dug into the mattress, her knees falling open as far as they would go.

After one long, luscious lick that caused Reggie to shudder, Gwen took her clit fully into her mouth, sucking with a relentlessness that threatened to bring Reggie to the brink of madness.

This was what had been missing from Reggie's life. Feeling like someone wanted her for her and not what Reggie could do for them. That was how everyone treated her. Truth be known, it was how Reggie viewed almost everyone around her. Relationships that were transactional.

It kept her safe, her heart locked away to avoid more pain. The fear of not truly being loved, of not belonging, had never made anyone worth the risk. But this woman, now, was worth anything. Was worth everything.

Reggie buried her hands in Gwen's hair, a cry of ecstasy battling its way up from deep within her throat. Lights behind her eyes started to explode like fireworks against a backdrop of stars. Reggie continued to hold onto Gwen's head but not to keep her in place. She needed to hold onto this woman. Now and forever.

Reggie's body shook.

Gwen didn't let up.

Reggie never wanted Gwen to stop. She wanted her to see Reggie. All of her. Every second she was alive. Flaws and all.

"Oh, my fucking god!" Reggie screamed, her body writhing until she went completely still.

For a few moments, all Reggie was aware of was the gentle feel of warm breath shifting across her sodden curls. A little bit later, Gwen snaked her way back up until she was supporting her weight on one arm, gazing down at Reggie, those sapphire eyes soothing her soul. Steadying her in this world that always seemed so turbulent. Not now. Everything was perfect. It should have terrified Reggie. Nothing could ever be perfect. Life had taught her that. Perhaps, though, the one thing missing the entire time was Gwen.

"Why were you so worried I was going to drown?" Gwen finally asked when their heart rates and breathing had slowed and the world had returned to some semblance of normal once more.

"It happened to Trevor. Seven years ago. It was my birthday—"

"I thought you were twins."

"We are, but our birthdays are technically a day apart. I was born minutes before midnight, and he was closer to one in the morning. When I'd turned thirty-five, but he was still thirty-four," Reggie explained. "I was teasing him—"

"Of course, you were," Gwen interjected in a humorous tone. "It's what you do best."

"Yeah, but I dared him to jump off our yacht and..." Reggie turned her head. "He went under. I had jumped at the same time and went in just fine. We'd done it hundreds of times in the past. I don't know what went wrong. When I realized he was struggling, I couldn't reach him. They finally pulled him out, but he's never been the same."

"Reggie, I'm so sorry." Gwen's voice cracked with emotion. "But that's not your fault."

"But it is. We were both drunk, and I threatened to tell Dad if Trevor chickened out. I-I—" Reggie's voice cracked. "It was the worst day of my life."

"He doesn't seem to hate you for it. Or if he does, I didn't pick up on it."

"He's never held it against me. I don't know if I would do the same." Reggie's shoulders shook.

Gwen pulled Reggie's back to her chest. "Hey, hey. It's okay. Trevor's fine."

"He's not, though. His brain injury isn't visible, but it's very real. We hid it from everyone. Dad is determined Trev take over the company, but he can't handle it, and he doesn't know how to tell Dad no."

"That's why you're trying to get the board to appoint you, instead." Gwen wrapped her arms around Reggie's chest. "You can't blame yourself. Your father is barbaric, raising all of you as if you were competing in the Hunger Games." Gwen kissed the back of Reggie's head. "Everything's going to be okay." She kissed Reggie's neck.

Reggie slowly swiveled her head to look into Gwen's eyes. "Do you really believe that?"

"I do. It would be nice if you did. You don't have to battle everything and everyone, every time you take a breath."

"I always feel safe with you. It's almost disconcerting how much I trust you." Reggie's head tilted, her lips right there.

"I hope you never lose that trust."

"I can't see how I would. You're a good person. Through

241

and through. I'm fucked up, Gwen. I should let you go now, before it's too late."

"Too late for what?"

"To save yourself. This family—it eats you alive. I don't want you to experience this pain."

"I'll be fine as long as I have you protecting me." Gwen kissed Reggie's forehead.

Reggie closed her eyes, reveling in the sensation. "I like that."

"Protecting me? Or the way I'm kissing your forehead?"

"Can I answer both?" Reggie let out a long, slow breath. Peace surrounded her. "Gwen?"

"Yes?" Gwen's voice was small and filled with sleep.

"I think… I love you," Reggie whispered. The peaceful feeling expanded.

"I think I love you, too," Gwen replied. "Actually, I know I do."

The peace that surrounded her expanded again, growing to encompass the whole universe. At that moment, everything was truly right with the world.

CHAPTER EIGHTEEN

At the buzzing of an alarm, Gwen rolled over in bed, smashing into a barrier. A lusciously soft one. With a smile on her lips, she snuggled closer, but instead of the breasts she'd been expecting, the side of her face made contact with something solid.

Cracking one eye open, she started. The hard thing turned out to be Reggie's hip bone. Reggie herself was wide awake, sitting up against a stack of pillows and staring down at her in an intense and disconcerting way.

"Jesus!" Gwen let out a nervous laugh. "I feel like a prey animal with a predator looking down."

"Does that mean someone's hoping to be eaten again?" Reggie gave her eyebrows an exaggerated wiggle. "I think I can make that happen."

Snorting at Reggie's silliness, even as her body flushed with memories of the night before, Gwen struggled to get into an upright position. "This bed refuses to let a person out."

"Yes, the mattress and I are working toward a common goal." Reggie swooped in to nibble Gwen's ear.

"I thought we had to run errands today," Gwen protested, even though she tilted her head to allow Reggie's lips greater access to her neck. "You said I had to go shopping."

She knew the way she said it made it sound like she had an appointment with a guillotine, which was nearly how it felt. Leaving this bed and facing the world might kill her.

"About that," Reggie purred. "I was thinking how nice it would be to stay in here a little longer. What I wouldn't give for an extra hour in bed with you."

"Why stop at an hour?" Gwen asked. "Why not the whole day?"

"A day?" Reggie's eyes widened, looking as if she'd never in her life contemplated playing hooky from life before. "I guess we could. The shops will still be there tomorrow."

"You know—" Gwen stopped talking long enough to pepper Reggie's throat with kisses. "We really don't have to go shopping tomorrow, either. I don't mind."

"Nice try."

"Oh, come on. We're adults, right? We can do what we want." Gwen wrapped her arms around Reggie, pulling her close for a kiss that landed on the side of her head.

Reggie squeaked, burying herself into the crook of Gwen's neck. "We are adults, which is why you're going to go shopping with me tomorrow without making a fuss. It has to be done."

"Fine." Gwen treated Reggie to her best pout before her expression brightened. "But the theory still applies, right? We can do what we want?"

"Within reason." Reggie rested her head on bent elbow. "Why?"

"I was thinking." Gwen swallowed, her stomach fluttering. "I know we said eighteen to twenty-four months in the contract, but that's a minimum, right? Not, like, a max?"

"I suppose that's true." A mixture of excitement and hope played out across Reggie's face before caution weighed down her brow. "Why do you ask?"

"Because... I don't know. It occurred to me that two years isn't a long time."

Reggie nodded. "It's really not. Did you have a different number in mind?"

"It seems unlucky to say," Gwen admitted. Even saying as much as she had so early in their relationship, or whatever it was that was happening between them, made her head spin. "Can we just go with... longer?"

"Longer?" Reggie sat silently, appearing deep in thought. "I can live with that."

"You're sure the uncertainty won't be too much for you?" Gwen asked in a teasing tone. "I know how you feel about a plan."

"I'm determined to live in the now. Right here, in bed, with you." Reggie let out a happy sigh. "What else matters in life?"

"I'm digging this side of you."

"Oh, yeah?" Reggie waggled her brows. "Show me."

Gwen was more than happy to comply.

"After all this shopping, I feel like... Which princess is it that has the animals make her dresses?" Gwen shifted the pile of bags in her arms as Reggie pressed the button to open the back of the SUV.

"Cinderella." Reggie shoved her bags in the trunk, stepping aside so Gwen could do the same. "How did you not know that?"

"I did know it. That was a test to see if your childhood was even more of a living nightmare than I already knew." Gwen shot Reggie a sly look as she nudged the woman with her shoulder. It was a thrill to be able to touch her like that and not have it be for the benefit of unseen photographers.

"Believe it or not, you can get Disney in hell," Reggie deadpanned, returning the nudge.

As Gwen walked around to open the vehicle's passenger door, Reggie slid into the driver's seat. It was an unusual occurrence, since Gwen knew Reggie always had a driver in the city. But today she'd said she wanted them to enjoy a day together and be truly alone. Which is exactly what they had done. At least, aside from all the tourists enjoying a Memorial Day stroll, plus the employees at the boutiques, and all the shoppers...

Bottom line, they were never alone. But being out and about at the end of a holiday weekend was starting to make Gwen appreciate the relative privacy of the Hawkins family compound. At least the small army of staff did their best to stay out of sight unless they were needed.

"I hope you're not shopped out." It was almost like Reggie could read her mind. "We have one more stop before we can head back."

"What else do I possibly need?" Gwen clicked her belt into place.

"How about this?" Reggie leaned over and gave Gwen a quick kiss.

"You're right. I did need that." The touch of Reggie's lips had brought a smile to Gwen's face and a rush of blood to her cheeks.

It was still such a new sensation, not just the public display of affection but knowing it was for real. They hadn't discussed exactly what had changed since they'd started sleeping together, but that something had was undeniable.

Reggie pressed the button to start the car. "I've never met a woman who turns down dinner at fancy restaurants and whines about shopping."

"Maybe that's what you've been doing wrong up until now," Gwen replied. She sighed as she recalled all the bags in the trunk. "It's so much money. It doesn't matter that you have it to spend. It's just—a lot. It feels wasteful, knowing how many people are truly in need."

Gwen had been one of those people most of her life. Constant struggling left its mark. If it hadn't been for her hardscrabble upbringing, Gwen wondered if she would have realized sooner the terrible things Kensington Datalytics was up to. But the promise of a high salary and bonuses had dazzled her and kept her from asking hard questions of herself for far too long. Compromising her values for money was a mistake she didn't want to make again.

"If that's how you feel, you're not going to like the next place we're going," Reggie said. "But it has to be done, and I do want your input."

Gwen lifted an eyebrow questioningly. "Consider me curious."

"That's the spirit." Reggie smiled, looking more than a little relieved Gwen hadn't put up a fight.

The drive was short, ending practically at the water's edge. There were two businesses that shared a small parking lot: a place called Beach Front Designs and an ice cream shack. Spotting what appeared to be jewelry displays in Beach Front's window, Gwen crossed her fingers for the latter.

"If I keep eating ice cream like we have this weekend," she said as she exited the car, "we'll have to return all my clothes and get them in the next size up."

"Oh, good, then you'll be happy to hear we're going to the jewelry store," Reggie replied.

"But I don't wear jewelry," Gwen whined. And yes, she knew Reggie would count this as more whining over things most women enjoyed. "I'd rather have ice cream."

"That's why I love you, but I'm sorry. There's one item of jewelry you're going to have to wear soon, whether you want to or not. It's in your contract."

The conversation left Gwen too dizzy to respond. She couldn't decide whether to melt over the casual way Reggie had said *I love you* or to bristle at the mention of that damned contract. Now that true feelings were involved, Gwen couldn't stand the reminder of how it had started. It felt almost sordid, even though they'd done nothing wrong.

Opening the shop door, Reggie ushered Gwen inside. The shop, while quaint, reeked of money. Handcrafted display cases dotted the interior, which was painted in the same muted seaside tones as every other place they'd visited. Gwen noted a sign on the door that read *By Appointment Only*. Reggie had obviously called ahead for a reservation, which meant the older man and younger woman waiting inside had given up their holiday just for them.

"Ms. Hawkins. We're so honored you've chosen us for this very special purchase." The older gentleman nodded to them both in greeting. "Your father is a valued client."

Gwen imagined he was, considering he'd bought jewelry for four wives. However, she kept this wisecrack to herself.

"I'm sure you'll handle this transaction with your usual discretion." Reggie shoved her sunglasses onto the top of her head before taking Gwen's hand in hers. "This is Gwen Murphy, my soon-to-be fiancée."

"Enchanted." The man nodded again, his manners reminding Gwen of an old school English butler. "My daughter, Alicia, will be happy to show Ms. Murphy some of our custom settings while I acquaint Ms. Hawkins with our selection of stones. Remind me, you said you were looking in the one to two range?"

"Yes, that's right," Reggie confirmed.

"One to two what?" Gwen asked. "Carats? Two would be way too large. Even one is probably—"

"Not carats," Reggie corrected, the quick shake of her head and lift of her brows signaling to Gwen to drop the subject.

Gwen couldn't let it go, asking in a hushed voice, "Are you talking one to two thousand dollars?"

"Gwen," Reggie warned, casting a glance at the proprietor. "We can talk about this another time."

"Why are you avoiding answering me?" Gwen pressed her lips together, a sinking feeling in her stomach. Surely, Reggie wasn't thinking more than that. This wasn't even a real engagement. Once again, the reminder of their situation cut to the quick.

"Go with Alicia and look at the settings," Reggie directed, her voice barely audible. "Let's not make a scene."

"Fine," Gwen agreed, but she didn't like it. And she didn't like the way this place reeked of bored society women with expensive taste. Who spent so much money on jewelry when there were much more worthy causes out there? It was disgusting.

The jeweler's daughter waited behind a case, a black velvet pillow on top of the glass. "Why don't you tell me about your style?" she asked with a smile. "Do you prefer yellow or white gold? Or perhaps platinum?"

"I don't know," Gwen admitted. "I don't really wear jewelry. Sorry."

"Quite all right," Alicia responded cheerfully. "Is there a piece of jewelry you've seen that you really like? You could describe it, and we'll start there."

Gwen closed her eyes, seeing a hazy image from her childhood. "My grandma had this ring, and it was like a pearl that sat on a crown of diamonds."

"That sounds lovely. Something like this?" The woman searched through one of the cases, returning with a ring that matched Gwen's memory, though grander by a factor of ten.

"That's a bit bigger than hers was, but close enough." Gwen smiled fondly at the ring. "May I see it?"

"Of course." Alicia handed Gwen the ring. "Try it on if you'd like. Your fingers are slender, so it might be a little big, but you'll get the idea."

Gwen slid the ring on, twisting her hand one way and then the other. "This is perfect. Reggie? Come take a look."

Leaving the counter where a dozen massive diamonds sparkled against a black cloth, Reggie dutifully trotted over to admire the ring. "It's beautiful. I like how the bottom part looks like a crown."

"My grandmother had a ring like this." Gwen slid the ring off, holding it up for Reggie to see. "I really love it."

"I knew you'd have fun once you got going." Reggie winked, sending sparks flying all the way to Gwen's toes. "Alicia, do you have any other settings similar to this one, with the crown shape?"

"A few," she said. "And we can always custom make something once you decide on the stone."

"Decide on... but I like this one," Gwen argued, putting the ring back on. She loved it even more every time she looked at it. "What's to decide on? Can't we just wrap it up and go?"

"Honey—" Reggie lowered her voice, which was not a good sign—"we need to remember that I'm not your grandfather. It's a beautiful ring, but as a Hawkins, there's a certain standard I'm held to by my peers. They would never take this, or us, seriously."

As Gwen stared down at the ring, a sinking feeling overcame her. The Hawkins family expectation were like a massive weight tied around her, pulling both her and Reggie further and further into blackness. They needed to cut those ties or they would never be free to be who they really were.

Slipping the ring off, she handed it back to Alicia and tried to disguise her regret with a smile. "I guess we'll keep looking."

"You know," Alicia's tone was kind, her expression full of sympathy, "pearls are considered bad luck on your wedding day. Did you know that?"

"No, I didn't." Gwen couldn't help thinking the woman was very good at her job, although she imagined most of the time that sympathy was directed at brides who wanted rings they couldn't afford, not the other way around.

"I promise you we can make a setting very similar to this one." Alicia's face brightened. "You'll love it. Let's see what my father and your lovely future wife have decided on for the stone, shall we?"

"So this one?" The jeweler separated one stone from the others as Gwen approached. "Excellent choice. 11.03-carat, round, ideal cut, D color and IF clarity. Truly a treasure."

"I agree. Well, what do you think?" Reggie slid her hand into Gwen's, giving it a squeeze.

"I…" Gwen stared at the massive rock, wanting to cry. A million girls would love to be in her place, and she would gladly trade with any of them. "It's huge. It's going to go all the way to my knuckle."

"With these beautiful, long fingers of yours, you can easily pull it off," Reggie said. "It's half the size of the one Alexis Ohanion gave Serena Williams."

"That one cost nearly three million," the jeweler said with a knowledgeable air.

"I heard it was a bit more," his daughter added conspiratorially.

"Three million *dollars*?" Gwen planted her hands on the glass counter top. "How much is this one?"

"Honey, I told you—"

"How much?" Gwen demanded again, her hands tightening into fists.

The jeweler frowned. "Would you two like a moment alone to discuss?"

"Yes, please," Reggie said with a thin-lipped smile. "Gwen, you're making a scene."

"How much does it cost?" Gwen deliberately mimicked the woman's phrasing and singsong tone.

Reggie shut her eyes. "With the stone and custom setting, around one-point-five."

"One-point-five... million dollars? That's obscene." There truly was no other word for it, and Gwen was in no mood to think of one for fear she'd unleash a string of obscenities that would stretch all the way to the moon. "Think of all the good that could be done with that much money."

"I've already explained why we need to do it this way," Reggie pleaded.

"But what about what I like?" Gwen sucked in a breath, trying to dispel some of the repulsion she felt toward the shimmering goose egg on the velvet pillow. "I know this was part of the plan, and I shouldn't care. It's just after last night..."

After last night, it had started to feel like this thing between them was real. And a real fiancée shouldn't feel like she wanted to throw up at the sight of her ring. A real couple would work together toward a solution they both could live with.

"I'm sorry." Reggie's face twisted with true anguish. "But we have to sell it for the plan to work. Don't forget you have fourteen million reasons to make it happen. Fourteen million you can spend on whatever good causes you choose."

"If there wasn't a plan..." Gwen started but thought better of it. She closed her mouth and breathed deeply, once, and then again. "Never mind."

"No, Gwen. What were you going to—"

"I'm being stupid." Gwen plastered a bright smile on her face as the jeweler returned. "Pre-engagement jitters, that's all. Who wouldn't be happy with a ring like this? It just took me by surprise. Really, it's beautiful."

Gwen swallowed down her disappointment as Reggie finalized things with the man.

If she hadn't signed that damn contract, maybe things would be different. They'd have time for their feelings to grow, and proving it was real wouldn't be such a burden. A 1.5-million-dollar burden, apparently. But they were in a rush, so that was how it had to be.

Buying a ring put them on a fast track, right at the point where Gwen desperately wanted to take it slow enough for real feelings to grow. That didn't mean they couldn't take the time they needed once the plan was through. Right?

Surely, that was true.

Deep down, there was a different question Gwen was too afraid to answer. Was she on the verge of compromising her values for money again?

CHAPTER NINETEEN

"Here. Let me take that from you." Ushering Gwen from the apartment's private elevator and into the foyer, Reggie eased Gwen's laptop bag off her shoulder. After hanging it on a nearby hook, she pulled the woman close for a kiss, followed by a tight embrace. "I've missed you. It feels like forever. Why haven't you come over before now?"

"I've missed you, too," Gwen said. "But I had to work."

"Work?" Reggie gave an exaggerated frown. "Who's the chairperson of your organization? I'm going to call her and give her a piece of my mind."

"I wouldn't, if I were you," Gwen teased. "She's in a very foul mood lately."

"Can you blame her? She's spent weeks cooped up in her apartment, all alone."

"It's been less than four days since we left Montauk."

"Are you sure? Time's been standing still since Dad had me frozen out of the office." The first thing Reggie had discovered upon returning to the city the Tuesday morning after Memorial Day was her Hawks Corp keycard had been deactivated. Security had met her at the elevator to escort her from the building.

"Any word about when you'll be allowed back in the office?"

"Nope. Still on house arrest." Reggie motioned for Gwen to follow her down the long hall toward the living room. "I've gotten the runaround all week. Everyone keeps telling me it's for my own safety, but I know BS when I smell it."

"One thing's for sure," Gwen said. "Clark hasn't let up with the hatred. I think he's ratcheting it up, and the right-wing trolls are amplifying it. It's probably for the best we're not going back to Montauk until next week."

"Better to lay low," Reggie agreed. The only thing that kept her from defying her father and marching right into Hawks Corp headquarters was knowing it could put Gwen in danger. She would do anything to keep this woman safe.

"Oh, did you know one of the charities the Hawkins Foundation has given some big grants to recently is right down the road in East Hampton?"

"I'm afraid I don't keep up with it as much as I should," Reggie admitted, embarrassed by how little attention she had paid to the organization Gwen was so passionate about.

"I'm thinking I'd like to go visit next time we're there."

"I think that's an excellent idea," Reggie encouraged. She vowed to make a bigger effort to pay attention to the family charity from now on, even if her father had only put her in charge of it out of spite. "You should definitely do that and find out all about it."

As they reached the living room, Gwen slowed, her eyes sweeping the tall ceilings and walls of windows that offered expansive views of the East River. "At last, I get to see the inner sanctum. Can you imagine what people would think if they found out we were getting engaged in a month, and this is the first time I've been in your apartment?"

"Better late than never." Of course, Reggie knew why she'd never invited Gwen up before, to avoid exactly what had happened the first time they were alone together for the weekend. But now that the proverbial horse was out of the barn, there was no reason in Reggie's mind not to spend as much time together as possible.

"When is all your stuff going to arrive from London? I'm shocked it's taken this long."

"What do you mean? It's been here for weeks." Reggie shoved her hands deep into the pockets of her jeans, viewing her Spartan decorating style with Gwen's fresh eyes. It came up lacking.

"Oh. I mean, if this is what you like... it's great." Gwen, usually a pro at being diplomatic, fell short this time.

"It has no personality, does it? Or color?" Now that she was really seeing it, Reggie was horrified she'd allowed herself to live this way for so long.

"It sort of looks like the whole thing came in a big box labelled *swanky rich person starter set*," Gwen opined.

Reggie's shoulders slumped. "This is why some of the board members want me to put down deeper roots, isn't it?"

"Let me put it this way," Gwen said gently. "If someone came in here when you weren't home, they would think a realtor had staged it for a quick sale."

"You never hold back, do you?" Reggie said with a laugh. "I hope you never do."

Gwen had been walking in a slow circle around the living room the whole time she'd been poking fun at

Reggie's apartment. Now she stopped in front of one of the built-in bookcases that flanked the fireplace and tilted her head.

"Hold on, now. This isn't standard issue." As Gwen reached for the knickknack on the shelf, Reggie raced across the room.

"Careful with that," Reggie breathed. "It's delicate."

Gwen held back as Reggie took the small glass object from the shelf and held it for her to see.

"Is this a blown glass Cinderella's coach?"

"It is." Reggie turned it carefully so the intricate designs caught the light. "I've had this since I was a kid."

"Who gave it to you?"

"No one. I won it. Maybe that's why it's one of the few things I cherish. Well, that and the memory that goes with it." Reggie hadn't thought of this in years. She had to take a second to get her bearings. "I guess I was seven when my parents split up. That summer, Trev and I were dying to go to the Hamptons, but we couldn't."

"Why not?"

"Uh, because Dad was there with our nanny."

"Why did your dad have the nanny—? Oh." Gwen's face fell.

Reggie couldn't help but laugh. "Wife number two, remember? My dad can be a very lazy man about certain things. He's married a nanny. An admin. Or two. It's amazing he met Rovena. None of us can figure out how or where."

"Maybe he has his own version of your countess," Gwen suggested.

Reggie snorted. "A bargain basement version, if that's so. Have you seen the way that woman dresses? Like someone who learned about the rich and famous by watching Real Housewives on television."

"Not his usual type?"

"No. With the notable exception of my mother—the reason I am cursed with being short and having dark hair—he prefers tall blonds." Reggie clasped a hand to her mouth as soon as she'd said it. "Oh God."

"Am *I* your father's type?" Gwen's expression was a picture of horror. "You have the same taste in women as your father?"

"Don't say that!" Reggie covered her ears. "I'm going to need boiling water and bleach to get that out of my head."

"Why don't we go back to your story?" Gwen said quickly. "I still don't know where that beautiful carriage came from."

"Oh, right. Back to that summer." Reggie was more than happy to change the subject. "Our nanny was pregnant with Stephanie. Not that *we* knew that. Mom did, naturally—hence the divorce—but Trevor and I had no clue. My parents' divorce was acrimonious, to say the least."

"I'm not surprised."

"The big thing Mom wouldn't budge on was Dad putting the Hampton cottages in our names. She didn't want any of his other children—she assumed, very correctly, that he'd have more—to take away the place Trevor and I loved so much." Reggie stared at the carriage, her eyes misting with emotion she rarely allowed herself to express. But with Gwen, she couldn't hold it in anymore.

"Take your time," Gwen said softly, allowing Reggie to recover.

"I don't think about my mom enough," Reggie admitted. "It's too hard. I miss her."

"I understand."

There was a seriousness to Gwen's tone that caught Reggie by surprise, especially since she knew Gwen's mom and dad were alive and well in Chicago. It occurred to her briefly that it was odd that Gwen never called her parents, but Reggie let the thought go. If Gwen wanted to talk about it with her, Reggie hoped she'd feel comfortable when the time was right.

"Anyway," she said, returning to her story, "that summer, since we couldn't go to our usual place by the ocean, Mom decided we would go to a different beach. She rented a cottage in a little seaside town in Massachusetts—and before you say anything, it was actually a cottage, not rich-people-code for mansion."

"Oh, yeah?" Gwen's eyebrows arched, daring Reggie to offer a definition.

"It was tiny. It had two bedrooms and one little bath. Trev and I slept in bunk beds."

"The horror!" Gwen giggled as Reggie gave her shoulder a playful sock.

"Are you kidding? It was awesome." Reggie let out a childlike laugh. "Every day, we would ride bikes, swim, and go to the arcade for Skee-Ball. I spent the entire summer saving my tickets because I wanted to buy this. It probably cost my mother a fortune in quarters, now that I think about it."

"I'll bet," Gwen agreed. "Those places are rigged against you. And it's like twenty tickets for a pack of gum."

"Exactly. I remember there was a matching castle, too. But it was way more tickets, and my mom had some limits, so I only got the coach."

"It's really pretty, even by itself."

"I've taken it everywhere." Reggie ran a fingertip lovingly along the glass. "Let me tell you, packing this baby isn't easy. But it's the one thing I must have to make my place feel like home."

"I'm glad you have it." Gwen squeezed Reggie's hand. "And that you have at least one undeniably happy memory from your childhood."

Reggie's phone buzzed, and the message on the screen snagged her attention. "Huh. It's my brother."

"What does he want?"

Reggie could only think of one thing, and it made her insides twist into a massive knot. "I can't believe he's sending Trevor here to do his dirty work."

"Who are you talking about? Your father?"

"Who else?" Reggie pressed a hand to her stomach, feeling worse by the minute. "Trev isn't the *stop by* kind of guy. Dad must have sent him."

"But why?"

"I think he's going to—" Instead of finishing the thought, Reggie ran a finger across her throat by way of illustration.

Gwen's eyes widened. "I really hope you're talking about getting fired."

"Me too."

There was a knock at the front door. Reggie and Gwen exchanged nervous glances before Reggie headed down the hall, motioning for Gwen to come, too. If she was going to get fired, she wanted a witness. While Gwen had come up the private elevator that opened directly into her apartment, Trevor had come up using the public elevator bank, so he was standing in the hallway outside the apartment, waiting.

"Who is it?" Reggie asked, purely to stall while she collected her nerves.

"Pizza delivery," her brother answered in a comically falsetto tone.

Reggie didn't budge, unable to decide if her brother would pair a joke with giving her the ax or not.

"Come on, Reg." Trevor pounded on the door. "Aren't you going to let me in?"

"Are you here to fire me?"

"What—?" There was a brief pause. "Jesus, Reggie. Of course not. I need your advice."

With an encouraging look from Gwen, Reggie opened the door. Her eyes lit up when she saw the big pizza box in her brother's hands. "Oh, thank goodness. You weren't kidding about the pizza."

"I would never joke about something so serious." Trevor cast a glance at Gwen and smiled. "Oh, hey! Good to see you."

"Likewise," Gwen replied.

Reggie took the box from her brother. "I'm sorry. Come on in."

"You sure?" Trevor teased. "You want to strip search me first?"

"No, thank you." Reggie grimaced. "It's been weird being so cut off. I'm not getting any emails. I can't send any, either." She led the way down the hallway in the opposite direction, past her study, to where the dining room and kitchen were located.

"Seriously?" Her brother's surprise seemed genuine, meaning he had not been kept in the loop on that decision. That had been a one-hundred-percent Reginald Hawkins special. "That's fucked up. I might know why, though."

"Other than Clark Maxwell trying to get me killed with his batshit lunatic rhetoric?"

"Yes, there's that," Trevor conceded. "But the Phoenix-Spotlight deal is about to blow up in Dad's face. Advertisers are bailing. Even the My Buddy guy is threatening to walk."

"Say it isn't so!" Reggie rolled her eyes at the mere mention of Hawks News' most stalwart advertiser. How anyone made a fortune from dog beds was a mystery to her.

"Yeah. I have to fly the dude to Paris this weekend for the French Open final to butter him up."

"Better you than me." Reggie thought for a moment. "You think he actually wants to cut ties?" If he did, that was bad news for Hawks Corp. Until now, that had been the one advertiser whose loyalty was as certain as the dogs who slept in their beds.

"Honestly? Nah." Trevor made a sound like he was blowing a raspberry. "I think he just wants to go to Paris in our PJ."

"Pajamas?" Gwen's face squished in adorable confusion.

"Private jet, dear," Reggie corrected, bopping her on the nose with her forefinger.

"You two are too much." Trevor used his own forefinger to pretend to gag himself. "But, yeah. I'm sick of cheap, rich assholes. Oh, hey, Gwen. I hope you like pizza. It's from Ray's."

"You didn't have it flown in fresh from Italy on your PJ?" Gwen asked with mock seriousness.

"Are you kidding me? New York pizza tops anywhere else on the planet." Trevor emphasized this with one of his killer grins, which made Reggie's heart lift. She didn't see that expression on her brother's face very often when they were in the office.

"Watch it. She's from Chicago. They take their pizza deadly seriously." Reggie blew a kiss to Gwen, knowing it was super sappy and not caring one bit.

Trevor held his hands up in a *don't shoot me* way, before he gave Gwen a hug. "I'm glad you're here. You can help me keep Reggie calm when I show her the video later on."

"Another Clark video?" Reggie asked.

"No. Do you have plates?"

"Of course, I have plates. They're in the cupboard where normal people keep plates." Reggie gave her brother a stern look. "Are you changing the subject? I feel like you're hiding something from me."

"What? Of course not." Trevor gave his best innocent look, which wasn't stellar. As a Hawkins, perhaps looking innocent didn't come naturally.

"You really think the loss of a few advertisers is what has Dad spooked?" An uneasiness came over Reggie as she considered how unlikely it was that this alone would leave such a mark on the old man.

"Dwight's dropping in the polls," Trevor admitted.

"That almost makes it worth getting exiled like a teenager being sent to my room."

"I'm jealous. Being around Dad these few days has been hell." Her brother's smile was gone. "He doesn't understand that not everyone in this country is cheering for a cuckoo crazy billionaire's son who thinks JFK, Jr. is going to come back to life in the nick of time to be his vice president when he runs." Trevor broke into a wide grin again, oddly putting Reggie at peace. While their cousin was drinking Hawks News cult water, her brother wasn't.

"Please tell me he doesn't really think that," Gwen said, putting a slice of pizza on the plate Trevor handed her.

Reggie made a face but couldn't do as Gwen asked, since she didn't want to lie. "What's this about a video, Trev?"

"I brought it with me," he said. "Do you have a TV?"

"No, I'm the only person in America without one." Reggie shook her head at her brother. "In the study. We can have the pizza in there."

Reggie led the way. Trevor, with considerable effort, fished his phone from the inside pocket of his blazer. He cast the video to the TV, and they all took seats so they could see.

"It's not the best quality," he said apologetically. "I took it with my phone during the meeting today, and I didn't want Dad to know."

"What is it?" Reggie squinted at the video, which shook in a way that made her feel seasick. She could just make out the face of a man who was standing in front of a screen in the boardroom on the executive floor of Hawks Corp headquarters. "Is that Dwight's campaign manager?"

"Yeah. Keep watching," Trevor said.

The light in the video dimmed, and a grainy image appeared from a projector onto the screen. It was impossible to make out the details, but when a narrator's voice boomed, Reggie recognized it as the political ad of Dwight's campaign rival.

"He's a straight shooter," the commercial began. "An everyday man. One who stood by his wife after the terrible car accident that left her paralyzed from the neck down. He stepped up to raise their two daughters, taking them to school and making their lunches."

There was a loud noise like a car crash.

Reggie jumped. "What the hell?"

"Shh." Trevor put a finger to his lips.

The voice returned. "That's what they've been feeding you, but it's all a lie."

On the screen, blurry but readable, was a text message purporting to be from the candidate: *I wish we went through with the divorce before the accident.*

Followed by another: *She's not what she used to be.*

Reggie slid her eyes to her brother, who stared intently at the screen.

The last was: *I'm trapped with a cripple.*

Reggie sucked in her breath when she saw that one. The wording alone was too shocking to ignore.

Then Dwight appeared, dressed in his signature navy blue suit and red tie. "With me, you get what you see. I'm Dwight Hawkins, and I approve this message."

"Holy shit," Reggie breathed. "Dad can't run this. Those text messages are obviously fake. That violates like a hundred campaign laws, not to mention common decency."

"Dad swears the texts are legit," Trevor said as he paused the video on the screen. "I guess Dwight's opponent sent them to a sister or something. I mean, hey, I don't know any spouse who hasn't needed to let off steam."

"If he sent them to his sister, how the hell did Dwight get them?" Reggie dug her nails into her palms, not liking where any of this was going. "Shit, is this another one of those wiretapping things, like the scandal in the UK awhile back?"

As Reggie was speaking, Gwen hopped up and went closer to the TV. "Huh. I didn't know your dad wore a hairpiece."

"What?" Reggie's head swiveled toward the screen. "He doesn't. He's as vain about that thick silver hair of his as any prom queen."

"I don't know," Gwen said diplomatically but looking far from convinced. "My grandmother wore a wig for years on account of her hair thinning from lupus, and I recognize this little line right here. See? That's the sign of a lace front wig that's coming loose."

"No way. Is he?" Reggie joined Gwen next to the screen, closing one eye and slanting her head nearly horizontal to the floor. It looked like nothing more than a tiny spot of flaking skin on her father's forehead, which thanks to the size of her screen, was larger than life. It was hard to tell for sure.

"Look at his shirt collar." Gwen pivoted to Reggie. "Do you remember what you told me?"

"About what?"

"About recognizing rich people by their clothes being perfectly tailored. There's an inch or more between the collar and your dad's neck."

"Oh, shit." Trevor sucked in his breath as he got up close to the screen, his face suddenly ashen. "Do you think it's back?"

"Is what back?" Gwen asked.

"Cancer." It was Trevor who uttered the dreaded word. "No one knew he had it. We kept it quiet, and he's been in remission. But, maybe now it's back."

Reggie shook her head, unwilling to believe it. "He told me no."

"When did you ask him?" Trevor sounded scared.

"January, on the way back from Davos."

"You mean when your father was ordering you to come home?" Gwen asked, her words heavy with meaning. "When he said he wanted to secure his succession plan because he might retire?"

Reggie squeezed her eyes shut. "Shit."

"I've gotta get going, Sis." Trevor's hands trembled more than usual as he made a break for the front door. It seemed he couldn't leave fast enough, like getting away from the place where the C-word had been uttered would make the whole thing go away. "I'll keep you up to date on what happens at the office and with Dwight's campaign."

"Yeah, okay." Reggie barely registered what she'd said. All she could hear in her head was the word *cancer*. Her dad had cancer.

"I should probably get going, too," Gwen said softly once Trevor had left. "Unless… do you want me to stay?"

"Yes." With no hesitation, Reggie grasped Gwen's hand, holding on tightly like it was the only thing keeping her grounded in a world spinning out of control. "Please don't go."

CHAPTER TWENTY

The squat brick building that housed East Hampton Helping Neighbors was less impressive than Gwen had imagined, considering the organization's high profile on the Hawkins Foundation's recipient list. Still, she shouldn't have expected different.

There was a definite dichotomy between the haves and have-nots in this summer paradise. This was a place that supported the workers, mostly immigrants, who provided household labor for the wealthy Hamptons summer residents. They weren't out to win any architectural awards. The fact that their offices were so humble was probably a good sign.

The walkway leading to the front door was cracked, weeds taking over.

Inside, the air was stilted with a few inadequately sized fans running, but the lack of air-conditioning was oppressive in the mid-June heat.

"Hello?" Gwen called out, half expecting her voice to echo. It was odd to find the place so empty. With new workers arriving every day, summertime was when Gwen would have expected them to be the busiest.

"I'm sorry, but we're not open today," a feminine voice called out as footsteps came toward Gwen from down the hall.

The hairs on the back of Gwen's head stood on end, a sudden tingle of warning that she couldn't put her finger on. At least, not until the woman came around the corner. Though she was dressed less casually today in slacks and a short-sleeve blouse, there was no mistaking this was the same person who had been waiting for Gwen in her old apartment in Queens.

"Jesus!" Gwen stepped back, one hand on the door. "Try anything, and I'll scream."

"No one will hear you." Leaning against the wall, the woman crossed her arms menacingly.

Gwen fumbled for her phone. "I'm calling the police!"

"Gwen, don't." The woman's posture shifted, becoming less intimidating and more defeated. "I didn't mean that as a threat. I meant it literally. No one will hear you because I'm the only one here. I've had to get rid of the rest of the staff."

Get rid of? Gwen's heart raced. Surely, the woman didn't mean that in a permanent sense, did she?

Phone still tightly clutched, Gwen's body shook, but she didn't complete her call. Not yet. "I don't understand. What the fuck are you doing here?"

"Funny. I was about to ask you the same thing." The woman frowned. "I would have remembered if there was anything on my calendar about you visiting."

"Sorry. It was an impromptu—wait. Why am I explaining myself to you? I have no idea who you are, other than someone with a habit of breaking and entering to threaten people." Gwen fixed the stranger with an expectant look. "I think you'd better explain yourself. Who are you?"

The woman let out a long, deep sigh. "My name is Anika Kapur."

"What are you doing here?"

"I work here." Anika took a step closer, but Gwen shook her head.

"Stay where you are, or I promise, I'll really call. Got it?"

"I understand." The woman raised her hands in the air. "Perhaps I should apologize. I handled our first meeting all wrong."

"Meeting?" Gwen couldn't help but laugh. "You make it sound like an afternoon with the Junior League. In reality, you broke into my apartment, threatened my family, blackmailed me, and scared the living shit out of me."

The color drained from the woman's face. "I regret that. Truly, I do. In my urgency to speak to you, I may have lost sight of decorum."

"That's a pretty big lapse. Whatever would Miss Manners think?" Gwen studied the woman with disbelief, and yet something about her rang true. "What could possibly have been that urgent that you needed to go to the lengths you did to speak with me?"

"Simply put? The opening for an associate director at the Hawkins Foundation was too great of an opportunity for us to pass up."

Gwen raised an eyebrow. "East Hampton Helping Neighbors was behind this?"

"No," Anika assured her with a shaky laugh. "This has nothing to do with the charity I work for. It's a separate organization I'm a part of, but I'd rather not say more than that right now." To emphasize the reason for her hesitation, Anika stared pointedly at Gwen's phone.

"I'm not turning it off, if that's what you're hoping for." Gwen clutched the device even tighter in her hand. "In fact, I should call Reggie this instant and get her help in having you removed from the premises."

"Please don't," Anika begged. "At least hear me out. I'll do my best to explain everything I can. In fact, if you're the type of person I think you are, this is something you'll want to hear."

"What does the type of person I am have to do with anything?" Gwen demanded. She couldn't begin to imagine what the woman meant or even if it should be taken as a compliment or an insult.

"As you know, I'm aware of your true background," Anika said. "I know the job you're doing now isn't a far stretch from what you might be doing if you hadn't gotten involved with... well, you know the company I mean."

Kensington Datalytics. Gwen filled in the blank silently in her head. "I have an interest in humanitarian relief and community development, if that's what you mean. In fact, that's why I was coming here today. I've been reviewing all of the foundation's grant recipients from the past five years, and when I realized how close you were to where I'm staying this summer—" she couldn't bring herself to call it her house, even though she and Reggie would soon be getting engaged—"I decided to swing by and check it out."

"What are your impressions?" Anika asked in a neutral tone.

"Honestly?" Gwen's eyes swept the interior space, which was no more inspiring than the outside had been. "This place is practically falling down. What happened with the money for architectural upgrades? Fresh paint? The new walkway?"

"All good questions," Anika said, "and only the tip of the iceberg. Come with me to the kitchen, if you think you can manage to trust me enough."

After a moment of hesitation, Gwen decided to go with her gut, which for some reason was telling her it would be okay. In this setting, the woman was a lot less menacing than she'd seemed in Queens.

Gwen took a step toward Anika, continuing to clutch her phone like a lifeline. "I don't understand why the building is completely empty today. What happened to the English language classes, or the community soup kitchen?"

"The English classes are on hold due to not being able to pay staff and having to let them all go. As for the soup kitchen and food pantry, you'll see in a moment."

"But the Hawkins Foundation has given you a quarter of a million dollars in just the past year. Forgive me for being blunt," Gwen chided, "but I'm no stranger to stretching far less than that to do a lot more."

"That's exactly why I wanted you to see," Anika said. "Come through here into the kitchen. Do you see this refrigerator?"

The kitchen was in even worse condition than outside. The laminated floor was stained and peeling from the concrete below. The refrigerator reminded her of the one in her grandparents' basement when she was a kid. It had barely worked, but her grandfather didn't want to throw out the hunk of junk.

"I don't get it. I saw the grant paperwork myself," Gwen said, unable to square what she was seeing with what she'd expected before her arrival. "There was a requisition order for a Norlake walk-in cooler and a check cut for almost twenty-thousand."

"Twenty thousand?" For a moment, Anika looked ready to cry. "When I heard from a friend at another nonprofit that there was a rumor we were supposed to get a new unit from the Hawkins Foundation, I was elated. This old thing only works half the time, and the food spoilage is costing a fortune. It's one reason the soup kitchen has been temporarily suspended. We can't risk people getting sick."

"But, what happened? The paperwork cleared our offices months ago, well before I started as associate director."

"You tell me. Whatever money is on your books sure as hell hasn't arrived here, let alone some fancy walk-in cooler. We've spoken with others—"

"By we, do you mean whatever group it is you are working with but won't say their name?"

"You catch on quickly," Anika confirmed. "There are other groups with accounts that are fishy. Other places the foundation supposedly supports where the folks on the ground have never so much as heard back about a grant application, let alone received funds. I have a list in my office of all the accounts."

"I'd like to see it," Gwen said.

"I'd like you to do more than look at it," Anika countered. "I want you to do some digging. It's the whole reason you're there."

"Or what?" Anger bubbled up in Gwen at the woman's demand. "You'll go after the people I love?"

"I told you already. I regret taking that line of—"

"Save it." Gwen put up a hand. "I can't do what you want, anyway. I don't have that kind of access to the records. The only one who does is Bitsie Donaldson."

"And Regina Hawkins."

"Oh sure." Gwen let out a bitter laugh. "You want me to ask Reggie if her family foundation is full of crooks?"

"I wouldn't *ask* her anything." Anika's tone was so mild Gwen almost missed the meaning of her words.

"Then how am I—" Gwen sucked in her breath. "You want me to go behind her back? No way. Reggie would never be a part of this. She's not like her dad." But even as she said it, Gwen was reminded of the many ways Reggie was like her father. This was a woman who had spent a fortune on a piece of jewelry. Were her priorities really what Gwen hoped they were?

They have to be. For all her faults, Gwen couldn't see Reggie being willing to shortchange a charitable organization that fed kids.

"You two seem very... close."

"We are." Gwen raised her chin, towering above the smaller woman. For once, she was extremely grateful for her height. "I'm telling you, without a doubt in my mind, that Reggie is not involved in this, whatever it is that's going on."

"Prove me wrong," Anika challenged. "That would be wonderful. I don't have to be right. Just help us figure out what's going on."

"I don't think I can spy on Reggie."

"I'm not asking you to spy on her," Anika said with a laugh. "Use her computer login to gain access to the bank records."

"You're not making it sound any better."

Anika wrung her hands, on the brink of total frustration. "Don't you care?"

"Of course, I do. Why else would I be here today?"

"Fine. Then you have to do something. We won't be able to keep the doors open much longer without the money we've been promised. The community will suffer if we close. They already are."

"I'll think about it. Send over the list of accounts if you must, but I have to get back now." Gwen left the building feeling as if the world was closing in on her.

Was she right in her estimation, or was the Reggie she knew a lie?

GWEN TAPPED HER BLUNT NAILS ON THE RED checkered tablecloth of the picnic table outside the clam shack. If Solène didn't arrive in the next four minutes and fifty-five seconds, Gwen would leave. She was already taking a huge chance with this meet-up minutes from the family compound. Sitting here all alone would draw attention. Just her luck, people would start tweeting that Gwen had a massive fight with Reggie and was drowning her sorrows with fried clams.

People were ridiculous.

If that were actually the truth, ice cream would be her choice. But the clams were good, and Gwen continued to nibble as the seconds ticked by.

"How do you do it?" Appearing from nowhere, Solène sat down as if nothing were amiss.

"Do what?" Gwen nearly choked on a clam in surprise.

"Eat fried food and still look amazing. I'm going to gain weight just looking at them."

"Please." Gwen half rolled her eyes. Her friend had

nothing to worry about. "Sorry to drag you out here. Were you in DC?"

"Yes, and it's okay. It's a lovely drive. What's going on?" Solène pulled a small notebook from her pocket, knowing without being told that whatever Gwen had to tell her would need to be written down.

"You know how you said you couldn't get—" Gwen casually looked left and right, checking for listening ears, before continuing—"the attention of *certain people.*"

By this, Gwen meant the people in government positions in DC, London, and Brussels who were the keys to finally releasing the dirt on Kensington Datalytics and the Polyphemus project into the wild without it exploding on them with the devastation of a nuclear bomb. If nothing else, Gwen had learned to have a greater appreciation for what investigative journalists faced when trying to bring a dangerous story like this one to light.

Solène leaned over the table, stealing a clam. "Go on."

"I might have something that will help." Gwen filled her in about Dwight's possible campaign ad and the text messages it employed. "As soon as Reggie said it sounded like wiretapping, I knew it had to be more than that. Don't you agree?"

"I've long suspected Reginald Hawkins was involved somehow." Solène spoke cautiously, but there was a gleam of hope in her eyes that hadn't been there when she arrived. "A lot of his personal enemies have been targeted by the program, more than could comfortably be called a coincidence. Not to mention some news scoops that defied logic."

Gwen gasped. "Why didn't you tell me that? I've been in the thick of it with the Hawkins for months."

"Because we keep everything siloed. To protect not just you but our sources." Solène let out an exasperated breath. "How was I supposed to know you'd fall in love with his daughter?"

"I didn't know that would happen, either!" Gwen exclaimed, shrinking as her friend gave her a gotcha look.

"You are in love with her, then." Solène poached another clam, chewing slowly.

"I did not call you out here today to discuss my love life," Gwen scolded. But she didn't deny it, because she couldn't.

"If we're able to implicate Reginald—"

"He's dying," Gwen interjected. "At least, there's a good chance. Did you know that?"

"No." Solène was clearly taken aback. "How do you know this?"

"Please, this part is off the record." Gwen waited for the journalist to agree. "He's had a brush with cancer before. Now he's losing weight, losing his hair. All the evidence points to it."

"I'm sorry, my friend. I know you love Reggie, but you have to leave. Now." There was a sense of urgency in Solène's tone despite her outwardly calm mannerisms. "We can set you up in New Mexico. You love green chiles."

"I can't leave Reggie." Gwen was adamant.

"Is she the successor?" Solène's expression was grim.

"That's what she wants."

"Then you have to leave."

"Why?"

"Because people are going to jail when all the dust settles from this bombshell."

"Not Reggie. She had nothing to do with this."

"Are you certain?" Solène's gaze burrowed deep beneath Gwen's skin, to the place all her doubts resided.

Gwen pressed her lips together, waiting to see what her gut would say, other than it wanted more clams. Finally, she let out a breath. "She wouldn't have anything to do with a spy program like Polyphemus."

"How do you know?"

The details of Reggie's long ago sex scandal with Lydia ran through her mind, but Gwen would never divulge the details. Not even to Solène. "I just do. She would never condone such dangerous invasion of privacy."

"What if she did? Would you still want to protect her?"

"If she's guilty? No." Was that the truth? Gwen's belly twisted, unsure how far she would go for Reggie if it turned out the woman wasn't who or what she believed. How far gone was she when it came to the woman she loved?

"I don't believe you." Apparently, her friend had reached a conclusion faster than Gwen. And she didn't look happy about it. "Has her money brought you over to the dark side?"

"Solène, no. Hawks Corp is without a doubt an evil organization. If it falls, I will dance on its grave for what it did to my grandfather. But I don't want Reggie or Trevor to go down with the ship. They're good people. You have to trust me on that." Gwen couldn't hide the desperate pleading in her tone, which matched the depths of her being.

"I can't guarantee who will get caught up in the web," Solène cautioned. "If the feds get involved—and I think they finally will be convinced to act now with this new information you've brought to light—people are going to turn on whomever they can to get lighter sentences. If

Reggie is involved and her dad dies—there's no one higher for her to turn on."

"Reggie would never turn on any of them." Gwen's heart sank at this basic truth.

Looking at the ocean she said a prayer, something she hadn't done since childhood. Reggie would take a bullet for her brother. That was for sure. It made Gwen love her all the more. Even if she was guilty. But Gwen hoped she wasn't with all her heart.

CHAPTER TWENTY-ONE

Standing in the large, open foyer of her Montauk cottage, Reggie checked the mirror one more time, her heart thrumming in her throat. It was only early evening, but the family compound was already filled with guests for the fireworks, and she could hear laughter from children playing despite all the windows being closed. After so many months, her plan was in the final stretch.

Reggie dabbed at a bead of sweat that spontaneously broke out on her forehead, right at the edge of her hairline.

"We're going to be late to the party," Gwen said. "You hate being late."

Jumping from the sudden noise, Reggie covered her heart. "I need to put a bell on you. Were you a spy in a former life?"

Gwen laughed, her eyes darting everywhere in imitation of a secret agent. "Maybe I was a cat."

"Oh no!" Reggie put a hand to her mouth, her heart beating wildly. "I'm not supposed to see you right now."

"Why not?"

"Isn't it bad luck?" Reggie felt a little lightheaded, her head swiveling for an easy spot to sit down. For lack of a better option, she leaned against the wall.

"You're thinking of the wedding day." Gwen kissed Reggie's forehead as she simultaneously peeled her from the wall. "Everything's going to be okay. I can't believe I have to say this to you of all people, but pull yourself together, Regina Hawkins."

Reggie inhaled shakily. "I'm sorry. I've never done this before."

"You've gotten engaged before," Gwen pointed out. "Twice."

"First of all," Reggie felt compelled to point out, "I was on the receiving end, not the question-popping side of the equation. Second, it was never to someone I loved."

Gwen's eyes misted, her facial features softening at this unintended but heartfelt declaration. "I love you, too."

"Are we rushing things?"

"Um, yes." Gwen laughed. "I mean, I can't lie. We absolutely are, which was all part of the plan. Remember?"

"Yeah, but it's not just a plan anymore. Is it?" Reggie swallowed, uncertainty flooding every inch of her.

"No. It's more."

"Okay." Reggie was oddly reassured by Gwen's simple assertion.

"I know we have to do this in front of a crowd for it to have the impact you want with the board," Gwen said in her most practical manner, "but when you ask, look at me. Pretend it's only us and none of the guests are even there."

"I feel like that's the same as the advice to pretend everyone is naked when you have to give a speech." Reggie shivered. That advice terrified her. Why would you want to be in a room with hundreds of naked people?

"Don't picture everyone naked," Gwen advised. "Just me."

"Now there's something I can fully endorse." Reggie took a step back. "While your dress is lovely, I can't wait to see what's underneath. I had Hector send over something special as a surprise. Are you wearing it?"

"I am, but have you already seen it?" Gwen playfully crossed her arms. "That's cheating."

"I swear I haven't." Reggie crossed her heart. "Let's roll, babe."

"Babe?" Gwen arched an eyebrow. "You've never called me that in your life."

"Nerves." Reggie's face morphed into a look of pure horror at the bizarre slipup. She sounded like she was hitting on some disco chick in a 1970s nightclub.

"Whatever you do tonight," Gwen warned, "don't say, *Will you marry me, babe?* I will kill you."

"Why did you go and put that into my head?" Reggie groaned. "You know that's all I'll be able to think of now."

As they left the house, Reggie surveyed the mass of humanity that had concentrated on the property. It was a who's who of every corporate tycoon, politician, celebrity, and journalist in America. If Reggie had a late stage capitalism bingo card to fill, she'd win anew with each sweep of her eyes across the crowd. And her father would be in the middle space, wearing a crown. King of the universe. But the king needed to be brought down.

"What do we do now?" Gwen's earlier bravado seemed to have taken a bruising now that they were actually out in the thick of things. "Can we go back inside?"

"Now, we mingle. Oh!" Reggie raised a hand, waving. "There's my baby brother."

"Trevor?" Gwen squinted, searching the crowd.

"No, my *real* baby brother." Reggie pulled Gwen by the hand toward a lanky kid of about fourteen. He had a coltish appearance, like his body and limbs had all decided to grow at different speeds without checking with him first. "Logan!"

"Hi, Reggie." Clearly out of his element, Logan seemed uncertain whether to shake hands or hug the sister who was old enough to be his mother. He put out an awkward hand as Reggie scooped him up like a momma bear, putting an end to the standoff.

"Logan, this is Gwen," Reggie said once she'd let him go so he could catch his breath.

"Nice to meet you, Logan." Gwen offered a sweet smile but kept her distance, provoking a look of pure relief from the young man's face.

"You've grown." Reggie tilted her head back. "A lot."

"Sorry." Logan wore a bashful grin. "I know I promised not to."

"What?" Gwen asked, laughing.

"When Logan left for school last year," Reggie explained, "I asked him not to outgrow me before he was fifteen. I'm tired of being the littlest Hawk in the nest."

"There's Little Baby D," Gwen not-so-helpfully tossed out.

Reggie glared, but Logan laughed.

"You're going to fit right in," he assured Gwen. "Can I get either of you a drink?"

"What a gentleman. A seltzer would be lovely." Gwen

smiled as Logan charged off like only a teenage boy could. "He's completely charming."

"Luckily, Dad played no role in raising him."

"I truly believe if you removed Reginald Hawkins's influence, your family wouldn't be half bad."

Removing her father was all part of the plan.

Reggie squirmed a bit, her heightened nerves having led to the unfortunate state of a prematurely full bladder. By this time, they'd made it too far across the compound that the path back to the cottage was blocked, though her father's place was close by.

"You know what? I need to hop inside Dad's house for a moment. Stay right here, okay?"

"Okay, but—"

"Please. I need to know you're here. Or I won't make it until tonight."

"I'm not going anywhere."

Gwen's promise soothed the panic in Reggie's soul, if not the urgency of her bladder. "If we don't find each other before then, we meet on the beach, right before the fireworks. You got that?"

"We've gone over the schedule a million times." Gwen rolled her eyes. "Go pee already."

"I never said I had to pee," Reggie whispered with a hiss.

"We all do it," Gwen taunted. "No need to be embarrassed."

"Oh my God, you're very annoying sometimes." Laughing, Reggie kissed Gwen's cheek. She whispered in her ear, "And I'm madly in love with you."

"You better be, or you're in big trouble." Gwen squeezed Reggie's hand, not seeming to want to let go. "Please don't be gone long. You aren't the only one who's nervous and would rather not be alone."

Reggie sealed the promise with a kiss before heading into her dad's house. It wasn't just that her bladder was full —darn Gwen for realizing what she was really up to. Reggie needed a moment alone, to get her head on right. In a matter of hours, she was going to propose to Gwen, a woman, in front of a collection of the most powerful and important people on the planet.

Not any woman, either. The one.

Reggie had finally, after all these years, fallen in love.

Life didn't get much better than that. Yet it would, because in addition to getting the woman of her dreams, Reggie would convince the board to put her at the head of Hawks Corp, her father's wishes be damned. At last, his malignant reign would come to an end, and Reggie could start the hard work of remaking the family business into something worthy of the Hawkins name.

On the way back from the bathroom, Reggie spied movement in her dad's office. She frowned, certain she'd seen him outside. But she hadn't seen Trevor. Her insides tightened, fearing the worst. If this was one of Trevor's bad days, he might require some coaxing to join the throng outside.

"Hey, Trevor?" Reggie pushed the office door open, stopping in her tracks, startled, as she took in what was going on.

It wasn't Trevor, but Rovena. She was putting a key in a locked box on Reginald's desk.

"What are you doing?" Reggie strode toward her, determined not to let her father's girlfriend get away with whatever she was up to. Reggie wasn't sure why, but she was certain the woman was up to something sneaky.

"Me? What are you doing?" Rovena scowled. "Last I heard, your father had forbidden you from coming inside his house."

"What's in that box?" Reggie demanded. "Show me right now, or I will call security. My father never lets anyone rummage through his things, not even family. And you definitely are not that."

"I told him this was a foolish idea." With a sigh, Rovena unlocked the box and lifted the lid to reveal dozens of bottles of pills. "There. Satisfied?"

"What the hell is this?" Reggie began to shake as the truth started to sink in. Right next to all the meds was a RN badge for Rovena with a smiling photo. Until this moment, some part of Reggie had been able to deny her father was sick again. "You're not his girlfriend, are you?"

Rovena stiffened. "I'm not in a position to answer that question."

"Good God." Reggie threw her hands in the air. "You've been hanging around this family too long. Why doesn't anyone ever answer simple questions?"

"I'm not at liberty to say."

"You don't have to." Reggie edged closer, picking up a bottle and peering at the label. "I assume you're providing round the clock care for him, since back before Thanksgiving when you first pretended to be dating."

"I can't say."

"Yeah, yeah." Reggie let out a frustrated groan. She should have felt a sense of triumph in figuring out what was going on, putting the pieces together, and beating her father at his game. Instead, she wanted to curl up in a ball and cry.

"Tell me one thing. How much time does he have left? A year?"

The woman stood as still as stone, not even blinking.

Reggie swallowed. "Six months?"

Whether she intended to give anything away or not, Rovena's eyelids fluttered, almost like a sign Reggie was getting closer.

Dread filled her as she asked the next question. "Is it less than six?"

Rovena's eyes drifted to the floor, her painted lips thinning into a line.

That was Reggie's answer. In less than six months, her father would be gone.

Dates and numbers began to race through Reggie's brain. The deal with Phoenix Media was supposed to go through in less than three months. He obviously planned to still be kicking, alive and able to usher that through to completion. He'd even gone so far as to back her idiot cousin Dwight for the senate to ensure the deal went through.

But why?

Because it was going to be his last big deal? Was that why her old man had been pushing so hard for it? Billions of dollars to the family and a guarantee that his beloved news division, and nothing else, was at the heart of his legacy?

What then? Would he make it to Christmas?

Reggie's head spun.

"I have to go." Reggie raced past Rovena, intent on only one thing. Gwen. Reggie needed to find Gwen. She stepped outside the house with that mission.

"Reggie! Get over here," her dad barked.

Caught red-handed.

Reggie skidded to a stop, bracing herself to face the father she knew was dying. Emotions warred within her. Banishing them all was impossible, so Reggie chose to take hold of the only one she knew what to do with. Anger.

Turning to her father, who was standing beside a guest she'd never met, Reggie narrowed her eyes. "You haven't spoken to me since Memorial Day. You want to talk now, after six weeks?"

"Six weeks. So what? I didn't realize I'd raised a sissy who needs Daddy to tuck her in bed every night." Reginald let out a hollow laugh, and the man standing beside him offered an uncomfortable smile. "I want you to meet Simon Wyeth."

"It's nice to meet you." Reggie put her hand out. She had no clue who the guy was, and her father clearly had no intention of telling her. A classic Reginald Hawkins power play.

"Likewise," Simon said, speaking with what Reggie recognized as an upper-class British accent, as he shook her hand. "Your father tells me you're recently back from London."

"That's right." *Which is more than I know about you,* Reggie couldn't help thinking.

"It's a shame we never met while you lived in London. A little bird told me you became a Tottenham fan when you lived there."

"Yes. Apparently, I like to suffer. It's a Hawkins' trait."

"Indeed." Simon laughed, carefree and not bowled over like most in her father's presence. "The next time you're over, I'll arrange box seats."

"Simon's involved in a lot of charitable work," her father interjected. He seemed to have grown impatient with not being the center of the conversation. "My daughter's recently taken over the Hawkins Foundation."

"Ah." Simon's smile brightened. "In that case, I expect we'll be doing quite a bit of business together. Including what we were just discussing."

The man turned to Reggie's father with eyebrows lifted. Reginald gave an almost imperceptible nod. Reggie had no idea what any of it meant, but she was wise enough to know that some sort of deal had been finalized in her presence.

Reggie made a point of checking her watch. "It's been nice to meet you, but I really must—"

"Yes, go," her father growled, obviously having no further use for her. Reggie might've been hurt by his tone if she wasn't already so used to being dismissed.

Still scanning the crowd for Gwen, Reggie spotted Aunt Val instead. The woman was standing with the three board members whom Gwen had christened Tom, Dick, and Harry. When Aunt Val caught Reggie's eye, she made a quick move to excuse herself and scurried over.

"The votes are falling into place," Aunt Val said with a smile, speaking in a low voice so as not to be overheard. "I'd like to get this nailed down before the annual meeting in October if we can."

"Are you thinking of calling a special meeting?" Reggie registered her surprise. She hadn't expected her aunt to move so quickly. Did she, too, have suspicions about her brother's health?

"Not quite yet, though it would be so tempting. We're all in town for this little party, after all. It would be so easy to pop back into the city for a quick gathering." Val's eyes twinkled as she gave Reggie a conspiratorial wink.

"If only we could be certain of the votes."

"You said you'll have an announcement later that should address those concerns we discussed before."

"Tonight," Reggie promised. "What do we think the breakdown is right now?"

"Reginald and Carl are definitely not on our side. You and I can be counted as yes votes, I assume." Reggie's aunt laughed. "As for the other nine, I can't see Stephanie turning on her dad, or Trevor—"

"Trevor's with us."

Aunt Val's eyebrows skyrocketed. "You're sure? Okay." There was a newfound sense of respect in the woman's tone. "The three gentleman I was just speaking with are leaning heavily our way. So that's six. That means of the other three, we only need one more. Two would be better."

"It'll be tight," Reggie acknowledged.

"Maybe by the end of summer," Val said.

That they were this close to a coup was a miracle. Then there was the revelation of her father's terminal diagnosis. This, Reggie held back for now, even from Val. It was too hard to say what such a wildcard would do to their chances to risk putting it in play unless they had to.

"I'll keep doing what I'm doing," Val said before returning to her schmoozing.

With thoughts of Gwen, Reggie searched all around her. The woman was nowhere to be seen. Her nerves jangled as the press of the crowd overwhelmed her. Where could Gwen be?

"Ms. Hawkins?" A woman Reggie had never met, with an accent that sounded vaguely French, had come up beside her. "If you care about Gwen, you need to come with me now. Before it's too late."

"GWEN!" REGGIE TORE THROUGH THE FRONT DOOR of her cottage, mindful of nothing but finding Gwen. "Where are you?"

Reggie reached the bedroom door, finding it closed. Muffled sounds came from within, among them something that sounded like sobbing. She tapped on the door, gently so as not to scare the woman on the other side. "Gwen, can I come in?"

"Only if you leave your phone in the kitchen."

That was not at all the response Reggie had expected, but she complied. After sprinting to the kitchen, putting her phone on the counter, and racing back upstairs, she tried again. "The phone's gone. Can I come in?"

"Yes, but close the door."

Gwen sat on the floor in the far corner, holding her knees as she rocked herself back and forth. A suitcase, open but empty, sat on the bed.

"He found me."

"Who? Is this about an ex?" Reggie rushed to kneel at Gwen's side, pulling her body close. "I knew from day one there was someone out there you were hiding from."

"No, there's no ex." Gwen wiped her eyes with the back of her hand. "But, Reggie, I can't keep lying to you. I'm not who you think I am."

"What? Of course, you are." Reggie kissed the top of Gwen's head. "Whatever is going on, nothing can change the way I feel about you."

"I think you should wait to say that until you hear everything." It was Gwen's total resignation, her deathly stillness, that finally got through to Reggie, letting her know

Gwen had something important—maybe life altering—to share.

Heart pounding, Reggie forced herself to sit across from Gwen and remain calm. Taking Gwen's hands, she kept her tone even as she said, "Tell me from the beginning."

"I don't know how." The words came out as a sob.

"Gwen—"

"That's not even my name." Gwen buried her face in her hands. "I'm not from Chicago. I'm not even a blond!"

Reggie was numb. "What's your name?"

"Wendy. Wendy Mancini."

"Mancini. That sounds Italian. I guess that explains not being blond." Reggie was talking nonsense, frowning as she tested the unfamiliar name on her tongue. "Should I call you Wendy?"

"Please don't." There was a steely resolve in Gwen's eyes as she lifted her chin. "I don't really feel like that's who I am anymore. I fell in love with you as Gwen. I'm Gwen now."

Reggie swallowed hard, a spark of relief in sight. Whatever else, Gwen was still in love with her. At least she knew that much. "Now that we've settled that, tell me what I need to know. Start with where you're from."

"I grew up dirt poor in a small town in Texas," Gwen began. "Mom was young and not married when she got pregnant with me. The whole thing about having happily married parents was a lie. I don't even know my dad. But it wasn't all bad. We lived with my grandparents from the time I was little. They were kind, fun, and loving. Then my grandfather lost his job. My mom became disabled. My grandmother got sick and eventually died."

"Lupus?" Reggie asked, wondering if that part was true and feeling ridiculously relieved when Gwen nodded.

"After that, things got bad. My grandfather got more and more like the fanatics he watched on TV." Gwen broke down into sobs. "Called me evil for being queer."

Reggie scooted closer, putting an arm around Gwen. "I'm sorry."

"I got lucky. I was a good student, and I got a scholarship to college. I ended up in the UK studying international humanitarian law at the University of Essex."

"Smarty-pants." Reggie experienced a twinge of sadness at only now discovering they'd lived within a few hours of each other. How much more didn't she know?

"After graduation, I took a job at a non-profit organization working with refugees. Not the one you saw on my resume but similar. By then, my grandfather had forced my mom to cut all ties with me, threatening to cut off the financial support she depends on." Gwen rested her head on Reggie's shoulder. "I haven't spoken to her in a year. I'm afraid if I call, he'll punish her for it."

"I'm so sorry," Reggie whispered against Gwen's hair as her head rested on Reggie's shoulder.

"Anyway, thanks to the low salaries at non-profits, I was working for peanuts. Totally burnt out. Then three years ago, a friend from university introduced me to a man who ran a company in London. He told me they were using massive data sets to fuel humanitarian projects such as improving the reach of HIV awareness and clean water campaigns in developing countries."

"You understood what he meant by all that?" Reggie asked, laughing uneasily at how incomprehensible Gwen's words had seemed.

"Not entirely," Gwen admitted. "But enough to see a genuine opportunity to fix some of the systemic issues that had frustrated me while working in humanitarian aid. I'd heard that the company had ties with some unsavory governments, and I knew they did political consulting, but I was willing to turn a blind eye for the chance to do some real good."

"What happened to change that?" Reggie sensed there must have been something Gwen's strong moral compass couldn't tolerate.

"Ironically, it was when I got promoted to Director of Business Development. Don't be too impressed. It was a fancy title, and I was making a good salary, but I was nowhere near the inner circle. Even so, I was close enough to see glimpses of the darker side of things."

"This led to what... going on the run?" Reggie could hardly believe she was saying the words. It sounded like something out of a spy novel instead of real life.

"Not at first. I didn't quite understand the information I'd uncovered, so I contacted a friend from university who's now an investigative journalist. We met up in Edinburgh under the guise of a class reunion so no one at my company would suspect. After she did some digging, she realized the full significance of what I'd stumbled on. My company had developed one of the most sophisticated and dangerous pieces of spyware ever created. One that could be put on any phone in the world."

"Like malware?" Reggie's heart beat faster, and she began to understand Gwen's insistence that she leave her phone outside the room.

"Sort of, but with traditional malware, you have to click on a link to get infected. You can teach people to avoid it. This is different."

"Undetectable?" Reggie swallowed, the dizzying

implications for personal privacy making her head spin as Gwen nodded.

"How they get it on the device is still a mystery, but once a phone is infected, they have total control of the device. They can go into all of your accounts. Turn on your camera. Listen to every conversation you have in real time. Track your location. If you text or call someone, they have it all. In the interest of greed, what started out as a top-secret military program is now being made available to anyone willing to pay the price. Like politicians looking for dirt on their opponents."

"Oh my God. Dwight's campaign ad. The text messages. It wasn't a wiretap." It was way worse. Reggie covered her mouth with her hand as she worked through the full horrifying scenario to its obvious conclusion. "My father is involved with this?"

"I didn't realize it until today, but I think so," Gwen confirmed. "The man who hired me, whose company is behind all of this. He's here."

Reggie gasped. "Here? You mean at the party?"

"I saw your dad talking to him. And you, too."

"Simon Wyeth." Reggie took a deep breath as all the pieces connected to form a startling whole. "Keep packing."

Gwen's face fell. "You think I should leave you?"

"Hell no." Reggie held Gwen in an embrace, kissing her like it was the very first time. If there was only one thing she knew, it was that she didn't want to so much as imagine a life without Gwen—or Wendy—in it. "I'm coming with you. We're heading back to the city tonight as soon as I talk to Val. I know exactly what we need to do."

CHAPTER TWENTY-TWO

I n the kitchen of her apartment early the next morning, Gwen whipped around toward the sink, coffee pot in hand. She nearly broke the fragile glass carafe on Reggie's head.

"I'm sorry!" Gwen couldn't stop herself from laughing. "I need some water to fill the pot."

"Sure, you do. There's got to be a better way to bump me off than that." Chuckling, Reggie eased the pot from Gwen's grasp. "I'll fill that up, dear. I'm closer to the sink. And why don't you have one of those single serve pod machines like the rest of us?"

"I don't know. Maybe because my kitchen was last updated in the 1990s," Gwen quipped. "Why don't you talk to the woman who moved me into this place?"

"If I see her," Reggie said, "I'll be sure to also tell her about the total lack of counter space in the kitchen and bathroom."

"Not quite what you're used to, is it?" Gwen reached

into the fridge for a stick of butter, one of the few items contained within.

"I'd rather be in this small kitchen with you than alone in my own. Plus, my family doesn't know anything about your apartment." Reggie grabbed the toast from the toaster as it dinged, handing it to Gwen on a plate she grabbed from the drain rack. "We're safest here."

Gwen wrinkled her nose at the toast, which was burnt to a fine char along the edges. Was this how Reggie preferred it, or had the woman never operated a toaster before?

"I doubt your family is aware my neighborhood exists at all," she said. "But that doesn't mean we're safe. Solène found me here."

"Ah, yes. The French woman. But she's an investigative journalist."

It was subtle, but that didn't mean Gwen didn't notice the jealousy in Reggie's tone at the mention of her ex. They'd had a chance to talk much more in depth on their late-night drive from the Hamptons to New York City, not trusting a helicopter ride to keep their journey as anonymous as joining the thousands of cars on the road.

During this time, Gwen had learned that Solène had been instrumental in helping Reggie find Gwen before she fled the Hawkins family compound in fear, all alone. Reggie had found out that Gwen and the French journalist had occasionally engaged in sexual activities some fifteen years prior. It had turned out not to be a well-balanced exchange of information.

"Your family runs most of the news operations in this shitty world." Gwen used her knife to peel off some of the black from the toast. She soon gave up and buttered it, carved bits and all. "Are you telling me they can't track us down on their own?"

"Shitty world? You don't normally talk like that. I thought I was the pessimist, and you were Miss Sunshine." Reggie added coffee grounds to the machine. Gwen wondered if she'd remembered the paper filter or even knew to use one. Witnessing Regina Hawkins without her usual entourage of office and household staff was eye-opening. And amusing.

"Maybe I'm coming around to your point of view." Gwen chomped into the toast, pulling a face at the bitterness on her tongue. "Yuck."

"I'm sorry. Breakfast is more Sherri's specialty. Once all this is over, we'll go away somewhere nice to recoup. You need a vacation." Reggie adjusted the dial on the toaster and put in two fresh pieces before taking the burnt disgrace from Gwen's hand and tossing it in the trash. "This is kinda fun, though. Don't you think? Making breakfast together. And, we keep bumping into each other." Reggie wrapped her arms around Gwen, who shot her an annoyed look but didn't make any move to wiggle free, especially not when Reggie nibbled her earlobe.

"How are you so calm?" Gwen struggled to keep her own voice even and panic-free. "You're about to participate in a corporate coup that's going to make international news. If it fails, your dad will probably find a way to send you to prison for all the shit he's been doing through the foundation he saddled you with. I'm betting that was his plan all along."

"I'm sure it was. Dad's always looking for scapegoats. Even if I get control of the company, there's still a chance of that happening." Some of the joviality had drained from

Reggie's voice, and it became clear to Gwen that it had mostly been an act.

Gwen leaned against the fridge, massaging her heart to keep it from stopping. "Why can't we go back to my original plan of disappearing? Get the hell out of Dodge? Maybe we could move to a small island. Surely, your family has one or two of those lying about."

"Sadly, they know the locations of those. It would be hard to hide."

"I know you hate boats, but hear me out. What if we stayed in the middle of the ocean?"

"How about the Bermuda Triangle?" Reggie's forced joviality had been replaced by sarcasm, which actually made Gwen feel more at ease.

"I'm game." Gwen closed her eyes, dreading the day ahead.

"Drink some coffee. After the drive here last night, you could use some caffeine. The toast is nearly done, and the smoke detector isn't going off, so I think I did it correctly this time." Reggie winked. "I'll butter it, and we can sit down before we both head off for battle."

Gwen took a seat on her couch, watching Reggie take care of tasks that she usually had people do for her. It would have been a charming scene of domesticity if she wasn't so worried for what was to come in the day ahead. "I never thought my last meal would be coffee and toast."

Reggie handed Gwen a plate. "Unfortunately, I didn't pack my travel caviar."

Gwen scrunched her face. "I'd legitimately rather eat Marmite, and that's not saying much. Be honest with me, are you nervous?"

"Yes." Reggie took a bite of toast.

Gwen wasn't quite sure honesty was what she was after if Reggie was going to deliver it so bluntly. "You're not showing it."

"Decades of training."

Gwen picked up her slice of toasted bread, admiring the perfectly golden color but unable to summon an appetite. "Remind me again how it will all play out."

"Without the engagement announcement and several weeks, if not months, to help certain board members feel more comfortable with me in the top leadership role, we're having to resort to the nuclear option. Twice."

"Your dad's cancer and Trevor's brain injury." Gwen knew the pain Reggie was trying to hide. No matter how necessary and ethical, it would seem like the worst possible betrayal. And while Reggie might have a complicated relationship with her father, she would crave his approval until the day he died. Probably beyond.

"Val's quietly rallying the troops to make it back to New York first thing this morning, which means, best-case scenario, Dad sleeps in and doesn't even know the meeting is happening until it's over."

"How likely is that?"

"Not very. The bastard wakes up before the crack of dawn."

"Sounds like someone else I know," Gwen said playfully. Reggie had gotten better about bounding out of bed to start working at 4:30 in the morning so that she would be there to snuggle when Gwen awoke, but there had yet to be a morning where Gwen was awake first. "And the worst-case scenario?"

"Worst-case, one of Val's maybe votes gets cold feet and

sides with Dad, who then gets me tossed off the board when my coup attempt fails."

"Which scenario is more likely?"

"I really wish I knew." Reggie sipped her drink. "How about you? Are you ready for your debut as a computer hacker?"

Gwen snorted at the description, even as nerves coiled in her belly at the thought of what she needed to do at work that day. "I'm not sure searching Bitsie's desk for her computer password qualifies as hacking—"

"How much you wanna bet it's 1-2-3-4-5-6? Or *password*?"

"You mean the actual word?" Gwen shook her head, realizing there was a greater than zero possibility of one of these things being true. "I wish for my sake it was going to be that easy, but I don't think we should get our hopes up. As important as it is to get into the foundation's records, it might not be possible. And even if I manage it, I might not find enough evidence to give Solène the smoking gun she needs."

"Good points." Reggie took another sip of coffee. "I bet you a fiver Bitsie keeps her password on a sticky note on her monitor."

"You're on." Gwen's brow furrowed, a sudden concern weighing her down. "By a fiver, you mean five dollars, right? I didn't just bet you the cost of a Manhattan apartment, did I?"

"I guess you'll find out." Reggie's silly grin hit Gwen exactly where she needed it, easing some of the tension from what was sure to be a harrowing day for them both.

GIVEN THE HOLIDAY, THE HAWKINS FOUNDATION'S office was a ghost town. Most everyone had taken at least the day off, and considering how many cocktails Gwen had personally witnessed the director downing at last night's party, she doubted Bitsie would be making an appearance for the rest of the week.

As Gwen sat at her desk, staring at the door to Bitsie's office, she worked on bucking up the nerve to do what she had to.

"Just walk over to her computer, and see what's what," she urged herself. The fact she was speaking out loud hardly mattered. The only two people working today had gone to lunch.

Sure, it sounded easy, but doubt shrouded her as every way the mission could go wrong played out in Gwen's mind. Maybe she should have accepted Solène's offer of help, but Reggie had insisted everyone keep to their own tasks. No fingerprints, she'd said. Had that been metaphorical? Gwen assumed so at the time, but now she wasn't sure. Perhaps it had been an error not to grab latex gloves.

Should she use a pencil to tap the keys on Bitsie's computer?

After several long seconds of indecision, Gwen finally sat down at Bitsie's computer, nudging the mouse to wake the monitor.

Now for the password.

Keeping her breathing steady, Gwen scanned the woman's desk for photos of children or a dog, preferably with a name prominently displayed.

No such luck.

She opened the desk drawers for a notebook that might contain a password.

Again, she came up empty.

Okay, Gwen. Think.

Remembering Reggie's bet, she tried 1-2-3-4-5-6 followed by *password*, striking out both times. She scanned the edges of the monitor, where many Post-it Notes framed the screen. Most of them were reminders about lunch and dinner engagements, but one clearly listed Bitsie's email address, followed by a string of letters, symbols, and numbers.

"Is it really going to be that easy?"

Gwen carefully typed the password into the computer, the mouse hovering over the enter button for at least ten seconds before she tried clicking it. The screen turned black for a second before Bitsie's desktop popped up, fully unlocked.

Seriously? Gwen started to laugh. Now she really hoped that bet had been for five bucks, or else she owed Reggie big time.

Gwen leaned closer to the monitor, opening the files on the desktop one by one. Given the woman was in charge of a charitable foundation with a considerable budget, there were shockingly few folders. Not for the first time, Gwen wondered how much actual work the woman accomplished. From what she'd seen, the answer was not much. But Gwen did know that all the financial transactions originated from this computer, so she continued her search.

Where would Gwen put records of money laundering if she were director of this organization?

Sadly, unlike with the password, Gwen didn't find a folder marked "white collar crimes."

Gwen blew out a breath in frustration, ready to call it quits. "I don't even know what I'm looking for."

"What was that?"

Gwen jumped. "Bitsie! What are you doing here?"

The woman was dressed for an afternoon at the country club, her oversized sunglasses sitting high on her head. Gwen was surprised she didn't still have them covering her eyes. After all that tequila, she must've had a killer headache.

"Oh, hey. It's just you." Bitsie giggled like a school girl. "Did Reginald make you come in today, too? Figures. He thinks I'm a ditz."

"I'm sure he doesn't think that about you." In truth, Gwen was certain he did, but it seemed impolite to agree.

"I'm glad you're here to help," the woman confessed. "Reginald can be such a bear about money, and I hate moving large sums on my own. Did he walk you through the process for making the transfers?"

"Uh, he said you would." Gwen's heart nearly exploded in her chest as she improvised a response.

"Just like a man, right? Of course, my husband always takes care of the money at home." Bitsie giggled again. She leaned over Gwen's shoulder, not seeming to register that the computer was unlocked, or that Gwen had no business sitting where she was. "Alrighty, then. First, you open this." Bitsie pointed to one of the icons on the computer. "This is the shortcut to the Foundation's bank account."

When the woman clicked on it, the eye watering sum that showed up on the dashboard made Gwen want to scream. It was one thing if it had all been destined for a worthy cause, but Simon Wycth was the very opposite of that.

"We need to move ten to this account number." Bitsie pointed to a string of numbers on one of the Post-it Notes.

Gwen stared in stunned silence at the banking information that sat right out in the open for anyone to see. "Is that it?"

"Oh, no," Bitsie answered in a singsong voice. "We have to move it to three more accounts. It takes time because you have to wait for the money to arrive. Banking is very complicated."

Yes, when it's illegal.

"Now then. We have to get the ball rolling."

"Uh-huh." Gwen's stomach soured as she prepared to watch any number of international laws being violated. "Is this for that refugee place in East Hampton?"

"No, that was a few months ago. This is for those poor children in the orphanage in Uganda."

Gwen saw red because it was one of the very same causes Simon had used on her to get her to believe he and Kensington Datalytics were the good guys. She'd been a fool, an easy target with a bleeding heart who couldn't stand to see suffering in the world. That she'd been charmed by a dapper man with a British accent and impeccable taste was mortifying.

Gwen forced her attention back to what Bitsie was doing, her cheeks burning. "So you move the money from this account, to which one?"

"To this one." Bitsie pointed to a different note.

"Do you mind if I write this down? I don't want to mess this up."

"Of course, dear. You can never be too careful." The director offered her a cheerful smile. "Knowing Reginald trusts you puts my mind at ease. I don't like having anything to do with the accounts."

"Just to be clear, when you say ten, you mean ten million

dollars?" Gwen swallowed as the other woman nodded like it was commonplace. "Is it always so much?"

"This is a fairly large grant," Bitsie conceded. "A bit unusual, I guess. But think of all the kids we're saving. Don't you hate the thought of kids going without food? Reginald is such a saint to do all he does."

Gwen tried not to think about the sick games the so-called saint had made his children play to earn their breakfast when they were young. She cringed inwardly as the woman clamped a hand on her shoulder. It was terribly uncomfortable, especially with several massive rocks adding to the weight, but it wasn't like Gwen could say much when she was literally being given step-by-step instructions for how the charity helped Reginald Hawkins commit wire fraud.

"You know what?" Gwen stopped the director before she could finalize what she was doing. "How about I take care of all this so you can go home?"

Bitsie straightened, a look of pure relief on her face. "Can I leave you to it? Carol's granddaughter is having a baby shower. I'd hate to be late."

"Sure thing, boss." Gwen flashed what she hoped was a winning smile. "I've got this handled."

As Bitsie flew out of the office, Gwen couldn't help noting that for an older woman, she could sure move fast when she was trying to avoid actual work. Left on her own, Gwen began transferring all of the information to a notebook—but definitely not finalizing any money transfers that would almost certainly lead to jail time if discovered. Routing numbers, accounts, transaction records. She finally had the smoking gun she needed to bring this nightmare to an end.

CHAPTER TWENTY-THREE

"A re we fucked?" Reggie studied Val's face, trying to read the deeply etched lines like she was reading tea leaves in the bottom of a cup. "We're fucked, aren't we?"

It was twenty-two minutes before two in the afternoon, and the boardroom at Hawks Corp headquarters remained mostly empty as the various members of the board attempted to make their way into the city from the Hawkins compound in whatever way they could. At the moment, with Tom, Dick, and Harry in attendance, plus Val, Reggie, and Trevor, they not only lacked the seven yes votes needed for victory, they didn't even have enough for a quorum.

"There's plenty of time yet." Val squeezed Reggie's hand. "Remember to breathe. The stakes are high, but we can't let fear consume us."

Reggie scoffed. "Easy for you to say. You're not the one who's going to end up dead if this goes wrong."

The door to the conference room opened, and Stephanie stumbled in, her giant mommy bag weighing down her shoulder. Why she always carried the thing was a mystery.

The woman employed multiple nannies, and Baby D wasn't even with her today.

But Reggie sensed that the designer diaper bag was an intrinsic part of her sister's identity. Mother, daughter, and wife. These were the roles that defined her, which is why her arrival was not great news. Unlike Trevor and Reggie, Stephanie would never go against their father's wishes.

Stephanie plunked her bag on the table before throwing herself into the seat across from Reggie. "I can't believe you people. How can you betray Dad like this?"

"It's for Dad's own good, and ours too." Reggie projected as much calm as she could. "He's been lying to us, and he's lying to himself if he thinks he can continue to keep secrets from the shareholders. It's my duty as an executive of Hawks Corp to act."

"Bullshit." Stephanie stared daggers at Reggie. "I have no idea what secrets you think Dad is keeping, but I have children, and if they did this to me, it'd kill me."

"It's complicated," Reggie began, pausing as Trevor entered the room, a box of candy from the break room vending machine clutched in one hand and a soda in the other, looking more like a kid on the way to a movie than a son about to commit corporate patricide. "Trev, explain to your sister, please."

Trevor flashed his charming smile at Stephanie and took a seat beside Reggie, setting down the candy and soda on the table. "Steph, listen. We're not trying to hurt Dad. But we can't pretend like everything's fine when it's not. We just want him to step down and focus on his health. The company needs a leader who can be fully present and make clear decisions."

"In other words, you," Stephanie shot back, assuming, as

most of the board members likely would, that Trevor would take control. "Trevor as CEO and Reggie as second in command. How convenient."

"This isn't about me or Trevor, or you for that matter," Reggie said. "It's about the company and its shareholders. If we don't take action now, it could lead to the downfall of Hawks Corp."

Stephanie shook her head. "You're all insane. Dad has devoted his entire life to this company. This is his legacy. He's not just going to give it up because you say he should."

Reggie leaned forward, her voice low and measured. "Stephanie, you don't understand. Dad isn't just risking his legacy. He's risking his life. He's almost eighty, and he's already had one brush with cancer."

"And he beat it. He's as healthy as a horse now." Stephanie tilted her chin defiantly. "He's Dad. That's what he does."

"He's human," Reggie countered. "What if he dies? Can you live with that on your conscience?"

Stephanie shut her eyes as if to block Reggie's question from her consciousness. "Without Dad at the helm, Hawks Corp stock takes a nosedive. How are Brandon and I going to raise four kids if all our money is gone?"

Reggie resisted the urge to roll her eyes. "All your money won't be gone."

"More of mine will be than yours." Stephanie's jaw clenched. "My mother didn't get me a Hamptons cottage in her divorce, don't forget. But why would you care? I know I've always been beneath you two. Just the daughter of the help, and you never let me forget it."

Reggie sucked in a breath at this unexpected accusation.

"What are you talking about? Trevor and I have never treated you that way."

"Like hell." Stephanie's eyes flashed. "You've never included me in anything. Ever since we were kids, when you two played the newspaper game every morning with Dad but not me. No one ever let me play. But don't worry. Dad told me why. He said you didn't want to be friends with your nanny's daughter. You're both just mean."

"Are you fucking serious right now with this?" Reggie trembled with emotions too disparate to identify. Had her father been playing all three of his children against each other this whole time?

"You've got it wrong, Steph." Trevor spoke in such a calm voice it was terrifying. "Dad wasn't playing a game with us. He made Reggie and me compete against each other every day for breakfast."

"Breakfast?" Stephanie repeated the word but seemed not to comprehend its meaning.

"Breakfast," Reggie confirmed. "The loser went to school hungry. It wasn't that we thought you were beneath us. Not ever. We didn't want you to have to deal with his sick games."

"I didn't—" Stephanie's expression was one of shock and disbelief as comprehension of this revised version of her childhood memories started to sink in.

"Carl and your father have arrived." Val bowed her head, her shoulders folding inward. "They're on their way up along with the final four members of the board."

"Lucky thirteen." Reggie swallowed, her heart sinking as she did the math. "Looks like we'll have a full house today."

That all four of the remaining members were heading up as part of her father's entourage did not bode well. One look at Val's face said she realized it, too. With thirteen in attendance, they needed seven votes to remove her father as CEO. By the looks of it, they only had six.

The boardroom door swung open. A sense of dread washed over Reggie as her father, her uncle, and the final four board members—Mark Light, Jesse Creaven, Kalid Bagheri, and Antony Fox—made their way into the room. As her father swaggered to his seat, the posse's postures were tense and rigid, their faces set in determined scowls. It was obvious that her father's soldiers were ready to tear Reggie and Val to shreds.

"You've really done it this time, haven't you?" Reginald's face darkened as he shifted his gaze between Reggie and Val. "You think you can take my life's work from me without a fight? I'm sure you understand the penalty for traitors. But if not, you'll soon find out."

Reggie felt her stomach churn as the situation escalated. It was clear their father had every intention of inflicting the most harm possible on anyone who crossed him. Not that she hadn't expected it, but even knowing how ill he was, his looming presence was as larger-than-life as ever.

"I think we should get this farce over with and vote now." Reginald met his eldest's eyes before shifting to her twin. "Or do my children want to further humiliate themselves in front of the entire board with whatever cockamamie bullshit they've invented to drag us all here in the middle of our holiday?"

"I think we should hear the facts," Val bravely waded in.

"Truth!" Her father slammed a fist onto the table, making the solid wood jump.

"You want truth?" Reggie spoke directly to the board

members who held her future in their hands. "How about explaining that your cancer's back, Dad?"

"For real?" Stephanie gasped. It was clear she'd thought Reggie's earlier mention of it had been hypothetical.

"How many of you knew that?" Reggie continued, as guilt twisted in her heart at what this revelation must be doing to her sister. "He's known for months, but it appears he never disclosed it to anyone on the board, in direct violation of company policy."

"That's a lie," Reginald declared. "And even if it wasn't, I'm entitled to privacy."

Reggie's uncle Carl turned to his brother, a flicker of doubt playing across his face. "Is it a lie?"

Reggie's father crossed his arms. "I don't have to answer that."

"You do if your cancer is back because we all know what it means after the last time," Carl pushed back.

"You're a doctor now, Carl?" Reginald demanded with a sneer. "You know what that means? I guess you must be God."

"How much time do you have left?" Carl wasn't going to let his brother's ridicule cow him.

"How much time do you have left?" Her father countered defiantly. He turned to Val. "And, you? Do you know how much?"

"I don't have cancer," Val said in an even tone. "Nor do I run this company, thanks to our misogynistic father."

"Are you dying, Dad?" Stephanie's voice wavered.

"He's beat it before. There's no reason to think he won't again." Mark Light, one board member Reggie was certain would never turn on her father, spoke with total calm.

The sentiment sparked some murmuring within the room, not all of which sounded convinced.

"An unsubstantiated cancer scare." Reginald chuckled, a hard glint of meanness beneath the surface. "Is that all you have? Pathetic. I know more about this company than all of you combined. No one here can fill my shoes."

"You living forever?" Val shot back. "You have to listen to reason. We just want what's best for the company."

Reginald's eyes burned with fury. "What's best for the company? You mean what's best for you, Val, the neglected eldest daughter. I should've known you'd team up with Reggie to overthrow me. You've always been selfish, always thinking about your own ambitions when our father chose me to lead. I won't let you destroy what I've built. Not while I'm still breathing."

"Dad, please," Stephanie pleaded, her voice shaking. "You need to take care of yourself."

"Who asked for your opinion?" Reginald's eyes narrowed as he regarded his younger daughter with open contempt. There was no mistaking the devastating pain in Stephanie's eyes as she sank back into her chair like a wounded puppy.

"I don't see any need for rash action," Mark said, clearly gearing up to make his case for the status quo. "I suggest we take a simple vote to firm up the succession plan today and nothing more. Reginald continues as CEO, and we make an official statement that Trevor is the next in line. That should calm any uneasiness in the market and stabilize the share price."

There was a deathly silence in the room as the board members considered this suggestion. Reggie's mind whirred. If they were unmoved by the return of her father's illness, this was the moment she needed to drop the bomb about Trevor's secret. But could she really do it now that rubber was hitting the road? Trevor had no idea what she intended, and the betrayal would be impossible for him to forgive.

Trevor stood, meeting her eye, before announcing in a loud voice, "I can't go along with that."

Realizing what her brother was about to do, Reggie put a hand on his arm. "Don't. It's not worth it."

"I have to, Reg."

"You'll ruin your future. I can't let you, especially since it's all my fault."

"What's your fault?" Trevor turned to face her full on. "What do you think you did?"

"I dared you to jump off the yacht. What happened to you is on me." Reggie buried her face in her hands, shame engulfing her.

Trevor sank back into his chair and placed a hand on Reggie's shoulder. "Are you telling me this entire time, you've blamed yourself for my accident?"

"What accident?" This time it was Kalid who spoke up, placing both palms on the table. "Will someone explain what's going on with this company?"

Trevor sat up straight, determination hardening his features. "Seven years ago, I suffered a traumatic brain injury after a swimming accident."

There was a general intake of breath as those outside the immediate family exchanged shocked and troubled expressions.

"Because I teased you and dared you to jump." Reggie blinked back hot tears as her brother vehemently shook his head.

"Reggie—I didn't jump because you dared me. I did it

because of him." Trevor pointed at their dad, and Reggie's heart clenched. "He was a level up, watching us. When you laughed because I didn't want to jump and then dove in—" Trevor gave a slight cough, like he was about to choke on his embarrassment. "If you could picture the anger and disappointment in Dad's eyes."

There was no need to picture it. Their father wore the same expression now, and from his complete lack of argument, Reggie knew this version of events was true.

"You let me blame myself this entire time, knowing it was you?" Reggie's eyes narrowed as she took in her father's smug face.

"You can't trust anything my idiot son says," Reginald spat. "Did you not hear what he said? He's brain damaged. Fucking noodles for brains."

"Then why were you planning to put Trevor in charge?" Mark asked, motioning for her father to respond and still seeming to expect a rational explanation to emerge.

"I don't have to explain anything to you," Reginald bellowed.

"Actually, you do," Antony said, speaking up for the first time. "You've been keeping all of us in the dark about serious issues, putting this entire company in jeopardy."

Ignoring the others, Reggie's father stared daggers at her. "You want my job? You don't even know what you're asking to take over. Polyphemus will eat you alive. I hope you look good in orange. At least you'll be among your own kind in prison. You can have as many girlfriends as you'd like."

"Wait. What are you talking about?" Stephanie demanded, looking more enraged now than Reggie had seen her, though the reason was unclear. "Did you say someone's going to jail because of Polyphemus? That's the name of the account you were going to give Brandon."

"Jesus, Dad." Reggie shook her head as she realized the man had been prepared to use his own son-in-law as a shield for his crimes. "Is there anyone you're not willing to fuck over? The man's got kids. You should know this. They're your grandkids."

"This isn't the moment for posturing and fretting," her father jeered. "This company needs real leadership. You can't do it. Trevor and Stephanie are lost causes. Only I can maintain control! Take me away, and I'll be sure to wreak havoc on all of you! Can you comprehend what I'm saying? Total destruction!"

"I think I've heard enough," Val said, her voice filling the room. "It's time to bring this matter to a vote."

"By all means, everyone can vote now. Hurry it up. I have dinner plans." As her father bared his too white teeth, Reggie realized they were dentures.

A burst of sadness stilled her heart.

He was an old man and probably dying. Here she was, battling him for the soul of the family company when she should have been finding a way to reconcile their differences while they still had time. But he'd left her no choice.

"Those in favor of removing Reginald Hawkins as CEO of Hawks Corp and replacing him with Regina Hawkins, please raise your hands," Val instructed.

Six hands went up around the room, including Reggie's own. Her heart sank. After all that had been revealed, not a single one of the others had changed their minds.

"Reginald, you know I've admired you all of my life." Mark steepled his fingers. "You've accomplished more than any of us in the room has done. You've got my vote."

Reggie's chest clenched. She'd lost, and her father had won. But just as her father's face puckered to gloat over his victory in earnest, a seventh hand joined them.

"I'm sorry, Dad." Stephanie's arm shook, but she kept it raised high all the same. "I'm with my brother and sister on this one."

"I'm surrounded by Judases. You have no idea what you've done. The first call I'm going to make is to the feds. Do you think my fingerprints are on this?" Reginald wheeled around to point a finger at his brother Carl's face. "Talk some sense into them, man!"

Rattled, Uncle Carl coughed, pushed his chair back and stared at the ground. But he didn't say a word in his brother's defense.

"Fuck all of you. Fuck you." Her father stumbled out of the room like a wounded rhino. "Fuck you."

Thunderstruck, no one spoke for many seconds, perhaps fearful Reginald Hawkins would burst into the room with another tirade. After it became apparent he was gone for good, the remaining board members quietly congratulated Reggie before filing out of the room, looking worse for the wear.

"You okay?" Trevor asked.

"I don't know what I am," Reggie admitted. "But I need our legal team ready to meet with me, like yesterday."

Trevor nodded. "Let me make some calls."

"I had no idea, Reg. No idea." Stephanie rose, shaking from head to toe.

"I'm proud of you, li'l sis." Overwhelmed by the courage Stephanie had shown, Reggie pulled her into a long, heartfelt embrace.

Eventually, Val was the last one in the room. "You did it, kiddo."

Reggie's smile did little to warm her insides. She'd done it, all right. But as she returned to her office in what should have been triumph, the real threat of legal consequences from her father's mess loomed ahead.

"Reggie!" A short time after the meeting had ended, Gwen bounded into Reggie's office. "How'd it go?"

"You're talking to the new CEO of Hawks Corp." Despite her overwhelming worry, Reggie's spirits lifted at the sight of the woman, though there was no disguising the heaviness in her tone.

Gwen pressed her lips together, a look of understanding on her face. "How does it feel to be put in charge of the Hindenburg?"

"Surreal. How did things go on your end?"

"I owe you five bucks."

A chuckle escaped Reggie's lips as she pieced together what Gwen meant. "Was it 1-2-3-4-5-6?"

"No. You may not believe this, but Bitsie walked me through the entire money laundering process and gave me the bank account numbers, which are on Post-it Notes on her fucking monitor for all to see. Along with her password. She's expecting me to transfer ten million dollars for her today."

"She didn't do it herself?"

"No. I'm not sure who Carol is, but her daughter has a baby shower. Bitsie didn't want to be late." Gwen rolled her eyes.

Reggie couldn't blame her. She was just as fed up with rich assholes. She'd had her fill for a lifetime. "Please tell me you didn't actually move any money."

"Of course not. Unlike my boss, I have a brain and a healthy desire to stay out of jail."

"Good." Reggie paused. "I don't want to worry you, but I think the Feds are getting involved. We may be heading to Washington soon."

"Washington? I know it was to be expected, but..."

"But we didn't expect it quite yet," Reggie finished for her. "I know. But we have to be prepared for anything that comes our way. Dad wants retribution, and that means taking everyone out. He's probably turning me in right now."

Gwen nodded, her brow furrowed in concern. "Do you think your father will really call the Feds about his own company? His own family?"

Reggie let out a deep sigh. "I wouldn't put it past him. He's always been willing to do whatever it takes to get ahead, even if it means hurting those closest to him."

"That's fucked up," Gwen muttered.

"It's the Hawkins family way." Reggie's words oozed bitterness. "I imagine you're just as relieved not to have gotten engaged to me last night, all things considered."

It was at that moment that Reggie recognized the true source of the weight in her chest. Now that she was CEO and no one would challenge her for it, her plan was complete. There was no longer an excuse to make Gwen agree to an engagement, let alone actually getting married. And if the woman had the sense God gave a flea, she'd run as far from the Hawkins family as quickly as she could.

CHAPTER TWENTY-FOUR

The mugginess of a late July morning in Washington, DC gave way to frigid air-conditioning as Gwen followed Reggie into the waiting car. This would be the second one they'd ridden in since their arrival at Dulles International Airport. Like the first, it was a dark sedan with tinted windows, the kind used by visiting diplomats and, as it turned out, people being escorted by federal agents to meetings in undisclosed locations within the nation's capital.

Gwen could've gone her whole life without knowing that, and she felt certain as she slid in beside Reggie that her companion felt the same.

"Nearly there now." Reggie squeezed Gwen's thigh.

"Are you sure we won't have to change cars again?" Leaning far to one side, Gwen rested her head against Reggie's shoulder. "Just getting to this appointment is shining a bright light on some serious mistakes in my life."

Gwen closed her eyes, concentrating on the bumps in the road. They'd flown in early that morning—by private jet for the sake of Reggie's sanity, but it still wasn't a restful journey. According to Reggie, Dwight's campaign was dead in the water, so there was no longer a concern for appearances, but the hour and twenty-nine-minute flying time was hardly enough to knock Reggie out with sleeping pills. Not if she wanted a clear head for a full day of questioning, and Gwen was counting on Reggie to help navigate these tricky waters.

Or a *conversation*, as the government representative had phrased it when directing both Gwen and Reggie to clear their calendars completely. Which branch or office of the government was being represented had been left troublingly vague, but the stable of company lawyers had cautioned that the details weren't something to concern them, and that in any case, compliance wasn't really optional.

"No one can know where we're going or who we're meeting," Reggie reminded Gwen, though it seemed this was meant to soothe Reggie's own nerves given the way her eyes flickered. "That's what will keep us safe, and ensure the meeting remains a secret. If it makes you feel better, the party we'll be meeting today is jumping through the same hoops."

When they'd left the airport, neither they nor their driver had known their destination. Only after the car was in motion did a call come with a randomly selected location. A second driver was tasked to take them from this spot— which turned out to be a roadside diner—to the secure site for their meeting. This was to make it more difficult for reporters to track where they were. Needless to say, all cell phones had been left behind.

"All the times in the past year when I've pictured this day, I never imagined this much subterfuge," Gwen admitted, her stomach tightening. "Will our lives ever be normal again after this?"

"Define normal," Reggie muttered. "With a successful coup completed, my family's charity on shaky legal ground, and my father on death's doorstep, I'm hard-pressed to understand the meaning of the word."

Gwen turned her head to face Reggie. "This will take some getting used to on my end because you and your family don't really do normal."

"They might not, but I do. Or try. Mine's just... different." Reggie nudged Gwen's side with an elbow. "It wasn't that long ago you wanted to run away to an island."

"I did." Gwen gave a trembling laugh, hinting at how nervous she was beneath her external calm. She'd been dreading this day for so long now. While she wanted to get it done, actually being in the car to accomplish that—it was too much.

"Past tense?" Reggie boosted her eyebrows. "Is it the island you've decided against or me?"

"Neither. I'd love to disappear to an island with you right now. But is that your idea of normal?"

"Sure. When we're done with all this today, I'll call the pilot to fuel up the jet."

"Yeah, that's totally normal." Gwen laughed and buoyed with relief that Reggie was still at her side despite their original plan having been pulverized by one complication after another. They hadn't discussed it yet, but Reggie had no need of her as a fake wife any longer. Gwen was afraid to bring it up. For all that she felt their relationship was real, she couldn't forget that for so long, Reggie had considered all human interactions to be transactional.

Reggie threaded her fingers with Gwen's, lifting Gwen's

hand to her lips. "Maybe not today, but when this is behind us, you tell me where. I'll take you anywhere you want to go."

The promise brought a flutter of hope to Gwen's chest. Maybe in this time they'd been together, Reggie had truly changed her tune. Gwen prayed it was so.

"Ladies, we're nearly there." The driver motioned to a parking structure looming in the distance. "There shouldn't be any reporters after the precautions we've taken, but to be safe, I suggest turning your heads away from the windows as we approach the garage.

They did as they were asked, and after the car circled down several levels, putting them deep below ground, they exited the car and were taken to an elevator. Instead of bringing them up, they descended.

"How far down do you think we are?" Gwen asked in a whisper, but Reggie shrugged, and the agent who accompanied them didn't say.

A man in a black suit waited in the corridor when they exited the elevator. They were ushered down a long, tile-lined hallway and into a room with only a table and four chairs.

"Have a seat," the man in the suit said. He left without additional directions or explanation.

"Friendly dude." Gwen took a seat, wringing her hands.

Reggie covered Gwen's hands with her own, holding them until the fingers went still before moving them to Gwen's lap. "It's going to be okay."

"I wish I'd never met Simon Wyeth." Gwen said the man's name like a curse.

"If you hadn't," Reggie pointed out, "we wouldn't have met."

"Are you sure?" Gwen gave her a searching look, the type she hoped Reggie could feel in the deepest parts of her. "It's hard not to think we would have, no matter what. Maybe we would have bumped into each other in a pub in London."

Reggie seemed about to speak, but the door opened. Another man entered, also dressed in a black suit. The theme song to the movie *Men in Black* played in Gwen's mind, and it was everything she could do not to ask if this place was hiding extraterrestrials.

"Good afternoon," the man said, sounding pleasant enough for whatever brand of spook he no doubt was.

Reggie dipped her head in greeting, and Gwen did the same. Neither of them seemed too keen to start talking unless they had to.

The man took a seat, folding his hands on the table. "All three of us have found ourselves in quite the pickle."

"All three?" Gwen raised an eyebrow, doubting this assessment immensely. Only one of them was on the interrogator's side of the table, and it wasn't Reggie or Gwen.

"I'm sure you know where things have gone south for you," he said with a chuckle that Gwen didn't entirely appreciate, "so I won't dwell on that just yet. Instead, I'm going to start with a little hypothetical. That okay?"

Again, Reggie and Gwen nodded. Gwen had a feeling the word hypothetical was being used ironically.

"You don't talk much," the agent said. "I like that."

"Do we need lawyers?" Gwen piped up, increasingly aware of just how much trouble she might be in. She was a whistleblower, sure, but that didn't mean they wouldn't find an excuse to pin blame on her, too. As coincidences went, unwittingly going to work for the non-profit agency that was laundering money for her former employer was a most unfortunate one.

The man pursed his lips. "Do you want your lawyers for a casual conversation?"

Gwen started to speak, but Reggie tapped her leg as a reminder this had already been cleared by the best legal minds money could buy. Or so Reggie kept saying.

"We're fine," Reggie said.

"Very good. So, hypothetically, let's say there were rumors of a certain product, like a piece of spyware made by a foreign company, perhaps. And people were saying this thing could revolutionize the surveillance game, make it easier to find terrorists and bad actors throughout the world."

"And obliterate personal privacy," Reggie added.

"That too," the agent conceded. "Now, it would be the official position of the United States of America that such a program didn't exist. That, in fact, it shouldn't exist. And that if by any chance it turned out it did exist, naturally the US government would never purchase, fund, use, or allow such a dangerous surveillance tool."

"Uh-huh." Gwen knew there was a *but* coming.

"However, we have three things causing us some problems. Here"—he made an X on the table with his finger—"is an investigative journalist writing an in-depth article that leaves little room to doubt the existence of the program. Over here"—he made another X—"are some text messages that most certainly could not have been obtained if such a product was not both real and also being made available for a scope that far exceeded the original intent of catching bad guys. And finally," this X was made much larger than the others, "we have the money trail you helpfully supplied us, which proves without a doubt that the Hawkins Foundation funneled money through back channels to Kensington Datalyics, who then poured that money into something called the Polyphemus project."

"I feel like things just became a lot less hypothetical," Reggie remarked.

The agent responded with a dry laugh. "Yes, and here's where it gets tricky. The United States government knows nothing about Polyphemus, so it's impossible that a US company could have contributed money toward it, and highly inconvenient to prosecute anyone for doing something that couldn't have happened. You see?"

"But all the evidence I gave Solène!" Gwen exclaimed. "The bank transactions!"

The man smiled, cold and hard. "Are, as I said, a huge problem. You see, if Polyphemus exists, we would, naturally, have to oppose it. We would never infringe on the constitutionally guaranteed rights of any citizen. But it's possible that some branches of the government are unaware of this memo."

"He's saying that government spies are already having a field day with Polyphemus," Reggie translated. "Isn't that right?"

"I'm sure I have no idea, but you see the pickle I'm in."

"I do." Reggie kept a hand on Gwen's leg, pressing it like that was the off switch to keep her from saying anything. From the faint smile on her lips, Reggie seemed oddly pleased with the direction this conversation was going while Gwen's mind continued to spin. But she knew one thing. She could trust Reggie. If Reggie wasn't concerned, there was a good reason for it, and Gwen would have to wait and see what it was.

"Our preferred position would be that there was no such thing as the Polyphemus Project," the agent said, and Gwen thought she detected a touch of wistfulness for the simplicity of this option.

"Are you going to stop Solène's article from publishing?" Gwen's legs tensed, and she found herself on the verge of bolting out of her chair at this possibility.

"We would never interfere with a free press. We protect rights."

Gwen did her best to hold in a snort, ending up sounding like she was sneezing.

"Bless you," the agent said. "As I was saying, that's our preferred position, but we can't always get what we want. Let me state again, we would never interfere with journalists. Freedom of the press is a cornerstone of American Democracy."

It was Reggie's turn to stifle a snort.

"Bless you," Gwen deadpanned.

The man continued, "This leaves us with our second-best option. This type of spyware is only used against terrorists and drug lords. It's irresponsible of any in the press to give the story any oxygen because it'll harm millions of innocent people. We need ways to fight the bad guys."

"What's your definition of a bad guy?" Gwen was grinding her teeth so hard she was certain Reggie could hear it.

"Terrorists and drug lords, ma'am." He turned to Reggie. "Surely, *you* understand what I'm saying, Ms. Hawkins."

"I do."

"I don't." Gwen spoke to Reggie, her tone demanding an explanation. "What's the subtext I'm missing?"

"He means the heads of news organizations all over the country, probably the world, are having meetings much like this one right now, being given subtle guidance as to how much air to give this Polyphemus story when it comes out."

"The best way to put out a fire is to deprive it of oxygen." The man refolded his hands on the table.

"Why should we agree to this?" Gwen demanded to know. "I've taken considerable personal risk to bring this information to light. Hawks Corp controls most of the country's news outlets. It seems to me the call on how much air this gets is up to her."

"Perhaps. But a lot of laws have been broken." The man drew a deep breath. "Reginald Hawkins—"

"I want to keep him out of this." The words were out of Gwen's mouth before she realized what she was saying. It was surprising even to her, but the more she'd thought about it, the less she wanted to see Reginald brought any lower than he already was. Not for his sake, but for Reggie's. As sweet as it would be to see him punished for what he'd done to thousands of people like Gwen's grandfather, she couldn't bear how much it would cause Reggie to suffer.

"Gwen," Reggie said in a gentle but scolding tone. "You can't protect him, and you certainly can't sacrifice yourself."

"Your father's dying." Gwen noted the way the agent's eyes widened a bit, just enough to confirm this was something the government didn't know. "It's true. I swear. There's little doubt he will be gone before this goes to trial, and under the circumstances, I don't see the benefit of making an old man spend his last months in prison, no matter how repugnant I might personally find him to be. Do you?"

"We don't want to put anyone in jail." There was a hint of compassion in the agent's tone that nearly brought a tear to Gwen's eye. "Frankly, we don't want this to get to that level, that the public would even feel the need for that to happen. If you see what I'm saying."

"I think I do," Reggie said calmly. "What do I need to do?"

"As your companion pointed out a moment ago, Hawks Corp controls the vast majority of this country's news media. Television, newspapers, cable. That's a powerful organization. One might say too much power to be in the hands of one family."

"What does that mean?" Gwen demanded of Reggie. "I'd like for you to spell it out."

Reggie gave Gwen an *everything is okay* look, whispering, "It's fine. We have to play the game. That's all."

"Game?" Gwen's brow creased as she hoped for more of an explanation. She didn't like the sound of games. It was too much like something Reggie's father would say. But Reggie had already turned her attention back to the agent.

"What would you say if I told you I'm working on a plan to cleave Hawks News from the rest of the organization?" Reggie sat back, waiting for the agent's reaction.

"Is that right?" It was the first time the man's smile reached his eyes. "I'd say it's nothing less than what I would expect of Reginald Hawkins' daughter. If I might say so, ma'am, aside from your father's less than legal activities, I've always admired him. He has a good head for business."

Gwen tensed, not liking where this conversation had gone. Was the agent suggesting Reggie and her father were alike? The similarities were there, for sure, but Gwen had hoped Reggie had grown beyond them. Maybe this was a mistake to believe. Given what Gwen knew of Reginald, Reggie being a chip off the old block was a terrifying thought.

"He's a ruthless S.O.B.," Reggie corrected. "But I have learned a lot from him. Enough to know when something is more valuable scrapped and sold for parts."

Gwen's lips thinned, forming a hard line. She liked the sound of this even less than before. Reggie had always seemed to fear turning into her father. Was she now embracing it?

"Parceling off your company's news division would be music to many people's ears," the agent said with an approving nod.

"And earn a pretty penny in the process," Reggie added.

Gwen's eyes widened. "But what about the Spotlight deal? If you sell off the news along with the entertainment assets, your family business will cease to exist. Even I can't expect that, as much as I've hated Hawks Corp all these years. Surely, the government can't expect it, either."

"The Spotlight deal fell apart the minute Phoenix Media found out my father had been forced out," Reggie explained, seeming not half as riled up over any of this as Gwen was. This was one of those times when the ice that sometimes seemed to flow through Reggie's veins was an asset, even if it sent a shiver down Gwen's spine. "That puts us back to square one when it comes to negotiating a deal. Hawks News is a toxic asset as a whole, but it has value in its parts."

"But, your father—"

Reggie held up a hand to stop Gwen's protest. "My father is no longer in control. I am. I'd rather turn my focus to a worthier legacy for the Hawkins family name. Besides, I do believe that's the only option that keeps every member of my family on the preferred side of the prison bars. And makes them each a few bil richer."

The mention of so much money felt ominous, but Gwen cast her worries aside for now. She needed to trust that Reggie was doing this for the right reasons. After a moment of deliberation, Gwen nodded, turning to the agent. "If that's what she wants, and it does what she said, I'm completely in agreement."

"Fantastic! This day is really looking up." The man slapped the tabletop before standing. "This has been very fruitful. We'll be in touch."

Reggie and Gwen stared at one another as the agent left the room.

"Is that it?" Gwen asked. "Will I need to testify? Do they want a statement?"

"I think that was it," Reggie said, her eyes registering Gwen's disappointment. "You were brave to be willing to do your part, but I think in the end, this was too big a deal to make a big deal over, if you get what I'm saying."

"Everyone gets away with it. No one gets punished," Gwen said, the weight of the day—not to mention the months of being on the run—pressing down on her. "Part of me can't help thinking it's not fair, but I can't bear the thought of you having to go through what it would take to bring your father to justice. And to be honest, I feel sorry for him in a way."

"Being pitied would feel as punishing to him as prison. At least Dwight's campaign is finished. Without funding from my father, Kensington's cash flow has dried up, and you can bet all eyes are on them now. As for Hawks News"

—Reggie smiled a little—"it's losing its teeth, thanks to you."

"No more poisoning America's grandfathers?" Gwen broke into a broad smile. "I guess that outcome will have to be good enough. At least for now."

"Not to mention growing the Hawkins family trust beyond even their loftiest dreams. Now there's a coup." Reggie stood, rolling her neck side to side, looking carefree. "I think it's time we went home to celebrate. You with me?"

"Sounds good," Gwen replied, only that wasn't exactly true. As much as she wanted to put all this behind her and focus on the future, she couldn't shake the feeling that something was still off.

Maybe it was the way Reggie was acting, supremely confident but also quietly calculating. Or maybe it was the mention of the Hawkins family legacy and the billions of dollars that would come with the sale of Hawks News. Whatever it was, Gwen couldn't ignore the nagging feeling deep in her soul that she was allowing herself to be blinded by the promise of riches without enough regard to her moral compass.

CHAPTER TWENTY-FIVE

"**A**re you sure you're ready for this?" Reggie stood next to Gwen at the imposing front door of her father's house.

"I feel like we had this conversation the last time we came here." Gwen offered a supportive smile. "The more important question is, are *you* ready for this?"

Reggie massaged the back of her neck. "I would rather tango with a leopard."

"I'll take that as a no," Gwen said with a chuckle. "But I might pay to watch you try to wrangle a wild cat around your father's upstairs ballroom."

"Kinda twisted, but I like it. Although, I think you've been around my family too much," Reggie said, unable to hold back a laugh. Gwen had that effect on her, even now, roughly fifteen minutes away from meeting her doom after Reginald Hawkins found out what she'd done in Washington. "Say, I was thinking. How would you like to tell my father I'm selling off his beloved news division? I'll pay you a million dollars."

"No, but I'll go in with you." Gwen looped her arm through Reggie's.

"What if I sweetened the deal with an ice cream from John's Drive-in?" Steeling her nerves, Reggie took a deep breath and rang the doorbell. "You know how much you love their chocolate raspberry truffle flavor."

"Tempting but still no."

A member of her father's security staff opened the door, gesturing them inside with a stern expression that made it clear he was fully aware of what had transpired at Hawks Corp and the role Reggie had played.

Unlike the last time they'd walked through the door, the house was mausoleum quiet.

Rovena was waiting on the second floor, wearing jeans and comfortable shoes, a lightweight sweater draped over her shoulders to ward off the chill from an overactive air-conditioner.

"He's in his office," she said. She'd lost her sharp edge now that the charade of her being Reginald's girlfriend was up. "Please try not to upset him. This is one of his better days, and he's feisty, looking for a fight."

"I'll keep that in mind." Reggie looked down the hallway, the patterned marble tiles seeming to stretch forever. This must have been how it felt for a condemned sailor moments before being forced to walk the plank. "Is he alone?"

"No one has been by in days," Rovena said.

The revelation brought with it a sense of sadness. Her father was old and dying. He should have been surrounded by family, enjoying the benefits of a life well-lived. Instead, he was certainly reaping what he had sown. Reggie wouldn't have wished this on her worst enemy, and Reginald Hawkins certainly wasn't that. For all the harm he'd caused, she couldn't even bring herself to hate him. He was her father, and deep down, she loved him despite herself.

"I guess it's now or never." Reggie hoped for the latter, but she was a Hawkins after all. Running scared wasn't in her blood.

Reggie and Gwen made their way to Reginald's office, where he sat in a leather chair, facing the wall of TVs. Every one of them was tuned to a different channel, each one muted. With nothing notable being reported, it seemed he'd done it out of habit more than anything. He turned as they entered the room, the leather of the chair crackling.

"What are you doing here? Come to twist the knife in my back even more?" His eyes narrowed with suspicion and anger.

"I came to talk to you, Dad." Reggie's voice was steady despite the fear that clutched at her insides. There was nothing more he could do to her, nothing he could threaten to take away, yet her terror was every much a reflex response as her father's need to stare at the flickering screens.

Reginald snorted. "Talk? After what you did in Washington? You must be out of your damn mind."

"I did what I had to do," Reggie said firmly. "You should be fucking grateful to me for it. And Gwen, too. It's mostly thanks to her you're not going to prison."

"You little bitch," Reginald spat, refusing so much as to look in Gwen's direction, as if her presence was a personal affront to him. "I should have known you were too weak to handle the responsibility of running this company. That's why Trevor was my choice for successor."

"If it was reversed and Trevor was standing in my shoes,

you'd be telling him you'd always wanted to name me." Reggie crossed her arms as she called her father's bluff. "I know how it is with you, how you operate. Finally, after forty-two years, I've figured out the rules to your twisted games."

"I didn't raise you to be this way," Reginald growled.

"You did, actually," Reggie shot back. "Never show fear. Always get the upper hand."

Reggie took her father in. How small he looked in the chair. He wasn't wearing his hair piece. Everything about him seemed shriveled and ancient. It had only been a month since the board meeting, but he looked like hell. It was hard to say which was killing him faster, cancer or retirement.

"Are you going to regale me on how you got this deal?" he demanded with a snarl. "Or are you here to gloat about how you've learned your lessons so well? Maybe you think you're better than me now."

"No, I'm here to tell you I'm selling off the news division. The one you've always used to push your political agenda." *The one you love so much you put it ahead of your own children,* she added silently.

Reginald's eyes widened. "What? You can't do that. It's the foundation of our family legacy."

"I already have," Reggie said coolly. "I've found a buyer who's willing to pay top dollar for it, no thanks to you and the illegal shit you've pulled."

"You can't do this, Regina," Reginald growled, his voice low and angry. "It's a mistake. You're ruining everything I've built."

"I'm saving our family's reputation from your bad decisions," Reggie said, her voice rising. "We deserve better.

Trev and me. Stephanie and Logan, and your little collection of alphabet grandchildren. We all deserve better than what you would've left behind. You can either accept this and try to repair your relationship with them all in the time you have left, or you can waste your precious breath lamenting something that's already gone."

"Who's the buyer?"

Apparently, Reggie's father was determined to do the latter, and all she could do was shake her head. "Phoenix Media, actually. Once they got over their initial snit about the share prices sinking and feeling left out in the cold, I was able to entice them back to the table."

"Don't be a fool," Reginald's voice boomed. "They're going to break the news up into pieces with a sledgehammer. It's why I never even considered letting them have it before."

"I'm counting on that, actually." Reggie reveled in her moment of triumph. While she'd agreed with Gwen that she didn't want to see her father in prison, that didn't mean he didn't deserve to be punished. "That news division is completely toxic. Not to mention, unless you're looking forward to an orange prison jumpsuit as much as you were looking forward to seeing me in one, this was the only way to clean up your mess to the satisfaction of the federal government."

"You've sold it all then. And sold your brother out, too." Her father's lip curved cruelly as he made another attempt at a kill shot. "I never thought you'd stab your own twin in the back."

"Of course, I wouldn't. Phoenix is carving out a role for Trevor at Spotlight, one that's perfectly suited to his strengths and abilities." Reggie swallowed back the bile that rose in her throat. "I once asked you to do that for me, remember? Turns out, it wasn't so hard. You just had to want to do it."

"What do you get out of all of this?" For once, her father appeared baffled, as if he couldn't comprehend what was going on. Was it the meds he was on, or was he truly that incapable of doing something for another person for the sake of making them happy?

"I get to start fresh. To build my life into something better, something that doesn't have your corruption and greed at its core. I get to make a difference in the world, without having to look over my shoulder at every turn, wondering if I'm going to be caught up in the next scandal you create." She held her father's gaze, unflinching, even as her heart pounded like a kettle drum. "I get to finally live up to my own potential, instead of being held back by your expectations and limitations. And I get to observe as you finally face the consequences of your actions by watching your legacy fall apart."

"You always were the smart one, Reggie. Others have wanted to, but you brought me down. I give you that much. You always knew how to play the game." He slumped back in his seat, admiration and defeat intermingling on his face. "From the moment you were born, when I stood in that hospital room and gave my name to you instead of your brother, I knew you had my killer instinct. Why do you think I've been so hard on you?"

"You were hard on me because you're a sadistic bastard who enjoys wielding power over others," Reggie informed him, speaking the full truth. "Don't try to turn it into some kind of *father knows best* narrative just because it suits you in retrospect."

"Fair enough," her father said with a smirk. "But don't forget I taught you everything you know. Without me, you wouldn't be where you are today."

Reggie shook her head. "No, Dad. Without you, I would have been better off. But you're right about one thing. You did teach me everything I know. And now, I'm going to use that knowledge to make a real difference in the world."

"Oh yeah? How?"

"The foundation. I know you gave it to me as a punishment, but I've grown to like it, and I think that's how I can make up for at least some of the mistakes I've made and the evil I've allowed to be done in my name."

"You sound like a damn idealist. Must be the influence of that girlfriend of yours." For the first time since they'd entered the room together, her father acknowledged Gwen's presence, though the look he gave her was anything but warm.

Reggie's jaw tightened as she saw Gwen take a slight step back. "You should be grateful for her influence. As I said before, she's the one who advocated for you with the Feds. Not me."

"Why would she do that? Money?"

Reggie stared at her father, feeling a mix of emotions. Part of her felt sorry for him, that he'd lived so many years with so little understanding of what mattered. But it was his own fault, and it was hard to feel pity for a man who had spent his life using and manipulating those around him the way he had.

"You remind her of her grandfather," Reggie finally said. "A man she still loves and pities, even though years of watching the monsters you brought to his TV screen every night turned him against her."

"Tell your girlfriend I don't need her pity."

"She's not just my girlfriend," Reggie said resolutely. "She's my partner. And like it or not, we're going to change the world together."

Reggie stood stock still, wishing more than anything she could catch a glimpse of Gwen's response. They hadn't discussed this plan yet. In fact, Reggie hadn't been a hundred percent certain until just now that this was the way she wanted to go. But it felt right, and she prayed Gwen thought so, too. But the last thing she was going to do was turn her back on her father to find out. What better way to end up with a knife in it?

"Change the world?" Her father chuckled darkly. "Good luck with that. You're going to realize soon enough that you can't change anything. The world is an unforgiving place, and you're just another powerless cog in the machine."

Reggie shook her head, unwilling to let her father's words get to her. "I refuse to believe that. People like you want the rest of us to think we're powerless, that nothing we do can make a difference. But I know better. Gwen's taught me better, shown me what can happen when people come together for a common goal. And I'm going to make the Hawkins Foundation a part of that change. Like it or not, Dad, that will be your legacy."

Her father sighed, his eyes closing as if he was too tired to argue anymore. "Fine, Regina. Do what you want. But don't come crying to me when you realize this is a pipe dream. You'll end up disappointed like all the other idealistic fools out there."

Reggie stood up from her seat, a sense of determination

filling her. "I don't need to keep listening to this. I've said what I came to say. I won't let you change my mind, and I won't let your mistakes define me or my future. I hope you find peace, Dad. I really do. And I forgive you."

With that, Reggie turned on her heel and walked out of the room, her heart pounding with a newfound sense of purpose. She felt a hand slip into hers and turned to see Gwen walking beside her as they approached the winding staircase. Instantly, a sense of peace filled her that had been sorely lacking when speaking with her father.

"Were you serious?" Gwen asked softly, hope beaming from her soft smile. "Do you really intend to put the family business behind you and work for the charitable foundation full time?"

Reggie nodded, a sense of amazement washing over her as she realized that was not only what she intended to do but what she wanted for her life more than anything else. "I have to replace Bitsie anyway. I can't exactly keep a director whose main skill is money laundering, even if it was unintentional. Actually, that makes it worse. And after dealing with her these past months, I'm not sure there's anyone I would trust enough to fill the role, other than me."

"What about your share of the family trust from this upcoming sale?" Gwen almost seemed to hold her breath as she waited for Reggie's response.

"I'm donating it all to the foundation, naturally," Reggie said firmly. "I was born with more privilege than anyone should enjoy, and I want to use the resources I've been given to make a meaningful impact in the world. I can't keep living with the guilt of being part of the problem. You're the one who taught me that, through the courage you showed in standing up to people like Simon Wyeth and my father."

Gwen squeezed her hand, her eyes flickering with admiration. "You're amazing, you know that? Most people talk a good game, but it's just that. Talk. I'll admit I sometimes worried you would be the same. I've never been happier to be wrong."

Reggie felt a blush creeping up her neck at the glowing words, but she hesitated to accept Gwen's compliment without pushing back. "I'm still more my father's daughter than I'd like to admit. I won't lie. It's not going to be easy to switch gears from earning billions to giving them away."

Gwen chuckled, the sound light and free. "That's what you have me for, right? The idealist, as your father would certainly call me."

"We make a good team."

"I might not have the head for running a multi-national business, but I do know a thing or two about people. And I know that you're capable of doing great things, Regina Hawkins. You have a heart of gold, and that's all that matters."

Reggie couldn't help but smile. "I want to build a charitable foundation the likes of which has never been seen before. I want to make a real impact, not throw my money at problems and hope they go away. I know I can do it with your help."

Gwen's eyes lit up, and she squeezed Reggie's hand tighter. "I want to be with you every step of the way. I have ideas. So many ideas."

"Why doesn't that surprise me?" Reggie laughed. "I feel like the prospect of you having ideas should scare the hell out of me, but oddly, it doesn't."

The two of them walked out of the house and onto Fifth Avenue, the sounds of the city filling their ears. Reggie felt a sense of excitement and fear, but more than anything, she felt alive. For the first time in a long time, she felt like she was on the right path, like she was making the choices that truly mattered.

She'd stood up to her father and come out victorious. But more important than that, she was finally free to be open about who she was and who she loved. After years of hiding this part of herself from the world, this was perhaps the most liberating thing of all.

"You know what the best part is going to be?" Reggie asked, a sly grin spreading across her lips as a vision formed in her head. "Going into Hawks News and personally delivering the word to Clark Maxwell that Hawks has been sold and he's out on his ass. Does that make me less of a good person in your estimation? Because I'm going to enjoy the fuck out of it."

"It makes me love you even more," Gwen assured her, eyes twinkling with the type of mischievousness that made Reggie weak in the knees. How had she gotten so lucky to have this incredible woman in her life?

"Thank you, Gwen." Reggie blinked but couldn't quite stop a single tear from escaping her eye and rolling down her cheek. "I don't think I could do any of this without you."

"Of course, you could," Gwen said, her tone gently teasing. "But why would you want to?"

Reggie laughed, joy overflowing. Unable to contain it, she leaned in to place a kiss on Gwen's lips. It started out a soft and gentle kiss, but the intensity of it soon built, taking Reggie's breath away.

She knew there were still so many obstacles ahead, so

many challenges to face, but in that moment, her heart swelled with love and happiness. She deepened the kiss, feeling a sense of hope and possibility that she hadn't felt in years. She was ready to take on the world, and with Gwen by her side, she knew she could do anything.

CHAPTER TWENTY-SIX

"I already explained." Standing at the entrance to the Zürich airport, Gwen crossed her arms and fixed Reggie with a look that dared her to complain some more. They had been through this argument a million times, and it had taken Gwen up to that morning to finally win. Now it seemed she'd declared victory too soon.

"But I hate flying commercial," Reggie complained some more, always willing to take Gwen up on a dare. "I've just completed a sale of the Hawkins media empire for a record-breaking, eye-wateringly large sum of money. What harm would one little hop across the pond in the PJ do? We could have it fueled up and ready in a jiff."

"You're incorrigible. You know that?" Gwen gasped, her eyes widening as she caught sight of someone familiar in the first class check-in line. "Oh my God!"

"What?" Reggie canted her head.

"That's Shane Paris," Gwen whispered, her pulse racing as she prepared to go from zero to fangirl in record time. "Over there, checking in for a flight."

Reggie squinted at the woman, who by now was gathering her bags and walking deeper into the terminal. "I don't think so."

"No, it is. I should know. She's my favorite singer of all time."

"I've heard," Reggie said with a groan. "But I'm telling you, it's not her."

"I can't believe we might be on the same plane as Shane Paris." Gwen's head spun as she pondered whether it would be too embarrassing to run over and ask the star for an autograph. "Do you think we are?"

"No," said Debbie Downer, aka Reggie, who seemed hell-bent on killing Gwen's buzz.

Gwen ignored Reggie's naysaying and soldiered on. "She's the biggest star on the planet. Her last album was voted as having the best love ballad of all time."

"Not sure I know that song."

"You do too." Gwen gave Reggie's shoulder a playful sock. "I listen to it all the time. If I'd known she was playing a concert in Zürich, I would have made us go. I wonder if it's still possible to get tickets to wherever she's playing next."

"I'm a bit old for concerts, and I really want to get checked in so I can get a drink," Reggie whimpered.

Gwen glared at Reggie. "You're so charming when you fly."

"I must be because it's how we met." Reggie batted her lashes, earning her another slug.

Gwen gave her breasts a wry glance. "You know how to a make a first impression. That's for sure."

"I sure do." Reggie beamed with pride.

Gwen crossed her arms. "I didn't say it was a good

impression."

"It worked out for me." As they stepped up to the check-in desk, Reggie asked, "You ready for some fondue and flaming coffee?"

"Will it improve your mood?"

"Time will tell," Reggie said with a shrug.

"You're impossible." Even though this was undoubtedly true, Gwen couldn't suppress a laugh. Something about Reggie being impossible was also completely impossible to resist.

"I could say the same about you."

They continued playfully bickering until they entered the first-class lounge. In an odd way, Gwen felt like she was coming home. Had it really been ten months since she and Reggie had met in this very spot?

"It's lovely to see you again, Ms. Hawkins and Ms. Murphy." The woman behind the counter turned out to be the very same person, Lauren, who had checked them in on their last visit. Gwen marveled silently at the coincidence.

Reggie eased her shoulder bag off. "Can this be brought to the dayroom while we get some refreshments?"

"Absolutely," Lauren said. "Leave everything to me."

"You ready, Princess?" Reggie waved for Gwen to enter the lounge.

"What about a bottle of wine this time?" Gwen asked.

"Anything you want."

"Your mood has definitely improved now that the bar is in sight," Gwen teased.

"Should we sit at our table?" Reggie's pace picked up speed as she took the lead. It was a habit she'd almost completely given up, but this time Gwen didn't mind. She smiled as she watched Reggie go directly to the table they'd sat at before.

"Aw, you remember." Gwen placed a hand on her heart.

"Of course, I do." There was an earnest tenderness in Reggie's tone that went straight to Gwen's soul. "I remember everything from that day. It's how I've gotten through these past few months, with all the difficult adjustments at the foundation, along with Dad's decline."

"It's been hard. But I have to admit I like this sentimental Reggie you've become lately," Gwen cooed. "Where have you been hiding her all day?"

Before Reggie could answer, a server came to take their drink order.

"Do you still have those flaming coffees?" Gwen asked.

"Of course, ma'am. Two?"

"No," Gwen was quick to say. She shot Reggie an apologetic glance. "Unless you want one. But last time you had that one with tea and rosehips."

"Of course," he replied.

"Oh, I wanted to order food, too." Gwen raised her hand to get his attention, but he was already too far away. However, to her surprise, another server appeared an instant later with a bubbling pot of fondue. "Oh, my goodness! Look, Reggie. Do you think they remembered our order from last time? Wouldn't it be wonderful if we could have the same room? I want to relive that day. Down to the last detail."

"Does that mean you'll leave me for a shower and then show up at my door in a robe?" Reggie waggled her eyebrows comically.

Gwen laughed. "Only if you play your cards right."

"I'll be on my best behavior."

The drinks arrived, and even though Gwen knew what was going to happen, she still squealed when the flames shot up from her cup. "This is perfect. Absolutely perfect. We couldn't have planned it better if we'd tried."

"Sometimes the most surprising things can lead you down the right path," Reggie said somewhat mysteriously, gazing into Gwen's eyes with an openness that still surprised her. The ice that had started off around Reggie's demeanor had melted completely along the way.

As they ate their fondue, there was music, so faint it was difficult to make it out, but it sounded so familiar. Finally, Gwen paused, straining to hear. "Is that—huh. I think they're playing Shane Paris's new album here in the lounge. This day is so full of coincidences it's uncanny."

"Totally uncanny." Reggie almost seemed to be holding back a smile. "Should I have them turn it up?"

"Can you?"

"Watch me." Reggie snapped her fingers.

Gwen laughed until, all of a sudden, Shane Paris herself rounded the corner with a guitar. At that point, Gwen made a squealing sound, jumped halfway out of her chair, and nearly ended up on her ass. "What the fuck?"

"Can you start at the top?" Reggie asked politely. "This is her favorite song, and I think she was too distracted by her mouth hanging open to fully appreciate it."

"Happy to oblige." The rock star laughed, holding out a hand toward Gwen. "I'm Shane by the way."

"Gw—" was all Gwen could get out.

Shane played the song, followed by three more. All of them were Gwen's favorites, and by now Gwen was certain this was not a coincidence. None of it was.

"Did you arrange this?" Gwen asked Reggie during one of the songs.

"How would I be able to pull that off? You only convinced me this morning to fly commercial." Reggie feigned innocence, but there was no fooling Gwen. Reggie was behind all of this for sure.

"But how then?" Gwen tried to run through every possible scenario for how this remarkable woman could have pulled off such a feat. "You're right. We weren't even supposed to end up here."

"I don't know about that." Reggie's words took on a philosophical tone. "I think we were always supposed to end up where we wanted to be the most."

"It was lovely meeting you, Gwen," Shane said when she finished her song. Applause rang out from several spots throughout the lounge as other passengers marveled at the impromptu concert. Gwen nodded, unable to say a word until they were alone.

"If you have any more surprises, can you tell me now?" Gwen begged.

"If I tell you about a surprise, it won't be a surprise." Reggie had an extra helping of teasing in her tone, which almost certainly meant she had more tricks up her sleeve.

"What I don't get is why this charade? Why did you act so pissy on the way here if this was your plan all along?"

"I wasn't being pissy," Reggie argued. "I was behaving as well as I could. I still hate flying, you know. Even if it is easier when you're there with me to hold my hand."

Gwen gazed at Reggie, her heart so full it was bursting. "I can't believe you. That was the nicest thing you've ever done, and you've done some really nice things. Like buying my mom an apartment a block away from us. I still can't believe how much we've reconnected since her move. It all feels like a dream."

"Anything for my girl. But, if you don't mind, I could use a nap before our flight. Do you think you could check on the room?"

Gwen went to find Lauren and ask if there was a room available. She was relieved to discover there was. But when she and Reggie arrived with their keycard and opened the door, she was shocked at what she saw.

"There are candles all over." Gwen walked in, taking in the sparkling, flickering flames. "Rose petals on the bed? A bottle of champagne? Oh, honey—" Gwen turned around, and her heart caught in her throat. Reggie was down on bent knee, holding a box, the lid still closed.

The whole day had been perfect, and this moment should have been, too. Only Gwen immediately noticed it was the box that held the 11-carat monstrosity she'd been meant to receive in July. It was mid-October now, but time had not made Gwen's heart grow any fonder of that hideously big rock. But she couldn't expect anyone, even Reggie, to get everything right.

"What's wrong?" Reggie didn't budge. "You seem troubled all of a sudden."

"Nothing." Gwen forced a smile. "I'm speechless. That's all."

"No, something's wrong." Reggie frowned. "Is it still too soon? I know it's under a year, still, but I thought—"

"Not too soon at all. It's just—this is quite the surprise. I'm overwhelmed. Everything has been perfect. Absolutely perfect." Gwen grinned because it had been. She'd learn to live with a diamond the size of Kentucky on her left hand. No biggie. "This is the best proposal ever."

"How do you know I'm proposing? Maybe I needed to tie my shoe."

"Can I just say yes so you can get up?" Gwen's eyes brimmed with tears.

"I had a speech." Reggie rose to her feet. "Do you want to hear it?"

"Do I need to? I see in your eyes how much you love me. I mean, you had Shane fricking Paris sing for me, but you knew me well enough to pop the question in private."

With that insane ring. But still. It was fine.

As Reggie started to open the ring box, Gwen braced for the sight of it, praying her smile would stay in place.

Ever so slowly, the lid rose until it revealed—

"Holy fucking shit! It's not that god-awful ring!" With a yip of delight, Gwen took the pearl ring on its diamond crown out of the box and held it up to the light.

"You had to be expecting that." Reggie laughed.

"No, I wasn't," Gwen admitted. "When I saw the box, I assumed it was the other one."

"You hated that ring."

Gwen fell into Reggie's arms, smothering her with kisses. "And I love you. Thank you. Thank you for knowing me, what I like, and being okay with it. Will you put it on?"

Reggie slipped the ring onto Gwen's finger.

"What happened to the other ring?"

Reggie shrugged. "I tossed it into the ocean."

"Regina Hawkins! What if some poor sea creature swallowed it and died?" All Gwen could think of was an unsuspecting whale coming by and choking on that terrible rock.

Reggie burst into laughter. "Seriously, honey? Sometimes it's just too easy. That was a scene from *Titanic*."

Gwen's cheeks tingled, but she had to laugh. "What did you do with it?"

"Where do you think the money came from to buy your mom's place?"

"Under your sofa cushions?" Gwen tilted her head. "I still haven't figured out how the whole billionaire thing works. And I don't plan to, because we're going to be giving it all away in record time now that you've given me free rein."

"I'm going to live to regret doing that," Reggie said with a groan.

"You love it," Gwen insisted. "And, I love you."

"I should hope so, or I wouldn't survive another day." Reggie gazed intently at Gwen. "I know you said yes, but I'm going to need something else to prove you won't leave."

"Not another contract." Gwen groaned.

"Sort of, but the type I much prefer with you and only you." Reggie captured Gwen's lips for the sweetest of kisses to seal the deal of a lifetime.

EPILOGUE

The plane was shaking so hard upon takeoff Reggie could feel her brain sloshing inside her skull. She slid her eyes over to Gwen as she white knuckled the armrests of the leather seat on their private jet. It was an unusual treat to fly on the trusty ol' PJ, and Reggie knew she should enjoy it, but she couldn't shake the terror that overwhelmed her.

"This part will be over soon," Gwen promised, looking unfazed by the racket the plane was making as it barreled down the runway.

"Hopefully not in a fiery blaze."

"Do you want to bury your head in my chest?" Gwen offered. "That helped last time."

Reggie's heart lurched into her throat as the plane lifted from the ground and rose higher and higher into the sky. The blue gave way to dark clouds, her brain locking onto the memory of the plane that had been struck by lightning. Her body shook as a familiar dread took up residence in the pit of her stomach.

There was no way around one simple fact: Reggie hated flying. No, that word wasn't strong enough. Abhorred. Despised. Detested. Loathed.

Only a crazy person would enjoy being so far away from solid ground. She wouldn't be doing it at all, except it was either this or get married in New York City where they would have to invite a thousand people, minimum. Given the choice between that version of hell and a flight to their destination wedding for only the most intimate of friends and family, Reggie was willing to make the sacrifice.

Without a word, Gwen's hand slipped into Reggie's, as if reading her mind. A wave of comfort washed over her. A soft smile played across Gwen's lips, soothing Reggie better than any anxiety drug. Gwen's blond hair cascaded in graceful waves around her face and the teal silk of Gwen's dress shimmered in the cabin's dull light, making Gwen look almost otherworldly. Reggie knew Gwen had worn it especially for Reggie because it was her favorite. The gesture was not unappreciated, nor was the distractingly low cut of the neckline. Under the circumstances, distractions were most welcome.

"The captain promised a smooth flight." Gwen spoke gently, gazing deeply into Reggie's eyes. "I'm right here. Nothing's going to happen to you. Not on my watch."

Reggie released a deep, cleansing breath as she locked onto Gwen's comforting eyes, as if they guided her to safety. Warmth spread throughout Reggie's body, booting out the fear. Wrapping her fingers around Gwen's hand, Reggie returned a smile. A real one.

Gwen squeezed Reggie's hand reassuringly. "We'll be there soon," she said softly. "Why don't you settle back and try to enjoy the flight?"

"Impossible," Reggie said. "Grin and bear it maybe, but I'm never going to enjoy it."

"Remind me; what do you usually do to make it through?" Gwen asked.

"Take a sleeping pill and pass out in the bedroom at the back of the plane," Reggie confessed.

"I forgot about the bedroom. Is it nice?" Gwen fluttered her eyelashes in a way that could almost pass for innocent if Reggie didn't know her too well by now to be fooled.

"It doesn't have the world's fanciest bed," Reggie responded, her body already tingling in delightful and unexpected ways at the prospect of giving Gwen a tour of the room later on. "Overall, I think it's decent. I'm usually comatose, so I don't feel like I can give you an accurate review."

"Comatose, huh? What a waste of a perfectly good bed and several hours of free time," Gwen teased. "But maybe you'll consider a glass of champagne in lieu of the sleeping pills, at least?"

Reggie nodded.

Gwen filled two glasses of champagne from the bottle that had been opened and put on ice in a silver bucket near their seats. The flight crew had specific instructions not to interrupt them during the flight.

The plane bobbled slightly, drawing Reggie's attention back to the window, the dark clouds gone. "Everything looks so small, like reality doesn't really exist right now."

"There's a pleasing thought. Why don't we lean into that?"

"What do you mean?" Reggie turned her head back to Gwen, the calming warmth returning like someone turned on a faucet.

"Life has been full-on. I, for one, would like to forget all of our troubles on earth for a little while and focus on what's really important."

"Dying?"

"We might need more than champagne." Gwen's laughter tickled Reggie's ears.

Reggie inhaled deeply, and Gwen's musky scent chased away her worries like a summer breeze dispersing clouds.

"It's weird. Together, I believe we can face anything." Reggie sipped the champagne.

"Why is that weird?"

"It's not something I have a lot of experience with. My experience has been even those who should be the most supportive are angling for what's best for them."

"I do have an agenda. I feel like I should be honest about that right now." Gwen nuzzled closer.

Reggie's heart fluttered. She loved nothing more than a good agenda. Especially the type she believed Gwen had in mind.

Gwen moved her hand up Reggie's arm, lightly tracing her fingers along her skin. Reggie shivered involuntarily, and Gwen leaned in closer. "I know a surefire way to make you forget all about your fear of flying," she whispered.

Reggie's breath hitched like it was the first time, and she savored the thrill of anticipation. What a change a year made. Before Gwen, everything in Reggie's life was transactional. Now that word left a bad taste in Reggie's mouth.

This wasn't a transaction. It was mind-blowing love.

Gwen leaned in and pressed her lips against Reggie's. The kiss was gentle but passionate, and Reggie let all thoughts fade away.

Gwen pulled away, her eyes twinkling. "Let me show you how much I love you."

There was another kiss. The sweetness on Gwen's lips was all Reggie had time to taste before Gwen's tongue was eagerly exploring inside her mouth. Since that first kiss in Switzerland, being this close to Gwen was intoxicating, and Reggie could never get enough.

"Why don't we take this to the bedroom?" Gwen reached for Reggie's hand, guiding her toward the private bedroom at the back of the plane. Gwen opened the door, the luxurious bed with satin sheets coming into view as if Reggie had never seen it before.

Given Reggie was usually drugged, it's possible she really hadn't.

Gwen pulled Reggie close, her body pressed against Reggie's while the door closed behind them. They escaped into a deep kiss, lowering themselves onto the bed as if they were one, not two.

Gwen continued kissing while she delicately unbuttoned Reggie's shirt. As the buttons popped open one by one, the desire surged through her veins. Her heart pounded in anticipation, heat radiating off her skin.

Gwen pressed herself against Reggie's body, kissing the exposed skin of Reggie's neck. The tender caress was like liquid fire, sending sparks of pleasure through Reggie's veins.

Gwen nudged the shirt off Reggie's shoulders, exposing naked skin and running her hands down Reggie's body, Gwen's fingertips tracing the curves of Reggie's form. Reggie leaned up, allowing Gwen to slip Reggie's shirt off. Gwen left a trail of soft kisses along the length of Reggie's collarbone.

Gwen continued to touch Reggie, her body heating up. Her eyes fluttered when Gwen's kisses moved from neck to chest. Gwen's lips were soft and warm against Reggie's skin, and her fear melted away as Gwen continued to explore exposed skin, each touch not solely washing away the fear, but stitching Reggie's heart whole.

Gwen moved lower, and Reggie pushed her head back, her breathing becoming short and shallow. Gwen's lips found Reggie's nipples. Reggie moaned softly when Gwen took one nipple into her mouth, flicking it with her tongue. With each passing moment, their bodies grew hotter and more attuned to each other's needs. Reggie gasped as Gwen began to suck and nibble, the sensation almost too much to bear.

Gwen traveled further down Reggie's body, lingering over Reggie's skin right above the waistline of her trousers, softly teasing and tasting until Reggie could barely contain herself, a desperate moan escaping her lips.

Gwen's hands undid Reggie's pants, slipping underneath, fingertips lightly tracing the area between Reggie's legs. Another moan escaped Reggie, her body trembling with pleasure. Gwen's touch was both gentle and passionate, and Reggie found herself lost in the sensations.

Reggie gasped when Gwen's fingers brushed against the most sensitive spot. Gwen grinned, apparently able to read Reggie's thoughts, although it probably wasn't hard to judge from Reggie's rapid breaths and gyrating hips.

Gwen's fingers found Reggie's center again, slowly exploring the folds. Between Gwen's fingers and the movement of the plane, all Reggie could do was hold on tightly, waiting for what was to come. Wanting it right away but never wanting it to end.

That was the thing about Gwen. Reggie could never get enough. She'd need a thousand lifetimes, and even that might not do it.

Reggie's breath quickened as Gwen moved her lips lower, her hot breath every so often blowing against Reggie's wetness.

Just when Reggie thought she couldn't take anymore, Gwen's lips finally landed on Reggie's clit. Gwen's tongue traced a slow, torturous circle around the tip of Reggie's pleasure and then slipped inside. Slowly at first but then with increasing speed, Gwen moved her mouth against Reggie, spurring sensations so intense she thought she'd explode.

Groaning with pleasure as Gwen worked against her swollen nub with a rhythm matched by a finger moving inside Reggie, a swell started to rise, in body and mind. Her fingers dug into the sheets as the promise of what was to come washed over her body.

Another finger found its way inside Reggie, her body shuddering with ecstasy. Gwen continued to tease and tantalize, her movements growing more urgent. Reggie's heart pounded throughout her entire body while Gwen expertly drove Reggie to the brink.

"Whatever you do, don't stop," Reggie could barely get the words out.

Gwen didn't.

The swell of a wave rose higher and higher, cresting the top for many blissful moments before it dove over the edge into an endless pool. Reggie's entire body quivered, her center moving with wild abandon.

With remarkable effort, Gwen stayed where Reggie needed her, the second orgasm overtaking Reggie.

"I fucking love you," Reggie said as her back bucked off the bed, her arms cradling Gwen's head, before Reggie collapsed back onto the mattress, her entire body spent.

Gwen moved back up Reggie's body, locking eyes. "I love you. More each day."

"I actually believe you." Reggie cupped Gwen's cheek.

"You better." Gwen kissed Reggie passionately, sealing the promise never to leave Reggie's side. "We're getting married in three days."

"You are full of surprises," Reggie said, kissing Gwen's temple. "All the times I've flown in this bed, I can't say I've ever done this."

"Part of me can't believe you've never taken advantage of having your own bedroom on a plane." Gwen's voice was soft and melodic, almost hypnotic. "But I can't lie. I like that your first time was with me. Hopefully not the last. I might be willing to fly on the PJ a time or two more, now that I know about this. I have a few more things I'd like to try."

"What else did you have in mind?"

"Do you still have that special tube of lipstick in your bag?" Gwen's mischievous grin and conspiratorial wink sent Reggie's eyebrows racing toward her scalp.

"Sadly, no," Reggie admitted. "But maybe there's something I can do to make up for this packing oversight?"

"I want to feel you inside me," Gwen whispered softly in reply.

Reggie's heart pounded as her still quivering fingers found their way to the zipper on Gwen's dress. She deftly slid it down until the fabric fell away, revealing Gwen's lacy bra. While she loved it, this wasn't the time for leaving any clothing on Gwen.

Reggie sighed at the sight of Gwen's breasts, perky and

inviting. Reggie made a move to take one nipple between her lips, sucking and biting it to life. She moved to the other, taking as long as humanly possible, but the need for more—everything pulled Reggie south, like gravity.

Reggie slid Gwen's panties down those long, sensuous legs. Reggie's mouth licked her way back up to Gwen's center, the scent of desire overwhelming Reggie, her emotions nearly stopping her in her tracks.

How could Reggie be this head over heels?

She pushed that question out of her mind, because the how didn't matter. Some things could never be explained or fully understood. What mattered was the here and now.

Reggie's mouth moved closer and closer, Gwen's heat sucking Reggie in. All of her.

The first taste, nearly sent Reggie into a tailspin, her emotions swelling deep inside. Her tongue traveled along Gwen's wet slit, guiding her to where Gwen needed Reggie.

As Reggie's mouth continued to work, she explored Gwen's wetness with the tips of her fingers, slowly entering, moving in deeper and deeper.

Gwen screamed out in pleasure, her back arching and her body shuddering at the apex of pleasure.

Reggie leaned back with a grin. "I just might get the hang of air travel now."

"That makes two of us," Gwen said with an answering smile. "I can hardly wait to see where else we'll go together."

"Anywhere you want," Reggie promised. "Forever."

A HUGE THANK YOU!

Thanks so much for reading *Flight Plan*!

Miranda and TB have cowritten so many books now and we're often asked how we manage to work so well together. What many don't realize is Miranda and TB go way back. How far back? We were actually born in the same hospital, just nine weeks apart, although TB keeps insisting it was seven weeks because math... While we may quibble about plot points, we're often laughing as we do.

For example, if you've been following TB's newsletters, you know she is obsessed with tits. By which, we are talking about the birds, and more specifically, with buying every possible t-shirt that has a tits or boobies (as in blue-footed boobies, another bird) joke on them. She does this in part because Miranda gets so embarrassed when she wears them in public.

For this book, TB kept threatening that the whole thing would be about boobs. It was TB's job to come up with the meet-cute in chapter one, and sure enough, it involved boobs, just as promised. But honestly, we think it's our best and funniest meet-cute to date.

If you enjoyed *Flight Plan*, TB would love some new tits shirts (or boobies), but since that's kind of hard to ship, a review on Amazon, Goodreads, BookBub, or your favorite book review site would be almost as nice. Even short reviews help immensely.

If you want to stay in touch with TB, sign up for her newsletter. She'll send you a free copy of *A Woman Lost*, book 1 in the A Woman Lost series, plus the bonus chapters and Tropical Heat (a short story), all of which are exclusive to subscribers.

You'll also be one of the first to hear about her many misadventures, like the time she accidentally ordered thirty pounds of oranges, instead of five. To be honest, that stuff happens to TB a lot, which explains why she owns three of the exact same Nice Tits T-shirt. Yes, we're still talking about birds here.

Here's the link to join: http://eepurl.com/hhBhXX

And, if you want to follow Miranda and find out what TB is really up to, sign up for her newsletter. Subscribers will receive her first book, *Telling Lies Online*, for free. For cat fans, she shares adorable photos of her felines, who are sisters and tag-team to destroy everything in Miranda's house. Luckily, they're adorable. Seriously, you don't want to miss out on Miranda's heartfelt and funny newsletters. Here's the link to join: mirandamacleod.com/list

Thanks again for reading *Flight Plan*. It's because of you that we are able to follow our dreams of being writers. It's a wonderful gift, and we appreciate each and every reader.

TB & Miranda

ABOUT THE AUTHORS

TB Markinson is an American who's recently returned to the US after a seven-year stint in the UK and Ireland. When she isn't writing, she's traveling the world, watching sports on the telly, visiting pubs in New England, or reading. Not necessarily in that order.

Visit TB's website (lesbianromancesbytbm.com) to say hello. On the *Lesbians Who Write* weekly podcast, she and Clare Lydon dish about the good, the bad, and the ugly of writing.

Originally from southern California, Miranda MacLeod now lives in New England and writes heartfelt romances and romantic comedies featuring witty and charmingly flawed women that you'll want to marry. Or just grab a coffee with, if that's more your thing.

Before becoming a writer, she spent way too many years in graduate school, worked in professional theater and film, and held temp jobs in just about every office building in downtown Boston. To find out about her upcoming releases, be sure to sign up for her mailing list at mirandamacleod.com.

TB and Miranda also co-own *I Heart SapphFic,* a website for authors and readers of sapphic fiction to stay up-to-date on all the latest sapphic fiction news. The duo won a Golden Crown Literary Award for *The AM Show* in 2022.

Printed in Great Britain
by Amazon